I0663527

Lilac Love - A Witchy Romantic Mystery

Glen Haven Series, Volume 1

Rosie Evylin

Published by Rosie Evylin, 2023.

This is a work of fiction. Similarities to real people, places, or events are entirely coincidental.

LILAC LOVE - A WITCHY ROMANTIC MYSTERY

First edition. November 19, 2023.

Copyright © 2023 Rosie Evylin.

ISBN: 978-1738619016

Written by Rosie Evylin.

To Andrew, for always loving and supporting me, and for teaching me that love can be magic even without spells.

To my family, for teaching me my love of stories.

To you the reader, thank you for reading this book! Lilac Love is an exploration of love, hope, and trust. I hope that it transports you to a magical world, just as it did for me.

1

Elsie

Elsie twisted her tea cup three times in an anti-clockwise direction, followed by a half a turn clockwise. Tipping it upside down, she let the last mouthful of tea fall into the saucer. She left the teacup upside down for sixty seconds and asked what the day had in store for her. Picking up the teacup once more, she gazed at the leaves at the bottom of her cup and frowned. A visit from a friend? That was interesting. Despite her best efforts, Elsie hadn't made any friends in Glen Haven yet. One of her friends from home could be visiting, but surely they'd have called first?

Still pondering, Elsie was about to take the teacup to the sink when she noticed two small lines of leaves at the bottom of the cup. A cross. Her heart sank. The cross represented trouble, even death, on the horizon. Its placement at the bottom of the cup indicated that it was foretelling something in the distant future, but nevertheless, Elsie didn't think she had the reserves to deal with any more negativity, not after dad, and gran, and the move. Life in Glen Haven had been harder than she'd expected when she first moved here. There weren't many people Elsie's age, and the Glen Haven crowd were difficult to get close with.

Philo padded in, his huge paws clattering on the smooth wooden floors. "Good morning, my friend."

Philo snuggled his colossal head into Elise's tummy, burrowing under her arm like a pig sniffing out truffles. *Morning Elsie, is it breakfast time yet?*

She managed a laugh and patted him affectionately. "Sure," she said, setting down his bowl and filling it with food. Philo snuffled up the food, then slurped water, his long pink tongue causing flecks of water to splash all over the floor.

"Philo," Elsie said reproachfully.

Sorry. Philo looked up at Elsie, his snout still held the remaining crumbs of his meal. Once Philo finished his breakfast, he looked at Elsie more carefully. *What's eating you?*

"Nothing" Elsie didn't want to worry Philo, he was still young, and she didn't even know what the cross meant yet. Philo just stared at Elsie, his honey brown eyes unblinking. "Fine!" Elsie said eventually. It was annoying having a pet who could read your moods, and sometimes even your mind. "There's a cross in the tea leaves." Philo visibly gulped, though whether that was from what Elsie had said, or he was simply still processing his food, she couldn't tell.

So, what are we going to do about it?

"I hadn't got that far yet."

Protection spell? Good luck charm?

"Good idea. I'll go to the forest and collect the ingredients." Pulling out her phone, Elsie made a list of everything she'd need: warlock's wart, clover, sage. She might make a discernment spell as well, so she added rosemary and a few other ingredients to her list. Philo leaned his body against Elsie in what she thought was an affectionate way. The doorbell rang, and he raced to the door, calling out about an intruder. Elsie sighed, following her young Familiar to the door.

2

Amanda

Amanda stood, panting, at the front door. She considered herself fairly fit, but that hill had nearly brought her to her knees. Of course number 13 had to be right at the very, very top of the footpath. She leaned her hip against a painted black railing and surveyed the house. It was white, with intricate black rails and black painted skirtings. The house was partially overgrown with ivy, and there were violet flowers growing up the vines. A huge tree stood to one side of the front door, its branches covered in brilliant purple flowers. A Royal Empress, she thought, though its petals were a darker shade of purple than she had seen before. The air smelt a little, with a subtle hint of something sweet Amanda couldn't place. Hitching the parcel she was carrying further under her arm, she approached and rang the small black bell once more, just in case the occupants were home but hadn't heard her ring. She heard a muffled "I'm coming," from inside the house.

The door opened and a polar bear launched itself at Amanda, nearly knocking her to the floor. Amanda closed her eyes in terror, wondering how this could possibly be the end. She felt heavy breath on her face, and opening her eyes for a moment, her vision was full of white teeth and black lips. She clamped her eyes closed again, regretting every decision that had led to this moment. "Philo, off!" a voice said sternly, and Amanda felt the heavy paws lift from her chest. Hesitantly, she opened her eyes and saw that Philo was not technically a polar bear, he was just the biggest dog she'd ever seen. Huge and white, with gigantic paws like sleds, and a tail that was now thwumping noisily on the bannister. Her attention was quickly drawn away from the dog beast and towards the stunning woman standing at the door, her hand perched angrily on her hip. She was petite, with olive skin and long black hair that reached almost to her waist. Amanda wasn't sure if her breath was still catching because of the walk up the hill, or because of the woman in front of her. Pulling herself together, she realised the woman was talking to her.

"I'm so, so sorry," the woman said, coming forward and looking at Amanda with earnest eyes that in this light somehow looked purple. "Philo is still a puppy. I don't think he quite knows his own size." She twirled a finger anxiously around her long, dark plait.

Amanda's heart was still hammering, but she rallied. "It's ok," she said. "I just wasn't prepared for a polar bear this far from the ocean. Is his name really filo? Like, the pastry?"

The woman beamed. "It's short for Philokrates, but that's a bit of a mouthful when you have a puppy running riot, so I shorten it to Philo. I'm a chef, so it seemed fitting." The woman held out her hand and Amanda shifted the box she was carrying under her arm to shake it. "I'm Elsie, by the way."

"Amanda."

"Nice to meet you. Are you new to Glen Haven? I don't think I've seen you before, and with my Amazon habit, that's saying something." Elsie smiled that self-deprecating smile, and Amanda knew instantly that she liked this woman.

"I just moved here," she admitted. "I'm staying in the BnB, the Bluebell Corner, while I figure out something a bit more permanent." Amanda tugged awkwardly at the hem of her shirt. She couldn't believe they'd made her wear this uniform; a tan polo neck shirt with red edging, complete with matching shorts that stopped just above her knobbly knees. She felt like a schoolboy, and in front of this casually chic goddess, Amanda felt suddenly rather self-conscious. Elsie was clad in a soft, flowing brown skirt that reached the floor, and above that she was wearing a cropped black t-shirt that showed off her phenomenal figure. Her fingers were covered with rings, and she gave off a distinctly bohemian vibe.

"Are you from Glen Haven originally?" Amanda asked, desperate to get the attention away from herself.

"Oh, I moved here about a year ago," Elsie said, tucking a stray strand of hair behind her ever so slightly pointed ear. "My grandmother passed away and left me this house. I've always loved the town, but I'm still getting used to being a permanent resident, rather than just a holiday visitor."

"Sorry to hear about your grandmother," Amanda said, trying not to be jealous that this woman, who must be about her own age if not slightly younger, apparently owned her own home outright. She seemed so settled, especially compared to Amanda; practically penniless and with nowhere to call home.

Maybe Elsie saw something of the fatigue in Amanda's eyes, because she said, "Will you come in for a cup of tea? That hill is exhausting to hike up, sorry!"

Amanda knew she should have said no. She liked this woman, but she wasn't here to make friends. In fact, her whole goal in moving to somewhere as remote as Glen Haven had been to get away from anyone who knew her. She was meant to be staying under the radar. Something about Elsie's manner, however, seemed to be casting a spell on her. She found herself saying, "Yes thanks, that'd be wonderful." And following the lithe woman into the mysterious house. She supposed one drink couldn't hurt.

3

Elsie

Elsie led the way through to the kitchen at the back of the house, Philo trailing behind her, tail thumping enthusiastically. The kitchen had high ceilings with a skylight above the big island in the middle. The cupboards were a deep grape, with silver handles in the shape of half-moons. There was also low-hanging silver orb lighting hung from the ceiling. The effect was that of a well-lit night sky. "I know," Elsie said, glancing back and seeing Amanda's surprised face. "It's a bit much. My grandmother was a little...extra."

Amanda smiled and shrugged. "It's cool. I like when people make things their own."

Elsie was relieved. She had invited plenty of people around for tea or coffee since moving into Lilac House, but the townsfolk hadn't been very warm in their reception to her. She was pretty sure that the only reason Beth and Reginald agreed to come in that one time was to snoop, and they had certainly judged her grandmother's kitchen. Amanda wasn't exactly effusive with praise, but she at least didn't seem to be looking around the house and finding Elsie somehow wanting. Yes, the house was different, but it reminded Elsie of her grandmother, and she loved it in all its quirkiness because of that.

"Have a seat," she said, waving Amanda towards one of the tall stools at the kitchen island. "OK, I have blueberry, blackcurrant and apple, cinnamon and apple, ginger, mint, lavender and lemon, vanilla rose..." Elsie trailed off as Amanda laughed.

"Wow, you have like a whole garden in that drawer, huh?"

Elsie blushed, but she saw Amanda was smiling warmly; Elsie wasn't the butt of a joke here.

"I'm rather fond of tea," Elsie admitted with a shy smile.

"I'm still a novice, so I'll have whatever you're having," Amanda said, and Elsie pulled down the vanilla rose, which she wouldn't usually give to guests who weren't regular tea-drinkers, but it smelt delicious, and it was so pretty with the pink rose buds which unfurled in the top. Elsie realised with a small start that she was trying to impress Amanda. *You cannot have a crush on the new girl in town,* she told herself sternly.

"So what brings you to Glen Haven?" she said, forcing herself not to get too absorbed by Amanda's soft smile and kind eyes. She was intrigued by this woman. She was beautiful, yes, but that wasn't what drew Elsie to her. Amanda seemed to be a walking contradiction; her sentences seemed clipped, almost self-protective, but then she had a face that was so open, and her smile was completely disarming. There was a strength to her, too, something about the way Amanda held herself, as if she knew that she could take care of herself if she needed to.

"Oh, I've always wanted to live here," Amanda said, surprising Elsie. "I've heard about the amazing hikes, especially Willow Falls and Pride's Peak."

"Ah, an outdoorsy person," Elsie said, remembering the toned calves she'd seen stretching out of the shorts which had hugged Amanda's hips just so. *Snap out of it!* She thought firmly, hoping Amanda didn't notice her blushing.

"Something like that," Amanda said, giving her a wry grin. "I've always loved hiking, being in the woods, or walking in the bracing wind along a beach."

"Sounds very healthy and rugged," Elsie said appreciatively. "Sadly, we don't have a beach in Glen Haven, but there's a river, and the forests here really are spectacular. Have you explored much yet?"

It turned out Amanda had already taken the Ridgeline walkway, which gave a stunning view out over the valley, with a glimpse of the sea in the distance. She hadn't yet been on any of the inland walks through the wood, though. "I was planning on going foraging on Monday," Elsie said without thinking. "You'd be welcome to join me if you like. I was thinking I would head into Viskande, wander towards Fairy Glen, then I tend to fossick around for an hour or so, so you could explore a little while I do that if you like?"

Elsie felt her sentence trail off at the end and was a little abashed. She knew foraging was a bit of a niche pass-time, and she had only just met Amanda. She might not be quite as eager as Elsie was for a friend! Before Elsie could start spiralling about getting carried away too fast, she realised with relief that Amanda's face had lit up. "That would be great, thank you! I've been wondering where the entrance to Viskande is, and hadn't yet been able to figure it out from my hiking app." She tucked a lock of mahogany hair behind her ear. "What do you forage for?"

"Oh, mushrooms usually, and herbs, and flowers for tea, that kind of thing." Elsie gave a shrug. Given her ominous tea leaves, she was actually on the lookout for Warlock's wart and a few other spell ingredients, but Amanda didn't need to know that.

4

Amanda

Amanda collapsed onto the lumpy bed at Bluebell Corner and let out a deep sigh. It had been another long day, but she was feeling a little better having had such a pleasant interaction with Elsie. She knew she couldn't let herself get too close to anyone, but maybe it would be ok to have made a friend, or the start of a friend, at least? Amanda didn't know why, but she was drawn to Elsie. She couldn't quite figure the woman out. She was a ball of energy, but she somehow made Amanda peaceful and at ease. Eyeing her things, she began mentally making a list of what she would need to bring on their outing tomorrow. She was excited to explore the forest with Elsie tomorrow. This was the reason she had come to Glen Haven- getting into the woods! Foraging had been an unexpected suggestion, but Amanda found the idea almost as intriguing as Elsie herself. She recalled the light that had come into Elsie's eyes when she talked about it, smiling to herself at the memory.

Amanda's phone beeped with an incoming text message, and she all the blood in her body turned to ice. Taking a deep breath, she picked up her phone and looked at the message on screen, not clicking into it, to ensure no 'read' message could be seen. She carefully swiped across the screen to delete the message before flopping back onto the bed with a thump. They still didn't know where she was, she was sure of that, otherwise they'd be here hammering on the door, rather than sending ominous text messages. Still, her buoyed mood was now gone.

She pulled her backpack out from under her bed and counted the diminishing stack of notes in there. This bed-and-breakfast wasn't exactly pricey, but her stores of money were running out fast. Plus, she should get a message to Pierce. Gritting her teeth, she pulled her hair into a bun atop her head and pulled out her laptop. Running her searches through several international VPNs so her progress couldn't be followed, she opened up a search engine and typed in 'Real Estate Agents.' She let out a long, sad sigh, then rolled her shoulders back and got to work.

5

Elsie

The next morning, Elsie opened up her shop, Pie in the Sky, whistling. "You're very chipper today," came a raspy voice behind her.

Elsie's heart sank in recognition. "Good morning, Beth," she said, plastering on a smile and turning to the angry- faced woman standing much too close to her on the footpath.

Beth Munroe was probably in her early sixties, but it was difficult to tell. Today she wore a red knitted hat pulled low over her wide face and a matching scarf and gloves. She also wore a voluminous blue coat that almost reached to the floor, and she was holding the lead on which a tiny sausage dog tugged impatiently.

"I see you decided to leave that mutt of yours at home," Beth said. Elsie had never brought Philo to the shop. Unlike the aged and extremely rotund Brutus, Philo was still a puppy, full of youthful exuberance. He would cause havoc in any kind of coffee shop, which Beth well knew. There had been one tiny negative interaction between Philo and Brutus, which was not at all Philo's fault, even if he had ended up with his sled-sized paws on the older dog's head, and Beth had been labelling her beloved familiar a 'vicious mutt' ever since.

That, and Elsie setting up what Mrs Munroe considered to be 'competition', had meant that the two hadn't exactly gotten off on the right foot. Elsie sighed, ignoring the jibe and instead choosing to move the conversation forward. "Not working today, Mrs Munroe?"

"Never work Sundays, it's the Lord's day," Beth replied testily.

"Oh, I didn't realise you went to St Andrew's." Elsie looked at her watch. It was a quarter past ten. "Isn't the service on now?"

"I'm a little under the weather today," Beth said, blustering. "So I thought I had better not be cooped up in close proximity with all those other good people." In a desperate attempt at getting to know the townsfolk, Elsie had been to St Andrew's on a couple of occasions, and it had certainly not been her impression that the church was filled with 'good people'. News spread in the town like wild-fire, and while everyone at the service had seemed to know who Elsie was, nobody seemed interested in getting to know her. Her efforts at building relationships in this town had so far been rather fruitless. Elsie was worried Pie in the Sky would suffer the same fate as her - rejected and alone, with only the reflection for company.

"I'm sorry to hear you're not feeling well," Elsie said. "Would you and Brutus like to come in for a cup of tea while I open up? I have a lovely ginger and chamomile blend which does wonders for the immune system."

"No, I would not," Beth said, drawing herself up straighter. "Nonsense stuff, all that. You'd never see me offering anything like that at the Bakehouse. English Breakfast tea or filter coffee. White or black, that's it. If the baking is good enough, that's all you need."

Elsie felt her good mood fading, and along with it, her resolve to be kind to this harsh woman. "Righto. Well, have a good day then." She opened the door, her good mood gone. She just wanted to get on with her day in peace. Business was hardly booming, but it was important to Elsie that she be ready with a range of tasty treats for anyone who graced her doorway.

"I don't know how you can sleep at night," Beth said, just before Elsie managed to close the door behind her. Not this again, surely? She turned, sighing.

"I'm sorry that you see my little shop as competition to your bakery," Elsie said. "I honestly think they're quite different. You do takeaways and I specialise in sit-in. You're mostly sweet breads and pastries, and I'm mostly pies and cupcakes. I think we cater to different tastes, and there's plenty of people in town in need of food and drink. We can certainly both operate happily side by side."

"You think you're better than me just because you have pretty tablecloths on the tables, do you?"

Well, at least she likes the tablecloths, Elsie thought.

"I don't think I'm better than you, Beth. I think we have plenty in common. We both love baking, we both enjoy making people happy..." She trailed off at the look of disgust on Mrs Munroe's face. Blessedly, at that moment, Brutus squatted down, indicating a need to relieve himself. Elsie knew that Beth never picked up Brutus's droppings; she simply tried to encourage him to do his business where others were unlikely to walk. "Come along, Brutus," Beth said, tugging hard on the diamante blue leash, which perfectly matched the collar around Brutus's bulging neck. The two shuffled off together, and Elsie sighed in relief as she finally stepped through into the sanctity of her little shop.

6

Amanda

Amanda arrived at Elsie's house on Monday morning at 7:30 on the dot, as agreed. She rang the doorbell and heard the scrambling of paws and barking coming closer. There was a loud curse from somewhere deep within the house, but it was drowned out by Philo's aggressive barking at the front door.

"Hi, Philo," Amanda called, and the barking changed to that of excitement. Well, I'm glad he likes me, Amanda thought, recalling the size of the teeth that had been so close to her face mere days before. Several minutes later, Elsie appeared, holding a coffee mug as big as her head, a small scowl on her pretty features. She was dressed in a black tank top that showed off her toned midriff, and silky grey pajama pants with a black satin robe draped around her shoulders.

"Come on in," she said groggily, and Amanda was suddenly worried she had the time wrong.

"Am I early?" she asked anxiously, following her into the kitchen once more. Elsie waved her hand for Amanda to take a seat as she thumped gracelessly onto the stool opposite her.

"No, no, you're not early," Elsie said apologetically. "It's early." Amanda remained confused, and Elsie must have guessed, because she continued. "We need to get started early, but I'm not really a morning person. Sorry." She slurped once again from her gigantic mug. "I'll be ok once I've had some more coffee."

Amanda smiled. "I know someone like that. He always wants to be a morning person, but he's an absolute nightmare until he's eaten and had three coffees. Then he's a delight." She dropped her smile and stopped talking. Why was she bringing up Pierce? "Anyway, I understand. You take your time."

Elsie smiled gratefully. "There's more coffee in the pot," she offered, but Amanda shook her head.

"I'm not going to take your lifeblood," she said, and Elsie looked relieved.

"Tea?" she asked instead. "I have an invigorating matcha and agar blend that packs quite a punch."

"That sounds great," Amanda said, standing, and placed her hand on Elsie's slender shoulder when she made to get up. "But I'll make it. You sit and wake up."

"Bless you," Elsie said into her mug, though whether it was to Amanda or to her coffee, it was hard to tell.

Amanda flicked on the glossy black kettle and reached into the cupboard above it for the mugs, as she'd seen Elsie do the day before. She took down one of the teapots from the row on the shelf below, admiring the earthy porcelain as she sat it on the counter. Then she opened the drawer below the kettle and gasped. "Wow, you really do have a thing for tea, huh?" she said, looking in astonishment at the drawer packed full of little boxes of neatly labelled tea. "I don't see the matcha," she said, scanning the thirty or so teas in the drawer. "Probably the next layer down," Elsie said, and then, as Amanda went to open the drawer below, she clarified. "It lifts out." The boxes were all in a large wooden tray, which Amanda carefully lifted to reveal another set of teas below the first. "Wow!" she said, placing the tray on the counter and pulling out the box marked matcha and agar in neat cursive. "This is next level stuff, pardon the pun." Elsie's face broke into a sleepy smile, and Amanda's cheeks flushed a little that Elsie had enjoyed her bad joke.

Amanda busied herself making tea while Elsie sipped at her coffee, cradling the ginormous mug like a precious newborn child. After a few minutes, Elsie stretched and said she was going to get dressed, and then they could go. Noticing the coffee pot was empty, Amanda busied herself refilling it. It bubbles away merrily, and Elsie emerged a few minutes later clad in black leggings and another crop top, over which she threw a cute forest green sweater that seemed to accentuate her tiny waist. She pulled on glossy black Doc Martin boots. Noticing the freshly brewed coffee, she smiled appreciatively at Amanda, grabbed two travel mugs out of yet another cupboard, and filled them from the pot, adding in something else Amanda couldn't see as she did so. She handed one mug to Amanda, kissed Philo on the top of his head with an assurance that they'd be back soon, and strode towards the door.

Amanda sipped the coffee on the walk down the winding path to Elsie's car, an old and slightly rusty pale blue VW Beetle. "What's in this?" She asked, awe in her voice. It was, without a doubt, the best coffee she'd ever tasted in her life. The rich coffee flavour was accented with hints of cherry and chocolate, and Elsie had obviously added milk and some sweetener, just as Amanda liked, without even asking her.

"Secret recipe," Elsie said, turning and winking at Amanda over her shoulder before continuing down the hill. "I have a knack for knowing what people like."

Amanda followed Elsie in awe, her heart ticking up a beat.

7

Amanda

The entrance to Viskande forest was off a side street that Amanda would never have seen had Elsie not been driving. The narrow, winding road looked like any other dirt path from the main road, but Elsie deftly navigated her little blue car along it, bumping and swaying. As they drove, Elsie came to life, the caffeine obviously having its desired effect. She pointed out birds, rare plants, and the entrances to other hikes as they drove. Elsie chatted amiably about the town and its residents, and particularly about how much she had loved it when she was younger. Weirdly, Amanda found herself wanting to tell Elsie more about herself too, but she kept her answers to Elsie's questions short, and she was grateful that the other woman didn't pry.

Before long they reached what could generously be called a car park, but was just an ever so slightly bigger piece of road. Elsie parked and led the way up the steep path. This part of the countryside was covered in pine forest. It was different to the native bush surrounding the rest of Glen Haven, and the pine forest was old enough that it didn't seem to be likely to be felled for timber any time soon. The trees towered above them, and Amanda breathed in the fresh piney air appreciatively. She loved being out in nature, and, while perhaps she hadn't told Elsie the whole story of why she had come to this tiny little town, she really was excited to explore the many hikes Glen Haven boasted.

The ground beneath them was covered in brown pine needles, the air still cold from the morning dew. There was a faint hint of mist at the tops of the trees that gave the whole place a slightly mysterious air. The pair walked in companionable silence, the path too steep to allow for easy breathing, let alone conversation. After a little while, it began to flatten out and Amanda saw a clearing ahead of them. She drew in a sharp breath. The clearing was carpeted with bluebells and dainty little flowers in purples and white that Amanda was surprised she didn't know the name of. There were mushrooms nestled under almost every tree, and the early morning sunlight filtered through the canopy above, casting the clearing in a glowing gold.

"Welcome," Elsie said, turning and beaming at Amanda, "to Fairy Glen."

Coming closer, Amanda saw little painted fairy doors at the bottom of the trees. Some were obviously decorated by children, with characters placed higgledy piggledy across them, while others looked almost professional. Amanda saw one that was painted red and white like a classic fairy toadstool, and another a shimmery violet, complete with tiny silver stars dotted across it. Something about that one reminded Amanda of Elsie. When she caught her eye, Elsie nodded. "It's a little bit of a town tradition," she said, moving farther forward into the grove and reaching down to pluck up a few of the mushrooms. Amanda noticed Elsie left plenty behind, taking just a handful from each cluster.

Just then, her mobile pinged, and Amanda's body went rigid. Pulling out her phone, she saw a new message. "*You can run, but you can't hide.*" Amanda's heart began to race. The messages were getting more frequent, more intense. "Are you alright?," Elsie asked, moving towards her.

"Yes fine, just, um, would you mind if I have a bit of an explore first, and then come back and do some foraging?" Amanda hoped her voice didn't give her away. "It's just so beautiful. I'd love to have a quick look around before the sun gets too hot." Elsie looked confused, but she rallied quickly. "Of course, foraging isn't that interesting anyway, to be honest."

Amanda wanted to protest that she thought foraging sounded incredibly interesting actually, but she had to get away, and fast. "There are three or four different routes from here," Elsie explained, pointing at a quaint sign which directed the way to each of the various trails and indicated the rough amount of time each would take to walk.

"Any recommendations?" Amanda asked, trying to keep the panic out of her voice.

"They're all great. As you haven't been in this forest at all, I'd recommend the lookout. It's wonderful walking through the trees and then looking out across all of Glen Haven. It's only about a twenty or thirty-minute walk each way."

Quickly, Amanda set off up the steep track, assuring Elsie she'd stick to the trail and would be back in less than an hour and a half, including photo stops. She felt terrible about bailing on Elsie like that, but she couldn't break down in front of the woman.

After a few minutes of speed-walking, she stood beside an old tree, resting her hand on its gnarled trunk, and took a few deep breaths, trying to steady herself as a tide of anxiety rose inside her. Amanda knew the chances of anyone tracking her down in this tiny village in the middle of nowhere were minute, but the thought of what would happen if they did invaded her mind like a rabid army. She clutched her head in pain, the beginnings of a migraine arriving at the edge of her vision.

Her phone pinged with another message, this time from Pierce. "Developments in the case. Need to talk. May need you to testify after all."

Bile rose in her throat, and Amanda closed her eyes, breathing hard. She reminded herself she was safe here, repeating the phrase over and over again in her mind. Nobody, not even Pierce, knew where she was. She could do this. Shifting to the ground, she rested her head against the huge pine tree and forced herself to take long, controlled breaths. She slowed her breathing, consciously making herself breathe in through her nose and out through her mouth, still leaning against the tree for balance.

The track was quiet and peaceful, and Amanda tried to allow herself to be absorbed by its beauty. The narrow, winding path was speckled with pine needles and the first yellow-gold leaves of autumn. High in the trees, she could hear birds singing. Five things I can see: The leaves on that tree, probably a Carmichaelia Aborea, the sunlight on the ground, the moss contrasting with the bark on that tree, my hands pressing against the tree trunk, a caterpillar on that manuka flower. Four things I can hear: a bird singing, the wind rustling in the trees, my heart racing, my breathing. Three things I can feel: the bark against the palm of my hands, the wind blowing my hair across my face...Amanda continued the exercise with all five senses as she had been taught, and eventually her breathing came back under control.

Eventually, she was able to move, and she continued along the track, taking in the views, trying to empty her mind. She loved the peacefulness of nature, and with her history with plants, she enjoyed looking out trees that were native to the South Island, or spotting a particular varietal she was fond of. She breathed slowly again, reminding herself she was grateful to be here.

Here, she was free. Free from her family, from what people expected of her, from people who thought they knew her, and what she had done.

She reached the summit in less than half an hour, and Elsie had been right, of course. It was breathtaking. Down below, she could see the picturesque town of Glen Haven stretched out below her. The meandering stream winding its way towards the town. The pretty brick buildings like that of an old movie, the whole thing surrounded by hills coated in trees of every shade of green imaginable, with a smattering of yellow, red, and orange. Looking down, Amanda was amazed by just how isolated and quiet the little town was. There really was nothing else made by human hands as far as the eye could see, apart from a few farms on the town outskirts, the unnaturally large paddocks and fields fading into the hillside beyond. She breathed out her first full breath in minutes. There was no way they would find her here. She was in the middle of nowhere. Besides, unless she went back and testified, they would have no reason to hunt her down. Sure, Pierce would be disappointed, but there was nothing he could do. He couldn't make her testify, not when he didn't even know where she was.

She was safe here. Here, she could start over, maybe even live some of the dreams she had had growing up that had always seemed to out of reach. Her heart pinged again at the thought of her nursery. She would have to be careful, she knew that. But she could do this, so long as she kept her wits about her.

Turning back, Amanda made quick progress down the hill. The forest had certainly helped to quell the anxiety in her, but she wasn't getting the same sense of satisfaction that she normally would from a walk like this. Maybe being with Elsie and trying the foraging would help ease her mind. The woman exuded a peaceful quality, and Amanda was fascinated to learn more about what the forest could provide. Amanda was used to gardening, to growing trees from saplings, or planting bulbs in the autumn to watch them bloom in the spring, but the idea of simply seeing what nature provided was much more, earthy, somehow. Something about that appealed to Amanda immensely, and she felt bad for running off as she had. She hoped Elsie would still be up to showing her the basics.

As she rounded the last bend, Amanda saw Elsie bending down to pluck something from the ground. She looked like she was surrounded in purple mist, and for a second Amanda could have sworn she saw sparks of gold flying from Elsie's fingers. Her migraine must have been worse than she had thought, if she was still seeing lights. Shaking her head to clear out the last of the anxiety, she strode over and called out to Elsie, who looked up with a start.

8

Elsie

E lsie dropped the spell she had been casting immediately, cursing herself for being so careless. She'd been completely engrossed in what she was doing and hadn't heard Amanda approaching at all. The plants were still growing, but Elsie could feel something not quite right in the forest. She had thought, for a moment, that she could feel something magical pulling at the plants. Once again Elsie cursed her lack of ability with the natural world. Grannie Margie would have known exactly what was going on here. She didn't have time to think about that now, though. Schooling her face into a smile, Elsie stood and looked at Amanda. "You're back early," she said, hoping she sounded light-hearted.

"It's a bit easier on the way back down," Amanda said.

As Amanda approached, Elsie noticed her face was a little pale. She didn't have the same vigour that she had that first day they had met, or even earlier that morning. Concentrating, Elsie could feel residual waves of anxiety coming off Amanda. "Are you alright?" She asked, closing the gap between them and reaching out a hand to squeeze Amanda's before she had time to think about the appropriateness of it. Amanda looked at her hand in surprise, and Elsie withdrew it quickly. "Did something happen?"

Her touch seemed to bring Amanda back to herself, and she shook her head as if to clear it. "No, no," she said. "Just a few gremlins from the past plaguing my brain."

For a second, Elsie thought Amanda meant literal gremlins, but of course she was speaking metaphorically. "Do you want to go?' she asked, still concerned. "We could head back to town now if you need some peace and quiet." She looked around and laughed. "Or maybe a little less peace and quiet?"

Amanda smiled weakly. "Would it be ok if I help you for a while?" She sounded less confident than Elsie had ever heard her. "I'd like to be outside still, just maybe...." She trailed off, and Elsie got the distinct impression that Amanda wasn't used to asking for help, let alone depending on anyone. But she wanted company, that much was clear.

"Actually, I could really do with some help," she said, thinking fast. Elsie could practically see the relief washing over Amanda's face, and she knew she'd read the situation correctly. Well, perhaps they would just do a bit more gathering then, the non-magical way.

9

Amanda

Amanda took off her shoes at the front door and followed Elsie through to the kitchen. Elsie dumped her bags on the counter and flicked on the kettle. "Fancy a cuppa and some pear and rhubarb pie?" she asked. "I made some yesterday." Amanda's mouth started watering at the mere idea of a homemade pie. She hadn't had homemade food that she hadn't made herself in, actually, she couldn't even think how long.

Amanda was surprised at how easy she felt in Elsie's company already. Usually it took her a long time to get comfortable with someone, but foraging and chatting with Elsie today had felt so natural. Elsie had explained the properties of so many different plants and how they could be used. She sounded like a botanist with all her knowledge! Amanda was impressed by Elsie, but she didn't feel intimidated by her. Elsie seemed a little chaotic, but she was kind and gentle; something Amanda wasn't used to. Somehow, the woman already felt like a friend. Amanda studied her as she pottered around the kitchen, pulling a huge pie out of the fridge, turning on the oven, and even whipping some coconut cream to go with it. Elsie floated around the kitchen like a fish gliding through water, only less wet and much better looking! Even in her leggings and crop top, Elsie looked elegant, her blue-black hair falling in a long braid down her back. She wore no makeup that Amanda could see, but her lips were a vibrant red. She looked so at ease in this environment, so in control. "How did you become a chef?" she asked, curious. "Have you always been into cooking?"

Elsie placed two plates piled with delicious looking pie on the table in front of them and scooped a generous portion of cream onto each before sitting down opposite Amanda. "Actually, I studied to be an accountant," she said, and Amanda stared at her in surprise. She did not get a 'numbers and order' kind of vibe from this boho-chic woman. Elsie must have seen the shocked look on Amanda's face. "I've always liked numbers, and I was actually really good at it," she said, laughing. "But I was living in the city at the time, and the pace of it got to me. I was working long hours, not getting enough sleep. I never saw my family."

"I'm sorry," Amanda said, seeing Elsie in a new light. "So what happened?"

"My dad died suddenly," Elsie said, swallowing hard. Amanda put down her fork, looking at her new friend gently. "I was so caught up in grief, I couldn't do anything. I couldn't eat, couldn't even get out of bed most days. Then one day, I was lying in bed binge-watching a baking show on Netflix, and I thought, 'I could do that.' So I got up, and I did. Once I'd started baking it was all I wanted to do, it became kind of, meditative to me. Work had been great, but when they called me after two months saying they wanted me back in the office, I just couldn't do it." Elsie wrapped her hands around her mug of tea, looking into the past. "Everyone thought I was mad, but I chucked in my job and started baking instead. I set up a little store at the weekend market selling pies and scones. After a while, I started making specialty teas as well. Things kind of grew from there."

Amanda reached out and squeezed Elsie's arm gently, not even thinking about it. Elsie smiled at her gratefully. Her skin was smooth and warm, and Amanda found that she rather liked touching it. Quickly, she removed her hand again. Amanda wasn't usually a physically affectionate person, so she wasn't really sure where that had come from, but she was so touched by Elsie's openness, by her vulnerability. "That's an incredibly brave thing to do," she said, and she meant it. Amanda knew firsthand how hard it was to follow your dreams. She had done it herself. Even though the nursery Amanda had worked so hard for had been taken from her abruptly, she was glad she had owned it for a little while. It was nice to know she could work hard and make something happen, no matter how unlikely. That thought was even more comforting now she was starting over in Glen Haven.

She spooned pie and cream into her mouth. Her eyes went wide, and she moaned in ecstasy. Cinnamon, pear, rhubarb, vanilla, and the thick but delectably light coconut cream. This pie was heaven. "This is incredible!"

Elsie smiled, digging into her own pie. "I'm glad you like it," she said. "This one is my variation of one of my grandmother's recipes."

"Your grandmother baked too?" Amanda asked..

"She's where I learned how to cook," Elsie said, that faraway look in her violet eyes again. "I used to come to Glen Haven every summer when I was little and stay with Grandma for the holidays. We would bake, go foraging in the woods, go for walks along the riverside. It was wonderful." Elsie's eyes were misty now.

"You must miss her," Amanda whispered.

"I do. I miss them both. But I love that living in granny's house means I feel closer to her again. I have so many wonderful memories in this place. It's also where my dad grew up, so it's nice to have that sense of being close to them both, in some way." Amanda held Elsie's gaze and thought she'd never met anyone quite like this intelligent, gentle woman in front of her.

Philo plopped his giant head into Elsie's lap and barked a huge, bellowing sound that echoed around the entire kitchen. Elsie laughed, patting him on the head and nuzzling him affectionately. "I know buddy. You're ready for some lunch, hey?" She rubbed her knuckles over his nose and Philo wagged his tail, smacking Amanda on the leg with the force of it.

Amanda followed Elsie out through the backdoor of the kitchen and stopped dead. In front of her, in a sprawling mass of green and yellow, was a chaotic mess which had obviously once been a garden. "Wow."

Elsie looked back. "Oh, yes." Elsie looked a little embarrassed now. "My grandmother was rather a green thumb, but I'm afraid I haven't inherited her skills." She picked her way along what Amanda assumed was a path, underneath all that overgrowth. "I've tried a few times, but the garden just won't seem to do as I ask. It's such a shame as I'd love to have more vegetables for my savoury pies, but alas." She waved her hand around at the mess in a look of surrender. "I'll either have to pay someone to do it, or rip it all up and put pavers down. But I don't really have the spare cash to do either," she said with a grimace.

"I could do it for you." Amanda surprised herself as the words left her mouth. "I love gardening. I used to run a nursery."

Elsie's eyes grew wide. "Seriously?" Then she looked sad again. "That's so kind, but as I said, I don't have the money to pay you. Unless...." She gave Amanda a strange look, and then, all in a rush, she said, "You're looking for somewhere to live, aren't you? I have a couple of spare rooms. You could stay here and just pay expenses, if you could help out in the garden, and maybe with a few odd jobs here and there about the place?"

"What?" Amanda asked, feeling relief washing over her body at the thought of having somewhere more long-term to live. Her back still ached from the lumpy BnB bed, and she was getting worried about the cost. The postie gig was temporary cover for the usual guy, Murray, who was injured, but Amanda didn't know how long it would be until he was back on his feet. Of course, now she was selling her beloved nursery, she would have some more cash, but that wouldn't last forever. This could be just what Amanda needed to establish herself properly in town. "That would be amazing!"

Amanda looked at her watch and swore. The Real Estate agent would be on the phone shortly, and Amanda wanted to be back in her room to have that discussion. "I have to get going, but shall we catch up tomorrow to go through the details?"

Elsie smiled. "Sounds great!" she said, walking Amanda back through the house and hugging her goodbye. Amanda found herself wrapping her arms snuggly around Elsie's slight frame, a feeling she hadn't felt in a long while growing in her stomach. "Come and see me at the shop. I'll text you the address."

As Amanda walked back down the hill, she reflected on what had been an eventful day. The messages from back home were still sitting heavily on her chest, but the forest had calmed her a little. Something about being in Elsie's house, and the woman herself, also helped to settle Amanda. Would living there put Elsie in danger? No, Amanda didn't think so. They wouldn't come after her so long as she didn't testify. So long as she stayed away, she was safe. Hopefully, her dad would be too.

She thought again of that night. Of overhearing her brother say that he wanted to take over his dad's gig for good. She shuddered at the memory, at the cold calculation in Theo's voice as he discussed destroying his own father. They were very, very bad men, and Amanda was glad to be clear of them. If she got even a whiff that they were on her tail, she would move on.

As she got in the van and drove through the quiet streets, Amanda realised just how much she wanted this fresh start to be the beginning of a whole new chapter. Sure, she would have to be careful, but she could afford to have a friend, couldn't she? For the first time since she had run away, Amanda felt hope begin to take root in her heart. Finally, maybe things were looking up.

10

Elsie

"What were you thinking?" Elsie asked her reflection exasperatedly. "You can't bring a total stranger into your home! You must be mad."

"You're not mad, you're lonely," her reflection replied, and Elsie jumped. She'd forgotten that she'd enchanted the mirror. Sometimes she needed someone to bounce ideas off, but there was nobody else in the house except Philo, and although the loveable mutt was very enthusiastic in his affection towards Elsie, their connection hadn't yet reached full conversation levels. Mirror-Elsie was right, she *was* lonely.

"But she's *human*," Elsie reminded her reflection. "This is a terrible idea." It wasn't as though witches could *never* be friends or, Elsie conceded in response to the raised eyebrow in the mirror, more than friends, with humans. It just wasn't usually a great idea. History hadn't exactly shown humans and witches to live together in harmony. Plus, people could be rather judgemental about things like the ability to levitate or brew a potion to turn a person into a toad. Witches all had very strict codes which they adhered to. Usually these included things like not turning people into toads, but humans didn't always find that as reassuring as one might think.

"You like her, though," mirror- Elsie cut into Elsie's thoughts. "And honestly, how often do you click with someone so quickly?"

It was true, Elsie had always been slow at making friends. She was quirky and a tad chaotic for most people, especially the somewhat more old-fashioned folk of Glen Haven. Elsie had hoped that they would welcome her, given that she had been coming to the town for years as a child, but the town was very slow to let new people in. Reginald hadn't helped, Elsie thought wryly.

On top of that, although Elsie craved connection, and wanted desperately to build relationships with people, she had learned to be cautious.

Few people 'got' her, and on the rare occasion she started getting close to someone, she became anxious and second-guessed it. Elsie had had a few too many negative experiences with humans who knew about her magic in the past, so now she was more cautious about opening up to humans. It was hard, as by nature Elsie was an open book, but she couldn't risk the harm that seemed to come when humans found out about her powers. As a result, she had probably pushed away the few people she had almost become friends with over the past year; putting up barriers just as they began to get closer, and sending some rather mixed-signals. She liked people, and she was always kind, but it was rare for her to instantly like someone as much as she'd liked Amanda.

"You need a friend," mirror-Elsie said. "You're sad and lonely, and if you stay locked up here in this house by yourself for much longer, you really will go mad." Elsie stuck her tongue out. Sometimes her reflection could be a little *too* honest. Her image changed tac- "just think how nice it will be to have the garden looking like a garden again," it said, and Elsie sighed wistfully. When her grandmother had lived here, the garden had been the pride of this house. Brick paths meandered among beds of flowers, vegetables, and herbs. A row of fruit trees lined the far end, producing oranges, apples, and pears all year round. Her grandmother had had green magic in spades. Elsie, on the other hand, couldn't even keep a cactus alive. It wasn't for lack of trying; she loved being in the forest, loved sitting in the garden appreciating the bursts of colour from the flowers and vegetables, but every time she tried to tend to them, something went wrong. Elsie didn't know if she was under watering or over watering, she didn't know how to prune or when to put down fertiliser. Plus, Elsie had been so busy trying to set up her business that she just hadn't had time to learn.

The deep purple Royal Empress out front was the only thing that still bloomed. Probably that was because Elsie had left it alone, trusting that the winter rains would keep it alive. She had watched in relief as it bloomed violet flowers again in the spring. Her dad had been green-thumbed like his mother, and Elsie wished that he or Grandma were still here to help her. She thought of her father's kind, narrow face, his quiet smile and his readiness to lend a hand. She missed him and Grandma so much.

They weren't here, though, and Amanda was. Who knew, maybe Amanda moving in would be the start of a new chapter in her life. Goodness knows that her integration into Glen Haven had been less smooth than she'd have liked. But maybe a friend, a *human* friend, could help her feel more at home here. And if she brought Grandma's old garden back to life as well, then so much the better.

Elsie set to work clearing out one of the spare bedrooms for Amanda, tidying away broomsticks and old tomes of spells that she hadn't yet gotten around to putting on the bookshelves. She packed up candles and herbs and her beloved cauldron.

Most of Elsie's magic was done in the kitchen, outside, or in her bedroom. Much of it wouldn't cause suspicion; just the mixing of ingredients while she murmured a few words. Nevertheless, she'd need to be careful now a human was moving in.

Elsie worked best as night; usually under a full moon, or at least at the witching hour. Amanda already knew she was a night owl, so she shouldn't be too surprised if Elsie was up 'baking' or 'brewing tea' at odd hours. Whisking the various candles and some vials of oils out of what was to be Amanda's room, Elsie realised she would need to give the whole house a spring clean, removing any evidence of magic before Amanda moved in. She sighed and set to work.

There was a study to the right at the top of the stairs, and Elsie piled all her magic paraphernalia in there. She floated everything through to the room, creating a levitating Congo-line, and encouraged it all to line up on the floor or in various cupboards around the room. Some things she needed to shrink to fit, but for the most part, she just embraced the higgledy-piggledy nature of the house. There was one small mishap to do with turning a wardrobe into a toad for a few moments, but overall the move went reasonably smoothly. Elsie was pretty good at magic, but, especially without anyone to practice with in town, and few reasons to cast significant spells, she was getting a little rusty. Witches honed their craft throughout their entire lifetime, and Elsie thought guiltily that she really should work harder at hers.

Finally, she cast a kind of reverse glamour spell to make the study look like just a dusty old room with a desk and a computer to anyone without magic who might open the door. Dusting her hands off, she looked around the room in satisfaction. She hadn't done much big magic since moving to Glen Haven, and it was nice to know that she still had it in her.

11

Amanda

A manda had learned her lesson from the foraging incident. She got up, had breakfast, went for a walk around the town, and timed her arrival at Elsie's shop for just before 11am. She was starving by the time she got there, and the rich aromas coming from the store were delectable. A jaunty sign above the door read "Pie in the Sky," and a corner of Amanda's mouth drew up as she pushed open the door. Clearly, she wasn't the only one around here who enjoyed a good, or perhaps a bad, pun.

A pretty sounding bell she couldn't see rang as she entered the shop. The store itself was small, not much more than a hole in the wall, with a scattering of pastel coloured tables and chairs outside, and half a dozen inside. She gazed around in interest. The space was light and bright, with sprays of white plastic flowers hanging from the ceiling and in tiny vases on every table. It should have looked tacky, but with the lanterns, mirrors, and quirky pictures on the walls, it created a soft, friendly atmosphere. A long cabinet took up almost half of the space. A riot of colour, it was filled with a dozen different kinds of pies, as well as a selection of sandwiches, cakes, slices, and cupcakes. Amanda's mouth watered at the sight, and her stomach growled in agreement.

As Amanda reached the counter, she decided on a peppery mushroom pie and a vanilla and lavender cupcake, complete with a frosted butterfly on top. It was a little more twee than she'd usually go for, but something about the lilac, sparkly butterfly appealed to her. Elsie came through a swinging wooden door which presumably led to the kitchen. Amanda could hear the muffled sound of dishes clattering around out the back. She gave Amanda a huge smile as she walked up to the till. "Welcome." She said, holding her hands out in a kind of 'ta da' gesture.

Amanda's heart ticked up a beat at the sight of Elsie. "Cool shop," she said, trying to hide her enthusiasm.

"You like it?" Elsie asked, more anxiously than Amanda would have expected. Now she felt like a dick.

"It's amazing. You've done a great job with the place."

Elsie beamed. "Thank you," she said, blushing. "I've been open for about seven months now, but it's been hard getting the locals to come in. They're very loyal to Beth's Bakehouse on the Main Road."

"But this place is extraordinary!" Amanda enthused, surprising herself with how much she liked it. It wasn't her usual vibe, but Amanda liked that the place had character. It reminded her of Elsie-pretty, calming, and intriguing.

"Thank you," Elsie said again, looking up at Amanda from under her eyelashes. "I have lots more ideas, but for now, it's about creating the brand and getting people to come in and keep coming back. Oh!" Elsie fished around in the hemp apron tied at her slender waist. "Here," she said, pulling out an ornate silver key on an orange ribbon and handing it to Amanda. "I realise I haven't shown you around properly yet, but if you want to start moving in while I'm at work, feel free. Just please don't let Philo out!"

"I think I can manage that," Amanda said, handing over some money.

Elsie rang up her order, continuing. "I've put you in the other bedroom with an ensuite. It's to the left at the top of the stairs and looks out over the back garden. Hope that works for you?" An ensuite!? This was sounding better and better.

"Perfect," Amanda said, pocketing her change. "Thank you, and thanks for this." She held up her food. "I'm really looking forward to it."

Amanda sat down at a table in the corner and dug into the pie enthusiastically. The rich creaminess of the mushrooms was cut through by the pepper. It was perfectly balanced and tasted like cosiness in a bite. I could get used to this. She had picked up a copy of the Glen Haven Times from the counter, and she spread it out in front of her. It was nice to just sit down, relax, and enjoy reading the paper. She hadn't done this in years.

Just then, a shadow fell across the newspaper, and Amanda looked up to see a tall, slim man with a ridiculous moustache staring down at her, a look of distaste on his face. "Hello?" she said, uncertainly.

The man pulled out a chair and sat down, uninvited. "You're the new post girl, aren't you?"

34

Amanda's hackles immediately went up. "I'm the new postwoman," she emphasised. "Yes."

Something flitted across the man's face as she said this, but he smiled toothily and continued. "I see. Well, I am Reginald Arnold the second." Amanda stifled a snort, hiding it behind a fake sneeze just in time. "I'm Editor-in-Chief at the Glen Haven Times."

"Pleased to meet you," Amanda lied, wondering why this self-aggrandising fellow was here.

"I hear you are staying at the BnB. Are you finding everything to your liking?"

News sure travelled fast in a small town. She'd been here less than two weeks!

"It's lovely," Amanda said, unwilling to comment on the lumpy mattress and noises in the night to this foul man. "But I'll be moving out shortly."

"Heading out of town so soon? What a shame. Still, Glen Haven isn't for everyone." Reginald shrugged and began to rise, unsuccessfully attempting to hide a smile.

Amanda remembered Elsie mentioning the townsfolk hadn't been very welcoming to her. She was beginning to understand what she meant. "Oh, no," Amanda responded, angry now. "I've sourced some more long-term accommodation." She smiled over-sweetly, and Reginald's eyes narrowed.

"I see," he said slowly, his bottom hovering in an awkward squat over the chair. After a moment, he thumped back down. "You won't mind me asking where you have managed to secure lodgings at such short notice?"

Amanda was annoyed with herself for goading this idiotic man. She knew he was harmless. She had met his type before; self-elected interfering townsperson. Sometimes, though, instead of ignoring them like she should, she just had to fight. Even more so when they were arrogant misogynists, as this one clearly was. "Actually, I do mind. It's not any of your business where I'm staying. Now, if you don't mind, I'm going to go back to reading my newspaper and enjoying my day off."

She picked up the newspaper pointedly and held it in front of her face. There was a sputtering sound, but when it became clear that Amanda wasn't backing down, Reginald stood with a huff, muttering, "I say, city people have no manners these days."

Amanda didn't bother to correct him that she wasn't a city person. She didn't even look up again until the thick smell of his aftershave had disappeared. Moments later, another shadow appeared across her newspaper. Amanda sighed and steeled herself internally, but she smelt the faint scent of cinnamon and jasmine, and when she looked up, it was to see the anxious face of Elsie. "Are you ok?" Elsie asked, "Reginald can be a bit..." She searched for the word. "Sharp."

"I'm fine," Amanda assured her, putting the newspaper down and indicating for Elsie to sit. Elsie plopped onto the chair heavily. "I'm not scared of bullies like him. What was he doing in here, though? It doesn't strike me that someone as foul as him would frequent a lovely shop like this." Elsie's face darkened, and Amanda noticed a tiny smudge of flour across her high cheekbone. Her fingers itched to dust it off.

"He doesn't come here very often, you're right." Elsie said, unconsciously wiping at her face and making the smudge bigger. "He just drops in now and then to criticise my food or, on the odd occasion I have customers, to comment loudly on how much better the food is at Beth's."

Amanda felt her face reddening with anger at this. "He what?" she asked, indignant.

"It's not too bad," Elsie said hurriedly. "Like I said, townsfolk are slow to warm up here. Reginald and Beth are some of the worst; they're determined to keep new people out of Glen Haven. Reginald ran a couple of pieces in the paper about how bad my food was when I first started, but I think he's run out of steam for that sort of thing. Nowadays he'll just pop by now and then to remind people that Beth's is better. I think sometimes he tries to use it as a place to collect town gossip, but as you might imagine, his presence does rather put people off." Amanda was getting outraged. She hated seeing people picking on or using others just because they were small or didn't fit in. This Reginald had clearly been throwing his weight around, and Amanda didn't like it.

"Still, you must be doing ok? All this food, a kitchen hand..."

"Kitchen hand?"

"Oh, I heard someone doing dishes out back, plus that tray of cupcakes in the cabinet has been refilled." Elsie's face froze for a moment, and then her smile was back. "Oh, that's just a dishwasher, and I had some more cupcakes to hand. It's just me." Elsie shrugged exaggeratedly. Amanda was confused. She could have sworn she had heard a tap being turned on and off and dishes being placed on the bench.

"How was your day?" Elsie asked, that cheery smile not quite reaching her eyes. "You probably know your way around Glen Haven better than me with your job!"

Amanda settled back into her chair. "It was good, thanks. I should probably have spent some more time looking for work, given the postie thing is only short term. Honestly, though, it was so nice just to relax for once." Amanda said, taking another bite of the pie and feeling her eyes roll heaven-ward. "This is amazing, by the way. As for knowing the town, I'm getting there," she said. "The town center is obviously not too big, but it's amazing how far into the hills some houses go. I had to drive for forty minutes the other day to deliver a parcel to somewhere called 'Holly Oakes Farm,' as if Glen Haven isn't remote enough!"

Elsie smiled. "Ah yes, the Burridge clan. They do tend to keep to themselves, from what I understand. My grandmother told me they come into the town about four times a year to stock up on various supplies and so on. But apart from that, they just keep to themselves out in the wilderness."

Elsie shuddered, but Amanda thought it sounded quite delightful. "I can certainly think of worse things than being stuck in nature with everything you need, only having to interact with other people quarterly, and in complete control of when you have to do so."

Elsie looked horrified. "Nature, sure. But can you imagine being by yourself for that long?" She asked, her eyes going round.

"Sounds like bliss!" At the look on Elsie's face, Amanda laughed heartily.

"I guess you must be a bit of an introvert," Elsie said, studying her with apparent interest.

Amanda shrugged. "I grew up learning to depend on myself. I like people sometimes, but I'm very comfortable in my own company. I guess I'm an introvert, though that's not to say I wouldn't value having a few close people in my life, a partner to spend my days and nights with...." Why was her face going red, and why was she babbling? She never usually talked this much! She wasn't trying to suggest to Elsie that they move away to the middle of

37

nowhere together. Though she could probably think of worse things.... "I'm just more used to being on my own, I guess," she finished weakly.

Elsie said, leaned forward, studying Amanda. "I'm ok on my own, but even though I grew up with just Mum and Dad, and my cousin Phoebe, I've always had people around. Mum and Dad seemed to bring in stray animals and stray people alike, so I'm pretty used to a bustling house. It took me a long time to get used to living on my own here, and even then I think I would have completely lost the plot if it wasn't for Philo."

Amanda laughed. "He sure has a lot of personality. How long have you had him?"

"Just over a year," Elsie said, with a smile. He came to me when he was just six months old."

"Came to you?" Amanda asked.

A strange look flitted across Elsie's face, but again, it was gone before Amanda could place it. Amanda was usually excellent at reading people; she had learned young to pay attention to tiny nuances in the way a person held themselves. Elsie, despite her friendliness and her charms, was much harder to figure out.

"He just turned up on my doorstep one day," Elsie said. "As soon as I laid eyes on him, I knew it was meant to be. He was skinny as a rake and shivering, but he warmed up to me pretty quickly."

"Gosh," Amanda said. "Do you think he was abused?"

"I'm not sure," Elsie said slowly. "There have been a few things that made me think maybe that was the case. How he looked when he turned up, for one thing. But also he's terrified of loud noises, goes into full on shakes and everything. I think maybe he had a bad experience with something or someone when he was just a little puppy."

"That's awful," Amanda said with feeling. Why couldn't people pick on people their own size for once? "You'd never know now, though. He's such a happy, friendly dog."

"He is," Elsie agreed, beaming. "He's come such a long way since then, and even though he's still a bit of a handful sometimes, he really is such a good boy."

Just then, the chime over the shop door tinkled, and Elsie leapt to her feet. "Sorry for disturbing your 'me time,'" she said. "Best get back to work!"

Amanda watched her retreating back with interest. Here was a woman who was hiding something. She knew, because she was one too.

12

Elsie

Elsie was putting chairs on tables ready to sweep the floor of the Pie in the Sky when she heard the chimes above the door. Instantly, the dishes wish were washing themselves out the back fell dormant in the sink. She had learned her lesson about disembodied dish-washing. "Cool consequential alert spell," an accented voice said, and Elsie looked up in surprise. In front of her stood a tall, sleek man with a narrow face and perfectly quaffed ash-blond hair. He wore a huge grin as he looked at Elsie, and she could feel the magic radiating off him in waves.

"Thanks!" She leaned the broom against the counter and walked towards him, shaking his hand. "I'm Elsie."

"Soren," the man said. Elsie guessed the accent was Scandinavian. Normally a complete stranger identifying a spell upon meeting her would send Elsie into a tailspin, but the magic coming off this man was so strong that Elsie knew he had to be a witch.

"Pleasure to meet you," Elsie said, surprised by how cool his touch was. "What brings you to Glen Haven?"

"My family is from here." The man said, pulling out a chair and sitting down opposite Elsie.

"Really?" Elsie knew she would have noticed Soren around town before now, and unless his family neither resembled him in magic nor looks, she hadn't come across them in all her years of visiting Glen Haven, either.

"We founded this town, that's why the forest is called Viskande." Elsie felt a flash of anger at this. She knew the indigenous people of New Zealand had been in these parts for hundreds of years. Soren presumably meant his family were among the first white settlers to come here in the 1800s. Elsie had often wondered why there were names in Glen Haven in Swedish - here was her answer.

"Glen Haven was founded by a witch family?" She asked, surprised.

"Witches and... others, yes," Soren said, waving his hand languidly and levitating one of Elsie's cupcakes into his hand. He raised an eyebrow at her, "do you mind?"

"Not at all," Elsie said hurriedly. It was so exciting to have another witch in her shop that she didn't even mind him not paying for the treat. It was awesome just to see someone else do what she could do.

"So your family is moving back?" Elsie felt a pang of excitement that a whole witch family could be moving to town. People she wouldn't have to pretend around, people who would understand her need to collect stardust under a full moon, or to make potions because the tea leaves were forbidding. Elsie shivered at the image of the cross, which was haunting her tea leaves almost every day now.

"Just me for now. The rest of my family is still in Stockholm." Soren looked at the ground for a moment, a frown on his face. "We are not terribly close, truth be told, but I hope they will join me in due course." Then he bit into the cherry chocolate cupcake. "This is rather good."

"Thank you." Elsie felt a flash of camaraderie with this man - away from his family, somewhere new, without any connections.

"We still have our old homestead here, so I've been able to settle in without too much bother. Though I am not used to living in such an isolated town."

Elsie grinned. The population of the entire South Island was probably about that of Stockholm. In fact, New Zealand was well known for having a higher sheep population than human population. Taking in Soren's sleek black trench coat, stylish shirt, and shiny shoes, she imagined he had come from a city. Glen Haven would be rather a shock to him then.

"Are you the only witch in town?" Soren asked, leaning back in his chair and looking at her appraisingly.

"As far as I know," Elsie replied, a little taken aback. "I could feel your powers as soon as you walked in the door, so I assume I would know if there were any other witches around."

Soren winked at her. "My powers are rather strong. They're easy to detect." Elsie blushed and Soren went on, "But so far, you're the only one whose powers I have sensed here."

Had Soren come looking for her because she was a witch? Elsie didn't think she'd ever been sought out before. That was certainly a pleasant change. As they exchanged numbers and Soren took his leave, her mind raced. OK, two people were too few for a coven, but still, it would be nice to have someone to do witchy things with.

13

Amanda

As she stood at the top of the hill, panting, Amanda took in her ornate new home. She noticed for the first time that there was a stained-glass image above the front door. It seemed to be a crescent moon and five stars. She couldn't believe this was where she would be living for the foreseeable future. It was certainly a far-cry from the tiny little run-down shack she had lived in next to her nursery.

Hearing Philo's bark as she approached, she called out a hello and pulled the ornate key from her pocket. Her favourite colour was orange, and she momentarily wondered if Elsie had known that when she gave her the key. But that was silly. "I have a knack for knowing what people want." Elsie's words came back to her, and Amanda shook herself. This was a living arrangement, nothing more. Bracing for the polar bear, she carefully ducked through into the entrance hall. She was greeted with a shower of enthusiastic barks and wet kisses.

Amanda didn't have much stuff. When she'd left, she had simply packed a bag with her most precious possessions, stuffed some clothes into a suitcase, and run. She now left the suitcase in the hallway, deciding to check out the house before unpacking. In the cold light of day, it seemed a little hasty for Amanda to be moving into a house she hadn't even fully seen before, with a woman she'd met just three times, including this morning. But she didn't have many better options. Elsie seemed nice, more than nice, if Amanda was honest. Besides, if it really all fell apart, she knew she could be packed up and on the road again in fifteen minutes flat.

The house was an old, two-story building, with the feel of a manor, but more the size of a large cottage. As you entered through the front door, there was a grand, winding staircase to the left, and a long entranceway in front, with several doors coming off it. Amanda knew you walked through the hallway to the end of the house to get to the kitchen, resplendent in its purple and silver glory. The door just before the kitchen was to a cosy lounge, complete with a fireplace and walls full of books. The mahogany floor was covered with a huge red rug, providing a warmth and softness to what could otherwise be quite an imposing room.

The mantelpiece above the fireplace held a photo of a slim, dark-haired man in his late fifties. The photo was in a delicate silver frame with a heart in the top left corner, and, approaching, Amanda knew that this man must be Elsie's late father. He had the same kind, almond-shaped eyes as Elsie, and his shiny dark hair mirrored hers. The cheek bones were a little different, sitting in a narrower face than Elsie's heart-shaped one, and his skin tone a little darker, but there was no mistaking the family resemblance. The mantel held three large candles of various shapes at one end, and another, a small, silver one in front of the photo. It was almost like an altar. Amanda felt a pang as she thought of her own father, and the crumpled photo she kept in an old novel, which she tried to pretend she had simply forgotten to throw away.

Opening the other doors along the hall, Amanda found a laundry, a hall cupboard, and a bathroom. Heading through to the kitchen at the back of the house, she saw an enormous slice of lemon meringue pie on the kitchen island with a lilac sticky note saying "welcome" written on it in elegant slanted letters. There was also a little drawing of a smiling hedgehog underneath. Amanda stared at the pie and the note, a warmth growing in her belly. She couldn't remember a time when anyone had ever done something like this for her before. When she moved in with Jo, the only romantic partner she had ever attempted to live with, all she had walked into was a sink full of dirty dishes and a text saying 'heading to the pub, don't wait up.' Probably a red flag, she thought, in hindsight.

She knew the pie would be left-over from the shop, but she was touched that Elsie had thought to leave her something, her favourite kind of pie, in fact. Her eyes kept being drawn back to the note with that adorable little hedgehog. The pie looked so amazing that Amanda paused her snooping of the house to sit down and eat it straight away.

Philo came over and placed his huge head on her lap as she ate. The first bite was pure bliss. Flaky pastry, tangy lemon curd with a hint of, was that basil? Wow! The flavour combination was utterly divine. It was all finished off with a light, slightly crisped meringue topping that melted in her mouth.

Amanda involuntarily let out a groan of pleasure. This pie was good. She didn't know how Elsie's shop wasn't swarming with people. If she knew there was a bakery that sold this kind of food in town, Amanda felt sure she would find it hard to leave!

Polishing off the delectable pie in record time, Amanda grabbed her suitcase and backpack and headed upstairs, Philo hot on her heels. Amanda sighed with pleasure as she opened the first door to the left at the top of the stairs. High ceilings, eggshell blue walls, and a big bay window at the other end with, yes, a view out to the garden. The tall, four-poster bed looked a little old-fashioned, but comfortable, and the ensuite even had a bath. This was luxury. Amanda hoped her gardening skills would be up to scratch. She suddenly felt rather conscious of having to earn her keep in a house this fancy.

Amanda was eager to get to work in the garden, keen to earn her keep. After quickly putting her few items of clothing away, Amanda and Philo headed back downstairs to assess the garden.

Somehow today, the overgrown mess was worse than she remembered, and Amanda knew she had her work cut out for her. However, she had never been one to shy away from hard work. Rolling up her sleeves, she assessed the situation. A rather overgrown patio with a sunshade melted into the meandering garden. The garden was a large, walled space with a tall elm and several tired looking fruit trees at the far end, and veggie beds that seemed to house nothing but weeds all around the outer edge of the space. It looked like there used to be a brick pathway somewhere underneath all the grass and weeds that coated the floor, and she could see a few hardy bushes still fighting to stay upright. Lavender hedges trimmed the pathway, and there was some sort of plant trying to grow over the walls, but it seemed to be fighting a losing battle at present.

The first thing she would need to do was get all the weeds out. Then, once she could see what was underneath all of this overgrowth, she could figure out a plan. It looked like there might have been vegetable gardens, flower beds, and herb gardens, as well as a grassy area, but it was hard to tell with the amount of mess and overgrowth that was going on here. Clearly, the garden had been neglected for some time. Amanda could tell that the garden would once have been beautiful, though.

Elsie had mentioned that there were some tools in the shed in the corner, so Amanda picked her way across to it and hauled the rusty door open. The shed itself was surprisingly tidy, with shelves covering every wall. There were stacks of wooden crates with symbols on them that Amanda didn't recognise, and there was an unusual, slightly aniseed scent in the air. After poking around for a bit, she found a crate with garden gloves and trowels in it. She also found an old yellow wheelbarrow at the back of the shed, its jaunty colouring standing out brightly in the dusty space.

Amanda hauled the wheelbarrow, gloves, and trowels out, and got to work, pulling up weeds and throwing them into the barrow, being careful to avoid anything that looked like it might be a salvageable plant.

It was hot work in the early autumn sunshine, and it wasn't long before Amanda pulled her sweaty plaid-shirt off and continued working in just her shorts and sports bra. Philo padded around enthusiastically, getting rather in the way, but having a lovely time doing so. After two hours, Amanda decided it was time for a break. Leaving her muddy boots at the door, she walked into the house to grab a drink.

14

Elsie

Elsie started at a noise from behind her. Turning, she saw Amanda walk through the back door in socks, shorts, and a sports bra, a blue and white checked shirt thrown casually over one shoulder. Her knees were covered in mud and leaves, and she had a smudge of dirt across her cheek. The turquoise ankle socks were pulled up, emphasising her strong calves, and in high-waisted shorts and a sports bra, her curvy figure was on display.

Wow. Elsie felt heat rush through her body. Calm down! She told her libido sternly. This was ridiculous. She was going to have to get used to having Amanda in her house. She certainly didn't mind seeing her bare arms and curvaceous figure, but she couldn't be ogling at her every time she entered a room, or things with her new friend were going to get awkward fast.

"Oh, hi!" Amanda said, noticing Elsie. Quickly, she threw her shirt back over her head and tied it at her waist.

"Hi," Elsie smiled warmly at Amanda, relieved, albeit disappointed, that the top had gone back on.

"Thank you so much for the pie." Amanda walked to the sink and got herself a glass of water. A bead of condensation dripped off the glass and down her cleavage, and Elsie had to tear her eyes away, shaking herself. "It was absolutely delicious."

"Hmm?"

"The pie," Amanda repeated. "It was the best lemon meringue pie I've ever had, and that's one of my absolute favourite desserts, so I assure you, I've had a few!"

"Oh!" Elsie pulled herself with some effort back into the conversation. "I'm so glad you liked it. I had a feeling lemon meringue might be your thing. It's a plant-based version of an old recipe of my grandma's I found, plus I added basil for a little something extra."

"I would never have thought that basil in a lemon meringue pie would work," Amanda said, tugging her high bun loose and letting her brown hair fall in soft waves to her collarbone. "But it was absolutely amazing." She leaned against the sink, downing another glass of water. "Did you say plant-based? I thought meringue was made from egg?"

Elsie sat at the kitchen island, a cup of tea held between both hands. It had been a long day at the shop, and she was tired. However, she was very excited by the idea of having someone to come home to, as well as Philo, of course. "Usually it is," she explained, "but there's this thing called aquafaba that you can use instead. It comes from chickpeas and," Seeing the horrified look on Amanda's face, Elsie laughed, "I know, I was completely unconvinced at first, but it works remarkably well! It's cheap, easy, animal-free, and it doesn't taste like chickpeas by the time you're done with it. Plus, then you can use the chickpeas for hummus!"

Amanda still didn't look convinced. "If I hadn't already devoured that pie, there's no way I would believe you." She said, shaking her head, "That is some kind of witchcraft."

Elsie froze.

But Amanda was grinning, and then she turned, washed her glass, and popped it to dry on the rack next to the sink. "I'm going to hit the shower. I'm pretty disgusting from the garden."

"I didn't expect you to get started so soon!" Elsie said, finally registering that, of course, that was why Amanda had come in hot and sweaty and covered in dirt.

"It was actually pretty fun." Amanda's eyes were alight, a broad smile spreading across her flushed, round cheeks. "I haven't done proper gardening for ages, not since—" Something flashed across Amanda's face. "Well, not for a long while, anyway. It was nice to be outside getting my hands dirty again."

Elsie decided she wouldn't push Amanda now on what she had been about to say, but made a mental note to come back to that. "I'm glad you're enjoying it. There's towels in the hallway cupboard. The shower itself is pretty self-explanatory. Are you hungry? I was thinking of making eggplant moussaka for dinner."

"That sounds incredible," Amanda said. "Though I have to warn you, I'm not much of a cook. I'll try my best to return the favour, but it won't

48

be anything as fancy as eggplant moussaka, I'm afraid." She began walking away and then turned, as if she'd just registered something. "Actually, if you're plant-based, my repertoire is probably even more limited. I might have some swatting up to do!"

"It's fine," Elsie said, waving away Amanda's concerns. "I enjoy cooking. I'll happily show you a few recipes if you like. I just hope you don't get too sick of pies. If we don't sell them at the store, then I sometimes end up taking them home."

"Based on the two I've had today, there's no way I'll get sick of them," Amanda said, throwing Elsie a wink that made her insides flutter. "But I'd be keen to learn some new recipes too, thanks! See you in a bit."

And she walked out, a tiny trail of leaves following after her. Elsie sighed. She had a feeling this was going to be both nicer and harder than she had thought.

15

Elsie

S oren strolled into Pie in the Sky late the following morning. He looked around the empty shop and quirked an eyebrow at her. "Slow day?" He asked.

Elsie's cheeks flushed. She had tried so hard to get Pie in the Sky off the ground, but people in Glen Haven just didn't seem prepared to break with their traditions of going to Beth's Bakehouse. Reginald's overbearing ways certainly hadn't helped, but Elsie knew that really it was just that the townsfolk didn't like her.

"What's wrong?" Soren asked, clearly sensing her discomfort.

"Oh, nothing," Elsie plastered on a smile. "Just, you know, slow few months. More than a few, honestly."

Soren shrugged. "So cast a spell to bring some people in." He said nonchalantly. "What's stopping you? Do you need some help with it?"

Elsie widened her eyes. "No, it's not that."

"What is it then?"

Elsie was confused. She didn't have that many adult witch friends, really just Phoebe, in America, but even at school, she had never come across a witch who would so casually suggest casting a spell on other people. Maybe they did things differently in Europe? "I don't cast spells on people." She said, not sure how to explain something she had always taken so for granted. "It's against my code. I don't use magic on people without their consent."

"Do the people in this town know you're a witch?" Soren asked, stepping back in surprise.

"No!"

"Well then, how could they consent to you using magic on them?"

"That's just it, they couldn't."

Soren shook his head. "This seems like a strange thing to me. You want more customers, you have a way to do that. You wouldn't be hurting anyone.

The worst thing that could happen would be people would get fed. What's wrong with that?" His furrowed brow was quite endearing.

Elsie shook her head. "That's not how I use my magic." She said, placing a chilli cinnamon donut on a plate for Soren and sitting opposite him. The advantage of her little shop being empty was that she had plenty of time to catch up with people, she supposed.

Soren looked bemused, but he didn't push the issue. He just dug hungrily into the donut.

"What are you up to today?" Elsie asked, keen to change the subject. "Are you settling into your family home ok?"

A flash of something crossed Soren's face, but he simply shrugged. "It is ok," he said, "the house needs a lot of cleaning, but I have some enchanted items on the way which should help with that." Elsie tried to hide her surprise. Enchanted items were not exactly rare, but they were expensive. Soren's family must be well off for him to have several on the way. "Will you be working while you're in town?" She asked, realising she had no idea what kind of work Soren did.

"Oh, no." Soren cut another piece off his donut. She had never seen someone eat a donut with a knife and fork before. "I'm on a kind of sabbatical. I taught at a magic school in Stockholm, but after a few years, I decided I needed a break. The students could be rather tiresome."

Elsie sighed internally. It must be nice to have everything you need. Enough money to just move to a different country and explore your family history for a while. Then a thought occurred to her.

"I haven't really done much magic since I left school." She began, "not big stuff anyway. I read my tea leaves each morning and I brew teas and potions, but," Elsie looked at the table, embarrassed.

"Would you like me to teach you?" Soren asked, his voice gentle.

Elsie looked up into his icy eyes. "Would you?"

"Of course!" Soren said, standing and clapping his hands. "I can feel that you have quite a lot of power. Untapped potential! Let me sort a few things out at the house and we can get started in a week or so. What do you say?"

Elsie grinned broadly. "That sounds wonderful, thank you!"

"I had better be going," Soren said, heading towards the door. "Thank you for the donut. See you soon!"

Elsie stared after him in amazement. This was too good to be true. A wonderful new flatmate to help with the garden, and now a witch friend to help teach her magic! Elsie had been so lonely for the past year that she had thought about giving up and moving home more times than she could count. Soren had arrived at exactly the right time.

16

Amanda

The following Sunday, Amanda awoke to the peaceful sound of birds in the trees and saw the hint of sun shining through the gap in her curtain. She turned off the lamp she had put under her bed- she always needed a little bit of light to be able to sleep. Amanda was surprised by how light the room still was once the lamp was off. Picking up her phone, she baulked. She hadn't slept in until 9am for as long as she could remember. Snuggling down into the soft bed and cosy duvet, she looked around the room contentedly.

Looking over at her bedside table, Amanda smiled at the blue hydrangeas Elsie had placed there the day she moved in. It was nice to feel so welcome somewhere. Amanda felt a jolt of anger at her brother for getting her into this mess, and at the people who were out to get her. Even here, she couldn't let her guard down, couldn't allow good things in. Her decision had cost her a lot, but she knew she wouldn't have been able to live with herself if she hadn't. Amanda's moral compass had always been strong despite, or perhaps because of, her father's rather dubious one. She sensed a kindred spirit in Elsie, whose plant-based, gentle ways seemed to be driven by her own strong values.

As she wandered downstairs, the sweet smell of pancakes wafted through the air. "Good morning," Elsie said when she walked into the kitchen. The slim woman had an apron around her waist with a picture of a whisk and mixing bowl and the words Whisky Business scrawled across it. She was pouring maple syrup over a pile of the fluffiest looking pancakes Amanda had ever seen.

"I hope you're hungry," Elsie said, and Amanda just stared at her.

"I promise I won't try to feed you every single meal of every day," she went on, a flash of concern darting across her face. "But we keep missing each other in the mornings, and I thought you might appreciate pancakes on your first morning off in Lilac House."

"Feel free to feed me every meal. I have to work to get this figure, you know." Amanda grabbed at her belly with both hands and smiled warmly at Elsie. She perched on a chair after Elsie waved away her offer of help. "Did you say Lilac House?"

"Yes," Elsie placed the pancakes down in the middle of the kitchen island. "Tea or coffee?"

Elsie was cradling her usual enormous mug of coffee. After ascertaining that there was definitely plenty of coffee left in the pot for both of them, Amanda opted for her preferred morning beverage. Elsie poured, then sat down at the kitchen island opposite her.

"I don't know if it was called that before my grandmother got the place. The history of this house is a little opaque, but she always called it Lilac House. When I was a little girl, I used to come and visit her in the springtime, and the garden walls were covered in lilac flowers. It was the most beautiful thing I'd ever seen." Elsie's eyes lit up at the memory. Then it seemed to shift and make her sad, and she changed the subject abruptly.

"Did you sleep ok?"

"Like the dead," Amanda said.

"What, standing up in a coffin?"

Amanda nearly spurted coffee all over Elsie's pretty elfish face. "What?"

Elsie just grinned and shrugged. "You know, like a vampire."

Amanda shook her head and laughed, digging into her pancakes. "And I thought I was the one with the terrible jokes."

"You are." Elsie grinned cheekily. "My jokes are comedy gold."

Amanda was going to make a funny retort when her world spun to a halt. "Oh, wow," she said as the fluffy, maple syrup soaked goodness melted in her mouth. "What're you up to today?" Elsie asked, the smile still in her eyes.

"I don't have any plans yet," Amanda admitted. She had vaguely thought about looking for some more permanent work. Amanda didn't know how long Murray would be off work for, and if she was going to settle in Glen Haven, she would need something more permanent soon. But she really wanted to make the most of the fine day. Autumn was beautiful here, and she wanted to enjoy the rust-coloured trees and sunshine before the winter weather set in. "I think I'd like to do a bit of exploring, and I probably should do some more work in the garden."

"You did hours on it yesterday!" Elsie said indignantly. "You're not to work yourself to the bone on that mess. You've been out there at least three times this week already! I was going to take Philo down to the river, if you fancy a walk?"

"The little stream that meanders through town?"

Elsie beamed like a child with a secret. "The stream is just the beginning," she said. "It leads to the river right at the other end of town." Her eyes lit up as she spoke, and Amanda found herself, not for the first time, reflecting on how pretty her face was, and how infectious her smile. "It's absolutely beautiful," she gushed. "Trees on one side, and nothing but the steep curve of the hills on the other."

Amanda realised she had been staring at Elsie's mouth. Hurriedly, she focussed on sopping up the last of the maple syrup with her pancake. Elsie continued, apparently without noticing. "There are usually only a few people walking their dogs, and apart from that, it's just the water and the birds."

"Sounds wonderful," Amanda said. "count me in. Speaking of Philo, where is he? I haven't seen him this morning."

As if on cue, a large ball of white fluff tore through the room, a flash of pink in his mouth. He took one look at their aghast faces and immediately ducked around the side of the kitchen island. "What's that in his mouth?" Amanda asked, just as realisation dawned. "Is that my bra?"

"Philo, no!" Elsie cried, jumping up from her seat and giving chase. Amanda ran after them. Philo, apparently thrilled with his new game, bolted back through the kitchen door and into the lounge. He tore through the room with the two women racing after him. Just as Amanda gained on him, he darted out of her reach, out through the lounge door, and up the stairs. Elsie ran after him, Amanda hot on her heels. Amanda could hear Elsie's desperate calls of "Philo, no!" and "Drop" as she reached the top of the landing. Elsie had stopped, with Philo cornered at the end of the hallway. "That's a good boy," she moved slowly towards him. "Give me the bra," she said, in that fake, sing-song voice that people use with children of whom they are clearly terrified. In a flash, Elsie dove at Philo, who tried to dart around her, but Elsie was too fast. She landed atop him and shoved her hand in his huge, fanged mouth, crying, "Drop!" determinedly. She prised the dog's jaws open, pulling a sopping wet, bright pink bra from within.

She held the lingerie out to Amanda, crimson faced. "I am so, so sorry. I forgot to warn you to keep your door shut. Philo is still in what Freud might describe as the 'oral fixation stage'. I hope he didn't ruin your lovely bra."

Amanda stood stunned for several long moments, holding a soaking bra in her hand. Then she bent over double and roared with laughter. She heard Elsie break into laughter beside her, and in moments the two were lying on the floor in stitches.

"He is a good dog sometimes, I promise," Elsie said, after several minutes, tears still streaming down her cheeks.

"It's fine," Amanda clutched her stomach from the pain of laughing so hard. "He's the only guy who's ever gotten into my bra." That sent them both into more hysterics, and it was a good five minutes before they finally managed to get back upright again.

It was almost 11 by the time they made it down to the river, and the sun was already high in the sky. Elsie had been right, it was otherworldly. The township of Glen Haven sat nestled between two hills, one covered in forest, and the other mostly farmland, dotted with a few trees here and there. They had walked the length of the entire little village in less than half an hour. Then they followed a path that eventually turned into a dirt track, which seemed to meander entirely of its own accord. Eventually, the path met with a river coming down from the mountains to the West, and they spent several very pleasant hours walking along it, Philo racing ahead of them. He bounded around enthusiastically, occasionally jumping into the icy cold water to chase ducks and various other birds that had, until their arrival, been enjoying the tranquility of the morning.

The trees above them cast a pleasant shade from the heat of the day. The river splashed noisily over rocks, and birds called to one another from the trees. Several times they heard the slow, heavy wings of a heron as it flew overhead, or alighted on a tree branch pointing out of the water. It was nothing short of breathtaking.

17

Elsie

"So what's the deal with Pie in the Sky?" Amanda asked as they wandered back through the town, Philo panting loudly behind them, his tail wagging furiously. He must have chased every duck on the entire river, but he didn't seem phased by his zero percent success rate.

"What do you mean, what's the deal?" Elsie asked, glancing at Amanda in confusion. She hadn't seen the enchanted pots had she? Elsie had only resorted to using magic in the shop on a couple of occasions, when she really was too exhausted to do it all herself, but Amanda was savvy.

"You have this amazing shop that sells extraordinarily good food," Elsie blushed, but Amanda didn't seem to notice. "You're open what, five or six days a week?" Elsie nodded. "Including being open late Tuesday, Friday, and Saturday, if what I read on the sign was right."

"You're very observant," Elsie commented, relieved the questioning didn't seem to be on magical lines, but wondering where this was going.

"But every time I've been in there, there's been an amazing cabinet full of food and maybe three people in there max. What's the deal?"

Elsie sighed. She had been having such a pleasant morning.

"It's like I said. The people in this town are very loyal. People feel that to come to Pie in the Sky would be betraying the locals."

"But you're a local!" Amanda exclaimed.

"Not to them I'm not. Sure, Granny Margie lived here all of my life, but she moved here herself. Most people in this town have lived here for generations. Heck, they barely accept the Donaldsons and they've been here for four generations now!"

Amanda shook her head in disbelief, and Elsie changed tack.

"That's actually why I started opening the shop in the evenings. Beth's Bakehouse closes at 3, and there aren't that many places for a nice hot drink and meal in the town. There's the pub, the Italian place, and that's kind of it.

I thought maybe if I wasn't competing with anyone else, they would be more ok with me."

"And has it worked?"

"A bit."

Elsie was still running the numbers on how the shop was doing under various different opening schedules. The evenings were definitely better, but unless she wanted to just become a restaurant, she needed people to come in during the day.

"These evening opening hours have nothing to do with you being a night owl and the idea of getting up at the crack of dawn not appealing to you, then?" Amanda smirked, and Elsie laughed.

"Well, that is a lucky coincidence," she conceded, bumping Amanda's shoulder teasingly.

"Honestly though, I tried opening the shop at 8, 7, even 6 in the morning, and nobody came in. People are very loyal to the locals, and Reginald does a good job of reminding people they could be at Beth's."

"Is Beth his partner or something?" Amanda asked, looking a little sick at any woman finding Reginald appealing.

"Worse," Elsie replied. "His sister. It was only when I started opening for lunch and dinners that I got any regular customers at all. At least in the evenings, I'm not really competing with anyone."

"Have many of the townsfolk even tasted your amazing teas and food?" Amanda asked.

"No." Elsie had been so hopeful when she moved here that she would make friends and become part of the community, but so far she had been treated as nothing but an outsider. "I've tried everything I can think of: coffee and cupcake deals, two for ones on Tuesdays, but even then it doesn't make a big difference. Besides, the minute Reginald shows his surly face in the store, all the customers vanish!"

Amanda's face was tight with anger now. "OK, I get it if Reginald is protecting his sister's business," she took a deep breath. "But what does he have against you doing lunches and dinners? Surely your market and Beth's are completely different?"

Elsie shook her head. "I'm not sure. I know the townsfolk are pretty exclusive, supporting their own, wary of outsiders and all that, but Reginald's vendetta against me seems to be personal."

Amanda looked at her with interest. "What do you mean?"

"Nothing I can really put my finger on," Elsie admitted. "But he said something about me being just like my grandmother once, so I'm wondering if there's some bad blood."

"You can't let someone like that bully you because of an old feud!" Amanda said, determination in her voice. Elsie was surprised at her new friend's vehemence. It was nice to feel like there was someone in her corner. The shop was Elsie's happy place, but the lack of customers was beginning to get to her. She couldn't keep paying the rent out of her savings forever. More than that, though, she wanted people to like her, wanted them to enjoy the fruits of her labour.

"I have an idea," Amanda said, a twinkle in her eye Elsie hadn't seen before. "It might be a little...unorthodox, but I think it's worth giving it a go."

18

Amanda

The following week, Amanda piled the boxes of baking in the van and set off towards the post office at the far end of town. It was one of those typical red and brown brick buildings that evoked memories of England in a time gone by. Amanda waved hello to Murray at the front desk on her way in and unlocked the door to the back, where she would collect the day's parcels and letters. It had taken her a little while to get used to the emptiness of this place. She guessed that's how it went in a remote small town—every store or workplace only had a few people who were responsible for running things for the whole town. Amanda came out of the back room with a sack full of letters and parcels, feeling rather like Santa Claus. She placed a box of cookies in front of Murray and went to move away.

"What's this?" he asked, his voice gruff and his grey moustache twitching disconcertingly. Murray's leg was propped up on a chair, and Amanda could see a pair of crutches propped beside him.

"Chamomile and lavender cookies," Amanda opened the box and popped one into her mouth, in case Murray needed an example to follow. "My flatmate made them. They're amazing."

Still looking unconvinced, Murray reluctantly plucked a cookie from the box and sniffed it. "Couldn't she have just made chocolate chip like a normal person?" he grumbled under his breath.

Amanda smiled. "Nothing about Elsie is normal, but trust me, these are good!"

Murray harrumphed, but Amanda saw him take a bite, and a look of delight quickly flitted across his face before he schooled it back into a frown.

"See?" she said, encouragingly. "Good, hey?"

"Not too bad for a cookie made of herbs and twigs," he grumbled, but Amanda noticed him taking another, bigger bite. Grinning, she waved goodbye and got into the van. She had left a flyer for Pie in the Sky at the bottom of the box. She wondered how long it would take for him to reach it.

Amanda was surprised by the amount of snail mail people in Glen Haven received. Ms Peggy, on the corner of town, got a letter every week from her sister in Australia. Mr Mills who lived on a farm at the edge of town seemed to have a new book come every few days, and she was quite convinced that Mr Edwards either had a shoe fetish or enjoyed dressing in high heels, based on the number of purchases he received from somewhere called Heels from Heaven.

Today, as she handed out letters and parcels to the townspeople, she also gave them a box of cookies, cupcakes, or some slices of Elsie's various pies. Although Amanda had told Elsie she had a plan and would need flyers and access to some of Pie in the Sky's food, she'd been intentionally vague about her plan. Amanda had chosen the wares carefully, and absolutely nothing in the boxes was sold at Beth's Bakehouse.

People were reluctant when she first brought out her boxes of treats, thinking she was trying to push sales on them. Once she explained they were free samples, the confused frowns remained, but nobody except Reginald actually refused. "What's this? Trying to rob my sister of her customers by using underhanded techniques?" he had boomed, making Amanda take a step back. Amanda had simply smiled and muttered a few consoling words as she walked away. It wasn't her responsibility to manage his outbursts.

Luckily, the other townsfolk were a bit more amenable to the free samples. Amanda noticed that the frowns quickly vanished once they tried the baked goods. "You say Margie's granddaughter made these?" Mrs Flaggherty asked, her croaky voice sounding dubious.

"That's right," Amanda responded eagerly. "She has a little store in town, pop by for a cup of tea and a piece of pie some time." She had placed flyers in the bottom of each box, and saw a few people peering at it curiously, their mouths full of the delicious baked goods, as she waved them goodbye.

Amanda's post run was finished by noon, as it usually was, so she headed into the Pie in the Sky for lunch. Funny, she thought, you would think I would want some space from Elsie and her vegan cooking, given that I see her every night. But somehow, I still look forward to seeing her each day.

Elsie looked up from behind the till when she entered and gave her a broad grin. "Right on time," she said, pulling an extra large piece of pie from the cabinet and placing a heaped portion of salad next to it. "Potato and pea curry," she said, putting the plate down on a tray for Amanda and waving her away as she tried to pay. "This one's a new recipe. You can be my guinea pig."

Amanda knew Elsie was being kind to her. Given she was now working and not paying rent, though, Amanda felt she should pay for something. She pointed at a fruit and nut slice. "At least let me get one of those." She pulled some cash from her wallet. "I thought I might go for a run along the river this afternoon. Want me to take Philo?"

"Would you?" Elsie asked, looking thrilled. "I know he'd appreciate the company, and he could do with the extra exercise. He's a bit strong on the lead though, so be careful he doesn't pull you over!"

"Maybe he'll help me get my distance up," Amanda joked. "Useful to have a sled dog on a run! I've not had a dog before. They're rather good company."

"Your flatmate is the best company, though, isn't she?" Elsie teased. Amanda pretended to look thoughtful for a moment, and Elsie hit her hand playfully, in a way that made Amanda's heart rate quicken just a little, before she agreed.

"How's business?" Amanda asked. "Same old, same old," Elsie said, with a sad smile. "We got a couple of tourists. I had a few people in for coffee and cupcakes around 11, but as you can see—" She waved her hand at the empty store. "It's now just me and you."

Just then, Murray walked in. He gave Amanda a nod. "Hey Murray," Amanda said. Winking at Elsie, she took a seat over the far side of the cafe.

19

Elsie

E lsie looked after Amanda in amazement. Murray coughed loudly, and she turned back to her newest customer. "What can I do for you, Murray?"

"Do you have a chicken pie? Or a mince and cheese?"

"All the food here is plant based," Elsie said gently, "but I think you might enjoy the mushroom and lentil potato top pie. I'll get you some gravy for it as well." Murray didn't look convinced, but Elsie was a natural salesperson. She turned on the charm, metaphorically speaking, of course. "How would you like a slice of my triple chocolate fudge cake for dessert?"

"Does it have hemp or something else hippy dippy in it?" Murray grumbled, pulling out his wallet.

"Just some cinnamon and a secret vegetable." Elsie grinned conspiratorially, "Tell you what, if you can tell me what it is I'll give you your money back." Murray grunted and took his food over to a table in the corner, as the door to the cafe swung open again.

In walked Mrs Finlayson, the school principal. "I simply had to come and get some of your cupcakes for our staff meeting," she said, gazing into the cabinet. "After Amanda gave me that sampler this morning, I thought it would be just the thing to cheer up the teachers for the first week back. Could you do me say a dozen?"

Elsie glanced over at Amanda, samplers! So that was what she had been up to.

"Of course," Elsie said, beamed - customers! "We have a range of flavours for you to choose from. Would you like, say, two of each?"

Mrs Finlayson ended up buying two dozen cupcakes, deciding she could bring any spares home for her knitting group that evening. She had almost completely cleared Elsie out of cupcakes! That was unprecedented.

As she left, Mrs Finlayson nodded to two more people coming in through the still open door. Mr Mills held the door for his wife, and the two entered, looking for all the world like they were out on a date. Elsie had only seen the Mills twice in the eighteen months that she had been in Glen Haven. They seemed to keep to themselves on the farm, and Elsie wondered what had brought them into town. Mr Mills settled Mrs Mills at a table, smiling at the flowers on the table, then came up to order. "Welcome to Pie in the Sky," Elsie said cheerfully. "How can I help?"

"Your chai and cinnamon cookies were incredible." Mr Mills said, beaming. "My wife and I shared some over our morning coffee. We haven't had such a pleasant morning together in a long time. We were quite...intimate." Elsie blushed a little, but she was pleased her cookies had had a positive effect.

"So you're in for lunch, are you?" She asked, her mind still reeling at the effect of Amanda's plan.

"We are. I think we'll share a slice of that delicious looking vegetable medley pie, and maybe some chocolate cake as well."

"Certainly," Elsie rang them up, and felt a little thrill as she looked around her shop. It might not have been bursting at the seams, but this was more business than she'd seen since arriving.

Amanda's faith in her was touching. Elsie loved seeing the happy looks on her customers' faces, and the money in the till made her feel a lot better, too. The lease for the shop wasn't cheap, and her savings wouldn't see her through forever. With a little more income and the fact that she and Amanda were now splitting bills, maybe she could keep her little store open. Would the new customers mean the townsfolk would start accepting her into the community, too?

20

Amanda

Weeding the garden had taken more than a week, but Amanda was pleased with her progress as she surveyed the freshly tilled garden soil. Tomorrow she would go to the garden centre at the end of town and fill up on new plants and seeds. Autumn was a good time for planting, and she was excited to see the garden bursting with colour. She smiled as she remembered that lunchtime at Pie in the Sky. Elsie had looked so thrilled to see her little shop filling with people, and Amanda was pleased to see her new friend looking happy.

Her cellphone buzzed, and she pulled it out of her back pocket. Blanching, she saw Pierce's name on the screen. With a pang of guilt, she swiped to disconnect the call. A heaviness she hadn't felt for a few days settled back onto her chest, and she decided to go for a run to clear her head.

The river was just as beautiful today as it had been the previous week with Elsie. A slight breeze came in from the other end of the hills, and Amanda watched, entranced, as the leaves spiralled and span in slow circles; a golden, red, and burnt orange halo above her head. Amanda was beginning to fall in love with this place. She hated that she couldn't afford to get too comfortable. There was nothing to say that they would find her, but she knew if they decided to track her down, she would need to pack up and run.

As she ran, Amanda thought about what to do about Pierce. He had been the officer assigned to her case when she called in the dead bodies. Amanda hadn't told them who had buried the bodies in her nursery grounds, but she figured Pierce could guess. Calling them in was one thing, but Amanda wasn't sure she wanted to rat on her brother, even if he did deserve it. Family had to count for something, surely?

Not that Theo seemed to think that. When Amanda had heard what he'd said about their father, Amanda had thought she might be sick. She'd told Pierce to keep her brother far, far away from her dad.

Pierce wanted Amanda to give a statement. He wasn't pleased with her for running away. Well, tough. She had done her bit, and now she was washing her hands of the whole thing. Even if the thugs hadn't been sending her ominous messages, reminding her to keep her mouth shut. Amanda just wanted out. Breathing hard, she tried to focus on the here and now. She was safe. She had done nothing wrong. Nobody knew where she was. She was safe.

She stopped abruptly once more, as Philo, for about the thousandth time, halted their run to sniff something exciting. Their run was a kind of a staccato combination of excited sprints and stopping to smell what seemed to be every single blade of grass along the way.

After about twenty minutes, just as they were hitting a comfortable stride, Philo barked, and she felt the lead wrench as he took off at great speed after something in the river. Amanda was strong, but this dog was clearly part husky, part tractor. She dug her heels in as he tugged her determinedly towards the river. Slipping and sliding on the rocky pathway, Amanda was soon on the bank of the river as Philo barked and tugged at the lead. Floating on the river was something slimy and white, and Amanda groaned as Philo leaped in after his prize, pulling her along with him.

It took all Amanda's strength to stay upright as he dragged her down the riverbed and into the river. She clung to the lead with all her might. Philo tugged her with such force Amanda nearly toppled over, and he moved determinedly towards his prey. Amanda's energy was spent, and she let out a groan as, despite all of her efforts, his jaws closed over the disgusting smelling object. "I am never taking you on a run again!" she grumbled at her companion.

"Can't you keep that wretched dog under control?" The angry voice made Amanda start. She stood, knee deep in the water, dripping wet and rather shaken. Philo stood next to her, panting happily, his mouth full of something foul smelling.

"I'm fine, thanks for asking," she said, unable to stop the comment flying from her mouth. The scowling face of Reginald Arnold appeared on the path above her, his upper lip curling in distaste. The face was soon followed by the rest of the hateful man.

"Sarcasm is the lowest form of wit." He said 'wit' with an emphasis on the w, and Amanda saw spittle arc through the air. She shuddered. Resisting the urge to make another sarcastic comment, she focused on trying to find a way out of the river. The banks were higher here than where she and Philo had ploughed in, their sides steep and muddy. Amanda scrambled up the river bank, Philo leaping easily ahead of her.

"Thanks for your help," she mumbled, as at last she stood on the path, out of breath and covered in mud.

"It is hardly my responsibility that you do not have control of that beast," Reginald said, in what Amanda was sure was a put-on English accent. She turned to walk in the other direction, Philo at her heels, when she heard him mumble something that sounded a lot like "living with that freak" under his breath.

"What did you say?" She spun around so fast that Philo yelped as his lead caught. She marched up to Reginald and looked him square in his shifty grey eyes.

"I said," he repeated, drawing himself up and squaring his shoulders. "I don't know what else I expected when you choose to live with that freak." Amanda's blood boiled, and she clenched her fists to prevent her from doing something that could get her arrested.

"Elsie is the nicest person I have ever met," she said hotly. "She only wants the best for people. Her entire shop is about making others happy. What on earth is your problem with her?"

"You'll find out soon enough," Reginald said, fire in his eyes. "I've seen her out in the woods at night gathering materials for her spells."

"Spells!" Amanda sputtered, barely believing her ears. "She's getting ingredients for her baking. She's a chef!"

Reginald just looked at her witheringly. Amanda had no energy left for this spiteful man, so she simply turned on her heel and marched away, fuming.

A witch! Of all the absurd things that vile man could believe, the idea that he thought Elsie was a witch was possibly the most outrageous. What century was he from!? Amanda stomped the entire way home, Philo pattering quietly behind her.

21

Elsie

*S*he stood up for you today you know.

"What do you mean?" Elsie asked, curled on the couch, watching Amanda's retreating form leaving to head up to bed.

That mean man Reginald, the one who always smells like wet dog, was insulting you. He was there when we went down to the river to go fishing. She got in his face, got very defensive of you indeed.

"I think that was meant to be a run, not a fishing trip," Elsie chided.

Either way.

Elsie thought for a moment, then: "She stood up for me?"

You seem rather pleased about that. Elsie stuck her tongue out at her Familiar, and he wagged his tail teasingly at her.

Elsie's got a crush, Elsie's got a crush.

"I do not!"

I can read your thoughts, remember?

"That's meant to be about helping me with my magic." Elsie sniped.

Love is magic.

"Since when did you get so soppy?"

I like her.

Elsie could almost have sworn that her dog shrugged as he said this.

She was just turning back to her book when she heard Philo's voice in her head again. *Maybe you should tell her how you feel.*

She put her book down again with a sigh. "You know I can't do that."

Why not?

"It wouldn't be fair to her, that's why not."

Amanda had made enough comments about her dating history that Elsie was pretty sure Amanda was a lesbian. But that didn't mean she would fancy Elsie.

Why wouldn't she fancy you? You're pretty for a human, plus you're an excellent cook.

"Oh, all the important things, huh? Thanks," Elsie jibed, quietly flattered by the compliment, even if it was rather, well, animal.

"Anyway, that's kind of the point. Even if she did like me, it wouldn't be the real me. She doesn't know I'm a witch." She whispered the word 'witch,' even though she could hear the shower going upstairs.

So tell her.

Elsie baulked.

Not straight away, Philo hurried on, *but you two are obviously becoming close. You're away from home. Phoebe is in America, your grandmother's gone, your dad is gone.* Elsie defied the tears that were forming in her eyes. Philo licked her hand affectionately, knowing the loss of her father still hurt. *You need someone to confide in who understands your witchy ways.*

"I've got you," Elsie said defiantly.

Of course you do, Philo said, climbing onto the couch beside her and laying his head across her lap. Elsie had tried to enforce a no dog on the couch rule, but that had gone out the window more or less immediately. When she was grieving her dad, if she wasn't baking, Elsie had been crying on the couch. Having Philo's huge, furry body to cuddle had been so comforting that when he'd climbed up next to her the first night after he had arrived, she'd simply looked at him, wrapped her arms around his neck, and bawled. *You will always have me. But you could have another friend, too. Just think about it.*

Elsie was quiet. She wanted to tell Amanda she was a witch. She hadn't had that desire for a long time, but she knew first-hand the pitfalls of being a witch. Magic wasn't easy, as much as it was wonderful. There were people out there who would not treat Elsie well if they knew her secret. It could put her life in danger. Magic was unpredictable, too. She knew she would never intentionally hurt someone with her powers. But the accidents that can happen when you're a witch are a lot worse than those that can happen when you don't have the power to, say, accidentally levitate a vase off a shelf at someone you're angry with. Elsie still winced at the memory of that fight with her mother when she was still a teenager, and very much growing into her powers.

Plus, she had watched her mother love a witch, had seen her pulled into the magical world, a world in which she would never belong. Her mother hadn't complained, but Elsie had seen the looks of longing as she and her father had gone into the forest to cast spells, or when she and Phoebe had brewed a potion together. It must have been hard not to join in; never to experience the rush of flying, or know the feeling of calling the stardust from the sky.

Elsie wanted to share her heart and her magic with someone. If that someone couldn't do magic themselves, would they ever really understand? Wasn't it cruel to show someone that another way of life existed when they couldn't be part of it? Not to mention the dangers associated with being a witch. Elsie was constantly on guard to ensure that nobody found out her secret, and while she was sure Amanda was trustworthy, even one tiny slip up could have catastrophic consequences. She didn't want to put that burden on Amanda. The witch hunting days of old might officially be over, but all that meant was that witch hunters went underground. Humans were pack creatures at heart, and if they got a whiff that Elsie was 'other', she knew they would turn on her.

22

Amanda

Glen Haven was a small town situated, as the name implied, between two hills. The hills on the North of the city were covered in native trees, which blended into the pine forest of Viskande. Given her interest in native plant life, Amanda had spent most of her time so far exploring the northern side of the village. The hills on the South of the village were barer, with more farmland. There were still a few good walking tracks there, however, if the brochures and reviews Amanda had read were to be believed. Amanda itched to continue exploring the woods. Today, though, she and Elsie were walking through the town.

So far, Amanda had only explored a small part of the Glen Haven proper, namely the Library, the Post Office, and Pie in the Sky. She hadn't precisely boycotted Beth's Bakehouse, but she'd certainly preferred to give her business to Elsie when she could. There was also a green grocer, run, fittingly, by a gentleman called Mr Peabody, and an old movie theatre, which only showed one film at a time and always smelt deliciously of popcorn every time Amanda walked past.

She knew there were a few other shops farther into the valley, including a vet, a doctor, the Pub, and one of those shops which sold various knickknacks nobody needed but that somehow never goes out of business. What Amanda really wanted, though, was a garden centre. The shed, plentiful as it was, didn't have all the mulch, fertiliser, seeds, bulbs, or plants that she needed to do Lilac House justice. So, on a crisp autumn morning, she and Elsie set off through the town.

From a distance, Higgs' Twigs looked like a quaint little garden shop with a greenhouse. As they approached, however, Amanda's heart sank. "Oh dear," Elsie said beside her, "it seems to have gone rather downhill." The little shop had a corrugated plastic roof over a few trees and ferns. Behind that was a rather sad looking greenhouse, housing a much smaller selection of plants than Amanda had expected.

The owner, Mrs Higgs, came out to greet them. Instead of the distant coolness of the other villagers, Mrs Higgs seemed rather sad and withdrawn. Amanda found the hair sticking out of the mole at the bottom of her chin particularly distracting as she tried to explain what she was after. Her heart broke for the woman as Mrs Higgs explained she was a recent widower. Mr Higgs had been the keen gardener, and the shop had been his dream. Her son was helping lug things around the store, but neither of them really had the heart, or the head, for the place.

Eventually, Amanda picked out a couple of bags of fertiliser, a few plants and seedlings. She also got some packets of vegetable bulbs that looked close to being dead, but possibly had a slight chance of life still left in them. She had wondered about buying some plants to create new hedges, but that didn't seem possible based on Mrs Higgs's current stock.

When Mrs Higgs rang up her order, Amanda pulled a wad of cash out of her wallet without thinking. "Whoa," Elsie said. "What have you been doing, dealing drugs?" Amanda could have kicked herself. How had she been so stupid as to let Elsie see her with so much cash? That was bound to raise suspicions.

"Oh, you know, small town, South Island. I didn't know if you'd all have card readers here or if it was more of a cash/bartering/I'll give you a goat for three loaves of bread kind of system," she joked.

Elsie laughed that sweet, melodic laugh, and Amanda exhaled. That had been a little too close. Amanda was subdued as they left the shop. She didn't like hiding things from Elsie. Most people, sure. She was used to being on her own and doing her own thing, used to keeping quiet about how her dad made money, or why she spent so much time at her neighbour's place. But with Elsie, hiding her past and the stress of her present, felt deceitful. Could she tell her new friend about what had happened? She didn't want to worry Elsie, and the less anyone knew, the better, but still. Amanda wondered if maybe she could let someone in. Sharing her secret with a particular kind, sparkling-eyed, sweet as the pies she makes someone might be just what Amanda needed.

Just then, Amanda noticed an old plot across the road, which looked completely overgrown.

"What's that?" she asked Elsie.

"I think it used to be the community garden."

They crossed over and Amanda noticed vegetable patches with stakes for climbing plants, a garden area with meshing to keep birds away, and a sign that read "Grandma Margie's Community Garden."

"Your grandmother started a community garden?" she asked in surprise.

"I guess so? I've actually never looked at it properly before. It makes sense, though. Granny had a very green thumb, and if she could do something for the community, she always would. What a pity that it's all grown over."

Something sparked in the back of Amanda's brain. This could be a way to help everyone out; to bring old and new townsfolk together, to help support the struggling farmers and provide more fresh produce for the whole town. Maybe she didn't have her nursery anymore, but she could use her skills and her love of plants to bring people together.

23

Amanda

As they walked back through the town, Elsie suggested popping into the Tui Tavern, the local pub, on their way home. The Tavern was a quaint old brick building, obviously built in the same era as the post office. It had that universal pub feeling about it. Faded arm chairs beside cosy fireplaces, a hint of the smell of slightly stale beer in the air, but also the delicious smell of fried chips and wood smoke. Elsie waved to the man behind the bar, a tall, well-built man in his late thirties, on their way in.

They took a seat at one of the fireplaces without a deer's head mounted above it, and Philo promptly curled up on the rug and fell asleep. Amanda could see Elsie avoiding looking at the animals on the other walls and felt a flash of protectiveness towards her gentle-hearted friend. After a few minutes, the barman walked over. "Evening ladies, how can I help ye this evening?" he asked in a gentle Irish accent.

"Hi, Sam," Elsie said, flashing the man that friendly smile. "A couple of mulled ciders, please, and what's your soup of the day?"

"Parsnip and cauliflower. It's really quite good, if I do say so myself."

Elsie glanced at Amanda, who nodded. She wasn't exactly flush with cash, but a pub dinner and a cider shouldn't break the bank, especially when she didn't have rent to pay anymore. She would just need to get serious soon about a more permanent job—if she was sticking around.

The soup didn't take long to arrive, and was accompanied by crusty garlic and herb bread. When Sam came back to collect the bowls they'd cleared in remarkably swift time, Amanda was curious. "Do you make the soup in-house?" she asked, and Sam smiled that lazy smile at her.

"We do, yeah. Declan and I make most of it ourselves."

"Where do you get your vegetables, if you don't mind me asking?"

Sam frowned looking a little uncomfortable. "Well, we used to get everything from Mr Peabody and old man Higgs, but since he passed away..."

Sam looked at bit awkward. "They don't have quite the stock that they used to, so we've had to get a bit creative. Mayfield is a two hour round trip, so we're not really sure how viable a plan it is long term."

"Hmm," Amanda said, her mind still quietly whirring.

Elsie's voice brought her out of her thoughts. "You could have some vegetables from our garden once we've got it up and running," she said, that playful glint in her eye. "Amanda is transforming the garden at Lilac House, and she bought so many vegetable bulbs today that I think she's planning on feeding the entire village."

Elsie laughed, but Sam looked at Amanda with interest. "I don't think that many of them will actually grow," Amanda insisted, shifting in her seat. "And you can go through a surprising amount of vegetables in one household if you're plant-based," she reminded Elsie pointedly. "But I might have another idea for you. Can I come and see you in a couple of days? I just need to work a few things out."

"Sure," Sam said, shrugging. "I'd appreciate any help ye can give. We might not always be packed, but we have a loyal group of regulars, and I hate the idea of selling them chips from frozen."

Elsie visibly shuddered. "Never let anyone stop you from producing the amazing chips you make here," she said emphatically. "I will personally pay the price of your potato stock if necessary."

"The shop doing that much better then, is it?" Sam asked, raising his eyebrows and laughing at Elsie.

Just then, the door chimed, and a couple walked in. Sam bobbed his head in a silent apology and headed over to greet them.

"You two seem friendly." Amanda tried not to sound jealous as she watched the attractive man walk away. "Oh yeah, Sam's nice," Elsie said. "He's relatively new to town, too." She shrugged. "We went on a date once, more because it seemed like a thing we should do than because it was something either of us was actually excited about. It was fine, but we both agreed we don't really have a huge amount in common. He's a great bartender, though, chatty and all that."

"Have you dated many people in town?" Amanda did not like the feeling that was sitting in her belly as she thought about Elsie going on dates with anyone else.

Elsie laughed. "Oh no. There aren't exactly many eligible bachelors in town. Or bachelorettes or bache-non-binary folk, for that matter." She said, more or less confirming Amanda's guess that Elsie was pansexual. She tried not to dwell on whether or not Elsie might consider her an eligible bachelorette.

After another drink and a plate of the famous fries, Amanda's mind drifted back outside. What if she could do something with this community garden? She was making good progress at Elsie's place. The soil at Lilac House was amazing. Amanda had never seen things grow so quickly and so well. The garden seemed to be its own little micro-climate. She didn't know how Elsie had had so little luck with it. Though, she reflected, the other woman had been rather busy setting up a business and grieving the loss of her father and grandmother.

Maybe the South Island had slightly different seasons to the far north, though. Things outside of Lilac House seemed to be dying much faster in Glen Haven than they would back home. The leaves turning orange and gold was one thing, but Amanda had seen three trees turned rotten on her run the day before, and that wasn't normal when it hadn't been raining all that much.

Amanda's brain itched to figure out the root of the problem. She missed the sense of satisfaction that came from the nursery. Figuring out the perfect conditions for each plant, checking to see if they each had enough, but not too much water, sunlight, and fertiliser. Amanda loved melding of the science of the seasons, the art of reading the soil and the seedling.

"What are you thinking about?" Elsie asked, and Amanda snapped back to the present — she had been miles away.

"I was just thinking about your grandmother's old community garden," she said, munching on what might possibly have been the best chips she had ever tasted. "I thought maybe people would benefit from somewhere to come together and plant vegetables, especially with Peabody's being low on stock. You know, get everyone to" she held up her fry, the corner of her mouth twitching up, "'chip' in to supplement their weekly groceries." Elsie groaned, but Amanda continued. "Autumn is a good time for planting broccoli, onions, and cauliflower. They'll take a little while to grow, but by spring we should have some lovely fresh crops. Once we get the basics sorted, we could expand to include a few more optional extras, like herbs."

"Herbs are not optional if you want your meals to taste like anything!" Elsie protested.

"I want to go back and have another look in full daylight," Amanda went on. "I think there might have been a few fruit trees at the back of the garden. If we prune them back now we might even get some fruit come summer. Why are you looking at me like that?"

Amanda suddenly felt embarrassed, as Elsie was staring at her peculiarly.

"Nothing," Elsie said, a warm smile on her face, "I've just never met anyone like you. You're so eager to get stuck in, to help people. Have you always been like that?"

Amanda flushed. "I guess so. Growing up, we didn't have much. I often went to stay next door at Ms Watters's. That's where I learned how to garden. My mum left when I was just a kid and my dad was..." She paused, not wanting to go into too much detail. "Not around very often. So Ms Watters would mind me most days. We would spend hours after school in her back garden, pruning, weeding, planting, watering. She taught me all about growing flowers and vegetables. She said if you had a plot of dirt and a little know-how, then you could look after yourself pretty well, no matter what else was going on. I think that's why I bought the nursery in the end."

Amanda fidgeted with a napkin. "Anyway, Ms Watters was always looking out for people. I wasn't the only stray kid she took in. The number of times that she would have a visitor pop around to the front door and she would call me, saying 'Mandy, just pull up a couple of carrots and some beetroot, there's a dear.' Or, 'Mandy, be a love and get Ms Ross some lettuce and potatoes, would you?' Honestly, I don't think Ms Watters actually ate any of the vegetables we grew herself. She fed me with them plenty of times, and she was always looking out for people in the neighbourhood. I guess I kind of learned to do the same."

Elsie was looking at Amanda with interest. "Sounds like you had an interesting childhood," she said.

"It had its ups and downs like anyone else's," Amanda shrugged, keen to move the conversation away from herself. She had already shared a lot more than she would have expected. What was it about Elsie that made her open up so much? "How about you? What's your deal? What on earth made someone as..." She searched for the right word—"bohemian," she landed on, "as you decide to go into accounting?"

Elsie laughed, taking another sip of her tea. "It's really not that interesting a story. My mum wanted me to have a 'profession', to make sure that I could look after myself. I think she was conscious of women in her mother's generation having few options and having to rely on their husbands for money. She grew up poor, and wanted me to understand money so I could always look after myself."

"What did she think about you going into baking?" Amanda asked, leaning forward.

Elsie's face clouded over. "Mum took dad's death pretty hard. To be honest, she didn't really seem to notice me at all after he died. She walked around their old house like a ghost."

Amanda was surprised at this. It had sounded like Elsie had grown up with two loving, supportive parents. Maybe things hadn't been as straightforward for her as she'd thought. "I'm sorry to hear that," she reached across and squeezed Elsie's knee sympathetically. Immediately, though, she let go again. Elsie's leg was toned and smooth, her skin like silk. Amanda had been trying to be friendly, but she had to admit, she was attracted to this woman, and now was not the time. If there ever was one, she thought miserably, as she remembered the two further missed calls from Pierce that morning.

24

Elsie

The following week, Elsie was behind the cabinet at Pie in the Sky, pretending she wasn't sneaking glances at Amanda whenever she could. Elsie looked up to see Amanda wince. She twisted her head back and forth, and rolled her shoulder, her face pained. Elsie finished placing the next tray of cupcakes into the cabinet, wiped her hands on her apron, and walked over to her friend. "Sore neck?" She asked, as Amanda looked up in surprise.

"Wha? Oh, yeah," Amanda said, still wriggling her back unhappily. "I think I must've pulled something unloading one of Mrs Higgs' parcels today. It was really heavy, but I wasn't exactly going to ask the old lady to give me a hand with it. My back is killing me now."

"Have you tried stretching it out, yoga or anything?" Elsie asked in concern.

"Have you seen me?" Amanda snorted. "I'm not exactly a yogini."

"Everybody can do yoga," Elsie said firmly. "Even if it's just the breathing techniques. But actually—" She appraised Amanda's strong, curvaceous frame. "I think you would find some postures quite easy, given how strong and fit you are."

Amanda looked taken aback.

"Here," Elsie said, moving one of the small empty tables out of the way. "Let me show you." She bent over into a downward dog position, her fingers stretching out on the floor, body in an inverted 'V' shape. "When my back is sore I do a few, simple vinyasas, like this." Elsie moved her upper body forward in a gentle wave, until she was parallel to the ground in a plank position, still supporting herself on her hands and toes. Then she put her knees to the ground, and, pulling her elbows in close to her sides, lowered down until her upper body was on the floor. She pushed up, arching her back downward, her face to the sky, legs flat on the ground. She stayed like that for another breath, before pushing herself to her knees, and then back into her downward dog, before jumping forward and standing again.

"Oh, I couldn't do that," Amanda said.

"Of course you can. Come on, I'll talk you through it."

Amanda was clearly a little uncomfortable, but there was nobody else in the shop, and Elsie knew yoga could help her friend immensely. "That's right, now lower your knees to the floor and gently bring your chest to the ground," she encouraged, as Amanda trepidatiously did a vinyasa flow. "That's it!" Elsie encouraged, as Amanda made it back to downward dog. "Let's do three together, and see how you feel afterwards," Elsie said, setting herself up in front of Amanda so she could watch in case she forgot the moves. She led Amanda through three vinyasa, telling her when to breathe in and out, holding the upward dog for a little longer each time. On the last time, she had Amanda twist her head to the left and the right in her upward dog, before pushing back into her downward dog without going back onto her knees. Then together they slowly rolled up to standing, allowing one vertebra at a time to settle into place.

"How do you feel?" she asked as they stood, faces slightly flushed.

Amanda rotated her neck slowly. "Actually, a lot better, thank you! Where did you learn yoga?"

"I spent a winter at an ashram a few years ago," Elsie replied, shrugging. "It's a beautiful practice, and I find it really helps to centre me, especially on days when I'm feeling panicked or like my muscles are seizing up."

"I can see why," Amanda said. "If you're not too busy, maybe you could teach me some more at home sometime?"

Something about the way Amanda said "home" made Elsie's heart warm. "Of course," she said, smiling. Just then, the chimes over the door went, and Murray walked in.

"Oh, hey Murray!" Amanda called out. "I've just been learning yoga."

"So I saw," Murray said, shaking his head, but Elsie noticed the corner of his mouth twitch up just a little.

"How can I help you, Murray?" Elsie asked, retying her apron and stepping back behind the counter.

"I wondered if you had any more of that pie I had last week." Elsie helped Murray pick out another pie, lentil curry this time. She was gratified to see him move to sit opposite Amanda at her table; twin newspapers mirroring each other as they read and ate their lunch together in silence.

Just then, Elsie felt the ground around her tremble, and a pain shot through her chest. She cried out. Amanda and Murray looked over at her, startled. From the look on their faces, neither of them had experienced anything. Fear rose in Elsie like a tide, as she realised what that must mean. Someone was practicing dark magic. And they were close by.

25

Amanda

Amanda sat up in bed. Her room was flooded with the light from the full moon outside — she must have forgotten to close the curtains when she passed out last night. Glancing at her phone, she could see it was 3.33 in the morning. As she got up to draw the curtains, she glanced out into the garden, and to her amazement, saw Elsie. She was sitting under the big elm tree and was looking intently into some sort of huge saucepan that was resting in front of her on what looked like a fire pit. What on earth is she doing?

She crept out of bed and went downstairs. The kitchen island was a disaster zone. Pots and pans overflowed with various colourful liquids; lavender, dill, and miscellaneous other plants were strewn across the bench hap-hazard; and there was a faint smell of something sweet still hanging in the air. What is Elsie up to?

She recalled the first day they had met, when Elsie talked about baking helping her to grieve her father's sudden passing. Amanda wondered if this was some sort of middle of the night, can't sleep sort of chaos baking. But why is she out in the garden?

Amanda carefully picked her way through the carnage of the kitchen and quietly opened the door to the back garden. Elsie had her eyes closed and was talking to herself. Amanda began to worry that she was having some kind of mental breakdown. The pot in front of her was bubbling away, a shiny black liquid rising to the top now and then. OK, don't startle her. Just stay calm. Let's see if you can help her snap out of this.

Amanda started towards Elsie, who still hadn't noticed her. Elsie reached up towards the sky, and gold and silver sparks seemed to flutter down into her hand. She sprinkled the particles into the pot, still muttering to herself as she did, stirring the liquid continually. As Amanda approached, she saw the black liquid in the pot turn a brilliant, shimmery gold!

"Elsie?" she breathed, and then she was lost for words. From upstairs she had seen that Elsie was sitting cross-legged behind the big brass pot. Now, she noticed that Elsie was, well, there was no other word for it. She was floating, hovering a good six inches off the ground, still serenely stirring, as if this were an everyday occurrence.

Elsie's eyes flew open, and she landed back on the ground with a thud. "Amanda!" she said. "What are you doing here?"

"I saw you out the window. I was worried. I, Elsie, were you... floating?"

"Levitating, technically." Elsie wiped sparkly dust off her hands and stood up. She peered into the pot and stirred it, the golden shimmery liquid not quite so bright as before.

"Levitating," Amanda repeated slowly. "And are you cooking out here? What's going on?"

Elsie looked at Amanda for a long moment. Amanda could tell that Elsie was contemplating her intently. She felt uncomfortable, but eventually, Elsie must have made up her mind. "I'm making a potion," she said. "It has to be done under a full moon, at the witching hour."

"The witching hour!?" Amanda could hear her voice rising by a full octave. What was Elsie talking about? "What..." Words failed her.

She saw Elsie take a deep breath. Then she said, "Amanda, I have to tell you something. I'm a witch."

26

Elsie

Amanda stared at her for a long time. "You're a witch," she said slowly.

"Yes," Elsie said, with a small shrug of her slender shoulders. She was trying to act cool, but desperately hoped she had read this right. She hadn't known Amanda all that long, but somehow she felt she could trust her. Philo had said this was a good idea, and Elsie had felt so supported by Amanda. But this was a very big deal. Now that her secret was out, she wondered if she had done the right thing.

"Don't take this the wrong way," Amanda said, and Elsie tensed. "But I didn't think witches really existed."

Elsie laughed. OK, so far this wasn't going as horribly as she'd feared. "We certainly don't advertise our presence much," she explained. "But yes, we do really exist."

"Is that why your eyes are purple?" Amanda asked.

Elsie was surprised. That was a pretty astute observation. "Yes, actually. It is."

"So you can do, like, full on magic? Sorry," Amanda hurried on. "I have like a million questions, but is that..."

Elsie held her arms out wide. "I'm an open book. Ask away. But maybe let's go inside first? I should put this potion away before it mixes with anything it's not meant to."

A bewildered looking Amanda followed Elsie into the kitchen. She stopped as they entered the room and pulled open the tea drawer. "The tea, is that a witch thing? It's a lot of tea."

"Sort of," Elsie replied, guiding Amanda to a seat, switching on the kettle, and then going back outside to bring in the cauldron before the potion turned. Waving her hand, she floated the cauldron down onto the granite countertop. She was aware Amanda kept staring. "Witches understand the natural properties of plants, like ginger for healing and lavender for tranquility. But the teas themselves aren't magic, they just utilise the natural properties to the best of their abilities. Oh, and I harvested a lot of them under a full moon, which amplifies their properties."

"So what was the deal with the full moon tonight?" Amanda asked, still looking a little white.

"The potion I'm making helps minimise the effects of anxiety and depression. It's called a hope spell. It needs to be brewed under a full moon and requires a sprinkling of star dust, so a clear night is best."

"A sprinkling of stardust," Amanda repeated dumbly.

Elsie set a cup of tea in front of Amanda. "Lavender for tranquility," she said, patting Amanda's hand gently. "I've also been making some protection potions." Elsie waved her hand absently at the kitchen counter which was still strewn with myriad herbs and oils, and the items tidied themselves into orderly piles, the oils lining up on a shelf, the herbs fluttering, pouring themselves into jars before hopping into the pantry.

Amanda stared.

"Where did you learn all this stuff? Like, did you go to a witchy school or something?" Amanda asked. Elsie was a little taken aback by the random, shotgun nature of Amanda's questions. Then again, the only other person she had told she was a witch was a boyfriend when she was 21, and his questions had been disappointingly focussed on what she could do, which quickly led to how he could use her. That relationship had knocked her back a fair bit, and Elsie had learned quickly to be much more discerning about who she talked to about witchy things. Elsie would take sporadic questioning over usury interrogation any day.

"I did go to a witchy school," she said, ladling portions of the potion into Tupperware containers. "I also inherited a few spell books from my dad."

"Your dad was a witch?"

"Yeah, my mum's a normy. My dad was a witch." Elsie pushed aside the thought of her mother. She had been in Glen Haven for a year now, and her mother had still not come to visit. Elsie heard from her occasionally, but after her dad died, their already strained relationship seemed to be worse.

"I thought witches were all women," Amanda said, her beautiful brow furrowed. "Maybe that's sexist of me."

"They mostly are," Elsie explained. "Magic isn't strictly genetic, but it is usually passed through the female side of the gene pool. If there isn't a girl born in a bloodline, then a boy or non-binary person might be born with magic powers."

"So, what's the difference between a witch and a wizard?"

Elsie laughed. "Wizard is just an out-dated term. We use witch for magical people of all genders these days."

"How enlightened," Amanda murmured thoughtfully into her tea. Philo plopped down on the floor beside Amanda, resting his enormous head on her lap, and Amanda stroked his nose absently.

"He doesn't usually trust people so quickly," Elsie said, smiling. Her Familiar had a good sense of things, and she was grateful that he liked Amanda so much. It had helped her feel like she could afford to open up to Amanda, too. She got up and reached into the pantry, pulling out a homemade dog treat. Philo's ears perked up, and his tail began thumping rhythmically on the floor.

"Do you make everything from scratch?" Amanda asked.

"Not everything," Elsie replied, handing Philo a treat and wiping her slightly drooly hand on her leggings. "But a lot of things now I know how. That way, I know exactly what's in something. Plus, now I have an industrial kitchen, it's a lot easier to make batches of things."

"I doubt the food inspectors would be thrilled to know you make dog food in the Pie in the Sky kitchen," teased Amanda. Elsie was pleased to see a little colour returning to her friend's face.

She laughed, "I don't make them there! But they're perfectly human friendly, all natural ingredients, they're practically cookies!"

Amanda didn't look convinced, so Elsie pulled another treat out of the container and popped it in her mouth. Philo and Amanda both looked at Elsie unimpressed, and she stuck her tongue out at them. A moment later, she ran over to Philo's bowl and spat the treat into it.

"That bad, huh?" Amanda laughed heartily.

"It's not that," Elsie replied.

She paused, but now she could actually tell Amanda things like this. A little thrill ran through her at the thought. "I think that's the batch I put a spell in for a shiny coat. I don't know how it will work on humans. Maybe it'll give me glossy hair, maybe it'll make all my leg hair extra thick and furry. I don't really want to risk that."

Amanda cackled with laughter, and Elsie felt happiness radiate through her. She really enjoyed having Amanda here. It was nice having someone to talk to, to cook for, to joke with (or in this case, to embarrass herself in front of). She even seemed to be taking the witch thing in her stride. For the first time since she moved to Glen Haven, Elsie finally felt like she had made a proper friend. It was just a pity that her body kept thinking it would be nice to be something more than friends.

27

Elsie

Elsie let Amanda in, flipped the shop sign to 'closed,' and together they began packing the tables and chairs away and moving them behind the counter. The small shop floor looked a fair amount bigger without the bistro tables and bunches of flowers taking up space. Seeing it empty like this reminded her of the blank space she had taken a chance on all those months ago. Things had been a little better since Amanda did her rounds with the sample boxes, but Elsie knew it would take more than a few free cookies to get the townsfolk to accept her. She hoped that this might be one of those steps; giving back to the community, getting a bit more money, and, hopefully, getting to know people better, too.

She lit incense and laid out a few yoga mats before plugging her phone into the shop's sound system. Soothing music filled the space. Next, she brought a heater out from the store-cupboard and placed it in the middle of the room. Within minutes, the shop had a warm, cosy atmosphere. She looked at her watch. It was exactly seven o'clock. She flipped the sign back over to 'open' and ensured the door was unlocked. Her stomach was in knots.

Amanda gave her an encouraging smile. "Even if it takes a little while to catch on, it'll be nice doing yoga together," she said, as if reading Elsie's anxious mind. When Amanda had found out that Elsie was a qualified yoga instructor, she'd urged Elsie to run a weekly yoga class in the shop after closing time. With Amanda's encouragement, she posted a sign for Tuesday night yoga classes on the community notice board.

After waiting another couple of minutes, Elsie sighed. "Shall we get started, then?" she asked, deflated. Amanda nodded and took her place on the mat facing Elsie's. Elsie had them sit on the mat and do deep breathing exercises, emphasising the importance of focusing on the breath and clearing the mind. After a few 'oms,' she started them with a few gentle sun salutations to warm up their bodies. While they were going through the second vinyasa, the chimes on the door sounded and a woman in her early forties came in, her mousey brown hair bedraggled from the wind. She was wearing bright orange yoga pants with a hole in the knee, and an old t-shirt that reached halfway down her thighs. She had a yoga mat under her arm and wore the frazzled look of women everywhere who are pulled in too many directions at once.

"Hello," Elsie said, smiling in what she hoped was a welcoming way. This woman's aura was sparkling, despite her evident fatigue. Elsie couldn't usually read non-magical folks' auras, but now and then a person was so in touch with their emotions, or so connected to a particular element, that their aura glowed through just like a witch's. Wanda's was a dazzling white gold, and Elsie knew that this woman was good.

"I'm so sorry I'm late," the woman said. "It's been a bit of a day." Elsie thought perhaps she had seen the woman down by the river once or twice before, pushing a pram up and down and singing softly to the child inside.

"That's no problem at all. We've only just started. I'm Elsie."

"Wanda," the woman said, spreading out her mat and giving Elsie a grateful smile.

"Welcome Wanda, to Pie in the Sky yoga." They began the sun salutation sequence again, and Elsie could tell that Wanda had practiced yoga before. They moved through some more sequences and finished with some twists and stretches, before lying on their mats in shavasana for the final few minutes of the class. Elsie had decided that an hour's class would be plenty for the first little while. She would love to take some more advanced classes, but she wasn't sure if there would be any interest in the classes, so she figured she would start small.

Wanda stayed for a cup of tea after the class. Elsie and Amanda learned she was a single mother living with her sister and her eighteen-month-old twins in a house down towards the other end of town. Elsie was surprised she hadn't met the woman before, but she supposed that as the only real community activity in Glen Haven was church, which she didn't attend, and the odd festival, where it was easy to miss people, there were few ways that she could have come into contact with her. Wanda's sister was the local librarian, and Wanda said that when she moved in with her after the children were born, the two of them took turns to run the library.

89

Just as Wanda was about to leave, Elsie had an idea. "We didn't sell these today. Will you take them home so they don't go to waste?" She asked, holding up two of her latest creations, pecan and maple donuts with sage icing.

"Oh, I couldn't," Wanda said, hesitantly, but Elsie was already packaging up the donuts in one of her compostable boxes.

"Of course you can," she said kindly, placing them in Wanda's hand. "Will we see you next week?"

"Yes, please," Wanda said. "I don't get to do many things for myself. Tracy's been great, but I feel bad asking her to look after the kids so that I can do something fun." Wanda worried at the hem of her t-shirt as she spoke. "Tuesday nights she has her book club at the house, though, and the kids usually have a nap from about 6-8, so this works perfectly."

Elsie beamed. "Wonderful. We look forward to seeing you then. Get home safely!"

Elsie and Amanda watched Wanda go.

"Well, I'd say that was quite a success," Amanda said, clearing away the teacups and taking them to the kitchen to wash.

"It was, wasn't it?" Elsie said excitedly. "I know we only had one person—"

"Two people," Amanda interjected. "I'm still a person even though I'm your flatmate."

"Two people," Elsie conceded with a smile. "But I think it was really worthwhile, don't you? Wanda seemed really pleased. And your practice is coming along beautifully."

Amanda's face was still a little flushed from the exertion. "I'm really enjoying it. Thank you," she said earnestly as she handed Elsie a clean teacup to dry. "My back feels so much better now, and it's a nice way to stretch out after a hike or a run."

Amanda paused at the sink, her eyes distant. "How long did it take you to master the 'clear your mind' stuff?" Elsie could tell from the way Amanda was pointedly not looking at her that this question perhaps meant more to her than she was letting on.

"It's always a work in progress," Elsie said carefully. "I've been practicing yoga for years, and of course attending the teacher training course in India helped incredibly. There's nothing quite like going to an ashram where all you have to do all day is eat, pray, do chores, and practice yoga, to calm your thoughts. But the point is for that meditative practice to be available to you even when things around you are busy. I found meditation helpful when my dad died, for example, and I use it in the shop when I'm anxious."

Amanda was looking at her with interest now. "You get anxious?"

"Sometimes," Elsie said. "Some days my mind runs in circles and I just can't get it under control, no matter how hard I try. On other days, I remember that controlling my mind isn't the point. Observing it is."

"Observing your mind?"

Elsie set the last of the teacups in the cupboard and leaned against the counter, pensive. "Thoughts and a busy mind aren't a problem in and of themselves. It's just that sometimes we get so caught up in our feelings or thoughts that we can't think rationally, or we feel as if we are losing control. The truth is, we never really have control."

Amanda was looking at her with hooded interest now. So Elsie continued. "But if we choose to slow our breathing down, sometimes we can shift to a place where we observe our minds, rather than being consumed by our thoughts. It's kind of like when I cast a spell, my mind isn't necessarily clear, there might be a million things still floating around in the background, but when I'm casting a spell, I need to bring forward the one or two key things I need to focus on and let the others slip to the background."

Just then, Amanda's phone buzzed. "And sometimes," she grumbled, "intrusive thoughts come from other people." She stepped back into the shop, looking at her phone with evident discomfort as Elsie turned off the lights in the kitchen. There's definitely something you're not telling me. What secrets are you hiding, Amanda George?

28

Amanda

E lsie walked into the kitchen looking like some sort of sexy pixie, and Amanda said so. The words were out of Amanda's mouth before she had a chance to review them. She blushed furiously and turned towards the coffee maker so Elsie wouldn't see her embarrassed face. "Don't be daft. Pixies basically wear lingerie and dance around mushrooms all day. I'm much too modestly dressed to be a pixie."

Amanda swallowed hard, refusing to think about Elsie dancing around in her lingerie. "What have you got on today, then?" she asked, trying to sound casual as she turned back around and handed Elsie another cup of coffee.

"Don't know," Elsie said, falling into a chair and picking at the corner of Amanda's toast. Amanda slid the plate across to Elsie. "Gosh sorry!" Elsie said, obviously just realising what she had been doing.

"It's fine," Amanda said, smiling. "I can make myself another slice of toast."

Elsie brought the toast to her mouth and then paused. "What's on this?" She asked skeptically.

Amanda turned back from placing bread in the toaster. "Peanut butter, banana, and date syrup. I used to use honey, but I've adapted, and I think the date syrup gives it an extra depth."

Elsie slowly lowered the bread back to the plate. "What kind of sacrilege is this?"

"You combine weird flavours in the shop all the time! How can you not have had peanut butter and banana before? It's possibly the best combination known to humankind."

"It's not the best combination known to witchfollk," Amanda heard Elsie mutter.

"Don't eat it if you don't want to." Amanda went to take the toast away from Elsie, but the other woman snatched it away with surprising alacrity. Elsie took a bite and Amanda gave a self-satisfied smile as she saw the look of surprise on her friend's face. It instantly transformed into a look of intense pleasure, and Amanda felt her insides turn to goo.

"Wow, that is good," Elsie said. Amanda was still reeling from the look that had crossed Elsie's face. Sexy pixie indeed.

"Maybe you should come and help at the shop." Elsie was looking at Amanda with interest. Clearly, the second coffee was kicking in.

"What?"

"I thought I was pretty creative with flavours, but I wouldn't have given that a try if you hadn't made me. Maybe I'm getting stale in my old age."

Amanda laughed. "You're six months younger than me, so now you're just offending us both." They had discovered one night that they were, in fact, exactly six months apart. Elsie was born September 13th, and Amanda was born March 13th.

"What with the community garden, this garden, and the postie job, I probably don't have heaps of time to..."

Elsie interrupted, "Amanda, it's OK, I'm kidding! So long as you're happy to be chief guinea pig extraordinaire."

Amanda grinned. "That is a role I will happily retain for the rest of my life." Why had she said that? Why did she keep implying that she wanted Elsie around for the rest of her life? I mean, she liked the woman, and being with her was always pleasant, and she could think of worse people to spend her life with...What was wrong with her!? Hurriedly moving on, Amanda continued, "I'm pleased to hear you're thinking about getting some support at the shop. I worry about you with your long days at the shop, and all that baking and cleaning."

Elsie winked at Amanda, "There are some benefits to being a witch, you know." She said, "though truth be told, having someone else to help out would be nice. I get a bit worried that the shop depends entirely on me for everything." Elsie glanced at one of the kitchen stools, which was piled high with her notebooks, a couple of jackets and several books. "I am a tad chaotic."

Amanda laughed. She happened to like Elsie's chaos, but she could certainly see her point.

"I'm sure the right person will come along at the right time," Elsie said in that very earth goddess, trust the stars kind of way she had.

"So what's with today's fancy outfit?" Amanda asked, trying not to stare as Elsie's lean legs peeking out from under her skirt.

"I don't know," Elsie said. "Maybe something important is going to happen today. Maybe it's just that my skirt was feeling left out. You'd have to ask them."

Amanda hadn't been expecting that! Swiping peanut butter across her own piece of toast and slicing banana to put on top, she shook her head in confusion. "This whole witchy woo woo thing is going to take me a while to get used to," she said.

"You love it, really," Elsie said, snatching the toast off Amanda's plate and stealing a bite before Amanda could stop her.

"Hey!" she said, giving Elsie's hand a mock slap. Elsie picked up the toast and turned away from Amanda, making out that she was going to take a bite. Amanda took the bait, reaching around her friend's slender waist and attempting to grab the toast from her. Her body zinged with electricity at the touch. Was Elsie flirting with her? She leaned her head over Elsie's shoulder and made to take a bite out of her toast. Elsie turned and Amanda found her lips pressed against the soft, warm skin of Elsie's cheek. She froze, and then stood back in shock. Just then, Elsie's phone rang. "It's mum," she said, an unreadable look on her face. Amanda nodded as Elsie walked out of the room, disappointed to eat the rest of her breakfast in peace.

29

Amanda

Amanda's mind was still very much on the softness of Elsie's cheek as she hooked Philo's lead onto his collar and started walking up the pathway towards Heaven's Gate.

Philo's pace was haphazard. He was either desperate to charge ahead and see what was just around the next corner, or, when Amanda relented and broke into a trot to keep up with him, he would stop, having found a particularly fascinating piece of grass which needed to be inspected and urinated on.

Amanda decided she could risk taking Philo off the leash for a little while. She unclipped him and the two walked through the forest, Philo's tail wagging in time with Amanda's heartbeat. The forest here was extraordinary. Trees towered above her head, their golden, red, and orange leaves rustling in the wind. Now and then there would be a bigger breeze, and Amanda would look up to see star-shaped leaves floating in lazy circles down towards her. It was nothing short of mesmerising.

She had been to the community garden, and had begun making plans for the space. Mrs Higgs had given her a couple of bags of fertiliser for free, which was incredibly generous, especially since Higgs' Twiggs was obviously not doing all that well since Mr Higgs passed. It felt strange to be making plans for a future here. Then again, she felt more at home in Lilac House than she had ever felt in her childhood home. She bent down to check on a sapling which seemed to be browning, despite the recent rain. That was strange.

After about an hour, they reached the top of the hill, and they looked out over the beautiful town of Glen Haven below. There was a small pond, something truly miraculous at the top of this steep incline. The water reflecting the blue sky and fluffy white clouds on its silvery surface. Amanda had brought some snacks, which she shared with a slobbery Philo. Amanda sighed contentedly. She might not have wanted to leave her nursery, but she was so glad to have found Glen Haven, and Elsie. There was something rather magical about this place, and she found her worries begin to, not vanish, but at least ease their tight grip around her throat.

Just as she was packing up her snacks to head back down the hill, Philo let out a bark and ran off down another, smaller path that Amanda hadn't noticed before. With a start, she raced after him, calling his name. Trust me to let my guard down for one minute, Amanda chided herself as she ran along the narrow path. I cannot lose that dog!

This pathway hadn't been as well kept as the one which brought her here, and she had to keep ducking her head to avoid having her eye gouged out by low tree branches.

Panting, she caught up to where Philo's barks were coming from. His tail was wagging, but less certainly now, and Amanda stared in horror at what he had found. What looked like a fire pit sat in a clearing just off the path, and in the centre of it was a pile of bones.

30

Amanda

Amanda stared, horrified. It didn't look like a full body, and she didn't think it was human. Maybe a deer? That was her best guess. Something about the way the bones were laid out sent a shiver down her spine. It looked as though someone had arranged them quite intentionally. As Amanda stepped closer, she saw strange runes drawn in the dirt around the fire-pit. Something was very, very wrong here. Philo barked again, making Amanda jump out of her skin. She looked up and saw a tall, hooded figure clad in black racing away from the scene.

Her blood turned to ice, and Amanda grabbed onto Philo's collar as he went to give chase. Nothing about this felt right, and she wanted to get as far away from here as she possibly could. Pulling Philo's lead, she raced back to the clearing at the top of the walk. The still waters which minutes ago had seemed so peaceful and held so much beauty now reflected back only her fears. Suddenly everything around her felt ominous. The trees and clouds were closing in, suffocating her. Amanda and Philo raced down the hill, her heart thundering.

Stumbling through the lounge door, Amanda was faced with the Lycra-clad behind of Elsie. Gentle music filled the air, and there was an intense smell of incense. Amanda was stunned for a second by the pert bottom before her. "Oh, hi," Elsie said, popping her face through her arms and staring upside down at Amanda. One look at Amanda's face and Elsie was on her feet in an instant, moving towards Amanda and taking her arm. She led her to the couch, her face a picture of concern. "What's wrong? You're white as a sheet."

"I think I just saw something very, very bad," Amanda said.

"Not the time to make a joke about my arse being a terrifying sight, I'm guessing?"

Amanda didn't even have the energy to laugh, and Elsie's face became grave. "I'll make us some tea. You look like you've had quite a shock." Elsie clicked her fingers, snuffing the candles and turning off the music in an instant. She went through to the kitchen. Amanda should have stayed on the couch, but she and Philo instinctively followed.

Despite the warmth of the kitchen, Amanda was shivering uncontrollably. Even Philo seemed to be off. Elsie settled Amanda on a stool, flicked on the kettle, and raced up the stairs. Philo placed his gigantic head on Amanda's lap and she patted him unconsciously, the softness of his fur a pleasant contrast to the cold hardness she had felt in her chest ever since seeing those bones.

Elsie came back down carrying two blankets, one bright blue and one deep purple. The purple one was covered in dog hair. She led her two frightened companions back to the lounge. She sat Amanda at one end of the couch, then gently wrapped the blue faux mink blanket around Amanda's shoulders, giving her a delicate kiss on her forehead as she did so. Amanda's heart fluttered. Elsie lay the purple blanket over Philo, and Amanda saw his breathing slow almost instantly. Elsie patted the couch and Philo jumped up, turned in a couple of circles like a purple ghost, and then lay down, the blanket covering him entirely. Not even his head poked out.

"It's his comfort blanket," Elsie said at Amanda's look.

Elsie went to the kitchen and returned with two steaming mugs. She set one in front of Amanda. "Lavender and chamomile tea. For the nerves." Amanda sipped gratefully, and it wasn't until she had finished the cup and Elsie had replaced it again that her friend asked her what had happened. As Amanda explained what she and Philo had discovered, Elsie's eyes grew wide with fear, and then dark with anger. She clutched the pendant around her neck as Amanda spoke. Amanda could practically feel the emotions coming off her in waves.

"It sounds like black magic to me," she said.

"Black magic?" Amanda didn't like the sound of that.

"Most witches believe in the sanctity of life and won't harm a living being, whether witch, human, werewolf, deer, whatever."

"Werewolf?" Amanda cut in faintly.

"There's not that many left," Elsie said, waving a hand dismissively. "But you know, even though witches are distrustful of werewolves, we still wouldn't hurt one unless it attacked us." Amanda shook her head, her addled brain struggling to catch up. "But an innocent animal being used as a sacrifice, that's pure black magic."

"You think it was sacrificed?" Ice ran down her spine.

"Can you remember what any of the runes looked like?"

"I only glanced at them to be honest, and then got the hell out of there, but I might be able to remember one or two."

Elsie grabbed a notepad and pencil from a drawer, and Amanda drew three shapes on it; a cross in a circle, a triangle with an eye in the middle, and something that looked like a sun with the centre coloured black.

"Stay here," Elsie commanded. Amanda wasn't sure if the order was directed at the dog or her. Either way, she had no more energy to move, so she and Philo remained huddled on the couch, listening to Elsie's footfall as she raced back upstairs. After several minutes of cursing and the sound of furniture being dragged around, Elsie came back down, holding a huge, ancient book. It was faded black and had a complicated, swirling-looking spiral on the front.

"Is that a book of spells?" Amanda asked in awe.

"This one is a bit of a history of magic as much as it is a spell book, though there are some spells in here, too." Elsie placed the book on the coffee table and knelt close enough to Amanda that she could smell the soft scent of cinnamon and jasmine on her skin. She rifled through the pages, muttering aloud to herself. "I'm sure I've seen it in here somewhere," she said, and then, "Ah ha!"

Amanda and Philo both looked at the page that Elsie pointed to. An icy shiver ran down Amanda's spine as she saw the words at the top of the page. "Divination by blood and bone," she read in a whisper.

"Whatever they were doing, they were trying to find something, or someone," Elsie said, her eyes wide.

31

Elsie

"Your pies always make me feel better," Amanda said through a mouthful of pastry. "Do you enchant them or something?"

Elsie busied herself in the kitchen cupboard, pulling out pots and pans for dinner. "Not really," she said, not looking at Amanda.

"Not really! You do enchant them!"

Elsie turned around, not wanting to have this conversation right now. She had been hoping they could forget about magic for the evening, or that Amanda could forget about it, at least. That experience in the forest might have put her completely off magic. Elsie didn't want her to change her mind about having a witch at home. But she didn't want to hide or be dishonest. She was finding she didn't want to hide anything from Amanda.

"It's not an enchantment, per se."

"What is it then?" Amanda asked, sounding interested, rather than horrified.

"I sometimes just bake in a little positive energy." Elsie blushed.. "Good luck, peace, clarity of thought, happiness, that sort of thing. It's more an intention than a spell, kind of like putting good vibes into them."

Amanda was looking at her with interest, and something else Elsie couldn't quite decipher. "You bake good vibes into your food?" she asked.

"Well, yes." Elsie said.

"People here haven't been very welcoming of you. Why are you so nice to them?"

Elsie shifted uncomfortably. "They haven't exactly been mean. Well, apart from Reginald, anyway. They're just not used to me yet."

Amanda tilted her head to one side. "I still don't understand."

Elsie said, twirled a long lock of her dark hair. "I just want the best for them. I know they're good people. I've seen them go about their lives. They care for one another, they care for these forests and mountains, and they might not care for me especially, just yet, but that doesn't mean I don't care about them." She looked at the ground, her voice not much more than a whisper.

"Elsie." Amanda said, taking a step towards her and lifted her chin up gently. "That's lovely."

"Really?"

"Yes. I block everyone out, run away from my problems, put up walls, and find it hard to trust people. You—" Amanda put a hand on each of Elsie's shoulders. Elsie was captivated by those hazel orbs, honey-coloured flecks shimmering in the light. "You let people in even when they might hurt you. You care about people, and you love and spread kindness and joy wherever you go. You're like this light that refuses to go out." She held Elsie's gaze, giving Elsie goosebumps. "You're amazing." Amanda gently tucked a lock of Elsie's hair behind her ear and Elsie's body warmed at Amanda's touch. She had never felt so seen, so cared for, so understood. Her heart fluttered, and she was so grateful to Amanda for sharing this with her.

They stood like that for a long moment, the space between them full of electricity. Then, blinking, Amanda stepped back. "What's in this pie, anyway?" She turned from Elsie and sat back down in front of her plate. Elsie's heart sank. Friends, just friends. She still felt the ghost of Amanda's hands on her arms, felt the gentle trace of her finger behind her ear. But she didn't want to lose her only friend because of silly feelings. Shaking herself inwardly, she turned towards Amanda. "Blueberry and rosemary," she said. "It's a good pick me up—rosemary for peace and good luck, and blueberries for happiness."

"I still feel like a rebel eating dessert before dinner," Amanda said, smiling, as she dug her spoon into the pie again.

"Well, you've had a shock," Elsie said, reminding herself of this and tamping down on the feelings bubbling up inside her. "How does lentil ragout sound?" She asked to change the subject.

"Delicious!" Amanda said. "There's more kale in the garden. I'll grab some."

Elsie began dicing garlic, as Amanda went out to the garden. Elsie was very grateful for this new ability to collect food from your own backyard - it was unreal.

When Amanda came back inside, she set about massaging the kale, as Elsie had shown her the week before. "So" said Amanda, her attention fixed on the kale. "What do we do about the dark magic?"

Elsie was surprised. She had expected Amanda to want nothing to do with the dark magic. Honestly, Elsie had thought that, as the only witch in town, she would be the one responsible for dealing with it, whatever that meant. It was nice that Amanda wanted to be part of finding a solution.

"I guess the first step is to figure out who is doing the dark magic." She said slowly. "They were obviously looking for something in the woods. If we can figure out what, maybe we can work out how to stop them."

"How do we do that?" Amanda asked, her honey brown eyes full of concern. Elsie wanted to reach out and hug her, but now wasn't the time.

"Let's look through the books in the house," she said. "That might give us a clue. In the meantime, we can cast a protection spell over Lilac House."

"A protection spell?"

"To keep the house or any of the magic in it from being discovered, and to prevent anyone with ill intent from coming in. I've brewed a few potions recently that might help, too."

"You brewed some potions on the off chance someone would come around casting evil magic?" Amanda asked, looking at Elsie in surprise.

Elsie realised she hadn't told Amanda about the cross that had been haunting her tea leaves for weeks. "The tea leaves said something bad might be coming."

"Great, can you ask them what it is, then?"

Elsie smiled wryly, "I'm afraid it doesn't work quite like that. Tea leaves are hard to interpret at the best of times. They rarely give a straight answer. Reading the leaves is all about the power of interpretation."

Amanda sighed. Elsie realised the kale was practically disintegrating, Amanda had massaged it so much. Gently, she took the bowl from her hands and placed it on the other side of the bench. "I think maybe you and Philo should just sit in the lounge. Don't you?" The poor woman was still in shock. The pie might have perked her up, but discussing dark magic and reading the future must be rather a lot for Amanda to take in, especially so soon after discovering witches even existed! Amanda looked at her with vacant eyes, and Elsie led her through to the couch.

32

Amanda

The following week, Amanda and Elsie were in the kitchen, making eggplant parmigiana. They had read through several of the magical tomes Elsie had, but there didn't seem to be anything else of relevance in them. Without knowing more about who the person using dark magic was, or what they were trying to achieve, it was impossible to make much progress. Nothing else dark or mysterious had happened in the preceding week, but Amanda knew Elsie was still anxious. She was just hoping the person who had cast the dark magic was already on their way to somewhere new.

"Every witch is different." Elsie explained as Amanda sliced eggplant. "Most witches have magic that draws predominantly from one of the four elements: earth, water, fire, and air." She carefully placed the slices of eggplant in an oiled pan as she spoke, cracking salt over them. "Gran and Dad were both earth witches, and they both had the green thumbs that come with that. Phoebe, my cousin, who I told you about, she's an earth witch too, but her speciality is animals. I should ask Soren what his element is, come to think of it. I wonder if he knows anything more about the dark magic."

"Who?"

Elsie looked surprised. "Did I not mention I had met another witch?"

Amanda looked at Elsie closely. She didn't know how unusual this was. It hadn't actually occurred to Amanda to ask how many witches were in town. "You didn't. Are there as lot of witches in Glen Haven, then?"

"Not as far as I know," Elsie set about grating some plant-based cheese into a bowl. "I could feel Soren's magic as soon as he walked into the shop, and often I will get a particular feeling about someone if they're magical, but not always. Especially if they have different magic to me, or they aren't very strong in their magic."

"Different kinds of magic?"

"I guess I mean different species, werewolves, vampires, that sort of thing. Though, like I was saying, there are different elements most witches connect to. I'm air. That's why I find levitating so natural. Most witches need brooms to fly, and that's fun too, but I can float without one. It's also why I can pull stardust and moonlight into my spells. Though that's also because I have an affinity with the night." She shook the eggplant in the pan, and then deftly turned them over just as they were turning a crisp golden brown. Amanda's mind was still reeling from the revelation that there was another witch in town. But Elsie was still talking.

"So, witches can use magic from other elements, but they will have a natural affinity with one element, maybe with a secondary affinity as well. Most witches cast spells that are harmless, positive even; wisdom, protection, glamour spells, that kind of thing. We usually need to use special ingredients and spell books for spells that aren't directly linked to our elements, or for more complex spells. That's what you saw that first time you saw me casting."

That day felt so long ago to Amanda now. Had it really only been a month? She took over grating the cheese as Elsie placed the cooked eggplant into a casserole dish. Elsie then set more eggplant slices into the pan to cook, the oil sizzling slightly as the damp surface of the purple vegetable touched the pan. "Some witches, though, want to do things that natural magic won't allow for. Dark stuff, curses, casting diseases, dark divination, even stealing someone's magic." She shivered, and Amanda watched her friend intentionally straighten her back again, as if she was drawing in strength.

"That's what I think that witch was doing when you saw her in the forest. Reading tea leaves gives you a general sense of what's to come, or can give you guidance about a question you hold in your mind. Dark Divination can be used much more specifically. Bone and blood divination, from what the grimoire says, are used for locating things, kind of like hunting." Elsie's faced looked pale as she explained. "You use the blood and bones of the hunted animal, along with some seriously dark runes and incantations, and you can conjure up a map to see where your prey is."

Amanda put a hand on Elsie's arm. She seemed really upset by the idea of a dark witch in Glen Haven. "Elsie," Amanda said hesitantly, "what if this Soren guy is the dark witch?" Elsie shook her head. "No, I don't think so.

Soren is lovely. You'll meet him. He's not the evil sort. He's got family history in Glen Haven. I think he's just here to reconnect with his ancestry."

Amanda didn't know anything about magic, but she knew from experience that bad guys were pretty good at pretending to be good. She could see from Elsie's face, though, that the topic was closed. For now, at least.

The mood was definitely low, and they ate their dinner on the couches in near silence. Eventually, Amanda couldn't take it anymore. She wished she hadn't told Elsie about the bones. Nothing else had happened since then, and she wondered if she was making a big deal out of nothing. "That's it," she said, after clearing away the plates and seeing Elsie staring into space bleakly. "There's nothing for it. We need a Dolly Dazzler."

Elsie raised an eyebrow at Amanda, who went into the kitchen and grabbed a whisk and a wooden spoon. Coming back into the lounge, she handed Elsie the purple silicone whisk and hooked her phone up to the lounge speakers. The opening bars of '9 to 5' filled the lounge. Amanda pulled Elsie up from the couch, spinning her around and singing loudly into her 'microphone': "I tumbled out of bed and stumbled to the kitchen." Elsie looked taken aback, but after a few seconds Amanda saw a small smile spread across her face and Elsie began singing along. Before long, they were making up terrible dance moves and singing at the top of their lungs. "This calls for an outfit change," Elsie said, and she snapped her fingers. Amanda's trademark jean shorts and checked shirt were replaced by a rhinestone covered denim jacket and low-cut white t-shirt over a voluminous fifties-style skirt. Elsie was now clad in skin-tight pleather pants and a shimmery black fitted top that sparkled like the stars.

Amanda whooped in glee! This was the kind of magic she could get behind! And she could stare at Elsie in those tight pants all night.

The two women twirled around the lounge, shimmying, swaying and finger snapping, and when the song ended, they fell on the couch laughing. "Thank you, I needed that," Elsie said.

"Oh, we are just getting started, sweetheart," Amanda said, in her best Elvis impression, as 'Jailhouse Rock' came on the speakers. Elsie's eyes sparkled, and she leapt back to her feet, clicking her fingers once more.

33

Elsie

Elsie had always known that drinking and enchanting was a bad idea. But she had wanted to show Amanda how good, fun even, magic could be. Plus, she had wanted to forget her worries, about the shop, about the dark magic, just for a little while. This morning, however, she remembered why she usually stuck to tea. Her head felt like it was underwater, and there was a truck driven by a reckless toddler driving around in her brain. The light that peeked through the gap in her curtains made her genuinely consider whether she could blight the sun. Philo's enormous face and pink tongue filled her vision, and she groaned again as he licked her face. When she didn't move, he gave an impatient bark, and she winced.

After dancing in the lounge, they had decided to keep the night going. Elsie couldn't remember whose idea it had been to walk down to the pub, but she was going to blame Amanda. She remembered them ordering at least three rounds of cocktails. It was possible Amanda had also done a few shots, and Elsie had a vague memory of a jukebox and some terrible lip-sync battles. She had a feeling at some point Sam might have gently cut them off. Elsie winced at the thought; she would have to make it up to him. She couldn't have the owner of the only pub in town unhappy with her.

Stumbling back up the hill together, Amanda had asked Elsie about her magic. Somehow they had gotten into a debate about whether you could bewitch a bath-bomb so that the glittery, sweet-smelling bubbles stayed bubbly forever. Elsie had been adamant that she had tried and failed to perfect such a spell for the past fifteen years, and that it was not possible. You either lost the smell, lost the glitter, or your bubbles turned bright green.

Elsie groaned again as she recalled what had happened next. But before she could kick herself any further, she heard a crash from Amanda's room and a whimper of pain. Dragging herself out of bed and sleepily wrapping her satin gown around her shoulders, she shuffled to Amanda's room, knocking quietly on the door so as not to amplify the drumming in her head. Amanda made a noise that might have been the words "come in,", so Elsie nudged the door open. There was a broken curtain rail and the sunlight streaming through temporarily blinded Elsie. Amanda was standing at the door to her ensuite, looking rather green. Elsie shuffled over to her, eyes shielded with her hand.

They stood together in the doorframe, surveying the damage. The ceiling was covered with a virulent green goo, broken porcelain was scattered across the floor, and everything seemed to be coated in a layer of glittery dust. Elsie rubbed her hand across her face, exhausted. "Sorry Amanda," she said, her voice still hoarse from alcohol and lack of sleep. "I think you'll have to use my bathroom for a while."

"Can't you just magic the mess away?" Amanda asked, turning towards Elsie. Elsie began shaking her head in response, but quickly realised that was a terrible idea. Instead, she just said, "Not all magical messes can be tidied up with a wave of a hand." She picked up a piece of porcelain and looked at the shattered remains of the bathtub in the middle of the floor. "We'll have to tidy it up ourselves, and then call a plumber to install a new bath."

The two continued staring at the mess in dismay. Eventually Elsie said, "Fancy some French toast?" Amanda's eyes didn't quite light up, but there seemed to be a little more hope in them than there had been a few moments before.

"I guess you proved your point, anyway." Amanda said, as they shuffled together towards the kitchen, Philo racing happily ahead of them, impatiently awaiting his breakfast. "I didn't realise you were so stubborn."

"It's the libra in me," Elsie said, shrugging.

"You're not going to tell me that star signs are real too, now, are you?" Amanda mumbled, holding her head and looking somewhat perplexed.

"Oh, come on," Elsie said, putting the coffee on and then pulling bread, aquafaba, vanilla, and sugar from the cupboards. "You must have had some experience with the mystical in the past, surely? Palm reading? Tarot?" Amanda shook her head. "Tea leaves?"

Amanda shrugged. "To be honest, I've always been a massive skeptic. If I hadn't seen you literally floating—"

"Levitating," Elsie cut in.

"Levitating," Amanda conceded with a small nod, her eyes still mostly closed against the light. "Then I probably still wouldn't believe magic was real."

"How do you feel about magic now?" Elsie asked. A knot tightening in her stomach. Amanda's introduction to magic hadn't exactly been the smoothest. Elsie wouldn't blame her if she grew to resent the stuff. An image of Elsie's mother crossed her vision, and she sighed. That wouldn't happen with Amanda, surely?

"Why do you ask?"

Elsie whisked ingredients in a bowl and then poured in almond milk and cinnamon. She opened a door to a cabinet that usually wasn't physically present in the kitchen, unless Elsie asked for it. Plucking out a small vial containing a brilliant blue liquid, she held it up to Amanda. "Something to help with the recovery?" she asked.

"At this point, I'll try anything," Amanda said. "So long as it won't make me grow fur."

Elsie laughed, relieved. "I promise this one is not canine-specific."

The canine in question was now running in circles around Elsie's ankles, barking loudly. Elsie reflected that she couldn't understand him so clearly when she was hung over. Nevertheless, she got the message. He was hungry. Amanda volunteered to feed Philo while Elsie made breakfast, and in no time the two women were perched at the kitchen island, greedily digging into the steaming cups of coffee and plates of French toast piled high with bananas and berry compote. Philo lapped happily at some extra banana and compote in a bowl.

Once they finished their food, Elsie looked at Amanda again. She must have been staring too intently, because suddenly Amanda looked nervous. "What?" she asked.

Elsie laughed. "You don't need to look so scared. I just wondered if you'd like me to read your tea leaves."

Amanda sat for a few moments, and Elsie was worried she had pushed the magic thing too far. Amanda had seemed so ok with it a moment ago. "What exactly does reading tea leaves involve?" Amanda asked after a few more moments of silence.

"It's honestly not scary or spooky," Elsie said, trying to reassure her. "We brew you some tea and you drink it, thinking about a particular question that you want answered. Once you've finished, you turn the tea cup anti clockwise three times and then a quarter turn to the right, still thinking about your question, before tipping it upside down onto a saucer. After ninety seconds, we turn the teacup back up again and I read the tea leaves for you."

"And what would it show?" Amanda asked.

Elsie studied her for a moment, trying to read what was in her tone. "If your question is specific enough, it can usually give you some kind of answer, though it takes a little while to understand what the various symbols might mean. If your question is more generic, then it will probably just show some things in your future, but it's harder to interpret without a question."

"Such as?"

"Say you ask what the future holds for you," Elsie said, getting up and beginning to prepare some tea. "You might have a cross in the bottom. Now the cross technically means death." Amanda looked horrified, and Elsie hurried on. "But it doesn't always literally mean death." Amanda looked confused, so Elsie tried again to explain. Explaining magic to normys wasn't always easy.

"Death could mean literal death," she tried to explain, "for you or for someone close to you." The idea of Amanda dying filled Elsie's throat with bile. She shook her head to clear it and continued. "But it could also mean the death of an opportunity, or death of a business or a relationship. So the more specific you can be with your question, the easier it will be to interpret the answer in the tea leaves."

Amanda nodded slowly. "Do you need to know what the question is to interpret the tea leaves?"

Elsie's eyebrows shot up. She was a little hurt, but she tried not to show it. "No, not technically. Though I might not be able to help you interpret the answer very well if I don't know what the question was."

"OK," Amanda said, a determined glint coming into her eyes. Elsie hadn't seen her look this hard before. She had no idea what type of question Amanda was thinking of. She looked both scared and a little scary.

Elsie poured the tea and Amanda did as directed, turning the cup slowly in her hands. She passed her empty teacup to Elsie to read. Elsie's mind was clouded with concern for her friend. Eventually, she felt the clarity that came through reading tea leaves coming over her, and she looked into the cup expectantly.

"Ok," she said. "I can see what I think is a key along the side. Now that can mean a range of things, such as new beginnings, home, or even something being lost. Do any of those make sense with your question?"

Amanda nodded her head, looking a little relieved. Elsie relaxed a little. She was pleased that there was good news in the leaves for her friend. "Then on the bottom, which is farther away time wise, we have an angel, which usually means someone is looking out for you." She glanced at Amanda again, and, assured that this meant something to her, continued. "Finally, on the sides, which is in the near future but not immediately, there is a person following another."

"That doesn't sound so good," Amanda said, her forehead wrinkling.

"It can mean a fresh path. Sometimes it means you're being followed, but often it's more metaphorical, like to do with family. A son might have it showing he is following in the footsteps of his father." Elsie thought she was being reassuring, but she could practically see the storm that crossed Amanda's eyes at the mention of family.

Amanda got up immediately, startling Philo as her chair clanged loudly on the floor. "Sorry," she said, hurriedly placing the chair back at the kitchen counter. "I'm just going to take a walk." She practically bolted from for the door.

Elsie looked after her in amazement. Something about the follower had made Amanda extremely nervous. Elsie looked at Philo. "What was that about?" She wondered aloud.

Not a fan of her family by the looks of things.

Elsie knew Amanda's dad hadn't exactly been the world's best father, but the look on her face as she left was genuine fear; but for who? Elsie realised with a sense of foreboding that she didn't know all that much about the woman she was living with.

34

Amanda

A manda dialled Pierce, thinking fast. He picked up on the second ring. "Finally. Where are you?" His voice was clipped and worried.

"Out of town," Amanda said evasively. "Listen, is my dad OK?"

"Your dad? As far as I know. Same unit. No change. Why, have you heard something?" Amanda could practically hear the cogs turning in Pierce's mind.

"Would you check on him for me, please?" she asked.

"You're not really in a position to be making demands."

"I said please." Amanda heard a snort down the phone, and some keys tapping. She was pacing the street like a caged animal. "Why are you at work on a Sunday, anyway?"

"Don't know if you heard." Pierce's voice sounded more distant now, as if he had put the phone down and placed her on speakerphone. "But I'm investigating a triple murder."

"They're not going to get any more dead if you take a day off," Amanda mumbled. The typing paused.

"Would you like me to wait until Monday to see what the status of your dad is?"

"Sorry," Amanda said. "I just, you know...."

"I know, I know." Pierce sighed. Amanda waited, and after a moment, he spoke again. "Ok, here we go. Hmm, that's weird. It looks like he's scheduled to be moved to Wiri next week."

Amanda stopped pacing. Her blood had turned to ice. Wiri was the prison her brother was in. "Wiri? They can't do that, surely. Does it say why?"

Pierce kept tapping away, more urgently this time. "I don't know," he said. "It says here for family reasons."

"He doesn't have any family!" Amanda practically screamed. "Apart from me and..."

"It looks like it specifically says that it's a request from his son to be closer."

"There should be a no-contact with my brother. Surely they wouldn't put them both in the same prison knowing my brother wants to kill my dad." Amanda tried to contain herself, but her heart was beating out of control.

"The no-contact has been lifted," Pierce said quietly.

"WHY?" This time Amanda did shout. Pierce was quiet for a minute, and Amanda's heart sank. "Is it because I didn't give evidence?" she whispered.

There was a long pause, and then, in a gentle voice, Pierce said, "There was no evidence of a threat, and without a signed statement from the source of the intel, the judge didn't think that the condition needed to be upheld. Nor did your father."

"You knew about this and you didn't tell me?"

Pierce's tone was sharp this time. "I've been trying to reach you. You haven't been answering my calls." There was a beat and then he went on, more gently. "But no, I didn't know. I knew they had lifted the non-contact, but I didn't think it mattered with them both in different prisons. I thought maybe your brother would try to contact Frank, but your dad didn't strike me as someone who would be easily fooled."

Amanda tugged her hair out of its bun, grabbing her hair in a fist and tugging at it in frustration. What was she going to do? "What if I sign an affidavit?" she blurted out.

35

Elsie

Amanda came back into the room looking dazed. "You ok?" Elsie asked cautiously. Amanda shrugged, collapsing into a stool at the kitchen island. "Want to talk about it?"

"Not really."

Elsie did what she always did in a crisis. She made tea. She placed a cup of chamomile and lavender tea in front of Amanda, alongside a plate of her famous lavender shortbread cookies. These ones had a little bit of chilli in them for some kick. Hopefully that would give Amanda a bit of energy to talk. Amanda mumbled something that Elsie thought was probably a thank you, and dipped her cookie vacantly into her tea.

She had a bad phone call.

"I can tell." Elsie said, rolling her eyes at Philo. "But you really shouldn't snoop."

Not my fault I have excellent hearing.

"Funny how that hearing seems to vanish completely when you're chasing a rabbit."

Philo looked away.

"It's still so weird that you can do that. Talk to him. Or, read his mind, or whatever."

"I wish I could read your mind right about now." Elsie said. Sitting down opposite Amanda and looking at her with concern.

"No pressure, but I hope you know you can tell me anything."

Amanda took a deep breath. "You know how I told you my family history is pretty complicated?"

"Yeah,"

"Well, part of the complication that I hadn't mentioned is that my brother is a maniac who wants to kill my dad."

Elsie stared at Amanda in horror. "What?"

113

Amanda nodded gloomily into her mug, munching on the cookies and spilling crumbs everywhere. A large, pink tongue came up from under the table and within an instant, the crumbs were gone. *Philo!* Elsie thought, rather than said.

Sorry

Elsie focussed her attention back on Amanda. "Your brother wants to kill your dad? Why?"

He hadn't sounded like the world's best dad, but wanting to kill someone was next-level stuff, especially for a family member.

"Theo's always been pretty head-strong. He thought dad was too soft, with all his rules about how he ran his business. Don't get me wrong, my dad was shady as anything, but Theo." Amanda visibly shivered, and Elsie put her hand on Amanda's arm. "Theo's just cruel. He got worse after dad went to jail. I left because he tried to drag me into his mess. But before I left, I heard him talking to one of his 'friends' about dad." Amanda was looking off into the distance, remembering something she clearly wished she had never been a part of. "He said that he'd 187 my dad if he ever got the chance. That he could do a much better job of running the company than dad had."

"187?"

Amanda almost rolled her eyes. "It's slang for murder. Something to do with American law, I don't know, it's a rap thing. Theo thinks he's so gangster."

Elsie could tell Amanda was trying to come across as more relaxed about this than she was.

"OK, I get that hearing your brother say that he wants to kill your dad would be awful. But would he really mean it? People say stuff like that all the time, don't they?"

Amanda dragged her finger across a drip on the countertop, pulling the tiny pool of water this way and that. "Oh, he meant it alright. Dad was never into that sort of stuff, and even Theo wouldn't have done it a few years ago. Lately, though, he's been out of control."

Elsie shivered. She couldn't imagine having someone like that in her family. Her dad had been wonderful. Phoebe, her cousin, had been Elsie's best friend since they were children, and her mum? Well, sure, Elsie and her mum had never exactly had the close mother-daughter friendship you

114

saw on Gilmore Girls, but she knew her mother wanted the best for her. It was shocking what Amanda had lived with. She'd known Amanda was hiding something, but she had no idea that all this time she had a possibly murderous brother! Something occurred to her then. "That would have been before you came to Glen Haven though, right? I'm not saying that it's not a huge deal, because obviously it is. But did something happen to make you extra worried about it now?"

Amanda put her face in her hands, pulling them down slowly. Elsie realised what she was about to say, just as she said it. "The tea leaves. I knew it had to be my brother following my dad. I called the officer I had warned about Theo. He said Theo is getting transferred to the same prison as my dad. Dad obviously just thinks his precious son is trying to move to be nearer him."

"But you're worried Theo is going to try to kill your dad?" Elsie breathed. And she thought her problems were tough.

"Exactly."

"What are you going to do?" Elsie asked, putting more cookies on Amanda's cleared plate. She had no way of knowing how to deal with this, but sugar and lavender couldn't hurt.

"I'm going to swear an affidavit."

"You're going to go on record about your brother wanting to kill your dad?"

"Pierce said that if I can swear an affidavit, he should be able to convince a judge not to release the name of the person who gave the information. The judge can review the file, and hopefully, based on my evidence, will stop Theo from being transferred. They'll put something innocuous on file, like the prison is over full or something, which is probably true anyway."

"Is it safe for you to do that?" Elsie was full of concern. If Amanda went on record about this, wouldn't that put her in more danger?

"It should be." Amanda didn't sound certain. "The file will be sealed, but there's always a chance someone will find out."

Elsie looked into Amanda's eyes. "You really want to do this?"

"No. But I have to. It's the only way to keep my dad safe."

Elsie nodded. "Would you like me to come with you?"

One side of Amanda's mouth pulled up just a little. "Thank you. That's so kind. But I don't want there to be any chance of you getting caught up in this. I think this is something I have to do on my own."

Elsie was going to argue, but Amanda was getting up.

"I'd better get to bed. It'll be a long day tomorrow." She turned as she reached the door. "Thanks, Elsie. I don't usually talk about this stuff with anyone. Thank you for not judging me."

Elsie's heart followed Amanda out the door.

36

Amanda

Amanda drove for two hours to get to the run down white building. The town seemed to be warmer than Glen Haven, though that did nothing to lift her mood. Her body shook with nerves as she gave her name at the reception and said she wanted to make a statement. The lady behind the counter looked at her over red cat-eyed spectacles that echoed the red of her lips. "Have you got an appointment, sweetie?" Amanda shook her head, and the woman tapped away at her computer. "Officer Patel is out at the minute. He should be back soon if you're happy to wait." The woman rolled the 'r' in 'officer' in that distinctly South Island way, and Amanda felt very far from home. The woman gestured to the faded, stained mint green waiting chairs and Amanda sat down. She wasn't a germaphobe. She was, however, conscious of how many people had been in a space, and she fastidiously avoided looking at the stains on the chairs as she sat down.

A tall Indian man in a police uniform walked in about ten minutes later, nodding to her as he approached the desk and murmured to Trudy, the woman with the red glasses. Amanda had almost picked the skin on her thumbs to the point of bleeding. She stood up as soon as the police officer walked in.

Amanda watched the two out of the corner of her eye and saw Officer Patel nod to Trudy and then approach her. Officer Patel held out his hand, a professional smile on his face.

"Ms Masters. I'm Officer Patel. I'm happy to take a statement in one of our interview rooms now, if you like. Alternatively, if the matter you wish to discuss is sensitive, we have a female officer coming in at 3." Amanda shook his hand and her head. "It's nothing like that," she said hurriedly. "I'm happy to speak to you now if you have the time."

Officer Patel inclined his head. "I'm afraid I'll need to ask you to come through our security check," he indicated towards a bag scanner and metal detector. "Standard policy these days." He smiled again, and Amanda placed her blue backpack into the tray and stepped through the detector. After passing through security, Officer Patel led her through a series of narrow, white corridors which smelt of coffee and sweat. He swiped a security card to let them through to a kind of office area and motioned for Amanda to enter. Amanda nearly tripped over her own feet as she walked. She had to count three steps to every breath to stop herself from hyperventilating.

They entered a painted blue hallway, with a couple of desks on one side and on the other, doors reading 'Interview Room 1,' 'Interview Room 2,' and so on. Officer Patel led her into one and motioned for her to take a seat. The room was sparsely furnished; just two chairs on either side of a Formica table, with a video recorder in one corner. "Do you want anything to drink?" he asked. Amanda's throat was dry, so she asked for water. Officer Patel motioned for her to sit. As she stared around the room, she wondered what she was doing here. If her brother found out that she was making this statement, she would be in huge trouble. Then again, she reminded herself grimly, if she didn't, Theo appeared set to kill their dad and take over the family business for good. The door opened again. Officer Patel sat down opposite her in the sterile room.

"OK Ms Masters," he said, uncapping a pen and flipping to a fresh page in his notebook. "Let's start at the beginning."

37

Elsie

The mid-year solstice was one of Elsie's favourite times of the year. Being in the Southern Hemisphere, June 22nd was the winter solstice, not the Summer Solstice. To Elsie's mind, that had its own delights. This year, the winter solstice was also going to be a full moon, which enhanced the magical properties available to witches that night. Elsie's stomach tightened as she realised that this would be her second solstice without her dad. Her dad had loved the Summer Solstice most of all. They would always travel to Lilac House, write their wishes for the year and their hopes for their loved ones on brightly coloured ribbons, and tie them to the elm tree in Grandma Margie's back garden. Winter Solstice was a bit more of a somber affair, but it suited the night owl in Elsie.

She began her preparations by gathering herbs and flowers and grinding them with a pestle and mortar. Her mind was everywhere. Amanda had been gone all day. Elsie was worried sick, but she reminded herself that Amanda was a grown woman, and that she would call her if she needed her. Elsie hadn't seen or felt any dark magic for a while now, and she was beginning to hope that whoever had cast that dark spell had moved on. However, she was taking no chances. She would enhance the protection spell over Lilac House to make sure that nothing could happen to them during the thinning of the veil.

Elsie sighed dejectedly into the pestle and mortar, dipping it into a pan. Phoebe was overseas, and her mum had, unsurprisingly, called to say that she was going abroad to visit Gloria, Elsie's aunt. That meant this would be Elsie's first solstice without either of her parents. Elsie tried to ignore the feeling of disappointment that her mother didn't want to spend the solstice with her. But then again, her mother wasn't magic, so the solstice didn't mean as much to her. She tried to tell herself that it was OK, she could make new friends and create new traditions. Plus, her mother had promised to visit once she was back.

Elsie was stirring a fragrant mixture of herbs and spices on the stove in the kitchen when she heard the front door open and close. She waited for Amanda to come into the kitchen, the unquestioned hub of the house, to say hello. Instead, she heard heavy footfalls on the stairs. Not a good sign. Amanda always came to say hello when she got home.

She continued with her preparations, placing a saucepan on the stove to begin the base for the mulled wine. Elsie liked her cinnamon and spices to soak in fruit juice, then rest together in the fridge for a week, before adding the wine on the day of so the fruit flavours really came through. She would make the wreaths later this week, to represent the circle of life. She was just opening the oven to check on the roasting vegetables inside when Amanda finally came into the room. "Sorry," she said, in a sullen tone Elsie hadn't heard from her friend before. "I'll just grab a cup of tea and some crackers and be out of your hair."

Elsie took in her friend. She looked exhausted. She had huge bags under her eyes, her shirt was wrinkled, and her hair was a mess. "Are you ok?" she asked cautiously.

Amanda sighed. "fine" she said, not holding Elsie's gaze. "Just a long day."

"Did it go ok at the Police station?" Amanda had taken the day off work, and had messaged Elsie when she arrived at the station safe and sound, but Elsie hadn't heard anything else from her all day.

"Fine," Amanda said again, grabbing a packet of crackers out of the cupboard.

"I'm making roast veggies."

"I'm not really hungry," Amanda said, just as her stomach growled. She continued towards the door.

Elsie was a little sad that her friend didn't want to have dinner with her, especially when she was so clearly hungry. Then her brain clicked to a conversation they had had a few weeks ago about introversion and extraversion, and Amanda's way of dealing with difficult situations. "There's leftover curry in the fridge if you fancy something a bit more substantial now." Elsie looked anxiously at her friend. Amanda didn't turn around, but Elsie could tell she was mentally weighing the pros and cons of this decision.

"I won't be offended if you eat it in your room," Elsie she said, and smiled when Amanda finally turned to face her.

Amanda's features were a little softer now, and Elsie breathed a gentle sigh of relief. "You sure you wouldn't mind?" Amanda asked, apologetically.

"Your introverted ways make no sense to me, but far be it from me to intervene in your method of processing."

Amanda smiled wryly. "You really do know me." She turned and grabbed the plate of curry from the fridge, blitzed it in the microwave, and headed towards the door, mug in one hand and steaming plate balanced carefully on the other. "Thank you," she said again, as she glanced over her shoulder at Elsie. "It's been a pretty exhausting couple of days. I appreciate you understanding."

Elsie walked over and placed a hand on Amanda's shoulder, giving it a gentle squeeze. "Take all the time you need. I'll be in the lounge watching Dharma and Gregg reruns for the foreseeable future if you feel like non-interactive company." The corner of Amanda's mouth quirked up, and she nodded and headed out the door.

Elsie heard her friend's footfall on the steps once again. She was glad Amanda had taken the curry. Still, she reflected, as she finished cooking a dinner that was now for one. She couldn't help but feel a little lonely. How was it she had been in Glen Haven for almost a year, and she only had one friend in the whole town?

38

Elsie

Elsie was just closing the shop when she heard a voice behind her. "Fancy seeing you here."

She turned and saw Soren leaning languidly against the shop wall, his ash blonde hair dazzling in the moonlight.

"Soren!" Elsie she said, starting. "You scared the life out of me. Why didn't you just come into the shop?"

"Sorry," Soren he said, moving towards her and embracing her., "You looked busy. I didn't want to disturb you."

"What are you doing here, anyway?" she said, her heart rate returning to normal.

"It's a beautiful evening," he said with a nonchalant shrug. "Perfect for casting. I thought we could go for a drive somewhere and practice some new spells." Elsie's heart leapt. It had been so long since she had had someone to cast spells with, and she missed the sense of camaraderie it brought. "Sounds good!" She said, then her heart sank.

"Oh, I forgot, it's pizza and Party of Five tonight at Lilac House."

Soren looked confused. "You are having a party with only five people?"

Elsie laughed. "No," she explained, "it's an old TV show. Amanda and I have gotten into the habit of bingeing like half a season while eating reheated frozen pizza most Fridays."

"I see," Soren said, still looking confused. "Surely if it is a television show you could watch it another time, yes? These things are now available for streaming, are they not?"

"They are," Elsie agreed slowly. Amanda wouldn't mind if she bailed on Pizza and Party just this once, surely? It wasn't every day that Elsie got a chance to cast spells with a fellow witch.

"Of course, if you would prefer to go home and watch television...." Soren began, but Elsie cut him off.

"No, it's fine. Let me just message my flatmate." She pulled out her phone and fired off a quick text, trying to ignore the knot of guilt that was sitting heavily in her stomach. "Ok," she said with a smile, pocketing her phone again. "Let's go."

Soren led her over to his car, a long, sleek, silver Mercedes. She got in and he passed her a scarf. "For your hair," he said, when she looked at him in confusion. Bewildered, she tied the scarf around her head, feeling very Old Hollywood Glamour. Soren adjusted the car heater, turning it up high to combat the cool of the night air. Then he pushed a button on the dashboard, and the car's roof slid off.

"You have a convertible!?" Elsie shrieked in delight. Soren just smiled, putting his foot on the accelerator and speeding off.

They drove out of Glen Haven, following the curve of the hills, the moon high in the sky lighting their path. Soren turned on the radio, and to Elsie's surprise, Elvis started playing. She hadn't expected him to be into old school music. They cruised the quiet roads for about half an hour before Soren pulled over at the side of a hill. Elsie looked out and saw a valley below. There were no houses around, and no sign of civilisation. Suddenly she realised that nobody, including her, knew where she was, and there was nobody here to help her if things went wrong. Soren looked over at her with a smile. "Shall we have some fun?"

He popped the boot and got out of the car. He's getting a shovel, he's going to kill and bury me, oh goddess what do I do!? Soren startled her by tapping on her window, and as she turned to look out she saw that he was holding something long and thin. Could that be the handle of a spade? Was he going to make it that obvious? Then with a huge sigh of relief, Elsie saw that at the end of the stick were bristles. They were broomsticks! "Have you ever been night-flying before?" he asked, a huge smile on his face.

Elsie hadn't flown in years. When she was at school, she had flown, of course; all the young witches had learned, or tried to. Not every witch could fly, but air witches like Elsie had a natural affinity with the sky. Elsie's father was terrible on a broom, so she had never really flown with him. At school, she had loved the feeling of pushing into the sky, feeling the wind on her face, and watching as the ground below grew further and further away. There was nothing in the whole world like the feeling of leaving the earth and soaring beneath the stars. Elsie levitated when she cast spells, as it helped her to concentrate, disconnecting her from the shackles of the earth, but she hadn't flown on a broom in a longer time than she cared to remember.

Glen Haven was a quiet place, but she got the feeling that people wouldn't take too kindly to spotting a witch flying past their window, and she couldn't risk anyone seeing her flying around town. There were, of course, plenty of remote places that she could have flown, but the chances of her being observed, though minuscule, were still there. Besides, she hadn't practised enough since school to feel confident going out in the middle of nowhere to fly on her own. What if something happened, and she was stuck at the bottom of a cliff with no way to call for help? What explanation would she give if she managed to call an ambulance? As much as it saddened her, she had decided that flying alone was simply too risky.

"What if someone sees us?" She asked Soren, whispering despite there being no-one in sight.

"All the way out here?" Soren smiled. "They won't. We will cast a luminous spell so that we can see where we are going, but if anyone sees it they will simply think there are strange lights in the sky, perhaps shooting stars or similar."

They were parked well off the road, and even on the drive, Elsie hadn't seen another car go by for at least half an hour. Plus, Soren was right; in the sky they would barely be visible. Her body filled with adrenaline at the idea of flying again. She took a final look around and then said, "Ok," grabbing a broom and taking off before she could talk herself out of it.

39

Amanda

The next day, Amanda walked into the office to collect the post as usual. "Morning, Murray," she called out as she walked through to the back. Murray responded with a wave and a grunt, that could possibly be interpreted as a hello. As she came back out with the day's post a few minutes later, Amanda noticed him stretching his leg out slowly and grimacing.

"Are you alright?" she asked, walking over with concern.

"Fine," the old man said, hastily folding his leg back up and placing it under the desk once more. Amanda saw him wince again as he did so.

"Is your leg still giving you a lot of grief?" she asked.

"It's not so bad," he said unconvincingly.

"What did the physio say? Did she give you some exercises to do?"

Murray mumbled something incoherent.

"What was that?"

"I haven't been to the physio," he said, turning to Amanda, his eyes like a defiant four-year-old. "All she's going to do is tell me to move my leg and charge me $400 for the privilege."

"Murray, your leg won't improve if you don't know what to do to help it get better," Amanda said with growing concern. "Don't you think you should at least give it a go?"

Murray grumbled something again.

Amanda pulled a flyer out of her postie bag and handed it to Murray. "What's this?" he asked huffily, though Amanda was 100% certain he could read.

"It's an ad for Elsie's yoga class. She runs it every Tuesday night at the Pie in the Sky. It's koha entry, so you just pay what you feel comfortable with."

"I don't do yoga," Murray said.

"No, I can tell." Amanda retorted. "But if you want to get that leg of yours moving again, I suggest you start." Then she strolled out the door, calling casually over her shoulder, "There are usually cookies."

The next day, Elsie and Amanda had just finished transforming the shop into a transcendent yoga studio when the door opened and none other than Murray walked in. Amanda could barely contain her surprise, but she sensed that making a big deal of this would put Murray off, so she simply waved at him and gave him what she hoped was a welcoming smile. Elsie wafted over and handed him a mat. Amanda noticed that Elsie, too was playing down Murray's presence; she directed him to take a place in the middle of the floor, ensuring he could see her well. Amanda saw her saying a few more words to him, probably about how to accommodate his leg injury. Then she wafted away again, like his presence here wasn't a cataclysmic event. Other people drifted in, and the space was almost full by 7pm.

It took all of Amanda's strength not to spend the whole yoga session looking over at Murray. The couple of times she did glance over, his face was a mask of concentration. She couldn't read him at all. Elsie took them through a slightly gentler yoga practice than the last few had been, with a few arm strength moves in the mix as well as the usual holds in warrior two, burning the legs, and a flow through to warrior three, which Elsie explained to the room at large was very good for strengthening muscles all the way from the ankle to the glutei. Elsie didn't even look at Murray when she said this. Amanda thought that throwing in the arm sequences could have been part of Elsie's plan all along, but she wondered if it had been to give Murray a little bit of an ego boost. The leg exercises might be very difficult for him, but he was a strong man, and his arm muscles still bulged in his shirt. Glancing over, Amanda noticed that he did seem to find some of the moves much easier than others. She saw a look of satisfaction on his face when he completed the upper body sequence with ease.

After class as usual, Elsie offered for anyone who wanted to stay behind and have a cup of tea. Murray looked like he was about to sneak out the door when Elsie added, "And I've got a new cookie recipe I wanted to try out on you all: caramel, cinnamon and ginger, my treat as a reward for your hard work today." Amanda stifled a laugh as Murray smoothly changed his determined march for the door to a complex showing of turning on the lights and then casually coming back to the group, as if that had been his intention all along. She noticed the corner of Elsie's mouth slide up slightly as well and caught her friend's eye. Elsie winked at her. Once again, Amanda's stomach was full of butterflies, and her face flushed red as she turned away quickly to hide her burning cheeks.

As always when they had new people at Spill the Tea—what Elsie had unofficially named their after yoga tea and chatting session—they each introduced themselves, giving their name, pronouns, and a little about themselves.

The class had grown in the few weeks that Elsie had been running it, and now there was a consistent group of half a dozen regulars, with more people trying it out each week. Wanda came when she could, and as well as that there was Tim, with the possible shoe addiction, and a couple of high school girls: Samantha and Sally.

There was also Lily, a softly spoken woman, probably in her mid-twenties. Amanda couldn't help but recognise something of herself in Lily. She had a feeling Lily had had to grow up a little too soon. Lily was a bright, artsy kid. Adult, Amanda reminded herself. She had bright purple hair and wore a lot of dark clothes and makeup. She was quiet, but on the odd occasion she did chip in, it was usually pretty insightful, or sharply amusing.

Murray said little over the tea and cookies, but they learned that his wife had passed away, and he had three adult sons, one of whom had two children of his own. According to Murray, they all lived out of town, but they came back every year for Christmas. Amanda saw Murray's usually stern face soften as he spoke about his family, and she realised the two of them might have the rough exterior, gooey insides thing in common. It was almost an hour later when people slowly began drifting out.

"See you next week, Murray?" Elsie called as he made for the door, three extra cookies folded into a napkin to take home.

Murray grumbled something that might have been, "We'll see." But he gave them a little wave as he walked out the door, and Amanda knew he would be returning. Yoga helped your body and mind feel a lot better. With everything going on at the moment, Amanda appreciated the opportunity to clear her mind and stretch her limbs. Even if he didn't come for the yoga,

Amanda had a feeling that Murray would be back for the possibility of more free samples.

40

Elsie

E lsie was prepping cookies for Pie in the Sky. These ones were star-shaped in honour of Matariki, the ascension of a particular cluster of stars which appeared in the sky at this time of year. This batch was thyme and lavender flavoured, but she was also experimenting with other flavours; matcha and cinnamon, brown sugar, hazelnut and orange, and some simple sugar cookies as well. Solstice was the following night, and Elsie was feeling out of sorts being away from her family, so she was stress baking.

Amanda walked into the kitchen from the garden. She had that fresh, bright look she always got when she had been gardening. Amanda took one look at the kitchen island coated in flour, the sink piled with dishes, and Elsie slowly unravelling, and her face fell. "There's a lot going on here. Are you ok?"

Elsie tried to keep the tears from her eyes. Amanda strode over and took Elsie's flour coated hands in her own, dirt covered ones. "Hey, hey." She squeezed Elsie's hands gently and tried to catch her eye. Elsie looked diligently at the floor, trying not to have Amanda catch her in the middle of a breakdown.

Amanda wrapped her arms around her, and she was instantly taken in by her warmth and soft, Burgundy smell. Suddenly, she was bawling into Amanda's neck. Amanda rubbed her back and made soft cooing noises like Elsie was some sort of baby bird. "I'm sorry," Elsie said, the sound muffled by Amanda's chest.

"You have nothing to apologise for," Amanda said, stroking her hair just like Elsie's mum used to when she had a nightmare., "Whatever it is, I'm here. We'll work it out."

After several minutes of snotty crying, Elsie finally got her breathing under control, and she released Amanda from her koala hold. "I'm sorry," she said again. "I'm trying to keep it together, but this is my first Solstice not at home, and it feels very weird not to have at least my mum around." Amanda turned off the oven and gently led Elsie to the lounge, as she kept talking.

"Solstice is one of the most important traditions in a witch's calendar," she explained. They sat together on the couch, their bodies turned to face one another. Philo jumped up and lay beside Elsie.

I'm here. He whispered, laying his head in her lap. Elsie stroked his soft fur gratefully.

I know, she thought, *and I'm so glad you are, it's just....* She sighed, then out loud said, "I miss my dad. I miss my grandmother. Everything is changing, and I don't feel like I can do everything on my own."

"What do you need to do?" Amanda asked. "Hang on, let me get some tea first, then you can tell me all about it." A soft, slightly self-conscious look crossed Amanda's face. "I know I'm not a witch." Amanda tucked a strand of Elsie's hair behind her ear gently. "But I would like to help and to—." She paused, as if searching for the right word—, "celebrate," she said questioningly, and Elsie nodded. "With you, if you would like that?"

Elsie felt as if something was blooming, unfurling in her heart. She swallowed hard. "I would like that very much indeed."

An hour later, they were sitting in the lounge on the rug in front of the fire, cross-legged, with an array of paper in front of them. Elsie had a system for everything. The spreadsheets and lists were colour-coded. Baking and other things she needed to do for her shop were in sky blue (haha). Magic stuff was purple, Philo was dark blue like his eyes, and family was red. She had made 'home' orange since Amanda had been living there, the colour she most associated with the woman. Elsie flushed just a tad as she explained her system to Amanda, hoping she wouldn't register Elsie's growing crush.

Amanda surveyed the lists. "There's a lot here. Let's start small. What's your favourite part about the Winter Solstice?" She asked, flipping through the various papers.

Elsie didn't hesitate. "Sitting around a firepit drinking hot chocolate or warm, spiced apple cider, and telling stories until the sun comes up."

"I think we can manage that," Amanda said

"But we don't even have a fire pit," Elsie said.

"I've seen you create fire with the snap of your fingers."

"It has to be real wood burning for the Winter Solstice." Elsie wasn't sure if this was an actual witchy rule, but the fire was an important tradition to her. Her dad had built a fire every Winter Solstice for as long as she could remember. She could feel her chest tightening at the idea of not having a fire.

"Well, what about your cauldron?" Amanda asked. "Surely we could fill that with wood? E could light a fire there and toast marshmallows or whatever the vegan equivalent is and stay up telling ghost stories all night."

"Actually, usually the ghosts are the ones who tell the stories,." Elsie said blandly. Then she burst out laughing at the look on Amanda's face. "I'm only kidding,." She reassured her quickly. "The veil between us and the spirit world is thinner from winter solstice until Beltane, but I don't think we'll have any ghosts come and visit us."

Amanda still didn't look convinced, so Elsie went on. She was feeling much better now she had Amanda helping her out. "Usually spirits stay in the house they died in, or sometimes they'll follow someone they care about, or come back to help them if they are in need. But there aren't any ghosts that I'm aware of in Lilac House. It will just be you and me staying up to watch the sunrise while chatting about whatever show we're binging on Netflix at the moment."

Amanda raised an eyebrow. "Why do you stay up until dawn?" She asked. "I know you're a night owl, but that seems like a bit much, even for you."

"It stems from an ancient druid tradition. Druids would keep watch all night to ensure that the sun rose the following morning. It's said that if the druids didn't stay up to watch for the sun, it could decide not to rise, and the earth would forever be cast into the shadow of darkness."

Amanda shivered. "OK. We can keep vigil for the sun for one night. Thank goodness the next day is Sunday and there's no post to be delivered! Another thing," Amanda added, picking up the Pie in the Sky spreadsheet and looking at the vast number of things Elsie still had to do. "Do you think now business is picking up you could hire an assistant? You've got so much to do, and I feel like if you had someone else who could handle a few things, it would help you a lot."

The Pie in the Sky had been doing better since Amanda's strategic marketing campaign. Elsie hadn't seen Reginald for a little while, either. That was odd, but Elsie wasn't going to dwell on it. "I hadn't thought about an assistant." She ran some numbers in her head. She probably could get someone to either open or close for her most days, and they could tackle the afternoon rush together. "That could work actually," she said slowly., "But is there anyone in town who needs a job?"

"What about the high school yoga kids?"

Elsie made a face., "Samantha and Sally are sweet, but they don't strike me as responsible enough to hold down a job, let alone open or close the store."

Amanda sighed. "That's true. Those two have their heads in the clouds most of the time." Elsie thought Amanda looked a little wistful at that. Then Amanda tilted her head to one side. "What about Lily?" She asked.

The quietly competent Lily's face swam into Elsie's mind, her goth makeup and faded purple hair framing a serious face. Elsie had only met the young woman a few times, but she was always polite, often offering to help pack up the yoga mats after class. Elsie thought she was in her early twenties, but couldn't be sure. There was an air of unassuming competence about her that Sally and Samantha didn't have. She seemed responsible enough. "That's a great idea! Do you think she would do it?"

"Only one way to find out," Amanda said, handing Elsie her phone.

41

Elsie

O nce Amanda had helped Elsie divide up and prioritise the tasks, it all seemed much more manageable. Elsie was excited by the idea of getting Lily to help in the shop, so much so that she had sent her a message tentatively floating the idea. Lily had come back instantly. *Seriously? I would LOVE that, thank you! I have exam leave soon so can do mornings or afternoons, whatever suits you best, and then I'll have the whole summer break so can pick up as many shifts as you like.* Then, moments later, *Thank you, this means a lot to me :)* That simple emoji had put a smile on Elsie's face too, and the message set the tone for the rest of the evening's preparations.

As well as the fire pit, Elsie wanted to do a sort of intention jar, where they would each write their hopes and intentions for the coming year on a piece of paper, fold it, and place it into a jar, which she had enchanted to sparkle, and from which they would take turns picking an intention each week until the summer solstice to keep them on track. Then there was the solstice feast, which was well under way, and the decorating of a tree. This year Elsie was planning to incorporate some of the traditional indigenous celebrations of Matariki, particularly, and fittingly for her, the remembrance of the dead.

Amanda walked in, her arms full of pine cones, berries, and even some holly leaves. She went back to the hall and came back a few moments later with a paper bag full of fruit and brightly coloured ribbons. "I hope this is what you had in mind," she said, as Elsie eagerly rifled through the bag.

"This is perfect!" Elsie squeaked. "Thank you." She held Amanda's gaze for a moment longer. "Seriously, thank you for indulging me in this." Was it Elsie's imagination, or did Amanda's face flush ever so slightly pink at that?

"It's no worries," Amanda said, ducking her head and making a show of pulling the items out of the bag and placing them in piles on the kitchen island. Her face was back to its normal hue when she looked up again. "Ok, where do we start?"

"Let's see," Elsie said, thinking out loud. "The vegetables are in the oven, the cookies are prepped. The mulled wine can be transferred to a crock-pot in the next hour or so. Apart from that, we just need to decorate the tree and do the intentions jar."

"Which tree were you thinking of decorating?" Amanda asked, pulling the last of the items from the bag and folding it before carefully putting it away. Elsie liked how at home Amanda was in this kitchen now — how it felt like *their* home. She shook her head at her silliness, and focussed on the question Amanda had asked.

"Well, traditionally we would dig up a tree, preferably an evergreen, and then we would bring it inside and plant it in a pot to decorate. Then we would plant it again in the new year. But I don't think we can realistically do that this year, so I thought maybe we could decorate the old elm in the garden?" It wasn't a perfect solution, but Elsie was trying to adapt.

"That sounds lovely," Amanda said. "the garden is nice and shielded from the wind, and it's not forecast to rain for a few days." Elsie smiled at how well her friend was taking all of this in her stride.

They got to work decorating the tree. It was handy that Elsie's element was air, as she could float the ribbons up and over the top branches on the elm. Next they nestled fruit amongst the branches, and Elsie even found a few hanging lanterns in the spare room, which she would light once the sun started to go down. "It's a lot like decorating a Christmas tree, isn't it?" Amanda said, as they put the finishing touches on their masterpiece.

"Actually, this is where that tradition came from," Elsie said, standing back with her hands on her hips as she surveyed their work. "In the northern hemisphere, the winter solstice is right around Christmas time, so they ended up merging the two traditions."

"And we get two occasions to decorate trees," Amanda said with a smile, stepping back next to Elsie. The two grinned stupidly at each other for a moment, and then Elsie came back to herself.

"Ok, I'll check on the food. You good for a bit?"

"Actually, I was just going to pop out for one last errand. That ok?" Amanda said, and Elsie nodded. She appreciated how much her friend was supporting her with this, but she didn't want it to stop her from having her own life. "Check back in in an hour or so?" she said.

"Deal."

The cookies came out beautifully, and the kitchen was so full of solstice fragrances when Elsie stepped inside that for a moment she was transported to the past, her mother, father, and grandmother all standing around her. Phoebe too. Swallowing down a lump in her throat, Elsie set to work. She finished up the roast vegetables, pulled together one of her famous not meat pies, and of course, made gravy. Phoebe called while Elsie was cooking to wish her a happy solstice. Elsie was pleased to hear from her cousin. She missed her a lot now she lived in America.

The hour flew by, and Elsie was just pulling her pie out of the oven, when she heard a kerfuffle at the front door. Taking off her oven gloves and wiping her hands on her "Witch, Please" apron, she went into the hall to see what the noise was.

She was greeted by the sight of Amanda hauling a tree in a pot into the hallway, huffing and puffing as she did so. The tree was perhaps two metres tall. Its trunk wasn't yet all that thick, but it had vibrant green foliage. Elsie's heart squeezed when she saw Amanda had decorated the tree with ribbons, bells, and berries. "Oh, hi," Amanda said, looking sheepishly out from behind the tree. "Sorry, I guess I didn't quite manage a stealthy entrance, did I?"

Elsie stared at her in wonderment. Amanda placed the tree on the floor and put her hands in her pockets, looking at her shoes, rubbing the toe of one across the ankle of the other. "I just thought. The elm tree is beautiful and all, but you said you wanted a tree that could be brought inside, so I thought, well." She pushed the tree forward a bit., "This is a baby kauri. Tradition has it that this kind of tree brought the world into existence— it's meant to be kind of a descendent of the tree of life. They live for like, thousands of years, and I thought maybe it would be a nice new tradition for you? If you look after it, you could even hand it down through the family, if you want kids or whatever, that is."

Elsie didn't think, she just ran forward and embraced Amanda. She felt the other woman's arms wrap around her tightly. She could feel the heat of her, smell the bergamot and sandalwood scent on her skin. "Thank you," Elsie said, breathless. "This is—", swallowing down the lump in her throat, she fought to continue. "So, so kind."

"I'm glad you like it," came Amanda's muffled voice in reply.

"Shall we put it in the lounge?" Elsie directed, as Amanda shuffled the tree into the living room. Then she raced into the kitchen to check on the gravy. Things were looking up.

They sat eating together at a little bistro table and chair set in the courtyard, Philo at their feet. The sun slowly set over the distant hills, turning the sky pale blue, then dusty pink, then orange lilac, until finally the dark violet turned to indigo and eventually to an inky black.

Amanda gathered up the dinner plates and brought out pillows and blankets. Elsie brought out two steaming mugs of hot mulled wine. They built a fire in the cauldron, and Elsie watched with satisfaction as the logs began to burn. In a moment of inspiration, she rushed back into the house and grabbed her colourful gel pens and a stack of silver-grey sticky notes. Amanda looked at her, a faint trace of amusement flitting across her features. "What have you thought of now?" She asked, her voice a little husky, a smile tugging at one corner of her mouth.

"We wrote out our hopes and aspirations for the new year," Elsie began, handing Amanda a stack of sticky notes and several of the pens. "But although the solstice is about new things, it's also about the ending of things. I thought we could write on these sticky notes the things we want to leave behind. Elsie grinned wickedly, "and then throw them into the fire."

Amanda took the lid off one of her gel pens and began to write. "People pleasing," Elsie said, writing the words with a flourish and throwing it into the flames. They watched it burn together.

"Keeping my guard up with people I care about," Amanda said quietly. Elsie watched as she threw the paper in the fire, a warmth blossoming in her chest to match the flames in the cauldron.

There was a heavy silence, so Elsie decided to lighten the mood a little. "Pushing the alarm button four times in the morning," she said, and Amanda groaned.

"*Four times*! What is wrong with you?"

"Hey!" Elsie said, shoving her companionably.

"Alright alright, maybe 'insulting people' should be one of mine."

"They have to be things you think you can actually achieve," Elsie said, poking her tongue out at Amanda. They went back and forth for a little while, and then Elsie noticed Amanda got quiet.

"Running," Amanda said, her voice a soft whisper.

"But you love to run!" Elsie said, looking at Amanda in confusion.

"Not that kind of running," Amanda said. And she stood in front of the cauldron for a long, long time before throwing the paper in and watching it curl up and burn.

Several hours later, Elsie held her mug of wine to her chest, warming herself with it. The fire was still burning, but it was softer now, and they could see the stars shining above. She placed her mug beside her and lay down on the soft grass, pulling the blanket higher over herself and sighing in contentment. This Solstice might not have been exactly the same as her last few, but it had been surprisingly, well, pleasant. She glanced at Amanda beside her and smiled. This woman, who seemed so rough on the outside, truly had the kindest heart of anyone Elsie had come across. She smiled to herself in the dark. Amanda lay down beside her, and for a second her fingers brushed Elsie's. They moved away again just as quickly, and Elsie felt a pang of disappointment in her chest. She thought back to Amanda's note, 'running'. This woman was slowly bewitching her. Her mind flicked back to her childhood, to the way her mother had slowly closed off over time, resentful of the magic she and her father possessed. Amanda was wonderful now, but she would get sick of her magic soon, and then Elsie would be alone again.

42

Amanda

A manda and Elsie lay looking at the stars, Philo lying just above their heads. "I always find the stars so reassuring." Amanda said into the quiet., "I remember when I was younger, I would sneak out into the yard and look up at them after a particularly bad night. Before my mum left, she taught me how to find the southern cross, so whenever I lay out there, I would look up in the sky and find the southern cross. It would help me feel, I don't know, grounded, somehow." Suddenly Amanda felt self-conscious, why was she telling Elsie this? "It's probably stupid."

Elsie reached out her hand and squeezed Amanda's. "It's not stupid," she said firmly. Their fingers stayed intertwined.

After a few minutes, it was Elsie's turn to break the silence. "Sounds like home was a little... complicated for you." She said tentatively.

Amanda laughed, but it was a mirthless laugh. "You could say that." Another pause. Amanda appreciated that Elsie didn't push her too hard to open up. But Elsie had been amazing about the Police station, and had trusted her with her own huge secret. Amanda had no idea how many people Elsie had told about being a witch, but she got the sense it wasn't many. She could trust Elsie with this, and it would be nice for someone other than Pierce to know her story.

"You've probably gathered by now that my dad wasn't exactly what you would call a 'good guy'," she began slowly. "He wasn't like Theo, but he was shady, always making business deals on the wrong side of the law. On-selling products that had 'fallen off the back of a truck,' that kind of thing. He was a pretty good dad when he was around. Cooked us dinners, checked our homework, all that kind of thing. But he travelled a lot for work. After mum left, he travelled even more. It sort of felt like Theo and I were orphans."

Amanda felt a gentle squeeze on her hand. She took a deep breath, continuing. "My brother, Theo, is older than me by five years. We didn't get along so well. When Dad was away, I would usually go to my neighbour Ms. Watters's house. I told you about her, the gardener?"

Elsie nodded. "She sounded wonderful," Elsie said softly in the darkness, still holding Amanda's hand.

"She was," Amanda agreed. Wondering how much more to say. "It was Ms. Watters who instilled in me a love of gardening. When I was old enough, I got a part-time job at a local cafe waiting tables. By the time I finished high school, I had saved up enough money to buy myself a little plot of land. I built up a nursery and supplied the local garden stores."

"Wow," Elsie said, and Amanda felt a rush of warmth at the pride in her voice.

She carried on, "I loved it. Things were OK while Dad was around, and I think he respected that I didn't want to go into the 'family business.' Then one day he got arrested, and everything changed."

Amanda paused, recalling the events that had turned her life completely upside down. "Theo thought he was the big man around town, he and started trying to step into dad's shoes. I heard through the grapevine that he was making dodgy deals and rubbing people up the wrong way. I think he thought he was doing a great job. He didn't realise dad's old partners were taking advantage of him, sizing him up to see if they could take over his patch, or use him to do their dirty work. Things got pretty bad after that." Amanda was tired of talking about this now. She didn't want to think about what had come next. "Anyway, what about you?"

There was a long pause. Then, "What about me?" Elsie asked, clearly choosing to give Amanda a break and not push the matter farther. Amanda felt a rush of gratitude.

"What was your childhood like? You're an only child, right? What's it like growing up as a witch?"

Elsie let out a small laugh., "I mean, I never knew any different, but let me see..." She was quiet for a moment, thinking. "I had a happy childhood. Yes, I'm an only child, but my cousin, Phoebe, came and lived with us every summer, so in some ways it felt like I had a sister, too."

Amanda had heard of Phoebe, but she didn't realise she and Elsie were quite that close. Thinking back, Amanda thought Elsie might have said Phoebe was in America now.

Elsie went on. "Phoebe is a few years older than me, and she's a witch too, so I always looked up to her. She was so kind and so cool. Very different from me. Even as an eleven-year-old she would dress in vintage clothes, doing her hair up in funky buns or quiffs from another era." Elsie laughed. "I tried to copy her sometimes, but the pin up look really wasn't for me." Amanda couldn't imagine sleek, chic Elsie trying to don the wide skirted, bright lipped looks of the fifties and sixties. She had an image cross her mind of a younger Elsie in her mother's heels, with makeup applied artlessly to her face, and chuckled. It was sweet.

"I know," Elsie said, turning and smiling at Amanda. "It took me a long time to learn that I could and should be my own person. I was completely distraught when Phoebe moved to Scotland for university." Amanda could hear the hurt in Elsie's voice. "She was my only real friend back then." Amanda hadn't expected that. "Mum and Dad were great, but I struggled when I was younger with self-confidence. Things with Phoebe were so easy. I knew she understood me because we were both witches. We were both so excited about our powers, but we had to hide them from everybody. Obviously, because of my mum, I knew witches sometimes opened up to normys, but it was hard to know where to start. I spent every day with Phoebe in the summer holidays, and it was the easiest thing in the world. Then she would go back home for the school term and I felt bereft. Kids at school were nice, but I didn't really know how to connect with them. Back then, magic was the most exciting thing in my life. If I couldn't talk to them about it, then I didn't know what to talk about."

Amanda felt another wave of gratitude that Elsie had opened up to her, and was spending this special day with her.

"Home life was pretty good, though," Elsie was saying. "Dad taught me spells. We spent weekends at the sea-side jumping waves like everyone else. The only difference was that we could cast a spell on ourselves to get rid of the sand, or to stop the chill of the wind and water from going deep into our bones." A soft, almost reverence came into Elsie's voice, and Amanda turned so she was lying on her side, mirroring Elsie. "That's the one thing I miss most about being here, apart from my parents, of course. The sea." Her eyes sparkled in the moonlight, and Amanda was momentarily rendered breathless by her beauty. Elsie's voice was wistful, full of happy memories.

"We would spend hours making sand castles, boogie boarding on waves, and turning each other into mermaids." Amanda sat up and shot a look at Elsie, and Elsie, registering, burst out laughing. "Not real mermaids! The same ones that you would have done, making a tail out of sand to cover someone's legs?"

Amanda lay back down, laughing as well. "I see. I thought for a second you were going to tell me mermaids were real, that they were just witches who wanted to level up their beach game."

"Oh, mermaids totally exist," Elsie said, with a sideways glance at her friend. Amanda didn't know what to believe, so she threw a pillow at Elsie's face, and they burst out laughing, beating each other with cushions, until, with a breathless voice, Elsie cried, "Look! The sun!" And sure enough, there it was, the first streams of yellow-gold light coming up over the Elm tree.

"Happy Near Year," Elsie said to Amanda.,

"Happy New Year," Amanda echoed, her voice thick with emotion.

43

Amanda

Amanda went to her room to lie down for a few hours before getting on with her day. Yawning, she stumbled up the stairs. She couldn't believe Elsie was going into the shop on zero hours' sleep, but at least she would have an endless supply of tea and coffee to keep her going. As she opened her door, Amanda saw something green on her pillow. Getting closer, she realised it was a wreath. It was stunning, with pine needles and pine cones woven into it, along with bright red holly berries, and tiny golden bells. Orange leaves were dotted along the wreath, and there were sprigs of rosemary tucked in to it, creating a beautiful fragrance. A little card attached to it was written on in Elsie's neat cursive. *Dear Amanda, Thank you for being such a dear friend. Your support and the way you have accepted me for all of who I am are extraordinary. Happy Solstice, love, Elsie xx.*

Amanda felt her heart squeeze as she read the note, trying not to fixate too much on those two little letters at the end. She smiled sleepily as she set the wreath on her bedside table, staring at it until her eyelids drooped closed.

Several hours later, Amanda had walked Philo, and was in Pie in The Sky having a late lunch. A bleary-eyed Elsie was out the back, as Lily had been keen to start that day, and was currently on the till. She seemed to be doing a good job, and Amanda smiled inwardly at the success Elsie was experiencing. The bell above the door chimed and a man Amanda had never seen walked in. She thought by now she knew pretty much everyone in Glen Haven, if not by name, then at least by sight. But this man looked very different to anyone she had seen around town.

He was tall and slender, dressed entirely in black, reminding Amanda of the Matrix, or, with his ash blonde hair, Draco Malfoy. His piercing blue eyes looked at Amanda appraisingly and filled with disdain. Just then, Elsie came out from the back kitchen, carrying a tray of pies. The man's face broke into a broad, friendly smile. "Hello" he said, in a velvet voice that made Amanda's skin crawl. Elsie's face lit up at the sight of him. Amanda watched with a jealous flush as the two began to chat animatedly.

She was at her regular table and had the newspaper out in front of her, but it was hard to focus on the *Glen Haven Times* with that glamorous man talking to Elsie. *Oh my goodness Amanda, pull it together!* She thought angrily to herself, you cannot be jealous of every single person Elsie talks to. Nevertheless, she kept one eye on them as she ate her sandwich and drank her coffee. After about fifteen minutes, the door swung open and Murray walked in. Finally, Elsie seemed to come back to reality. Amanda saw her and Soren hug each other goodbye, and her body went rigid. With a swish of his ridiculous trench coat, he was gone.

"Who was that?" Murray asked, pulling up a chair opposite Amanda and sitting down, a massive slice of pie in front of him. So Murray didn't recognise him either. Interesting.

"Apparently his name is Soren." Amanda said, trying to keep the disgust from her voice.

"You don't trust him, hey?" Murray said. "Just remember we didn't trust either of you two when you first came to town, and look how wrong we were." Murray put an enormous mouthful of pie into his mouth.

"Hmmm" Amanda said, noncommittally. Maybe Murray was right. She knew she was judging a book by its cover, but something about Soren just made her skin tingle, and not in a good way.

"How's the leg?" She asked Murray, changing the subject. Murray stood up, and to Amanda's great surprise, reached down and touched his toes. Then he stood back up again and kicked out wildly in front of himself, beaming.

"Coming right lassie, coming right!" He said, rather more enthusiastically than Amanda had ever seen him before. Amanda sat, shell-shocked for a second, before bursting out laughing.

"That's great news!" She enthused. "All that yoga must be paying off!"

"I haven't felt this good in years." Murray confessed, sitting back down and tucking into his pie with relish.

Just then, the heavens seemed to open, and Amanda looked outside to see a sudden flash of rain pouring down. "It certainly feels like winter." Amanda she said, shivering.

"At least we're on the other side of the shortest day now,." Murray said.

Amanda was a little surprised by the old man's optimism. "You're in a good mood today." She said, looking at him more closely. "Something up?"

Murray flushed. "You mind your business," he said gruffly. Amanda hid a smile behind her cup of tea. It was nice to see Murray in a better mood. Maybe this year really would be better than the last one. Then again, she thought grimly, reflecting on her family situation, it could hardly be worse.

44

Elsie

Elsie soared through the air on her broomstick, relishing the feeling of freedom that flying provided. She and Soren had been out flying three or four times now, and Elsie was feeling more confident on her broom again. After that first time, she always brought her own broomstick for flying. She hadn't used it in so long it had taken a while for Elsie to find it under all the magical paraphernalia in her spare room. She really should tidy up at some point, she thought vaguely.

Living in Glen Haven, Elsie hadn't totally disregarded her magical side, but she certainly wasn't practicing magic as much as she had been back home. She still read her tea leaves every day, and did minor spells, but a lot of her connection to her magic had been quieted since her grandmother and dad died. With her closest friend, her cousin Phoebe, in America, Elsie had missed having someone to do magical things with. Having Soren here was such a pleasure.

Soren's broom, however, was another story. It was fine to fly on, but there was something about the familiarity of her own broom that made her feel much more at home. Soren's broom sometimes seemed to have a mind of its own, taking her just a little higher or faster than she wanted. Her broom, by contrast, was almost an extension of her own body. She would lean ever so slightly to the left and the broom would turn, knowing exactly how much or little she wanted to turn. She could lean forwards to go faster, but the broom would gather speed gradually, rather than going from 0 to 100 in an instant, and nearly throwing her off.

Elsie's broom had been a gift from her grandmother, another fond flyer, and she felt an extra connection with her when she was in the air. Elsie loved living in Lilac House, especially now that Amanda had arrived. She smiled at the thought of their blossoming friendship.

She thought back to the lovely evening they had spent on Winter Solstice. Amanda had been so supportive. Opening up to her the way she had felt really special. Elsie reminded herself that her mother had been interested in their magic at first, too. But eventually she had grown bitter about it. Much better for Elsie to do witchy things with Soren.

Soren flew towards her suddenly, interrupting her thoughts. "Race you to that tree!" he bellowed, pointing at a tall nikau palm far below. Elsie wasn't a fan of diving. She was a more slow and steady kind of person herself, but Soren was already off, plummeting straight down towards the ground, uttering a "yehooo" as he went. Shaking her head at his antics, Elsie followed at a fast, but less break-neck speed. As she was nearing the tree Soren had pointed to, she heard a scream. Was he ok? She urged her broom down faster, and when she arrived, she saw Soren standing opposite two humans, his wand pointed directly at them. "We've got to get out of here," he said, grabbing her hand and pulling her through the forest on foot.

"What happened?" Elsie asked, glancing back over her shoulder at the two people standing, wide eyed and unblinking, in the spot that Soren had left them.

"They saw me flying," Soren said, his pace fast, his voice low. "I had to wipe their memories, but we need to get out of here before they come to and see us again."

"You did *what!?*" Elsie exclaimed, stopping dead in her tracks. Soren grabbed her hand and pulled her onwards, not allowing her to slow down.

"I had no choice," he said in hushed tones.

"We never should have come here." Elsie said, placing her head in her hands. Soren finally turned around and looked at her.

"I know it's not ideal," he said, gentleness creeping into his tone. "But the chances of anyone being out here were minute. It's unfortunate, but the effects on them will be minimal."

"It's not minimal to wipe someone's memory! They wouldn't have seen us at all if we were only flying, instead of diving,." Elsie said miserably.

"We weren't to know that,"

"You can't just go around wiping people's memories, though," Elsie said, horrified that he was taking this so easily.

"What else would you have had me do?" He snapped, his eyes like ice. "Let them go, knowing we were witches? Have them lock us up for testing, or burnt at the stake like they did our ancestors?"

"I'm not saying that, I just—"

"I did what I had to do to keep us safe," Soren said, his chin pointing upward.

"You should thank me for protecting you."

"Thank you?" Elsie nearly cried. "You used magic on those people, *serious* magic."

"It was just a small spell." Soren shrugged his shoulders. "They're just normys. Why do you care so much? I thought you said the people here don't even like you?"

Elsie felt extremely uncomfortable at this. "They don't — well, I think some of them are starting to actually, but that's hardly the point. We can't go around using magic on people just because they're human or we don't like them."

"What harm is it doing?" Soren asked, and Elsie had to admit that, in all likelihood, it was doing them very little harm indeed. Sure, there were some spells which led to pretty bad consequences, and from what she knew of memory spells, there was a higher risk of damaging other parts of a person's brain, but Soren was a well-practiced witch, and seemed confident that the spell had gone ok.

"You definitely don't think they got hurt?" She asked sceptically.

"I have done this spell many times," Soren said, smiling his charming smile at her. "They will not know what happened to them."

"OK," Elsie said, "but I think that's enough flying for one day."

"I agree, and it's quite a hike to get back to the car." Soren said, leading the way through the forest.

45

Elsie

E lsie groaned as light inexplicably filled her vision. She opened her eyes wearily to see Amanda had thrown open the curtains and was standing at the foot of her bed. Philo bounded into the room, tail threatening to wag itself off as usual. "Uuuugh," was all Elsie could manage.

"Good morning to you too," Amanda said cheerily, pulling the covers off Elsie's face and wafting a very large mug of coffee in front of her nose. The coffee smelt perfect, just as Elsie liked it, strong, with a dash of almond milk, cinnamon, and vanilla. She reached for it, and Amanda pulled it away. Elsie let out a sound similar to that of a feral cat, and Amanda laughed. "Sit up, and then you can have some," she instructed. Cursing her 'morning person' friend under her breath, but loud enough for Amanda to hear, Elsie begrudgingly pulled herself to sit upright in the bed, reaching out for the coffee mug with a desperate need.

"Right," Amanda said, once it was safely deposited in Elsie's grasp, and she had taken a few settling sips. "Today, we are going on a road trip."

"What?" Elsie's head was still foggy, and she had to try hard to keep her eyes open and focus on what Amanda was saying.

"I've done the maths, and it looks like we can get to the West Coast in about two hours. It's not exactly summer, so I can't guarantee that swimming will be on the cards, but we can walk along the beach, build sandcastles, drink tea, and generally try not to be blown over by the reputable West Coast Wind."

Elsie stared at her friend. "We're going to the beach? Today?" Her brain wasn't yet fully online.

"Yep, I've booked the day off. Murray's son is going to cover for me. The store isn't open on Mondays anyway, and I've already packed us lunch." "Get up, put some clothes on, and let's go."

148

Then she was gone. Elsie was left staring after her, wondering if she had dreamed the whole thing. The wide-open curtains and the coffee cup in her hand seemed to indicate it had probably been real. "We can take Philo too," Amanda called up the stairs. "Dogs are allowed on the beaches in the off-season." Well, that explained Philo's excitement then. Her Familiar was tugging at her hand, tail wagging faster than a hummingbird's wings, as he tried to pull her out of bed. Slugging down some more life-fuel, Elsie clambered out of bed to get ready for their beach day.

It took rather a while for Elsie to have a second cup of coffee, shower, read her tea leaves, and pack a beach bag. However, before the clock struck nine, they were on the road, a flask of rose hip and jasmine tea between them, Philo barking happily from the boot.

The journey took them through Arthur's pass, the lush greenery of the forest thick on either side of them. About half way through the pass, Amanda pulled the car into a lookout point and they got out of the car to stare in wonder at the sight before them. To their left, a waterfall gushed, white foam splashing gaily against the rocks as it tumbled towards the valley floor. To their right, the forest rose, majestic. Ahead, they could see the valley stretching out below. The tiny road followed a river that meandered carefree amongst the various nooks and crannies of the hillside.

Amanda handed Elsie a sandwich, looking out to the valley below them. "Wow," Elsie sighed, taking a grateful bite.

"My dad took me here once," Amanda said quietly. "It was our last trip together after my mum left. My brother has just got his licence so he decided to drive himself, thank goodness. That's when I first heard of Glen Haven, and decided I wanted to do those hikes some day."

They heard a screeching sound from behind them. The pair turned in unison to see a huge, olive-green parrot perched on top of the car, tipping over and using its beak in what looked like an attempt to prise the rubber from the window frame. "Shoo!" Amanda said, racing towards the kea and waving her hands wildly. The bird turned and looked at Amanda in surprise, then continued on with its task of destroying the window, entirely unperturbed. While they were staring at the destruction, another bird flew down and took half the sandwich right out of Elsie's hand! "What on earth!?" Elsie cried in surprise.

"Kea — they're worse than a small tornado," Amanda said, laughing. "Let's hit the road again before they nick all our stuff and we're stranded here in a broken car."

Elsie was in the front seat before Amanda even had time to open her door, and they were on the road again in moments. Elsie looked over at Amanda and burst out laughing. "I have never met a bird that bold before!" She said, tears streaming down her face.

Amanda was laughing too. Kea were native to the South Island, and they were very rare. That patch of Arthur's Pass was one of the few places you would come across them. "They're very intelligent," Amanda said.

"That's what scares me!"

The surrounding countryside was like something out of a fairytale. This was one of the most beautiful drives Elsie had done in her life. She couldn't believe it was so close to her new home. Waterfalls crashed beside them. Native bush with palm trees peaking through the top of the canopy towered on either side of the road. There were more shades of green than she would have ever thought possible.

They wove their way through the winding roads, and eventually the landscape around them changed. Gently rolling hills replaced the towering forests, and in little more than an hour, they were driving along a stunning coastline. It was rugged and rough, with waves crashing against rocks, spurts of white foam shooting into the air.

"I'll be honest," Amanda said, as she drove down a narrow, sandy pathway which promised to take them to the beach. "I don't think it will be much of a day even for paddling."

Elsie laughed. "I'm kind of relieved to hear you say that," she said, as Amanda pulled up on the side of the road. "I could probably cast a spell to keep our toes warm, but I don't fancy our chances against those waves."

"Walk along the beach and have a snack in the car. Sound OK?" Amanda asked, grabbing her ancient puffer jacket from the boot and handing Elsie her wine coloured one.

"You read my mind," Elsie smiled.

The wind buffeted at them, but Elsie cast a spell to stop the sand blowing in their eyes. "I can see why you like the beach so much if you don't need to worry about sand getting into every single crevice," Amanda called against the wind. "My memories of the beach mostly involve me finding sand in my hair for weeks later. That and the gritty taste of sand in my food. A whole new meaning to sandwiches," she deadpanned.

Elsie let out a groan, but she was smiling. "What, you think dad jokes should be exclusive to men with kids?" Amanda continued. "That's not very inclusive of you, Elsie. I think men get quite enough, thank you."

Elsie pushed against Amanda playfully, and Amanda pushed back. Soon they were running, laughing and screeching down the beach, scaring the birds and acting like children.

Philo was in his element, chasing seagulls and barking happily. Now and then he ran into the sea, splashing in the waves as he tore after birds who would simply take flight the instant he got close to them. "I think he likes the beach!" Elsie laughed, as he ran up to them, still barking happily. As Philo stood next to them, he twitched, and Elsie cried, "NO!" just as he shook himself all over them, drenching the pair in salty water. Philo ran off again down the beach before Elsie could tell him off. *Sorry!* Philo said to Elsie as he ran. *It was instinct. I couldn't help it!* Elsie just shook her head. Having a young, exuberant dog for a familiar seemed an awful lot like just having a young, exuberant dog, she thought.

Amanda's cooking skills might have still been a work in progress, but she had done a good job of packing lunch. There were sandwiches, fruit, crisps, and a few other odds and ends. Elsie had been teaching her to bake, and Amanda had included in their cache of food some slightly crumbly, but honestly rather tasty, lavender sugar cookies. Elsie was touched by how much effort her friend had put into the day. Most importantly, Amanda had brought an array of Elsie's various flavoured teas, decanted into little labelled pouches. She had a camping stove so they could boil water, and after lunch the three of them spent several pleasant hours wandering up and down the massive expanse of beach, staring out at the stormy sea; the humans with cups of tea clasped in their icy hands. The vast expanse of ocean with nothing to see for miles was truly a sight to be seen, and Elsie felt her soul lightening in a way that it hadn't in over a year. Not since her dad passed over.

She thought of her mum, that she had't come to visit. That they barely ever even spoke on the phone. They were, if possible, even more distant now than she had been when her dad was alive. She thought of her grandmother, and summers at her house, doing incantations in the back garden. She thought of her dad, the trips they used to take to the beach as a family with Phoebe. Her heart broke a little at all that she had lost. As Amanda raced after Philo in front of her, Elsie drew in a deep, salty breath. Maybe she didn't have much family left, but that didn't mean she couldn't make a new one. Letting out a howl, she tore down the beach after them.

46

Amanda

Night was close to falling when Amanda and Elsie began the journey back to Glen Haven. As Amanda was about to turn onto the main road, Elsie let out a squeal beside her. "Turn here!" She practically yelled. Amanda, shocked, turned the wheel sharply as commanded. They drove down a long, unlit road, and then Elsie pointed., "There!" She cried.

Amanda pulled into a small car park. Putting the car in park, she turned urgently. "What's wrong?"

"Look!" Elsie cried, her face a picture of delight. "Glow worms!" She pointed to a sign which read 'glow worm dell,' and Amanda breathed a sigh of relief. "You scared me half to death," she grumbled, but Elsie was already pulling on her arm.

"I've always wanted to see glow worms!" She said, a childlike gleam of excitement in her eyes that Amanda found ridiculously endearing. With a growing sense of dread, Amanda allowed herself to be led from the car down a path towards a vast cave. Philo, exhausted from a day bounding up and down the beach chasing sticks, splashing in the waves, and generally living his best doggy life, seemed perfectly content to remain asleep in the car's boot with the windows cracked.

They followed soft lighting down a stone pathway, the hill on one side of them covered with a soft, damp moss. Rivulets of water ran down the rock-side, and the air smelt cold and damp. Eventually they reached the mouth of the cave, and Amanda grabbed Elsie's hand reflexively. She didn't love the dark, never had. She couldn't help but feel overwhelmed in dark, confined spaces.

Elsie led her gently into the cave. Amanda could feel her heart rate quicken, and she reflexively closed her eyes, focussing on her breathing as she let Elsie lead her. She imagined it wasn't actually dark; she was just creating that sensation by closing her eyes. They walked several paces into the cave, and then Elsie stopped. "Woooow," she whispered, her voice full of awe, and Amanda risked opening her eyes. It was as though she had stepped into another world. Above and all around her, turquoise lights pulsed in the darkness. She felt simultaneously like she was in outer space, and as if she was underwater.

Stalactites hung from the ceiling, softly lit by the gentle glow of the worms. "Oh my..." Amanda started. The lights closest to her went out instantly, and Elsie hissed quietly. "They don't like noise. Whisper."

Amanda held a hand to her mouth, watching, enraptured, as slowly, the bright lights around her came back on. "This is amazing." She whispered, when she felt it was safe to do so. Elsie squeezed her hand again, pulling her in for a side hug, and then leading her further into the cave. The place was almost completely empty. From what Amanda could tell, there were just one or two couples or groups wandering around the cave as well. Now that her eyes were adjusting to the dark, she saw how huge the space was. It seemed to have one main room, with several others separated off it. Elsie led her through the maze of inter-connected chambers. Amanda's heart was in her throat, but the light from the glowworms, and the warmth of Elsie's hand, helped her feel grounded. She remembered looking at the stars with Elsie on Winter Solstice.

They wound their way through the cave, for Amanda didn't know how long. Time didn't seem to exist in this mystical space. As they were heading back towards the entrance to the cave, someone bumped into Amanda and Elsie, and their hands fell apart. She heard a shuffle and a small crash, and then a man's voice swore loudly from somewhere near her feet, his voice a booming echo in the expanse. All the glow-worm lights went out at once, and everything went black. Amanda could feel her chest tighten, her breathing becoming shallower. "Elsie," she called out, not caring about the noise now.

"I'm here." Elsie's voice seemed far away.

"Elsie!" she all but screamed, flailing her arms around and looking frantically for the way out. There was no light anywhere, and Amanda could feel the panic rising in her like a tide. She thought she heard Elsie reply, but she was so turned around she had no idea which direction it even came from. How was she going to get out?

She bumped into something solid and sharp. That must be the wall of the cave, she thought, her body recoiling from the wet, jagged surface. "Elsie!" she whimpered, despair roiling in her like a snake, her voice was softer this time, as her breathing became even more difficult. She smelt the faint scent of cinnamon and jasmine as an arm moved around her waist. Amanda tried desperately to focus on her breathing as Elsie led her out, talking to her the whole time.

"I'm here. It's OK. You're safe. We're getting out. I've got you." Elsie said the phrases over and over in Amanda's ear like a mantra. "Look down," Elsie whispered, and Amanda looked into their joined hands to see a soft golden light, warm like a fire. "I'll get us out," Elsie said, "and we'll have light on the way. You're not alone, and we're getting out." Elsie led Amanda through the cave, and eventually Amanda saw the lights of the car park. She stumbled towards the exit of the cave and collapsed as soon as she reached the open air.

She drew in a huge breath, panting on all fours. After a few minutes, Elsie guided her gently over to the car. Amanda stood leaning against it, her breath coming in sharp bursts. She pushed her hands against the cool metal, searching for solidity. "More light," Amanda managed to get out, and Elsie quickly jumped in the car and turned on the headlights. Light poured down onto the tarmac and Amanda sank into it like it was air to starved lungs.

She was sweating. Despite the cool of the night, her whole body was drenched, and she shook as if from a fever. "What can I do?" Amanda heard Elsie's voice from far away. She just shook her head. There was nothing that could be done at this stage. Falling to the ground, she allowed her body to convulse, trying to focus on her breath. She felt like her chest was going to explode, and it was a long time before she gained any control over her breathing. Eventually, she pulled herself into a sitting position on the floor, her back against the car, looking out at the empty space in front of her. She reminded herself she was safe, she was free.

47

Elsie

It took a long time before Amanda got her breathing under control. Elsie felt helpless, sitting beside her, unable to do anything. She reached out her hand and Amanda held onto it. Her hand was clammy, and Elsie could see the tears streaming down her face. She felt as if her heart might burst with concern and affection for this woman. Elsie had heard somewhere that breathing slowly with someone who was having a panic attack, which she assumed was what was happening with Amanda, could help them. Feeling a little unsure, she sat in front of Amanda and took long, slow, deliberate breaths, in through her nose, and out through her mouth. She exaggerated the sounds slightly, kind of like yogic breathing. Eventually, she heard Amanda's breathing matching hers.

After about fifteen minutes, when the car park had emptied, and Elsie was cold enough to have muttered a warming spell under her breath to keep the worst of the chill off them, Amanda stood up, letting go of Elsie's hand with a squeeze. She began walking the four sides of the carpark with a kind of dazed determination. When she came near, Elsie could hear Amanda muttering under her breath to herself, "you're safe, you're free." Her heart broke. What had happened to her?

She waited quietly by the car, and after three laps, Amanda came back and stood in front of her. Her face was white as a sheet, and her breathing was still ragged, but she didn't seem to be completely out of control, as she had before. "Are you OK to drive us back?" Amanda asked, her gaze on the floor.

"Of course," Elsie said, relieved that Amanda wasn't going to try to drive in this state. Amanda quietly handed over the keys and got into the passenger side of the car.

The drive home was considerably more sombre than the drive there. Elsie put on a gentle acoustic playlist, hoping that the soft melodies would help to soothe Amanda's mind. Hopefully, the slow tempos would help her with her breathing, too. She glanced at her friend a few times, and saw her staring out of the window, a harrowed look on her face. After what felt like an age, Amanda spoke softly, still staring out the window.

"When I was twelve, my dad went away on a business trip. My brother was sixteen, and he wanted to have some friends over. Back then I was a bit of a goodie two shoes, so I told him he shouldn't have friends over without dad's permission. I said if I saw anyone I'd tell dad." Amanda took a breath. "He didn't like me standing up to him like that. He already pushed me around a lot, but that night, things were different. He got real mad." Amanda's voice was shaky, and Elsie could only just hear her over the music, but she didn't dare turn it down or change anything, for fear of interrupting Amanda's train of thought.

"He had a few drinks. He was always drinking, Theo. Thought it made him cool. I heard a knock on the door and all of a sudden, Theo grabbed me by the arm, throwing me into the downstairs coat closet. It was small, dark, and incredibly cramped. There was no light, and coat hangers dug into my sides. The floor was littered with shoes and there was barely any room for me to stand up. He locked the door and left me in there. I think it was about seven hours before he let me out, casual as can be. 'See, you never saw any of my friends,' was all he said when he unlocked the door. I had been screaming and crying for hours, and eventually I think I tried to fall asleep, but I could hardly sit down. I just sort of leant against the door, sobbing. I had wet myself." Elsie's heart broke for Amanda.

"Theo looked at me like nothing at all had happened. He just unlocked the door and left. I started going to Ms Watters' any time dad went away after that, but I've been bad with enclosed spaces ever since."

Elsie could feel the tears streaming down her cheeks. She had no idea what to say. "I am so, so sorry that happened to you," was all she could manage. She squeezed Amanda's hand, desperate to pull her into her arms, but not wanting to confine the woman at all after what had just happened.

"At least he's in jail now," Amanda said, still talking to the countryside moving past her window. "Will he be in jail for a while?" Elsie asked. Not wanting to pressure her, but allowing her to keep talking if she wanted to.

"It depends on the trial," Amanda said, a shadow crossing her face. "If I don't testify, then who knows? Maybe there will be enough evidence, maybe there won't."

"But he doesn't know you're here?"

"Nobody does. Not even the Police."

"That must be hard, being in hiding like that."

Amanda nodded. "It is. I'm careful. I always feel like I'm looking over my shoulder. But in some ways, I feel like I'm more myself in Glen Haven."

Elsie made a noise to encourage Amanda to keep talking.

"At home, I was always Frank's son, or Theo's sister. Neither reputation was exactly something I was eager for. Here, I get to be me. No expectations."

Elsie squeezed Amanda's hand again, and Amanda lapsed into silence. She wondered if she would hear more, but it seemed Amanda was done sharing. She returned Elsie's squeeze, but just continued looking blankly out the window.

"How are you feeling?" Elsie asked a few minutes later. "Do you want some tea or anything? If you have any more of that lavender and chamomile, it might help to soothe your nervous system after the shock it's had." Amanda hadn't actually confirmed she'd had a panic attack, but whatever it was, her nervous system was certainly out of whack. Elsie wished she could do more than just offer some tea, but at least Amanda might find that to be of some comfort.

"Don't want to stop," Amanda said, her words still a little stilted.

"That's ok" Elsie said. "Here, let me...." She crooked a finger towards the box in the back, and a pouch of lavender and chamomile came floating out, hovering between the two women. "Why don't you pop that and some water into your flask?"

Amanda put the tea bag and water into the flask, the look of exhaustion on her face changing to one of intrigue as Elsie held her index finger to the side of the flask for a few seconds. "Try that," she said, and Amanda took a sip. "That's really good, thank you." Then, a few moments later, it obviously occurred to Amanda what Elsie had done.

"You can heat the water without the camping stove!?" she asked, incredulously.

Elsie felt a little sheepish., "Well, yes...."

"Why did you let me spend so long today lighting the stupid stove, then?" Amanda demanded.

"I thought it was so sweet that you had brought it, and besides, it would have been a little tiring to have done spells all day," Elsie said, knowing that she wasn't sounding all that convincing.

Amanda rolled her eyes at her. "Sometimes," she said, with what Elsie hoped was a humorous hint of exasperation in her voice, "you're too nice for your own good."

48

Amanda

Amanda slipped under the bubbles, basking in the sumptuous scents of lavender and sage. She could see why Elsie rated this so highly, it was surprisingly peaceful.

It always took a while to recover from a panic attack, and Amanda had come home from work feeling like she had run a marathon. She had remembered Elsie saying that a bubble bath could cure a great many woes, so here she was.

Normally Amanda didn't go in for this kind of lounging around, with scented candles and fragrant bubbles stuff. She always had too much to do, and too much on her mind. She had to admit, though, something about the bubbles, the smells, the way the light from the candles reflected on the water, it all helped her to pull herself out of her head more easily than she might otherwise have been able to.

Ducking her head under the water, Amanda closed her eyes and floated, clearing her mind and trying to focus on nothing but the feeling of her body suspended in the water. Eventually, she pulled her head back above the water, keeping her eyes closed as she breathed slowly. There had been so much going on in the past few weeks, with her brother, her dad, and the dark magic. It was wonderful to take some time to clear her mind and simply be.

The door flew open and Elsie's bum wiggled through. Amanda cried out in alarm, but Elsie, her whole body now in the bathroom, seemed to be in another world. She had purple headphones encasing her face, and Amanda guessed she was bopping along to the latest hit. Amanda waved, trying to get Elsie's attention, but she was facing away from Amanda, and just kept shimmying along, oblivious. Amanda's heart-rate ratcheted up, and when Elsie boogied over to the toilet and made to pull down her leggings, Amanda leapt from the water, waving her arms and hollering at the top of her lungs. Elsie must have heard or seen something, because she froze, staring at Amanda, and then she was shouting herself, presumably also trying to be heard over the deafening music that was limited to her headphones.

"What are you doing here!?" Elsie bellowed, as Amanda, realising that she was now standing, completely exposed, grabbed a towel and threw it around herself. "I thought you were at work."

"I thought *you* were at work," Amanda responded, and then had to repeat herself once Elsie registered she was still wearing the noise canceling headphones and took them off.

"We completely sold out of stock, so I finished a little early. I got Lily to close up." Elsie said, looking pleased with herself.

"Well, I ... finished early too." Amanda said,

Elsie looked at her more closely now, concern in her eyes. "You ok? Did something happen?" She asked.

"No. Nothing new, anyway," Amanda sighed, shaking her head a little. She hated how weak she felt. Amanda was used to getting on with things; putting her head down and carrying on. She couldn't understand why she was finding it so hard to do that now.

Elsie reached out and took Amanda's hand, holding it in her own. She led her out of the bathroom and over to the bed and sat her down, sitting next to her and turning to face her, those big, violet eyes wide with concern. Amanda felt a lump in her throat.

"Amanda, you've been through a lot. It would be fair enough if you're feeling overwhelmed. I don't know why your brother is in jail, or exactly what's going on, but from what you have told me, it's a lot. I know you're a private person, but you don't have to shoulder all of this on your own." Elsie's voice was gentle, her hand on Amanda's bare shoulder bringing goosebumps to her skin. "You're skittish and anxious, and I can see in your aura that there's a shadow hanging over you." She tucked Amanda's wet hair behind her ear and Amanda felt her breath catch for just a moment. *Snap out of it*, she told her body sternly. *Now is not the time.*

"Is it something to do with whatever you're running away from?" Elsie asked, with terrifying insight.

"H-how did you know I'm running away from anything?" Amanda asked, but Elsie just shrugged.

"Witch," she said simply, and Amanda had to laugh. What a strange world she had found herself in that her best friend was a witch!

"Also," Elsie went on, "it was your solstice resolution, remember?"

Amanda had forgotten that. She was surprised that she'd opened up to Elsie then, that she wanted to open up to her now. Amanda hadn't had a best friend before, and perhaps that was the thought that pushed her to say something. "There are some bad people who are after me," she began. "They don't know where I am or what my name is. That is to say, Amanda George isn't my real name—my name is really Amanda Masters."

Amanda heard Elsie do a sharp intake of breath, but she didn't say anything, which Amanda appreciated.

"I told you my brother and dad are in jail, right? What I didn't mention is that my brother is in jail because of me." Amanda had never said that aloud to anyone before. It was hard to admit it, even to herself. Theo was a bad person, Amanda could recognise that. But he was still her family. She felt guilt and sadness curdle in her stomach, but she forced herself to continue.

"After my dad went to jail, my brother's attitude got out of hand. He was hanging out with people who were in a completely different league than him, and he got caught up in some seriously shady stuff. One day, he and some dodgy guys turned up at my nursery with—," she swallowed hard, feeling the waves of nausea wash over her. Elsie held her hand and waited, and in a few moments Amanda continued. "They turned up with a dead body that they wanted to bury on my property."

"Oh my," Amanda heard Elsie whisper. "What did you do?"

"I watched them do it. Then, as soon as they left, I packed a bag and called the cops." Amanda toyed with the hem of the towel, remembering that horrible evening. "Pierce, the guy who keeps calling me, had me in a safe house for a little while. Then I got a call in the middle of the night. It was Pierce. He was frantic, he said Theo's 'friends' had found out where I was and I had to make a run for it." Elsie's eyes went wide, but she squeezed Amanda's hand to continue. "He told me to go to the Police station, but by then I knew I just had to get out of town, so I got on a bus and came here. I don't know how they knew it was me. Maybe they didn't for sure, but someone wanted to scare me, and they did an excellent job."

She explained that Theo's so-called friends had been sending her threatening messages, warning her that if she testified, she'd be in trouble. "Never from a traceable number, and never explicit enough to actually count as a threat to my life if it was ever traced back to them. But the message was pretty clear."

"Pierce said my statement the other day did the trick, and my dad's transfer to Wiri has been cancelled, but I'm so tired of being on guard all the time. The thugs don't know where I am, and so long as I don't testify, I don't *think* they'll actually come after me. But it's exhausting. I feel so alone."

Amanda said the last sentence to her knees, a hot tear running down her cheek. She had been trying so hard to keep it together, to start afresh and to put her old life behind her. Now she was worried that she would never be free.

"Oh Amanda," Elsie said, when Amanda finished talking. "I'm so sorry." She pulled Amanda into an embrace, and once again Amanda felt warmth rush through her body. She was suddenly very aware that she was wearing nothing but a towel. As they pulled out of the embrace, their faces lingered close to one another. Amanda could feel Elsie's breath on her lips, could smell the soft, sweet scent of cinnamon and sugar that so often lingered on her when she came home from the bakery, mixed in with her usual jasmine scent.

Amanda's eyes met Elsie's, and she watched as Elsie's eyes lowered, moving slowly down her towel-clad body, then back up, coming to rest on her lips. Amanda subconsciously ran her tongue around her mouth, which had gone suddenly dry, and saw Elsie's eyes flare as they followed the movement. It felt like they were suspended in time, held mere centimetres from touching. Amanda closed her eyes and leaned in, leaving a minuscule gap between them. She felt the soft warmth of Elsie's breath on her lips. Then the doorbell rang. Philo charged through the door, barking like a dog possessed.

They bolted apart, and Elsie leapt up "I'll see what the problem is. See you downstairs," she called over her shoulders, her eyes not quite meeting Amanda's.

"Yes, yup, good," was all Amanda could manage, and then Elsie and Philo were gone, and Amanda was left staring at the empty doorway, heart racing. What had just happened?

49

Elsie

Philo was barking angrily at the door. Elsie hadn't even noticed herself walking down the stairs, her mind was so preoccupied. Had she and Amanda really been about to kiss? Sparks shimmered up and down her body at the thought. She opened the door to see Soren standing out on the footpath, looking up at the house curiously.

"Hi," she said. It was nice to see him, but her mind kept drifting back upstairs to Amanda in that towel.

"Hello," Soren said, smiling up at her, his white teeth sparkling despite the grey of the day.

"What are you doing here?" Elsie didn't mean to sound rude. Her mind was just preoccupied.

Soren's face fell. "I thought we had plans." He said, looking at the ground. Had they made plans and Elsie had forgotten? She felt awful! She was more chaotic than normal at the moment.

"Did we? I'm sorry." Elsie hesitated. She wanted to go upstairs and talk to Amanda, see what that almost kiss had meant. But she didn't even know what she wanted it to mean. She liked Amanda. A lot. She had seen how hard it was for a normy to be with a witch, though, and she didn't want to end up like her parents had been; her dad always going off to do witchy things, her mum feeling left out and becoming increasingly withdrawn. Amanda already had a tendency to run when things got tough, she had admitted as much herself. Maybe a magical distraction was just what Elsie needed. "What are we doing?"

"Spell casting, of course!" Soren said. "I found an empty field the other day. It would be perfect for practicing in."

"OK, great." Elsie was still distracted, and Philo's loud barks weren't helping matters. "Do you want to come in and wait while I..." she suddenly thought how bad it would look to Amanda if Elsie had almost kissed her, and

164

then within minutes had a man in the kitchen. Not that she saw Soren like that at all. Elsie supposed he had that kind of sleek, polished look that some people liked, and he was handsome, but Elsie's heart was filled with nothing but Amanda these days. Still, it might be better if Soren waited outside so as not to give Amanda the wrong idea.

Soren seemed to read Elsie's mind. "I'll wait out here. It's quite a pleasant day." It was freezing cold, but Elsie supposed that compared to the cold in Sweden, the New Zealand winter was probably nothing. It wasn't windy or raining at least.

"Ok, down in a minute." She said, racing back inside and throwing on some different clothes. Elsie hesitated at Amanda's door, where she could hear movement. She knew she should knock and explain that she was going out. But she didn't really know what to say to Amanda right now. Instead, she settled for scrawling her a note, saying she'd forgotten she had plans, and suggesting they catch up soon. She hesitated at the end of the note. Should she do her usual two kisses? Or would that see presumptuous? For all Elsie knew, Amanda was regretting their almost-kiss, and Elsie didn't want to make things more awkward than they already would be. She settled for a hedgehog holding up a cupcake, and then, with a quick peck on Philo's head, she was gone.

50

Amanda

A few days later, Amanda strode out of the bathroom into Elsie's room. "Why do you have kids' toothpaste?" She asked, grinning. Amanda had done a lot of thinking since the almost-kiss the other day, and she had decided overly friendly and optimistic was the way to go forward. She *really* liked Elsie, and had been so excited when they nearly kissed, but when she'd come out of her room after putting some clothes on, Elsie was gone, with nothing but a note to say she'd see her later. It was pretty obvious Elsie was regretting their almost-kiss. Amanda didn't want to make things awkward, so she plastered a wide grin across her face, determined to get rid of the weird vibe that had been brewing between them for days.

"It tastes better," Elsie replied with a shrug. "I bought adult toothpaste when I moved out of home, but I don't really like mint, and one day I thought, 'kids get way better toothpaste flavours and colours. People are even more obsessive about kids' teeth than they are about adults' teeth, so their toothpaste must be good for preventing cavities.'" She raised her chin, "I also realised that as an adult, I can choose whatever toothpaste I want, and nobody can stop me." She had an extremely cute, defiant glint in her eye as she stood there and defended her decision to buy children's toothpaste. "So I've been buying kids toothpaste ever since. It always tastes better, and sometimes it even has sparkles."

Amanda burst out laughing. "You have got to be one of the quirkiest people I know," she said, looping her arm around Elsie's waist and giving her a squeeze.

"I mean, I am a witch," Elsie said in response, squeezing Amanda back. "I feel like that's quite a strong starting point.".

Amanda laughed, then flushed. She had done a good job of staying light, but a terrible job of not flirting. She liked the easy closeness that had developed between her and Elsie, but she had to be careful not to misread it like she had the other night.

"OK if I have a quick shower?" She asked, standing up again quickly.

"Of course. I promise I won't barge in this time!" Elsie's face was pink, and Amanda felt her own cheeks flushing as she recalled being literally naked in such close proximity to this woman. *Get a grip*! She chastised herself. She decided to have a very cold shower.

"**H**ave you got much on this weekend?" Elsie asked, as Amanda came out of the bathroom again fifteen minutes later, dressed in pj shorts and a tank top, towel drying her hair dry.

"Work Saturday as usual, then I said I'd pop down to the community garden for a couple of hours if you fancy joining me?"

"Love to," Elsie said with a broad smile. "It's amazing what you've been able to do with that place already. On Sunday I wondered if you wanted to go up Pride's Peak, if you fancy getting into the hills a bit?"

Amanda beamed. This was much better! Back on track, good friends, hiking together. She tried not to feel too smug that Elsie hadn't invited Soren. "That sounds amazing!" Pride's Peak had been on her list of places to explore since she arrived in Glen Haven, but as it was an all-day hike, and she had been so busy with work, Lilac House, and the community garden, she hadn't explored it yet. It was also known for being very exposed to the South-easterly winds, so you had to be careful about when to go.

"I checked the forecast," Elsie was saying, "and it looks like it will be calm but really cold. Have you got some thermals?" As the two began planning for their walk, Amanda could feel her excitement building. Pride's Peak was one of the highest points in this part of the country, with 360 degree views, and, if you went at the right time of the year, even a waterfall.

She was also, she admitted to herself, very grateful that Elsie was making positive plans to do something together. Amanda didn't want to be jealous of Soren, and she knew that's what this was. He could give Elsie something that she never could, and Amanda felt sick in her stomach at the idea of Soren sweeping Elsie off her feet.

Pride's Peak was something she and Elsie could do together though, and Amanda was glad that she would get to spend the whole day with no-one but Elsie and Philo.

"Hey, did Lily seem off to you at yoga last night?" Elsie asked, just as Amanda was about to head out the door.

Amanda stopped and thought. "I hadn't noticed anything at the time," she began, "but now that you mention it, she seemed pretty tired, and quite preoccupied. She's always quiet, but come to think of it, I don't know if she said anything at all. Has she been ok in the shop?"

"Yeah, she's been fine," Elsie said, a furrow in her brown that Amanda itched to rub her thumb across. "She's getting better at talking to customers, and her work ethic is excellent. She just seems...." Elsie paused, searching for the right word.

"Sad and like she had a lot on her mind?" Amanda asked.

Elsie nodded, "yes, exactly. I get the feeling there's something bothering her, but I'm not quite sure what. I wish I knew what to do."

Amanda leaned against the doorframe, considering. "If I know you, and I'd like to think I know you quite well now—" She smiled down at Elsie, who looked unreasonably gorgeous in her slinky purple pyjamas, —"then I'd say you're already doing the right things. Talk to her, be friendly, but don't push her. Let her know you're interested, but don't ask too many probing questions. Open up to her a little, so she knows she can trust you." Elsie smiled at Amanda, and she felt her insides melt.

"Thank you. That's excellent advice. You're pretty good at this, you know."

"Good at what?" Amanda asked, surprised by the compliment.

"Looking after people."

Amanda laughed bitterly. "I'm good at looking after myself," she said, thinking of all the times she had had to fend for herself, of the steps she'd had to take just to stay safe here. "I'm not sure the people around me have much hope."

"Well, you make *my* life better," Elsie said matter-of-factly. "So thank you."

Amanda's heart gave a squeeze, and she nodded at Elsie, taking her exit. If she didn't know better, she could have sworn that her affection and desire had been reflected in Elsie's eyes.

51

Elsie

Lily dragged the broom across the floor while Elsie cashed up the till. It had been a busy day, and she was grateful that Lily had stayed late to help her close up. Besides, this gave Elsie an opportunity to chat with the young woman.

"Thanks again for your help today," she said, as she counted bills.

"No problem." Lily shrugged, not taking her eyes off her work.

Elsie persisted. "How are you finding working here?"

"It's cool. Thanks again for the opportunity," Lily said, this time looking up at Elsie with earnest eyes.

"And the rest of life? Studies, all good?" Elsie knew Lily was studying extramurally. She didn't really understand why a young woman in her early twenties would choose to stay in Glen Haven and study entirely online. But then, Elsie reminded herself, not everyone was as extraverted as she was.

Lily shrugged, and Elsie idly wondered if the girl's shoulders ever got sore from that pivotal form of communication. OK, let's see if another tac works. "You live with your grandparents, right?" Elsie asked, "down on Willow Lane?" Lily looked up, concern flashing across her features, and Elsie realised too late that what she thought of as small talk could be considered quite invasive by someone as private as Lily. She tried to backtrack and get onto safer ground. "Sorry, I'm not trying to stalk you!" She said, letting out a laugh that she hoped didn't sound as frightening to Lily as it did to her own ears. "Sometimes I take my dog Philo down there as a short-cut to get to the river." Lily looked less concerned now, but still wasn't volunteering any information, so Elsie ploughed on. "I love living up in the hills, but there's something about the river that I find really calming. It must be nice living so close to it." Lily's face softened, and Elsie saw a sense of peace come across it.

"Yeah, I love being so close to the water." She said wistfully. "Actually, I think I might have seen you and your dog, Philo, did you say? Down there before. Is that short for Philokrates?" Elsie stared at the young woman in amazement. "Yes, it is. How on earth did you know that?"

"Classics major." Lily shrugged again, but she kept looking at Elsie this time, so she considered it to be a win. "He's cute."

"Thanks," Elsie said, beaming. "Do you have any pets?"

"I have a cat, Percy. He's a pain in the butt, but I love him." Lily's face was full of fondness. Elsie felt much better to be on safe ground now, pet talk she could do! The two women chatted pets and families for a few more minutes, Lily sweeping and Elsie finalising the last few things behind the counter. Finally, Lily swept her hair off her face and replaced the broom out back, sweeping up the pile with a dustpan and brush. As she stood back up, Elsie caught a glimpse of a pendant around the girl's neck, and her breath caught. "Pretty necklace," she said in what she hoped was a casual tone.

"Oh, thanks," Lily said, tucking the pendant below her shirt again and turning quickly away to empty the dustpan into the bin. Well, that was interesting. Elsie thought. She would need to consult the grimoires again tonight.

52

Amanda

Amanda looked up as Elsie walked into the house. She frowned in concern as Elsie came and sat at the kitchen island. "You look like you've seen a ghost," Amanda said, going to the kettle and turning it on.

"It's Lily," Elsie said, her anguished voice coming out more of a squeak than she Amanda would have thought possible.

"You found out what's wrong?" Amanda asked, confused. "Isn't that a good thing?"

"Not exactly," Elsie said, remembering the glimpse of the pendant she had seen and wondering if there was any way she had misconstrued what was going on. "She was wearing a talisman."

"A what?" Amanda set a cup of lavender and chamomile tea in front of Elsie.

"Thank you." Elsie said, looking at Amanda in surprise. "How did you know what tea I wanted?" That was odd. Amanda had known that Elsie was stressed. Whenever Elsie was stressed, she drank this blend of tea, so Amanda had made it for her without even thinking. *You are getting way too close to this woman*, she warned herself. But the look on Elsie's face tore her back to the present moment.

"A talisman," Elsie said. "It's an enchanted amulet. It's used to hide someone's magic."

"Lily's a witch?" Amanda asked, shocked.

"She must be," Elsie said. "Why else would you wear something to block magical people sensing your magic unless you didn't want to be discovered?"

"But why wouldn't she want anyone to know she was a witch?" Amanda asked.

"The only reason I can think of is that it's her casting those evil spells."

The room was heavy with silence for a moment. Amanda couldn't imagine it. "She always seemed so nice," she said. "Quiet, sure, and obviously there's the whole goth thing, but I never thought she was, you know, evil."

Elsie was shaking her head. "Me neither. But then, I guess the amulet would stop me from reading that, too."

"You can use an amulet to stop another witch from knowing you're evil?"

Elsie shrugged. "The point of an amulet, or talisman, is that it hides your true nature. It hides your magic, and can also hide your intentions."

Amanda stopped abruptly. She turned Elsie to face her and held her by the shoulders, looking down into those deep, violet eyes. "You have to fire her," she said. She felt like the room was closing in on her, the very thought that her suggestion for Elsie to hire Lily might have put her in danger! Amanda could have kicked herself.

"I can't just fire her," Elsie said. "We have employment laws. Plus, she knows I noticed the amulet; she'll know I know. Besides, it's better to get to know her and to figure out her plan. It could be the only way to get ahead of this thing."

If it had been anyone other than Elsie, Amanda would likely have agreed. But the idea of Elsie spending a single minute alone with an evil witch made Amanda want to go into bodyguard mode. She wondered how easy it would be to get a gun, off the record, obviously. "We'll find another way." Amanda said, her jaw clenched.

"Like what?" Elsie asked, raising her narrow chin stubbornly. "Besides, if I tip her off that I know, I'll be in more danger than if I don't. Keep your enemies close, and all that."

Amanda frowned. Else was probably right, but she didn't like it.

"Well, just — don't be alone with her, ok? Next time either you close up by yourself or she does, no starting early just the two of you or closing together. Or call me and I'll come by as well."

"Yes, mum," Elsie said, sticking out her tongue at Amanda. The feelings rushing through Amanda's body right now were far from motherly. She was glad to see Elsie in a lighter mood than she had been, though. One corner of her mouth hitched up as Elsie continued to make silly faces at her. What was it about this woman that drove Amanda so crazy?

53

Amanda

The two set off as early as Elsie could handle on Sunday morning, which, to be honest, was about 9:30. They had the biggest flask of coffee Amanda had ever seen in the car between them, and an exuberant puppy in the boot. Amanda had packed their bags with water, and Elsie had stocked them up on snacks; muffins, sandwiches, nuts, and an abundance of fruit. It was about an hour's drive out of town to get to the start of Pride's Peak, and they passed most of the time in pleasant silence, as Elsie was very much still waking up. Amanda was quite content to drive and look out the window, taking in the changing views outside.

The landscape outside turned from forest to farmland, and then they were surrounded by a jungle of ferns and native palms. Eventually, they pulled off the main road and began a long ascent up a steep track. The road twisted and turned, and several times Amanda wondered what would happen if another car came down hill towards them. The road was blessedly quiet, however, and Elsie directed Amanda to a track off the already tiny road. Amanda was grateful for her four-wheel drive, as she wasn't convinced Elsie's Beetle would have managed the steep incline and muddy roads.

They set off up the hill, Philo bounding jubilantly ahead of them. Amanda was in complete awe of their surroundings. Ferns towered overhead, whilst other, smaller varieties carpeted the entire forest floor. The air was alive with birdsong, and now and then they could hear the heavy 'whoosh' of a kereru's wings. They scrambled over huge tree roots and marvelled at the rough, black bark of the pungas. The air was frosty. Even though the incline was steep, both Amanda and Elsie were layered up. The forecast for the day had been clear, but you could never tell with the weather down here, so they were in thermals and sturdy hiking boots. Amanda had even packed ponchos for them both in case of unexpected rain.

Conversation flowed easily between them, now that Elsie's coffee had kicked in.

"Did you hike much growing up?" Amanda asked, as they stood and caught their breath beneath a huge manuka.

"A little," Elsie replied. "Dad was really into it. He was a big fan of the outdoors, and Mum has always been very into nature and any hippy stuff. Every year Dad would pack us up, Phoebe too, and we would drive somewhere new. We've been to the southernmost point of the island, walked the hidden beach coves right up north, and explored plenty of other places in between. I may not be a green witch, but I definitely appreciate nature and have always been fascinated by the properties of plants."

"Was it your dad who taught you that, too? It's kind of somewhere between magic and medicine, is that right?"

"Exactly," Elsie said. "Normys can use herbs and plant life, and can learn the various things that help plants to work well together, but witches can also infuse those ingredients with a little bit of magic to accentuate the natural properties. Dad taught me a lot about it, but so did Grandma. Even Mum has a keen interest in herbs and natural remedies." It had surprised Amanda that Elsie's mum wasn't a witch. She could certainly understand how someone as earthy and hippy as Elsie described her would end up jelling with an earth witch, though. Elsie didn't talk about her mum all that much. Amanda got the feeling things were a little more complicated there than Elsie would like.

"We also learned the basics at school, but because I'm an air witch, I spent more time focussing on things like flying, levitating things, and other more air-centric skills."

"Your school sounds wild,." Amanda said. "I wish we'd learned about plants when I was growing up. It was a steep learning curve when I started the nursery!"

Elsie laughed. "I know the basics, but I'm useless at keeping things alive. You saw the state of the garden before you got your hands on it! I can't believe you're not an earth witch yourself with the way you've brought that back to life."

Amanda glowed at the compliment. She was pleased with the progress at Lilac House. You couldn't yet see a lot of the work that she had done. The plants and flowers she had planted as seeds or bulbs wouldn't be visible until the spring, but the hedges were looking promising, the trees were thriving, and the whole place was much more tidy. The lilac climbing all over the walls was close to budding, and she knew that come springtime, the place would be beautiful.

"Oh, look!" Elsie knelt down and pointed out some tiny brown mushrooms growing on a crumbling log. "Woodear mushrooms." She pulled a mesh bag from her backpack and carefully plucked half a dozen mushrooms, placing them delicately in the bag before pulling the drawstring and replacing it.

Amanda laughed. "Are you ever not on duty?" She teased.

"They're very hard to find!" Elsie responded, poking out her tongue. Amanda smirked at her. A little farther up the track, Elsie grabbed a tiny pair of pruning scissors from her bag and cut some leaves from another tree. "This is Kawakawa," she said, holding up a spade shaped leaf that looked to be more hole than leaf. "We haven't had any in Glen Haven for the past year. I make a Kawakawa and elderberry tea that is delicious. It's very good for you too, with detoxifying properties."

"I know what Kawakawa is," Amanda said, taking a bite of the sharp, peppery citrus leaf. "But I didn't realise it had healing properties. Is it true that you can pick which leaves are best based on how holey they are?"

Elsie nodded, picking several more leaves and placing them carefully in her backpack. "The caterpillars pick the ones that are the best, that's why they're full of holes. The other ones are fine, but the flavour is a little more bitter, and the leaves are not yet really ripe enough for them to be so good at healing."

Amanda was fascinated. She had always loved learning about how plants grew, and how to help them grow, but she had never learned about how plants could help people.

About an hour into their hike, Amanda suggested they stop for a snack. "Great idea," Elsie said. "Let's just go a few more minutes. I think there's a nice spot for picnicking up ahead."

Amanda would have been happy to just squat beside the path and eat her sandwich, but a few minutes later they rounded a bend, and her breath caught in her chest. "Wow," was all she could manage.

"Thought you would like it," Elsie said, beaming like a Cheshire Cat. "Welcome to Rainbow Falls."

"Why is it called—" Amanda began, but just then a cloud shifted above them and the sun shone directly onto the waterfall, creating a rainbow effect from the water spray. It was nothing short of magical.

"If it was summer, we might be brave enough to go swimming, but given that I saw your teeth chattering when we started this walk, maybe it's not the best time to go for a dip." An image of Elsie in a snug black one-piece flitted across Amanda's mind, but she caught herself in time. It was freezing, the temperature was forecast to drop below zero, and there was simply no way that Amanda was getting into that water today. Plus, she had to stop thinking of Elsie as anything other than a friend. She had made her view on the subject clear, and Amanda would not pressure her.

In summer, if she was still around, she decided she would love to come back. It was weird, Amanda thought, — thinking about the future more, making plans, expecting that she might be in the same place. She had never understood what having a home would feel like, but Glen Haven, well, Lilac House, to be more precise, was beginning to feel like one. She smiled at the thought that she and Elsie could grow old together in that house.

Although of course she had no idea what Elsie might think of that idea. She assumed one day a handsome person would come to town and be totally swept away by Elsie, as she had to admit she had been. The only difference would be that Elsie might reciprocate their feelings. Maybe that person had already arrived. Amanda thought sadly, thinking of the tall, handsome man who had chatted so amiably with Elsie at Pie in the Sky. A witch with heritage in the town; he would be everything Elsie wanted. Amanda knew what it was like to be cast aside for someone else. Her mother had left with no note, no word of goodbye. She knew Elsie wouldn't be that cruel, but if she fell in love with someone else, presumably there would be no room for Amanda any longer.

Amanda tried to look on the bright side. She and Elsie could still be friends. She could find somewhere else to live in Glen Haven once she saved up a bit more. It was a pleasant town, and she felt like she was slowly getting to know people, to create roots, as it were.

A sharp bark from Philo interrupted Amanda's reverie as he raced off up the hill. "Oh, what's he up to now?" Elsie sighed, making chase.

54

Elsie

It was a rabbit. Philo advised Elsie when they finally caught up to him.

A rabbit. Of course. That was well worth interrupting the romantic moment she and Amanda might have been having beside the rainbow falls.

Don't be grumpy, Philo pleaded. Elsie decided she couldn't really be upset with him, when she knew she would never have gotten up the nerve to kiss Amanda, no matter how much she wanted to. Witches and normys didn't mix well. Elsie knew that. She didn't want to drag Amanda down the way her mother had been.

The way Amanda's cheeks had pinked from the exertion of climbing the hill had taken Elsie's breath away. She might not have known what was going through Amanda's head when she mentioned swimming in the pool, but she could have sworn she saw the other woman's pupils dilate just a little. Elsie knew she would be mentally dissecting that look for the coming days.

The path became even steeper after Rainbow Falls, and talking decreased to a minimum. After an hour of solid uphill climbing, watching the forest around them turn from ferns and palms to taller, more sturdy native trees, they rounded a corner, and Elsie heard Amanda gasp.

Coming up behind her, Elsie stood and stared. The ground in front of them was coated in a layer of white, and snow was falling in lazy circles above them. It looked just like a snow globe, as snowflakes floated to the ground. Elsie had to blink a few times to make sure it was real. They stood transfixed for several moments. Elsie, for one, had only ever seen snow on that one ill-fated family vacation to the mountains. She had never seen snow fall from the sky on a regular walk before. It was utterly mesmerising.

Elsie squealed, breaking the spell. She turned in a full circle, her arms out wide, face to the sky. "It's snowing!" She cried, somewhat stating the obvious.

Elsie grinned at Amanda. "I wasn't expecting this! We don't often get snow in Glen Haven. I guess I had heard it snowed down here, but it never occurred to me we might get to see it." Elsie felt like a kid in a Christmas movie.

Amanda, too, looked delighted at the surprise. "I've never seen snow before," she said, in a quiet voice so full of wonder Elsie wanted to freeze the moment forever. She rarely saw this side of Amanda, where she was open and vulnerable. Elise knew there was a lot more to Amanda than met the eye, but she preferred to keep her walls up and her cards held close to her chest. It was a rare and precious thing indeed to share a moment like this together.

Way out in front of and below them, the gorge stretched out, framed by two white tipped trees. The sun reflected off the snow on the grass, creating brilliant sparkles like diamonds all over the valley floor. The trees on the surrounding sides were coated in a fine layer of snow, and flowers dusted white bobbed their colourful heads in the breeze.

Philo let out a bark, approaching the snow with trepidation. He sniffed at the ground suspiciously, and Elsie could feel the confusion and concern in him. "It's OK Philo," she said reassuringly. "It's snow. Go on. I think you'll like it." Philo took a few hesitant steps forward and then put a paw gently on the snowy ground. He looked back at Elsie, who nodded. Philo stepped forward again, and then he was off! He bounded about, tossing his head in the air, leaping into the deepest patches of snow, tail wagging frantically. *It's so cold, so soft!* His voice in her head was full of glee. "I guess that's the husky in him," Elsie laughed, as Philo raced about like a toddler on speed, zooming around in circles, barking in excitement.

"He's pretty cute," Amanda said, taking out her phone and snapping a photo of the dog as he ran towards them, snout covered in snow, before he feinted away at the last moment, eyes bright with fun. "Oh! Stay there," Amanda said. Elsie had assumed she was talking to Philo, but as she turned to look at Amanda, she saw the phone was directed at her. "You look so beautiful with the sun on your face like that and snowflakes in your hair. I just thought maybe I could capture the moment, do you mind?"

Elsie hoped Amanda couldn't see her blush at the compliment. She gave a shrug, and Amanda began directing. "Turn back slightly that way, yes, just like that." Amanda snapped a few photographs and Elsie tried her hardest not to look like a deer in headlights. "Beautiful," Amanda said again, her eyes holding Elsie's for just a beat longer than expected. "You look absolutely beautiful." Elsie's heart thudded in her chest. The air felt suddenly electric, and Elsie's whole body warmed, despite the cold.

She took a step closer to Amanda without even consciously intending to. Amanda held the phone out so Elsie could see the photo, and Elsie was surprised. She was looking off into the distance, the winter's sun brightening her face. Her hair had a fine layer of fluffy white snow all along it, a crown at the top of her head, and flakes spread out down her ponytail. Elsie wasn't overly self-conscious about her looks, but she didn't often feel truly beautiful. In this photo, she looked, there was no other word for it, she looked beautiful. She smiled at Amanda in amazement. Then she took the phone. "Your turn," she said, trying hard to keep the intensity that she felt inside from seeping into her voice. Amanda blinked once or twice, but then obediently stepped between the trees, framing herself perfectly, though she looked rather ill at ease. Amanda stood facing the valley, and then at the last moment, turned her head back to smile at Elsie. Elsie could barely breathe; that look seemed to be an invitation. She took the photo, her brain firing so fast it felt like it might explode.

Amanda beckoned her over, and they took a selfie together, smiling at the camera. The field stretched out behind them, snow in their hair. Amanda pecked Elsie on the cheek for one of the photos, and Elsie felt her whole face flush. She turned and looked at Amanda, fighting with her body not to pull Amanda into a proper kiss. Amanda turned to face her, still close from their photo. Elsie could smell the faint hint of coffee on her breath, and the sandalwood shower gel on her skin. She noticed a lock of wet hair had slid out of Amanda's ponytail. Gently, she tucked it back behind her ear. Amanda held her gaze for a long moment and then, quietly, she said,. "If it's ok with you, I would very much like to kiss you." Elsie was rendered unable to speak, so she simply nodded. All at once, Amanda's lips were on hers.

They were warm and soft, and they kissed her gently at first, testing. Elsie responded, her lips eager for Amanda's, and soon the kiss was deeper, more passionate. Amanda had one hand resting just below Elsie's shoulder blade, pulling her in. The other was in her hair, her fingers sliding along the back of her head, and then slipping down behind her ear before cradling her face gently. Elsie let out an involuntary moan as Amanda's tongue slid inside her mouth, and she met it greedily with her own. Elsie closed her eyes and saw colours flashing behind her eyelids, reds and pinks and purples. She held both hands around Amanda's face, kissing her over and over again.

Eventually, they broke apart, gasping for breath. Elsie's chest was heaving, and she could see that Amanda's was too. "I have wanted to do that for so long," Amanda said.

"You have!?"

"Of course," Amanda said, her eyes still dark from—was that desire? Her body flushed warm again from the thought. It looked like more than that, though — there was a softness underneath the flame. This wasn't only a physical pull. She could tell, now that Amanda was allowing herself to be seen, that there was much more to this than a mere kiss.

"I think I've wanted to kiss you since the day we met," Amanda admitted, a shy grin on her face. "But the more I got to know you, the more I realised what a wonderful person you are." She seemed to be about to say more, but then stopped abruptly. "I'm sorry, I realise I don't actually know what you think about this. I know you said I can kiss you, but....,"

"What are my intentions?" Elsie asked with a cheeky smile. Amanda's face relaxed just a little.

"Something like that. I don't want to ruin our friendship. And I don't think I could really keep this just casual."

"I have been trying to convince myself that I don't have a crush on you for the longest time." Elsie admitted, feeling oddly liberated by the confession. "That day, when I saw you in the bath, I nearly died. I could hardly sleep that night because all I could see was this image of you covered in bubbles every time I closed my eyes." She saw a mixture of amusement and concern on Amanda's face and hurried on, not wanting to give her the wrong impression. "But it's not just that I'm insanely attracted to you physically. I really *like* you. You're smart, you're generous, you're strong. You're so independent, and yet you're always helping others. You have this rock solid exterior and the softest insides of anyone I've ever known. I spend every day with you, and I still can't get enough of you."

"So what does this mean?" Amanda asked, her face radiant with what Elsie thought might actually be joy.

"I think it means — Amanda, will you be my girlfriend?" Elsie felt anxiety race in her chest as she watched Amanda's face. It went from happy, to sad, to determined all in a matter of moments.

"I want that," Amanda said, taking Elsie's hand in both of her own and pressing it to her lips. "More than anything else in the world. But the things in my past, they could mean danger, for me, and for anyone else that gets close to me. The last thing in this world I want to do is put you in danger."

Amanda's tone had turned serious, and there was a protective glint in her eye. "Your brother and his goons don't know where we are, right?" Amanda shook her head. "And I have magic which we can use to help keep us safe." Amanda looked down at her sadly.

"That's another thing. What about your magic?"

"What about my magic?" Elsie asked. Surely Amanda wouldn't ask her to give it up.

"Don't you want to be with someone who has magic too? Someone who can go flying with you, or casting, or —" Amanda's voice trailed off as Elsie kissed her again softly. "I thought I wanted that." She admitted, "but I don't need that, not really. OK, so you can't fly with me. But you support me with my magic, heck you stayed up until dawn for the winter solstice even though your bedtime is usually like eight o'clock."

"Nine." Mumbled Amanda, nuzzling softly into the side of Elsie's neck and sending tingles down her spine.

Elsie pulled back and looked Amanda in the eye. "I know it's complicated. Heck, a queer couple in Glen Haven will probably raise a few eyebrows too, but you're everything I want. I know we can make this work." Now that she knew Amanda felt the same way, Elsie wasn't going to let fear stop them from being together. She felt a rod of steel in her spine as she looked at Amanda and said, "Whatever happens, we can face it together."

Amanda enveloped her in a hug, and soon their mouths found each other again. They kissed for a long, long time, until eventually Amanda pulled away. "I hate to break this apart, and *believe* me, I mean that — " Elsie felt her insides liquify at the look Amanda gave her —, "but I think we should probably head back before it gets dark, or we turn into icicles, or both." Elsie laughed, giving Amanda one more happy kiss on the cheek, before racing back to the path, calling to Philo as she ran.

55

Amanda

As they descended the hill together, Amanda's heart was a chaotic mess of joy and anxiety. She looked around the forest happily, and was surprised to realise that the trees here seemed to be in much better health than those in Glen Haven.

"Elsie," she began, not wanting to ruin the buoyant mood, but aware that something seemed to be awry. "Have you noticed that the trees in Glen Haven are dying?"

"Well, of course, it's winter." Elsie said, looking back at Amanda in confusion.

"Not losing their leaves and hibernating until the springtime." Amanda said, embarrassed that it had taken until now before she realised the extent of what was happening. "But actually dying. I saw three trees that were rotten when I went for my last run. And now that I think about it, a lot of the other trees have started looking quite sick. Plus, you said Mr Peabody was struggling with his usual supply of groceries because the crops weren't so good this year."

Elsie looked at Amanda, concern on her face. "I've only been here for one winter before, she said, catching up to Amanda and looking around at the trees. But I think you're right, last year the trees reacted differently. How widespread do you think it is?"

"The community garden is going ok" she said slowly, "but it's taking longer than I would have expected for anything to grow, and I've had to re-till the same patch about four times because the soil has turned icy. I thought it was just the weather, but it seems like it's only happening in Glen Haven. You don't suppose it could be connected to the dark magic, do you?"

Elsie's face visibly paled. "It could be," she said hesitantly. I don't know much about dark magic, but I know some of it drains the life from things. So it could be." She reached out and grabbed Amanda's hand. "I have an idea."

56

Elsie

"Elsie?"

Her cousin's face filled the screen, hair strewn around it like a red Medusa.

"Hey cuz, oh shoot, did I wake you?"

Phoebe rolled her eyes, which Elsie noted were still traced in what she assumed was last night's eye liner. "No, I'm wide awake at 4 in the morning." Elsie was pretty sure it was closer to midnight in New York, but she didn't push the point.

"I'm sorry! Now that I have you, though. Something weird is going on in Glen Haven. Look at this." They were in Viskande forest, about halfway up the main path. She placed the phone close to the ground, filling the screen with the sight of the blackened tree they had found.

"That doesn't look good," Phoebe said, sounding more alert. "But if it's only one tree, I don't think you need to worry about it. It's winter, right? Sometimes the trees just can't handle the cold of the South."

Elsie brought the camera back up to her face and was about to answer when Phoebe's voice dropped to a whisper. "Elsie, there's someone behind you," then, more loudly, "such a lovely forest, I sure do miss it!"

Elsie looked behind her, "oh, that's Amanda," she said, unable to stop the grin from spreading across her face. Phoebe squealed down the line, and on the screen Elsie saw Amanda's head pop up. "She's my girlfriend." Phoebe's squeal was even louder this time, and Elsie's cheeks hurt from the broadness of her smile. "OK, I have sooooo many questions!" Phoebe said, sitting up and revealing a bright red nightie.

"And you will get answers," Elsie promised. "But right now, what can you tell us about the trees?"

Phoebe made a noise close to a growl, but as an earth witch, Elsie knew she would be worried about what was happening. "It looks like its power has been drained somehow," Phoebe said, her brow crinkling with concern. "It's hard to tell without being there to touch the plant myself, but if I had to guess, I'd say there was some sort of parasite."

Elsie explained about the bones and the pain she had felt in Pie in the Sky. Phoebe's face went white. "Are you telling me this was caused by magic?"

"Is it possible?" Elsie asked. "The tree feels sad, and like there's a darkness in it. It feels like magic to me, but I've never come across anything like this before."

"Neither have I." Phoebe said, but then her eyes grew wide. "Elsie, do you remember Granny Margie's friend, what was her name, Esther? Eve? telling us about the great blight of 1913?"

The memory of a woman with short-cropped grey hair and a string of pearls around her neck came to Elsie. "I think I remember her, Edith?"

Phoebe clicked her fingers, "Edith, that's the one!"

"I don't remember the story, though." Elsie was two years younger than her cousin. It had never really mattered, but sometimes Phoebe's memories from childhood were clearer than Elsie's.

"It was something about all the trees in the town dying. There must be a record of it; you could try the library, perhaps?"

"Good idea." Elsie said, a feeling of foreboding rising in her.

"And Else," her cousin's voice was full of concern.

"Yeah?"

"Be careful, ok?"

"Of course."

Elsie ended the call and headed over to Amanda, who was crouched at the bottom of another dead tree, examining the ground. "It's cold." She said, looking up at Elsie with concern. Amanda had dug a small hole under the tree, presumably to examine the dirt. Elsie shivered at the sight of the black dirt. Something very, very bad was happening.

57

Elsie

As they walked back towards the car, Amanda grabbed Elsie's hand. "Don't tell Soren about the dark magic."

"What?"

"I know you like him, trust him, even, but he's a witch."

"You don't trust witches?" Elsie felt something inside her snap. Had she misread this situation all along?

"It's not that," Amanda said, her honey flecked eyes full of concern.

"What then?"

"We know the dark magic is being caused by a witch, right?"

Elsie nodded.

"Until we know for sure that it's not Soren, I think we should keep this between us."

"So what am I meant to do, just not hang out with my only friend in town?"

Amanda looked taken aback. Shoot, that's not what Elsie had meant. "My only *witch* friend in town," she corrected, but from the look on Amanda's face, the damage was already done. "Amanda, I-"

"I'm not saying don't hang out with him." Amanda interrupted, not meeting Elsie's gaze. "You said you haven't used powerful magic in a while right? It makes sense to practise with him. But, until we know for sure that he's trustworthy, don't say anything. Please?" Amanda's voice was soft, and Elsie reached out for her. "Please." Amanda said again. At Elsie's nod, Amanda stepped in and embraced her. "Thank you."

When they arrived at the library, a tall, blonde woman was inside stacking books. She looked up and gave them a warm smile. "Hello, I'm Catherine. Welcome to the library." Elsie couldn't believe she had been in the city for a year and hadn't made it into the library yet. No time for that now, though. She introduced herself and Amanda and told Catherine what they wanted to look up. The woman's finely plucked eyebrows raised as Elsie mentioned the blight, but she simply nodded and led them to an old reference section, telling them to sing out if they needed any help.

The reference section held copies of every Glen Haven Times published since the newspaper was established, which, fortunately for Elsie and Amanda, was 1900. They found the two volumes marked 1913, and took one each. Elsie did a double-take when she saw the publisher's photo on the back page on one from March of that year. It looked exactly like Reginald Arnold. Her thoughts were interrupted, however, by Amanda shouting, "found something." Only to look over at Catherine and whisper, "sorry! Found something." Elsie smiled and walked over.

Amanda had found an article dated 1 June 1913, and Elsie saw that there was mention that the trees and crops seemed to be struggling more than usual that winter. Turning a few pages, she saw that there was another article about an alarming number of trees found rotting in the famous forest. At the bottom of the page Elsie also spotted a heading about a farmer who claimed his sheep were disappearing. There was speculation about wolves, which was ridiculous because there weren't any wolves in New Zealand. Turning the page, Elsie saw that from springtime there seemed to be no more trouble.

They spent the next half hour looking through the articles, but they found nothing more. No reason was given for the blight, and it was localised to the Glen Haven area. Elsie felt a tingling in her spine. Had there been dark magic here before? Catherine came over and told them that the library was closing, so they thanked her and left. "Did Catherine remind you of someone?" Elsie asked absently, as they walked back to the car.

"Isn't she Wanda's sister?" Of course, that was it. She had thought the woman seemed familiar. That explained it. The woman looked a few years older than Wanda, but now that Elsie thought about it, the two women clearly shared the same genes. She wondered how she hadn't noticed immediately. Then again, she thought, looking across at Amanda's worried features, she did have rather a lot on her mind at the moment.

58

Amanda

The next day, after her postie run, Amanda popped into the Pie in the Sky for lunch. She was meeting Wanda, Murray, Sally, and Samantha to talk about the community garden. After her revelation the previous day, Amanda had been anxious to keep an even closer eye on the plant life in Glen Haven than she had been. Work on the community garden was going OK, but in the winter it was, understandably, reasonably slow. She couldn't do anything on days when it was pouring down with rain. Plus, fitting in the community garden around Lilac House, the postie run, and trying to decipher the many magical tomes in Elsie's house took some juggling.

If Amanda was honest with herself, though, she knew she had prioritised being at Lilac House whenever possible in case she got to see Elsie. Now, though, she had renewed vigour for the garden, and she was fortunate enough to have some keen helpers from yoga to make a plan that would, with a bit of luck, work for the whole community.

They were sitting at a corner table chatting amiably over pie and salad while Elsie kept up a busy lunch shift. Lily was working the till like a pro, but something about the way she kept glancing over at Elsie made Amanda curious. Did Lily have a crush? Amanda couldn't blame her, but she found it disconcerting the amount of time the girl spent staring at Elsie when her back was turned. Then, of course, Amanda realised she was doing the same thing, so she brought her attention back to the table.

Laid out in front of them were the plans for the community garden, complete with vegetable patch, herb garden, and even a community seating area with shade from some fruit tees. For a quaint town with so much nature around it, Amanda had been surprised that there weren't more community spaces.

"Here comes trouble," Wanda said, pushing the pram with her two sleeping children in it with her foot like an absolute pro. Reginaold Arnold strode in, his face flushed with anger.

"What's his problem now?" Amanda grumbled under her breath.

"You!" He said, pointing at Amanda, a blob of spittle hanging onto the edge of his ghastly moustache. Amanda took a deep breath, so as not to break the finger that was resting much closer to her face than was appropriate.

"Hello Reginald," she said in a sing-song voice designed to cause annoyance. "We're just having some lunch, but by all means, please join us." Reginald's face flashed with confusion for a moment, before anger replaced it again, and his cheeks, if possible, grew more ruddy.

"It has been brought to my attention that you have taken it upon yourself to dally with the space that was formerly the community garden."

Amanda was confused. "I've been doing some weeding and planting," she said uncertainly. "I've shown a few people some basic gardening, and now we're planning a few more vegetable patches. That's not a crime, is it?"

Reginald puffed himself up, his chest expanding so much that the buttons on his inexplicably formal shirt strained. "If you do not have the council's permission to use public property, then it is trespass and vandalism."

"The garden was overgrown and abandoned," she said, standing to look Reginald in the eye. She didn't like the way he was towering over her, too close for comfort. "All I've been doing is planting and trying to help. That's not vandalism, that's community service."

"Getting your grubby fingers all over the town, just like Margie did," Reginald snarled.

Amanda felt her own cheeks redden with anger, and she noticed Wanda standing beside her. "I think we could do with being a little more polite about the dead, don't you Reginald?" Wanda said, with a meaningful look that Amanda couldn't interpret. Wanda's voice was polite, but it had the firmness of a mother of twins. It was not to be messed with. Reginald jumped, clearly only noticing Wanda for the first time in that very moment.

"Ms Broadmeadow. How nice to see you," Reginald stammered, his tone changing instantly at the sight of the diminutive woman. Amanda stared at him in shock. Was he being *polite*?

"As Amanda said, Regi, we're in the middle of a planning lunch. Would you be so kind as to tell us how we might go about getting the permission of the council, and then perhaps we could get back to our meal in peace?" Reginald looked like he would rather eat dirt, but Wanda folded her arms across her chest in a manner that suggested her question had been entirely rhetorical.

"Well, you can apply through the usual channels." Reginald said, which meant absolutely nothing to Amanda.

"Do you mean there's like, a website, or something that I can put an application in through?" She tried.

Reginald scoffed. "We are a country town, Ms George. A discussion with the townsfolk at the Town Hall would be necessary before the council could consider your application. Once they have heard all sides of the argument, it may, at its discretion, grant its approval for you to utilise the community garden."

Amanda's mind reeled. Was this guy serious? She would have to get up in front of the whole town and say that she wanted permission to work on the community garden before she could grow a few vegetables? For their benefit? "It's a community garden," she said, struggling to keep the incredulity out of her voice. "Surely it can be used by the community for gardening, as the name implies?"

Reginald looked over his long nose at her disdainfully. "It has been over a year and a half since that land was used as a community garden. According to the by-laws of this town, the land reverts to being council land if it goes unused for its specified purpose for 18 months or longer. As such, you will have to apply for permission to use the council land as a community garden. Currently, it is not so designated."

Amanda wondered for a moment if Reginald had previously had dreams of being a lawyer or a police officer, or perhaps he had aspirations of being the town mayor. When these dreams didn't come to be, he instead took on the role of town busybody.

She sighed. "When is the next meeting at the Town Hall then?"

"There's one in two weeks' time." Reginald said haughtily.

191

"Can you please put me on the list, or whatever?" Amanda she asked, dreading the idea of speaking in public, but determined not to let this nasty man get one over on her.

Reginald nodded. "I shall publish it in this week's copy of the Times," he said, then he gave a strange little half-bow towards Wanda, and left.

"What was that all about?" Elsie said, coming over and collapsing into a chair next to Amanda.

"Just another case of Reginald being Reginald," Amanda said, sighing. "Do you know anything about Town Hall meetings?"

Elsie's face lit up, "Oh yes, I've been to a few since I came to town. They're such fun. People present petitions to the town and they get questioned. Everyone yells and gets carried away. It's really quite an occasion. Oh dear Amanda, what's wrong?" Amanda could feel her face losing colour as she thought about standing up in front of all of those people.

"Reginald has said that Amanda can't use the community garden without getting approval from the town," Wanda explained.

"But the community garden was previously a community garden." Elsie looked as confused as Amanda felt.

"It doesn't seem that Reginald is swayed by arguments involving logic." Amanda said heavily. One on one, Amanda was pretty bold, but talking in front of an entire room full of people? That was a very different story.

59

Amanda

"Today," Elsie said, wrapping an apron around her waist and tossing one to Amanda, who caught it easily and slipped it around her waist anxiously. "We are making cupcakes."

"Shouldn't we start with something simple?" Amanda asked, remembering the beautiful creations in Pie in the Sky, complete with butterfly or heart decorations.

"Don't worry," Elsie said with a gentle smile which practically melted Amanda's heart. "These ones will be simple. A coffee walnut cupcake with cinnamon coffee icing."

"That doesn't sound simple..." Amanda said nervously.

"Trust me, you'll be fine." Elsie gave Amanda a quick peck on the cheek as she walked past her and Amanda was putty in the woman's hands. Elsie got to work, pulling out a mixing bowl, and various other items of kitchen paraphernalia Amanda didn't know the names of. Next, Elsie went to the cupboard and brought out flour, sugar, oil, a bottle of yellow vinegar, cinnamon, baking soda, and walnuts. From the fridge, she grabbed cold brewed coffee and soy milk.

"Ok, we're going to start by sifting the flour into this bowl." She handed Amanda a sieve and the flour and passed over some measuring cups. Elsie laughed. "You don't need to look so scared. The worst that can happen is we make a bad batch of cupcakes."

"But won't you be disappointed if that happens?" Amanda asked in a small voice. Elsie moved in front of Amanda, her hands warm on Amanda's waist.

"No," she said simply. "This is your first time making cupcakes. Everybody has to start somewhere! And anyway," Elsie reached up and kissed Amanda gently on the tip of her nose, "I don't like you for what you can or can't do. I like you for who you are." A wicked smile crossed Elsie's face. "though it helps that you can garden well."

Amanda laughed, feeling her shoulders relax ever so slightly. "Just so you know," pulling Elsie back towards her as the woman turned to go. "I don't like you because you can bake, either. But there is one thing about you that makes me like you even more."

Elsie pursed her lips. "And what's that?" she asked, hands on her hips. Amanda smiled at the fierce, petite woman before her.

"You are," Amanda said, lifting Elsie's chin and nibbling Elsie's lower lip ever so slightly, "an excellent kisser."

There was a fairly long interruption to the baking while the two kissed as if their lives depended on it. Eventually, they remembered why they were in the kitchen, and Elsie read out the instructions from her little book of handwritten recipes. Purple, obviously.

Amanda tried to follow her directions the best she could, though Elsie had to explain some terms to her. She appreciated Elsie didn't tease her for not knowing what 'beating the mixture' meant. With her mum gone and her dad often absent, Amanda had had little opportunity to learn to cook, let alone bake, growing up. Despite Amanda's trepidations, before long they had twelve brown speckled rounds of cupcake batter ready to go into the oven.

Elsie set the timer, and they got to work on the icing. "Is baking much like what you do with spells?" Amanda asked, as she measured icing sugar into a small bowl and added vanilla, margarine, cinnamon, and some instant coffee.

Elsie thought for a few seconds. "Yeah, I think it is. Baking and casting are both a combination of science and art. When you first start baking or casting, you follow a recipe. You can think that you've followed it exactly, but then you mess one little thing up and the whole thing turns out wrong; your cupcakes don't rise, you accidentally turn your cat blue instead of casting a waterproofing spell on its fur, that sort of thing."

Amanda laughed, wondering if that example had been from Elsie's own experience.

"Then after a while you get a feel for things. You can follow a recipe or a spell exactly, but you can also make changes to taste, like adding basil to lemon poppy seed muffins, or enhancing a good luck spell to make it a protective one. Sometimes it takes trial and error, but you gradually get more of a feel for what will and won't work. Then you can even get to a point where you make up recipes or spells from scratch. You have enough of a framework to know that a cake is going to need flour, sugar, oil, and so on, just as you'll learn the basic ingredients of a spell. Then you can make up what goes into it, depending on what you're after."

"That's incredibly cool," Amanda said, as she carefully mixed the icing ingredients, and Elsie took their cupcakes out of the oven.

"It's fun," Elsie said with a grin. "Once you know the basic rules, you can have a lot of fun with baking and casting."

"I can think of something else that's a lot of fun," Amanda said, leaning over and kissing Elsie slowly on the lips.

"Oh, yeah?" Elsie's eyes were dancing as she looked up at Amanda. "Think that's another skill we need to practice?" A smile tugged across Amanda's face.

"I think you'll find me to be a very dedicated student."

60

Elsie

As they approached the Town Hall, Elsie could hear voices and feel the buzz of excitement coming from the building. The Town Hall was made of old red brick, but fortunately the inside had been renovated recently, with double glazing and heat pumps. Before they were installed last year, everyone had gone to Town Hall meetings in their full winter coats. They had even kept meetings to a half hour maximum in winter so that nobody caught pneumonia. Now the building had been renovated, Town Halls could go for hours, and townsfolk would often sit around gossiping after a session was officially over.

Elsie felt the waves of panic emanating from Amanda. She squeezed her hand. "You're going to be fine," Elsie said to her reassuringly, as they entered the already packed hall and found seats. "People love the community garden."

"But Reginald hates me, and he holds a lot of sway," Amanda said, her teeth practically chattering from the stress.

"Reginald's bark is worse than his bite," Wanda said, and Elsie looked at her curiously. "Do you know Reginald well?" she asked. But the woman was already bustling into her seat and greeting her neighbour, so she must not have heard Elsie's question.

Glen Haven was too small to have its own mayor, so the mayor from the neighbouring town, Plimmer Valley, was shared across the two townships. The deputy mayor, Hayley Simmons, lived in Glen Haven, and was assisting Mayor Fairly to chair the meeting. Mayor Fairly banged his gavel to bring the crowd to order. Elsie would have laughed at how very small town it all was, except that poor Amanda looked like she might spontaneously combust from worry. "You've got this," Elsie whispered, squeezing Amanda's hand once more.

There were several items on the agenda for the evening. Paula was petitioning for solar panels to be placed on the library roof. There was a discussion about the annual Halloween fete, the location of which alternated between Glen Haven and Plimmer Valley. Finally, there was Amanda's request to use the community garden as ... a community garden. Most of the town seemed in favour of the solar panels, although there was a lot of discussion about where they would be and whether they would be 'an eyesore.' The Halloween fete similarly garnered a lot of attention. This year the fete would be held in Glen Haven, with a committee of volunteers in charge of running the events, and townsfolk from both Glen Haven and Plimmer Valley providing stands.

Finally, Mayor Fairly announced their item, "Proposal for use of the community garden." Amanda stood shakily to her feet. "Hi everyone, I'm Amanda M-George," she said.

"Speak up," came a voice from the back of the hall. Amanda turned awkwardly, trying to face everyone in the hall at once. "I'm Amanda George," she said again, a little louder this time. "I want to use the community garden as a community garden." She swallowed hard, looking down at Elsie, who nodded at her encouragingly. "I used to own a nursery up north, so I have some experience with gardening. Everyone would be welcome to help with the gardening, and the crops would go to the community."

"And what do you want from the town?" Mayor Fairly asked.

"Nothing," Amanda said. "I mean, I was told I needed permission because the gardens used to be community gardens, but now they're not?" She trailed off and Reginald Arnold stood to his feet.

"Have you, or have you not, already been using the community garden?" Reginald asked, with the air of someone conducting a cross examination in court. Elsie saw Amanda's cheeks go an even deeper shade of red.

"I didn't know I needed permission," she said. "The sign said community garden, so I—"

"And how exactly do you intend to manage this garden?" Reginald asked, interrupting Amanda.

"Well," Amanda paused, "I don't know, really. It probably depends on what the townspeople want. I'm happy to run it myself, or to run some workshops on gardening, or—"

"It doesn't sound like you've thought about this at all," Reginald sneered. "And where will you get the resources for the gardening things?"

"Um," Amanda said. "So far I've just bought a few things from Mrs Higgs' place."

"So you're going to personally fund the garden for the whole town?" Reginald asked sarcastically.

Amanda was looking increasingly uncomfortable, gripping the seam of her jeans. Her neck was tomato red, and Elsie felt terrible for her. "I guess people could all contribute to the garden?" Amanda began hesitantly.

"You guess?" Reginald said haughtily. "You come here asking for permission to use the garden, but you don't even know how it will be run, who will upkeep it, or how to afford the required supplies? Sounds like a very well thought-through plan indeed." He grinned widely at the room at large, spreading his hands as if to say 'ta-da.'

Amanda's hands were shaking, and Elsie had had enough. She stood up next to Amanda. "Do you have any actual objections to this project, Reginald?" she asked, with more force in her voice than she had ever used in this town before. Usually Elsie was careful to play mediator, but she had put up with Reginald's bullying for too long. Messing with Elsie was one thing. Messing with Amanda? That she wouldn't stand for.

"Amanda is asking permission to use an unused common space for the same thing that it has previously been used for. She wants the townsfolk to be a part of figuring out how that works, because she is doing this *for* the townspeople. Maybe it will take some trial and error, but the *worst*-case scenario here is that it doesn't work and the community garden ends up unused and overgrown again. So the worst-case is the status quo." Elsie looked around the hall and saw that a few people were nodding. Samantha and Sally even gave her a thumbs up. "But if it works, and I have no doubt it will, because Amanda has been transforming the garden at Lilac House and it looks amazing, then that's a *good* thing for the town. We could have extra fruit, vegetables and herbs, there could be beautiful flowers, people could learn new skills. This is a *good* idea, and there's no reason not to do it."

Reginald opened his mouth huffily to respond, but Wanda started clapping loudly, and soon the whole town hall had joined in. Elsie flushed. Had she done that? She looked at Amanda, and they broke into mirroring smiles. "Order," Mayor Fairly said, banging his gavel once more. Elsie and Amanda sat down.

"I'm inclined to agree that this is a no-lose situation," Mayor Fairly said, after conferring with deputy mayor Simmons. "However, we shall put it to a vote. Those in favour of allowing Ms George to use the community garden for its intended purpose?" Almost the entire village raised their hands. "Those against?" Reginald and Beth raised their hands, mouths pursed like they had just eaten something sour. "The Motion passes." Mayor Fairly said, banging the gavel down.

Ms Simmons spoke then. "Ms George, if you could report back to the Town Hall about how things are progressing, we would appreciate it." She said, her eyes kind. Elsie didn't really know Deputy Mayor Simmons, but she seemed nice. Next to her, Amanda was nodding.

"Is there any other business before we adjourn?" Mayor Fairly asked in his booming voice. A man Elsie didn't recognise stood at the back of the hall.

"Yes, Bob?" Deputy Mayor Simmons said.

"Two of my cows have gone missing,." Bob said, "Keith said he's missing a couple of sheep as well. We haven't seen anything, but there may be poachers about."

Elsie didn't know why, but a tingling in her toes told her that this was something bad. She half-listened as the town discussed possible reasons the animals had gone missing. This was something to do with the black magic though, Elsie knew it. She looked around the hall, and her gaze landed on Lily, who was fidgeting with something at her neck and looking anxious. What was that about?

Elsie was startled out of her thoughts by the banging of Mayor Fairly's gavel to announce the end of the meeting. Elsie didn't have any proof about the animals being linked with the dark magic, but after the Dark Divination, and the dying plants, she was pretty sure it was all connected. She needed to get to the bottom of this, and soon.

61

Elsie

Amanda was ecstatic on the way home from the Town hall, and Elsie didn't want to dampen her mood by bringing up the dark magic just yet. It was so rare to see Amanda on such a high. "Thank you," she had said, again and again on their walk home from the Town Hall. Wanda, whose house was on the way back to Lilac House, fell in beside them. Once they were out of sight of most of the villagers, Amanda really let loose. She whooped and jumped up and down - there was even a fist punch. Elsie laughed, delighted to see her favourite person so happy.

Wanda's sister was away doing research for the next few days. The twins had been quiet for most of the Town Hall, but they were making a lot of noise now. Elsie took one look at Wanda's worn-out face, glanced over at Amanda to check she'd be ok with it, and immediately invited the woman over for dinner.

They had been getting to know various people from the yoga class over Spill the Tea, but it was nice to spend one-on-one time with Wanda. Something about the woman felt vaguely familiar to Elsie, and she wondered if perhaps Wanda reminded her of an old teacher.

They made tacos for dinner to celebrate, and the three women and Philo sat out on the back patio to eat, watching the setting sun. The twins had woken up were happily pottering around the back garden under their mother's watchful eye. Philo seemed to have taken a particular liking to them, and was being gentler than Elsie had ever seen him be, lying on the ground and letting the children climb all over him. He licked their faces until they giggled with glee, and even letting them share his toys. Wanda drew the line at letting the boys put the dog toys in their mouths, which seemed reasonable.

The garden at Lilac House seemed to exist in an ecosystem all of its own. Some of the early spring flowers were even beginning to come out. The lilacs themselves were a little more reluctant, but there were tulips and daffodils waving contentedly in the breeze. The flower beds were a riot of colour from all the pansies, poppies, and other brightly coloured florals Amanda had planted.

It was delightful in the evening sun, the scent of jasmine heavy in the air. Elsie knew that the pleasantness would be short-lived. Tomorrow, she would tell Amanda about her fears of what had happened to those animals. For now, though, she wanted to just enjoy the moment. They sat outside eating tacos and chatting amiably for hours.

The air got unbearably cold after sunset, so they moved to the lounge and ate a self-saucing chocolate pudding Wanda had whipped up for dessert. The recipe tasted just like her grandmother's, its warmth comforting to her heart, as well as her body. Not long after that, Wanda headed home to bed, thanking them for their hospitality. Amanda and Elsie were left curled up in the lounge under a blanket.

"Thank you for what you did for me today,." Amanda said, turning and kissing Elsie softly on the lips. "I was so scared. It meant a lot to me that you stood up for me like that."

"Of course!" Elsie said. "I know you could have handled it, but Reginald was being such a brat. I just can't stand that guy!"

"You were brilliant, though," Amanda said, taking Elsie's face in her hands and kissing her more deeply. Elsie's insides wriggled in pleasure. They got lost in each other for a while, kissing on the couch, and Elsie thought her heart might explode at the happiness blooming inside her chest. Eventually, when their hands were roving and their breathing was getting heavier, Elsie grabbed Amanda's hand and led her to her room.

62

Amanda

Amanda woke up curled around Elsie, her arm slung protectively over the other woman's slender frame. She smiled to herself, and lay there, taking in Elsie's room. She had a dressing table at the other end of the room and a chair in one corner which was covered haphazardly with clothes. Amanda could see jeans, a faded green cardigan, a bright purple bra, and several simple black singlets. Her own clothes lay on the floor, and Amanda blinked several times, still unable to believe this was really happening. On the other side of the room was a huge mahogany wardrobe, in which most of Elsie's clothes were displayed. Tidy, organised, from the looks of it, by both clothing type and colour. A smile floated on her lips. She appreciated the odd mixture of chaos and order that Elsie represented.

Her room smelt of the incense she so often burned, and there were candles on just about every surface; the bedside table, the tall shelf next to the window, the dresser.

They spent a lazy morning in bed, and eventually made their way downstairs for coffee and food. Philo made it clear to both Elsie and Amanda that it was past time to feed him. Rain sleeted down outside the windows, and Elsie looked over at Amanda. "Not much of a day for outdoor adventures." Amanda had to agree. She had hoped to get down to the community garden today, and to do some more planting at Lilac House, but this weather meant neither of those things was possible.

"I can't help that it's raining," Elsie said to Philo, who was looking rather forlornly outside.

That reminded Amanda. "I meant to ask you last night, but I got a bit distracted," Amanda's smile was echoed in Elsie's own, and for a moment her eyes lingered on the woman's lips, and she considered simply going back upstairs to bed. With an effort, she decided she wanted to show Elsie that she was interested in her as a person, or a witch, a person witch? That she was interested in who Elsie was, she settled on, as well as being interested in kissing her. With some effort, she kept her mind on topic.

"So, how exactly does a Familiar work? Like, they can understand you, and you can understand them? Do they have magical powers as well, or what?"

Elsie smiled. "I don't know how to explain it exactly," she said. "They're just something I've always grown up around. I think they're magic, but they can't cast spells in the way witches can. They mostly have powers connected to their witch." Elsie got up and seemed reflexively to pull out baking things. She summoned flour and sugar from the pantry and a few ingredients from the fridge. She began the process Amanda now recognised as making sweet pastry. "My dad had a cat, and we assumed she would become my Familiar when he—" She paused for a second, touching her finger to the amber necklace she always wore, then continued—, "passed on."

"But she didn't?" Amanda prompted gently, not wanting to cause her friend more hurt thinking about this difficult time.

"No, Lady Spencer connected instantly with my cousin Phoebe when she came to visit just after the funeral."

Amanda made a conscious choice to bite down on the laugh at a cat being called Lady Spencer, seeing that wasn't the most crucial part of this conversation. "Is that usual?" Amanda she asked.

"It can happen," Elsie said, a little guardedly, perching on the edge of a kitchen stool. "But it's not exactly common. As an only child, with only one parent who is a witch, it seemed strange that my dad's cat would connect with Phoebe, rather than me. But that's what happened. Then about a month later Philo just kind of turned up, and I knew he was meant for me." Elsie looked down at the young dog with affection, and he came and sat next to her, his head on her lap. Unthinkingly, Elsie waved her hand, and the lid of the dog treat jar on the bench unwound itself. Two dog treats floated into Elsie's hand, from which Philo greedily gulped them.

"So did he tell you that or...?" Amanda felt incredibly ignorant asking these questions, but she hadn't come across a psychic connection with animals before.

"Oh no, when he first arrived, we couldn't speak to each other at all." Elsie rolled out the pastry expertly, placing it over a pie tin and pushing it gently into the edges. She dumped in a heap of pastry balls, and popped the shell in the oven, before moving fluidly to the stove and heaping cherries, lemon, and sugar into a pan. "I sort of felt something inside me. A connection. It's hard to explain." She looked at Philo for a moment, then said, "Yes, exactly." She looked at Amanda again., "It was kind of like a jolt in my tummy. Not the same as falling in love, but kind of in the same place." Amanda's heart fluttered at the 'l' word, but she forced her face to remain neutral.

Elsie continued, apparently not noticing the whirlwind of thoughts she had caused in Amanda's brain. "It took a long time before I could understand words from him, but right away I got a sense of how he was feeling." She stirred the fruit mixture and rolled out another piece of pastry, taking a knife and slicing it into long lines, about an inch thick each. "The first time he talked to me, I was drying dishes in the kitchen. Suddenly there was this voice in my head saying I had better be planning on feeding him soon, as he was starving." Elsie flashed Amanda a smile. "I was so startled I dropped the glass I was drying. Then I had to tidy that up before feeding Philo. He was most unimpressed, weren't you, boy?" She ruffled the animal's hair affectionately.

"And now?" Amanda asked.

"Our psychic connections gets stronger every day," Elsie said. "We have a connection even when we're not in the same space. Sometimes he can send me messages and hear me from across a distance, just not for a prolonged period yet." She pulled the partially cooked pastry case out of the oven and began spooning the fruit mixture into it. "He can understand most conversations that happen around him, not just me, from what I understand. Sometimes he can read my mind, and I think he usually knows my mood and where I am as well."

"Kind of like a personal GPS," Amanda joked.

"Something like that," Elsie laughed.

"And you can understand him?"

Elsie was quiet for a moment. She patted down the pie filling and then wove a lattice of pastry on top. "It's strange," she said, "sometimes I can understand him perfectly. We have full conversations, it's just like you and me. But then other times, I know the gist of what he's trying to get at, but I just can't quite get the words. I think it's because I've been a bit slack at practicing my magic since dad passed." Elsie looked at the pie, and Amanda noticed her hands moving to her necklace again.

"That's incredible," she said.

Elsie was quiet, and Amanda went to her, wrapping her arms around her neck and placing her chin atop her head. She held her like that for a long moment, before saying, "is everything ok? Did I say something to upset you?"

Elsie stepped back and looked up at Amanda. "It's not that," she said, an unreadable look on her face. "It's about the dark magic."

Amanda felt a panic in her chest, but she tried to be calm for Elsie's sake. "What about the dark magic?" She asked.

Elsie told Amanda that she thought the animals who had gone missing might have been sacrificed by the dark witch. Amanda felt sick at the thought, and she clung to Elsie more tightly.

"What do we do?" She asked, feeling completely out of her depth.

"I don't know," Elsie cried into her chest. "I don't know what they want. I don't know who it is. It seems like it's getting worse, but I have no idea what their end game is. Plus, I'm out of practice casting big magic. Amanda, I'm so scared, I feel so alone."

"I'm here," Amanda said softly into Elsie's hair.

Elsie looked up at her, "I know you are," she breathed. The unspoken words hung in the air between them, "but you can't help because you're not a witch."

63

Elsie

Elsie was rushed off her feet. Pie in the Sky was busier than she had seen it in a long time, no doubt because Beth had come down with some sort of illness, so her bakehouse was closed for a few days. Elsie didn't know what was wrong with Beth, but she had asked Amanda to drop off a few teas and cookies to her house as a get well soon gesture. Apparently Beth hadn't been overly impressed by what she had termed 'rubbing my nose in it that your shop is open and mine isn't.' Elsie wiped a hand across her brow, she still couldn't understand why Beth was so determined to see her as an enemy.

Pie in the Sky was teeming, though, and Elsie was extremely grateful Amanda had convinced her to get in an extra helper- even if that helper was possibly a dark witch. Lily was running the till like a smiling drill sergeant to keep the customers moving and stop the queue from reaching out the door. If nothing else, a queue out the door would make the shop cold from the brisk spring air. For her part, Elsie was racing around like a hummingbird, arms a blur as she plated up food, poured teas, made coffees, and then delivered them to the various tables for consumption.

Just as the lunchtime rush was beginning to feel more manageable, Lily turned to Elsie, her face pale. "What's wrong?" Elsie asked in concern.,

"There's been an emergency, I'm so sorry Elsie, I have to go." Elsie nodded her head numbly as Lily untied her apron and raced out of the shop, turning to cast an apologetic smile over her shoulder as she raced out the door.

"Woah there!" Elsie heard Amanda's voice and her heart lightened just a little. Lily ducked under Amanda's arm and out of the store. "What was that about?" Amanda asked, walking up to Elsie and giving her a quick hug.

Elsie looked around Pie in the Sky and tried to keep the tears from bubbling up inside her. Empty dishes were piled high on the one or two tables which weren't currently occupied. Only about half of the customers had both their food and their drinks, and several of them were looking at

Elsie expectantly. Then there was the queue which was beginning to back up again just from the couple of minutes that Elsie had been standing there. "Lily had to go," Elsie said quietly. "Some sort of family emergency I think."

Amanda took one look around the shop, and one look at Elsie. She picked up the apron from the counter where Lily had left it and tied it around her waist. It barely fit around Amanda's circumference, but it hugged her curves appealingly. Elsie stared at her for a moment, but Amanda was already moving. "Alright," she said. "You run the till for now and I'll carry out the food and clear the dishes." Elsie nodded numbly once more, but Amanda was already hurrying over to the tables, picking up and deftly carrying a mountain of dishes out the back, where Elsie could hear them being stacked in the dishwasher.

Elsie breathed a sigh of relief and stood behind the till, taking the next person's order. Behind her, Amanda came back out, easily sweeping through the store, collecting dishes, nodding to customers. Then she was down the other end of the counter where the food prep station was, taking the printed dockets as they came out of the little machine so she could heat and plate up the various food orders.

The two worked like a well-oiled machine for an hour or so, stealing smiles whenever they could. Once the rush calmed down, Amanda pecked Elsie on the cheek, and with a gentle dangle of chimes, she was gone.

The rest of the day passed by in a more manageable blur. Elsie was dead on her feet when she got to Lilac House that evening. She pushed open the door and was greeted by the smell of fresh flowers. Smiling, she walked through the house and noticed a vase on the mantelpiece in the lounge, as well as one on the kitchen island. They were overflowing with a fragrant array of jasmine, irises, and daffodils. Elsie beamed. She knew that spring wouldn't really be here for a few more weeks, but it was so uplifting to see the first blossoms. The colourful sight and the beautiful smell were just what she needed after a long week.

She pushed open her bedroom door and saw the a third beautiful bouquet of flowers on her bedside table, and her heart lifted even higher. The note simply said 'hoping to bring some brightness into your day. A x'

Elsie's heart melted as she read the note, and smelt the beautiful flowers. Amanda knew her well, knew how much flowers cheered her. Not only had she helped her in the shop, which had seriously saved Elsie's butt, but the fact that she had then come home and done this for Elsie was—, Elsie's eyes filled with tears. It was incredibly thoughtful of Amanda.

Elsie walked into the kitchen to see Amanda spooning huge ladles of what looked like a creamy pumpkin soup into two large bowls. "Hi!" Amanda said, coming over and kissing Elsie on the lips. "How was your day?" For a second Elsie thought she might have been dreaming. Had she really come home to a house full of flowers, and dinner cooked by this incredible woman? Amanda pulled crusty pieces of bread from the toaster, slathering it with not-butter. Elsie's mouth watered, and she sat down at the kitchen island, grateful and exhausted.

64

Elsie

S oren led the way into an elegant Victorian Villa. The floorboards creaked
as they walked through the long dark hallway. As her eyes adjusted to the
dark, Elsie could see the layout of the house was not dissimilar to Lilac
House, with the living areas downstairs and the bedrooms upstairs. However
this villa was much, much bigger. One wall of the hallway was lined with
portraits of people in black robes. "Is this your family?" Elsie asked, stopping
at a portrait of a woman sitting in a chair, a small child on her knee and one
more standing on either side of her. A slim man with a shock of black hair
stood behind her, his hand on her shoulder. It was clearly one of those school
portraits that everyone got in the 90's, but this one had the air of a royal
family posing for their official portrait.

Soren stopped to look at the photo, and a flash of something Elsie
couldn't discern crossed his face. It was perhaps something unpleasant,
though, she thought. Family trouble? She wondered. Maybe they had that in
common, too.

"Yes," Soren said, after a moment. "That is my mother, and my father." He
pointed to the woman and man in the portrait in turn. "That is my brother
Ebbe, and that is Ivar." Pointing at the two boys on either side of the woman
now.

"And this little baby on your mum's lap is you?" Soren didn't answer, he
just continued on down the hallway. At the far end, the hallway opened into
a grand entrance hall, and Elsie realised they must have entered through the
back door. A narrow table sat against one wall. On it was set a large black
candelabra. A huge mirror in an ornate silver frame above it, reflected the
candlelight back eerily.

About halfway down the long hallway, Soren stopped. "This is my
family's casting room," he said, opening the door and revealing a room lit
entirely in red, though Elsie could see no lights anywhere. Mahogany

bookshelves lined the walls, filled with ancient looking volumes. There was a table covered in candles of all shapes and colours. Another held cauldrons, with rows and rows of gleaming vials lined up neatly behind it. The vials weren't exactly every colour of the rainbow, but there were plenty of virulent, almost fluorescent greens, several in brilliant shades of yellow and orange, one or two in a deep indigo, and disconcertingly, vial upon vial in the dark red shade of blood.

At the front of the room stood an altar. Elsie felt a shiver run down her spine, though she didn't know if it was from excitement or something else. The room had the distinct feel of magic to it. The hairs on her arms prickled, and she felt as if there was electricity running through her veins. Soren turned back and smiled that brilliant smile at her. "Shall we begin by looking through some of the books of spells?" He waved a hand, summoning two huge black books over from the bookshelves onto one of the workbenches in the middle of the room.

"Is that a Book of Shadows?" Elsie asked, spotting the symbols on the front of the first book.

"It is, this book has been passed down from my great, great grandfather through the Dahl family, and now it rests with us." Soren opened the book, and without touching it, turned the pages slowly.

"See anything you would like to try?" He asked Elsie.

Elsie stared, enraptured, as Soren turned the pages. There were spells of enchantment, spells for travel, spells for intellect, potions to make someone grow taller, to erase a memory, and to exert influence. About two-thirds of the way through the book, Elsie held up her hand. Soren stopped turning the pages, and Elsie peered at the double page spread. "A spell to make others like you,' she read in gentle wonder. "Does this really work?"

Soren looked at her analytically. Elsie had the feeling he was considering her, weighing her up, or perhaps trying to understand something about her. After a moment, his look of intense curiosity was replaced by a broad, clear smile. "Shall we try it and find out?" He asked.

Elsie swallowed. She didn't use spells on other people, ever. She felt that that was clearly on the wrong side of consent. Stamping down the pang of guilt she felt that Soren had wiped those people's memories, Elsie looked at the page with growing interest. This spell was cast on yourself, to make *you* more appealing to another. That would be OK, surely? Elsie cast spells on herself all the time.

The face of Reginald Arnold drifted before her eyes. Even if the spell doesn't make him like me, it would be nice if he could stop disliking me quite so actively. "Ok," she said eventually, and Soren's smile, if possible, grew even wider.

"Ok!" He clapped his hands like a happy toddler. "Go and choose a cauldron, and I'll start gathering the ingredients." He wandered over to the table piled with vials and began selecting a few, which he floated over to the table on which the Book of Shadows still rested. Elsie, still somewhat in awe of this magical haven, walked over to the corner in which the cauldrons were kept. There was a collection of cauldrons in all possible sizes and shapes, made from every material imaginable. From gleaming new copper cauldrons, to an ancient black one which might genuinely have been used in the days of the witch hunts. Elsie tried not to envy Soren for the strong magical familial connections he clearly had.

After several moments of contemplation, and a lot of awe, Elsie selected a small, slightly worn copper cauldron, and levitated it over to the work bench. Soren had assembled an array of glowing vials and several bunches of dried herbs. There was also some twine, a few fresh leaves, and what looked suspiciously like a rabbit's foot. Elsie swallowed again. Soren, oblivious to her discomfort, began reading out the instructions for the spell. "First, we take the ambelicustus and pour it into the cauldron while it is still cold." He handed Elsie an amber coloured fluid, and she poured it gently into the cauldron. "Then we sprinkle in a little rosemary, and a shake of sage." He duly passed the ingredients to Elsie, who poured them in also. "Now slowly warm the cauldron, stirring the mixture anti-clockwise, and calling forth the image of the person whom you seek to influence." He said.

"I'm not so sure about this," Elsie said, that pang of discomfort evident in her chest again.

"Elsie," Soren said, in a kind, patient tone. "What is it that you are worried about?"

"It's my code. I don't think using magic on other people without their agreement is ethical." She said, glancing into his ice-blue eyes. She hated disappointing him, but this was important.

Soren looked thoughtful for a moment. "Tell me, Elsie," he said. "Do you ever smile brightly at someone when they come into your shop?"

"Of course I do," Elsie said.

"And why is that?"

"Because I want them to feel welcome," Elsie said,

"And do you arrange your shop in a particular way so that it looks pretty and appealing to people who are walking by?"

"Well, yes," she admitted.

Soren nodded again. "And do you ever bake cookies or other delicious baked goods, and time it so that the smell of those delicacies will be wafting outside just at the time the townsfolk are walking to work, or on their way home?"

"Yes, of course I do," Elsie said. "That's just good marketing."

"It is," Soren agreed. "But it is also you using your special skills to influence people in order to get something that you want."

Elsie made a face, but Soren continued. "You're not using your skills for evil, you're just using them to encourage people—, to help tip them over that last edge from thinking about stepping inside, to coming in and buying that cookie or slice of pie. It's the same with this. You're not using your magic to try to make people obey your every whim, you're just using your skills to encourage them to like you a bit more." Soren shrugged, "It doesn't seem very different to me."

He made a good point, Elsie thought. She looked back at the Book of Shadows and another shiver of excitement ran down her spine as she thought about getting to do magic from a book that must be over a century old, passed down through generations of witches. "OK," she said after a moment. "You're right. It's not like I'm going to use the spell for evil, just to encourage Reginald to be a little less rude!".

Soren smiled brightly at her. "Exactly," he said, turning back to the book. "What could be wrong with that?"

65

Amanda

A manda woke at 6 without an alarm. She was curled around Elsie's slim frame, and a smile spread across her face as she looked at her. Elsie's hair was down, spread in a long curtain down one side of her beautiful face. Her little button nose wriggled ever so slightly now and then. Amanda imagined her dreaming she was a top chef, wafting the smells of her delicious meals into her nostrils as she stirred pots and sautéed vegetables. She brushed the hair off Elsie's face gently, and planted a soft kiss on her forehead, before sliding out of bed, pulling on yesterday's clothes from the floor, and heading out to get ready for work.

H er postie run flew past in a blur. Amanda spent the day daydreaming about how nice it was to be with Elsie. Amanda had had a couple of girlfriends in the past, but she tended to pick people who didn't treat her particularly well. When things ended so badly with Jo, a feisty truck driver Amanda had dated for about six months before finding out that she was still seeing her ex, Amanda decided that relationships weren't really for her. The risk of heartache wasn't worth it in her mind. She was surprised by how comfortable she felt with Elsie, given she hadn't known her all that long.

As she was arriving home, Elsie messaged to say she was going spell casting with Soren after work, but that she would be home for dinner. Amanda was trying very hard not to be jealous of Soren. She knew Elsie needed to practise her magic, and that Soren, a literal magic scholar, was best-placed to teach her. Something about the man still grated on Amanda, though she figured that was just jealousy that someone so attractive was spending time with Elsie. Someone who could understand Elsie's witchcraft in a way that Amanda never could.

To distract herself, Amanda attempted to make dinner. She had learned a few dishes from Elsie, but today she thought she would try something new. She sautéed onions and spices in a pan, and slowly added chickpeas, vegetables, and more tinned tomatoes than she thought was reasonable. She triple-checked the recipe, and was pretty sure that she had things right, even if the curry was a rather obnoxious shade of red. Satisfied that the curry would do best to simmer until Elsie got home, Amanda settled down in the lounge with Philo.

By 8, she hadn't heard from Elsie, and Amanda was starving. She spooned some food into a bowl and was surprised by how lonely she felt without Elsie's presence. Normally a lover of time to herself, Amanda was growing used to having Elsie around. At 10 o'clock, Elsie messaged to apologise for losing track of time. She said that she and Soren were almost finished with a particularly difficult potion they were making, but Amanda couldn't keep her eyes open any longer. Climbing the stairs, she fell into bed, and dreamed of Elsie and Soren flying happily on a broomstick together, Elsie leaning into Soren's arms.

66

Elsie

Reginald hadn't been into the Pie in the Sky for a few days, apparently leaving Elsie alone while his sister was under the weather. The following day, however, he charged into Pie in the Sky with a look which could only mean trouble across his face.

Reginald stepped inside, giving a disdainful look around the shop before clearing his throat loudly, gaining the attention of everyone inside. "As I'm sure you are all aware, my sister Beth has been rather unwell recently. We are still determining the cause of this illness." With this, he cast a distrustful glance at Elsie, as if she had somehow been involved in Beth's sickness! Old people in the winter got sick, that's just what happened. Elsie fumed internally.

Reginald was still talking to the shop at large. "However, Beth's Bakehouse is once again open for business, so you may now return to the town's *original*—" Reginald seemed to infuse that single word with an incredible amount of spite and judgement—, "bakery."

Customers shuffled to their feet, retreating out under Reginald's steely gaze. "Reginald," Elsie said, walking over to him and plastering what she hoped was a friendly but mildly threatening smile. "May I ask that you not come into my shop just to cause trouble?" Reginald huffed loudly, but Elsie wasn't scared of him anymore, not after standing up to him at the community hall. She continued, "Kindly either buy something, or leave."

Reginald looked like he was going to say something, but his face transformed. Elsie watched in amazement as his angry features softened. He smiled amiably at her and inclined his head. "Fair enough, Ms. Hazelwood," he said. "I apologise. That was rather abrupt of me."

Elsie stared at Reginald in amazement. Then slowly, realisation spread over her. For the last few days, she had daubed a couple of drops of the spell she and Soren had made on her wrists and neck as she got ready each morning. She had kind of gotten into the habit of it, even though she hadn't actually seen what the effects of it would be because Reginald had been busy taking care of his sister. Now, it seemed, the spell was working.

She stared in astonishment as Reginald walked over to the counter and began surveying her array of cakes and pies. "These all look very good," he said, leaning over to see inside the cabinet better. "Perhaps I shall take a selection into the office." Elsie walked, half-dazed, behind the counter, and loaded a takeaway box full of several cupcakes, slices of cakes, tartlets, and eclairs. The chimes above the door rang, and she looked up to see Amanda walking in, eyeing Reginald like she was ready for a fight. She paused, hovering by the door as she saw Elsie ringing up the items for him.

"Thank you very much Reginald, have a nice day," Elsie said, and the old man actually tipped his hat to her on his way out!

Amanda's face was a picture of confusion as she watched him leave, a cake box under one arm. "That was weird," she said. "What do you think has gotten into him?"

Elsie blanched. She knew Reginald's interactions with her today were to do with the potion she and Soren had brewed. With Amanda standing in front of her looking so innocent, Elsie felt shame bubble up within her, and she couldn't meet Amanda's eye.

Amanda must have picked up that something was wrong, because Elsie could see her tilting her head to one side, appraising her. "What?" Amanda said simply.,

"Um," Elsie began. Why was she feeling so uncomfortable about this? She had agreed with Soren's analysis when he talked to her about the spell. Plus, it was nothing short of amazing the difference that it had made to how Reginald treated her! Even so, guilt roiled in her stomach, and she felt like her chest was full of rocks. Amanda was really looking at her now, a worried look on her face. Looking around the shop to make sure nobody was listening, Elsie took a deep breath and then blurted out in a whisper, "Soren and I might have cast a spell to make me more...palatable...to him?" Her voice went up at the end like this was a question, not a statement of what she had, in fact, definitely done.

Amanda looked aghast. "You did *what*?"

"It was just a little harmless one," Elsie squeaked.

"What happened to 'I don't do magic without the consent of the other person'?" Amanda asked, her face a mask of fury and hurt.

"I didn't cast the spell on *him*," Elsie said desperately., "I cast it on *me*."

"Sounds like semantics," Amanda said, turning on her heel. "I have to get to the gardens." She said, without further ceremony. "See you later."

And with that, she was gone.

Elsie felt like there was a wrecking ball made of nails hammering against the insides of her stomach. She stared at the door, the chimes still jangling angrily in response to Amanda's not quite slam of the door.

Had it really been that bad? She knew she wasn't all that keen on casting spells on other people, but it was so nice having Reginald treat her like a human being, not a problem, for once. She was allowed to want people to like her. She wasn't being mean or manipulative, she wasn't using her powers for evil. The man had bought cake for heaven's sake. It wasn't exactly earth shattering. Still, she couldn't get the look on Amanda's face out of her mind.

67

Amanda

The Community Garden wasn't what you might call buzzing with people, but it was, Amanda reflected, more popular than she had initially expected. Mrs Higgs and her son had come along in support, and Elsie had been there as often as she could be. Truth be told, Elsie's support was more moral than practical, but Amanda had appreciated it, anyway. There was still plenty of time for Elsie to learn actual gardening skills. Thus far, the woman seemed to kill plants just by looking at them.

Amanda's chest tightened as she thought about Elsie. She was in bed by the time Elsie got home last night, and had gone to work before Elsie was up this morning. Deep down, Amanda knew she had avoided Elsie. She knew she should have handled things better, should have tried to talk to Elsie about what was going on and how she was feeling. Even the idea of it made her feel sick. Amanda wasn't used to talking about her feelings. It just wasn't the done thing. Sure, when her mum had been around, Amanda had sometimes run to her with a scraped knee or a bleeding toe, but nobody in her family had ever exactly been forthcoming about their feelings. Heck, the first Amanda had known her mum was unhappy was when her dad had come downstairs one morning with a note in his hand saying that Christine had left them, gone in the middle of the night, no phone number or forwarding address.

Amanda had cried, knowing that with her mother gone, Theo would only get worse. Her dad had simply slapped her on the back and said, "Chin up, kid. She'll be 'right," as he walked out the kitchen door without a backward glance. Amanda had been fending for herself ever since that day.

Amanda would have to learn to talk though, if she wanted there to be any hope of something with Elsie. It was unfair for her to have run out on Elsie like she had. She knew that. But she had been scared. She was still scared. Her feelings for the woman were getting stronger every day, and the idea that

Elsie wasn't really who she said she was terrified Amanda. She didn't have room for morally grey people in her life.

Regardless, Amanda decided she needed to air things out with Elsie. She owed the woman the benefit of the doubt.

On top of her worries about Elsie, thoughts of the dark magic which seemed to be blighting the earth in Glen Haven invaded Amanda's mind. Phoebe had told Elsie that although normys couldn't use magic, thinking and feeling positive thoughts as they planted would help give the new plants the best chance against the dark magic. Despite her concerns, Amanda dragged her mind back to the present, determined to sow positive energy into the soil.

Today, they were going to be planting! They had spent a lot of time clearing and tilling and it was finally time for the fun bit: putting new things into the ground and helping them to grow. The Higgs's had kindly brought over a few bags of extra fertiliser from their shop, and Amanda assembled the troops. Today, they would plant vegetables, herbs, and even a few flowers for the spring. The stock from Higgs' Twiggs hadn't been expansive, but Amanda had purchased broccoli, kale, cabbage, leek, and parsnip, as well as a few hardy herbs, including sage, rosemary and mint.

She handed these out to Sam, Sally, Samantha, and Lily, who got to work digging in the freshly tilled dirt, sprinkling the seeds in carefully, covering them back over as Amanda instructed, and sprinkling just a touch of water on top. The vegetables would need an extra layer of protection over them to see them through the worst of the winter, but Amanda could handle that once the seeds were in. On the far corner where the flowerbeds would be, Murray and Wanda stood chatting amiably with some of the other yoga folk. They would be planting sturdy flowers: pansies, snowdrops, and cyclamen. There would also be jasmine and lavender to encourage bees to visit. Sam had also secured a separate patch, which he would use to grow vegetables for the pub. Amanda was confident that the whole town would get behind the cause to ensure the Tui Tavern never ran out of its famous beer battered fries.

As the day went on, more people came out to help. It was one of those winter mornings which promised that spring was just around the corner. The air was bitingly cold, but the sky was a pale, forget-me-not blue, and although Amanda could see her breath when she got up this morning, there was a hint of warmth in the sun on her back as she worked. Several of the Church-going families came along after the service, and Amanda recognised others from her postie run.

She did the rounds, keeping an eye on each group and checking in if they needed any help. As she neared Sally, Samantha, and Lily, Amanda saw Lily hold her palm to the dirt and close her eyes. That was odd, Amanda thought. Lily looked down at the dirt, then said something to the other two and walked briskly away.

Approaching, Amanda asked Sally and Samantha where Lily had gone. "Oh, she said something urgent had come up, and she had to go," Sally said, barely glancing up at Amanda, as she concentrated on sprinkling just the right number of seeds in the gap she had made with the edge of her hand. Amanda glanced over at the patch Lily had been working on and saw something shiny. Getting closer, she strained to see what was sparkling in the winter sunlight. As she did, her whole body stiffened. Where Lily had placed her hands, the ground was covered with ice.

68

Elsie

Elsie strode towards the strong, curvaceous woman directing the proceedings in the garden. Her heart was hammering, and her stomach was full of butterflies. Amanda looked over and met her eye. She gestured for them to speak over in a quieter corner of the garden. When Amanda turned and faced Elsie, she took a deep breath and spoke before she could overthink this too much. "I'm sorry," she said, and then paused. Amanda had spoken the words at the same time. They stared at each other for a moment, recalibrating.

"I'm sorry for not talking to you when I was upset. That was childish of me," Amanda said, looking at the floor, her hands twisting around each other. Relief flooded through Elsie. She had known Amanda was flighty, and a part of her was worried that their relationship was over before it had even really started.

"It was," Elsie said, "But I should have been more considerate to you. I know you don't like Soren, but -,"

"I don't like him, you're right," Amanda cut her off, "I don't trust him. I think he's a slime ball, and I don't think he's a very good person." Elsie was going to interrupt, but Amanda held up her hand. "I'm telling you, I have a bad feeling about him. But I'm not your keeper, and nor do I want to be. I am telling you now that he has nefarious intentions. I don't trust him, but I do trust you. I know you won't cheat on me, or at least, I hope you won't, and I trust you to tell me if your feelings for me—," she swallowed hard—, "or him, change."

"Amanda, I—," Elsie's heart ached. She could never feel that way about Soren. And her feelings for Amanda were growing every day. "I'm crazy about you. With the dark magic, and a new witch friend, I'm sorry I got a bit caught up in everything." She stepped closer and was thrilled when Amanda wrapped her arms around her.

"Me too," Amanda said, pulling Elsie in closer and planting a kiss atop her head. "I didn't mean to get all intense. He's this super hot guy. He's got magical powers just like you. He's so stylish and put together. Truth be told, I was probably jealous, as well as upset with you."

Elsie looked up into Amanda's eyes and their lips met. "I'm mad about you, Amanda," she said, pulling back, face serious. "I'm sorry I gave you any reason to doubt that."

And then Amanda had swept Elsie off her feet and was spinning her around. Elsie laughed, and they kissed, deeper this time, as Amanda placed her back on the ground. Amanda smelled like sandalwood and earth, and Elsie wanted to wrap herself in the woman like a blanket.

"I missed you," Amanda said.

"We live in the same house!" Elsie chided. But her tummy did a little flip, and she bumped her nose to Amanda's. "I missed you too."

Elsie interlaced their fingers, kissing each of Amanda's fingers in turn. In this moment, she felt like everything was right with the world. Then a shadow fell across Amanda's face. "What's wrong?"

Amanda shook her head. "not here," she said quietly. "I'll see you tonight, at home?" Elsie nodded, realising now Amanda was there, Lilac House really did feel like home.

Amanda placed one more gentle kiss to her lips, before turning back towards her troops. Elsie watched her retreating form and knew that a part of her own heart had gone with her.

69

Amanda

Lying in bed with Elsie cradled between her arms, Amanda felt the need to say something. "Sorry for going off without talking to you," she began, stroking a pattern delicately up and down Elsie's arm. "I was taken aback and needed some time to process. I shouldn't have gone off in a huff, though. I'll try not to do that in the future."

Elsie spun to face her, nuzzling Amanda's nose with her own, and gently kissing Amanda's lips. "Sorry for being so defensive. Soren and I made the potion a while back, and that's the first time I've seen Reginald since we made it. I had kind of forgotten about it, but honestly, it was so nice. He stormed into the shop and basically tried to boot everyone out."

Amanda groaned, "He didn't?" she said, rubbing a hand roughly across her face, "what a ..."

"My thoughts exactly," Elsie said, nipping Amanda's bottom lip gently between her teeth. A spark fizzed down Amanda's body. "But then the spell seemed to work, and all of a sudden he was treating me decently, talking to me like I was a real human-being and respecting that Pie in the Sky is my workplace. It was so nice having him actually recognise that his behaviour wasn't ok. Then when you criticised me for it it felt like you were telling me you thought I deserved to be treated badly, even when I had a way to stop it."

Amanda stroked Elsie's hair and planted a kiss gently on top of her head. "I didn't in any way mean to imply that you should let him walk all over you." Amanda hated the way Reginald had spoken to Elsie. She had been tempted to take him outside and deal with him herself on more than one occasion. "I was just taken off-guard. You had been so clear with me that you would never use magic on someone without their consent, and there you were, using magic on Reginald and acting like it's no big deal. I have too many shady people in my past to be OK with people shifting moral grounds on the fly."

Elsie's hands slid up and down Amanda's back, her voice soft as her touch. "I'm sorry. I should have explained myself so much better. I think I was maybe feeling a little surprised myself, and then I heard your concerns as being about me not being worth treating well, not a curiosity about how I had changed my mind. It felt a bit controlling."

Panic flared in Amanda. "I'm sorry, that was never, ever my intention." She still felt uncomfortable that Elsie had used her magic to influence someone else, even if she had technically used the magic on herself, not Reginald. But she would never want Elsie to feel like she was trying to control her.

She knew that Elsie's relationship with Reginald was especially challenging. She also thought she knew Elsie. She was still the kind, selfless woman who had invited Amanda to stay on that fateful day at the beginning of autumn.

"I know, " Elsie said, slipping her hands around Amanda's neck and kissing her on the lips. Elsie's lips were warm, and her sweet scent lit up Amanda's senses.

"For the record," Amanda said, slipping her tongue into Elsie's mouth and kissing her more passionately. "I think you deserve to be treated very, *very* well."

70

Elsie

The Pie in the Sky was quiet again the next day, and Elsie got home to find a letter from the landlord, saying that the rent for the shop would be put up the following month. Her mood was low as she contemplated the future of her little shop. On top of that, Amanda had filled her in on the icy ground where Lily had been working at the community gardens earlier in the week. Elsie was usually a pretty optimistic person, but it was hard to feel hopeful at the moment.

After dinner, a gardener's pie which Amanda had made and which was surprisingly good, despite the mashed potatoes being a little crisped on top, they moved into the lounge and curled up on the couch together. Elsie squeezed comfortably between Philo and Amanda. *At least I have these two*, she thought, taking a moment to appreciate the warmth of her Familiar and her girlfriend. The word still sent a shiver of happiness down Elsie's spine whenever she thought about it. Amanda was a bright spark in an otherwise dark time.

They sat in silent contemplation for a while, before eventually Amanda turned to Elsie, a look of determination on her Rhadamanthine features.

"It's student night at Flicks tonight."

Elsie raised an eyebrow at her. "We're not students."

"No, but Lily is."

Elsie sat up, "You want to follow her?"

"We know she studies film, and I heard her say she goes to Flicks at least once a week. Seems like a pretty good bet that she'll be there. We could just, keep an eye on her? See if we can figure out what she's doing?" Amanda's hand was warm around Elsie's cold one. "Research doesn't seem to be getting us very far. Maybe it's time we try a more direct approach."

Research had revealed a little. There had been a freak blizzard in Glen Haven in 1913, and before that the trees had been dying, animals went missing, and so on. From what they could piece together from various news articles and googling the town's history, there was a massive blizzard in which many animals and plants died, not to mention at least fifteen of Glen Haven's small human population. After the winter had passed though, the newspapers spoke of the warmest September on record, and the spring was reported to be one of the most prosperous in over fifty years.

It seemed relevant, but Elsie was inclined to agree. It was time to do something practical and see what they could discover. They checked the screening times online, and there was a film starting in half an hour. Elsie smelt of coffee and body odour, so she dragged herself through the shower, emerging fifteen minutes later clean, dressed in dark jeans, brown ankle boots and a floaty white t-shirt. She grabbed a scarf and her tan trench coat from the door on the way out, feeling much more like herself.

71

Amanda

Amanda had never seen someone look so good in a simple pair of jeans and t-shirt. Then again, Amanda had never met anyone quite like Elsie before. Amanda held the door for her, momentarily feeling like they were going on a date, rather than a witch stakeout. Philo had been given a Kong, which Amanda had learned by now was a very sturdy dog toy designed for canines with the toughest of teeth, filled with peanut butter. Elsie assured the pup that they would be back soon, but he simply wagged his tail and stuck his nose as far as he could in the chew toy. Amanda couldn't read his mind, but she was pretty sure he was happy enough to one left alone for a little while.

The movie was in French, and Amanda had a time trying to keep up with the subtitles and the action simultaneously. After a while she got the hang of it, and it was a rather endearing film about two sisters who were separated at birth but found each other through a series of unexpected events, and a lot of courage. Amanda was surprised to find herself wiping a tear from her eye as the sisters embraced at the end, and Elsie picked up her hand, kissing her palm gently.

Before Amanda had time to process her feelings, she spotted a shock of bright purple hair leaving out the front entrance to the theatre. Nudging Elsie, she rose, and the two quietly exited the theatre behind her.

Lily checked her watch, and then hugged her friend goodbye before walking down the street, hood up, hands stuffed in her pockets. As they rounded a corner, they saw Lily speed up. Silently, Amanda and Elsie increased their speed. They followed at a distance, watching as she raced along the street, and then turned down another. After a while, they reached another fork in the road, but Lily was nowhere to be seen. Amanda looked left and right, searching for anything that might indicate where she had gone, but there was nothing! They were about to turn around and head back, when overhead they saw a flash of blue light, and Elsie cried out, clutching her chest in pain. Somewhere in the distance, Amanda heard another cry of pain, though human or animal she couldn't be sure.

She rushed to Elsie's side, heart hammering as she gently lowered her to the ground. "What happened?" Amanda asked, dread and bile rising in her stomach.

"I don't know," Elsie said, breathing hard. "But someone just used some very bad magic."

"OK, time to go home." Amanda said, "can you stand up?"

Elsie shook her head. "We can't go home yet," she said, her face still white.

"Elsie, you look like a ghost. You need to get home and rest, maybe get some sugar in you or something." Amanda knew she hadn't directly caused Elsie's pain, but she couldn't help but feel responsible. "Following Lily was a terrible idea. Let's get home and regroup."

Elsie remained on the ground, her breathing slowly coming back to normal. "Not yet. We need to see what she did."

"That sounds like a terrible idea," Amanda said again, watching with growing concern as Elsie hauled herself to her feet and began walking in the direction the sound had come from. Elsie kept walking, and Amanda sighed, knowing her protestations were falling on deaf ears. They walked for another few minutes, Elsie seemingly following the scent of something, almost like a magical trail. Amanda raised an eyebrow when Elsie climbed a stile and began walking through a field, but one look at Elsie's determined face told her that arguing would be futile.

The ground was sodden, and Elsie waved a hand at their shoes. Amanda noticed that her feet didn't sink into the mud so much anymore, and was surprised to see her shoes remained clean despite the slushiness of the field. A few metres ahead of her, Elsie stopped. Amanda could see the woman's back stiffen as she looked down at the ground. Hurrying over to stand beside her, a small sound escaped Amanda's lips. There, on the ground in front of them, lying in the mud, was a dead calf. Elsie knelt next to the creature and felt it, tears streaming down her eyes. "She's icy cold," she whispered, voice thick with tears. She looked up at Amanda and her eyes blazed. "This was dark magic. Probably by a Dark Ice Witch" she said. Amanda could feel the sadness and anger coming off her, and knelt to the ground, cradling Elsie in her arms. Her heart ached for the calf, and for the pain Elsie was in. Amanda realised that she would do anything not to have Elsie feel this kind of pain again. A voice in her head whispered that you protect those you love. That word floated around Amanda's mind while they stood huddled in the rain.

After several minutes, Elsie stood, sniffling. "There's nothing we can do for her," she said, tears still running down her sharp cheekbones. "But I will figure out who did this. This cannot go on." Amanda hadn't heard Elsie sound so angry before. They could work out a plan soon. For now, she took Elsie's hand, and in silence, they made their way home.

72

Elsie

E lsie had called Phoebe the moment she got in. Her cousin's voice was groggy and irritated when she answered the phone, but at the tears in Elsie's voice, she came to quickly. Elsie explained what had happened, with Phoebe on speakerphone, so Amanda could hear the conversation too.

"It sounds like whoever it is is drawing the energy from the earth, the plants, and even the animals." Phoebe said, when Elsie updated her.

"They can do that?"

"Dark witches can. Though you would have to be very powerful."

Elsie wondered if Lily would be powerful enough for something like that. Then again, she remembered the amulet the woman wore. For all Elsie knew, Lily could be some kind of dark prodigy.

"I think it's time to call the Witch's Council." Phoebe said.

T he Witch's Council was an unknown commodity. Elsie had learned about it a little when she was at school, but, rather than the clear (if messy) structures of the New Zealand Government, the Witch's Council was mysterious to say the least. Elsie filled a cauldron with clear water, and trawled sage across its surface, whispering the words she had been taught as a child. The surface of the water turned green, then blue, then purple, before becoming an inky black that reflected Elsie's image back to herself. A few moments later, a face appeared in the water. The face was androgynous, with no distinguishable features. It was utterly stunning, and yet at the same time so beautiful that if pressed, all that Elsie would be able to say to describe it would be that its features were plain and symmetrical. Before she had time to ponder this further, the face spoke. "Who summons the Witch's Council?" Elsie swallowed, "I, Elsie," she coughed again, having managed little more than a squeak the first time around. The mystery face was apparently used to this. It waited impassively as Elsie tried again. "I, Elsie Hazelwood, first born of Huan and Nancy Hazelwood, seek consult with the Witch's Council."

"Speak, Witch Hazelwood," the voice said.

"There is dark magic in our town. We believe that someone is drawing the energy from the earth and its creatures in an attempt to gain more power."

The visage's expression clouded, and Elsie knew that it was displeased, despite no obvious change to its face. "I see," the face said slowly. It turned to the side, as if listening. There was what Elsie could only assume was a discussion with others she couldn't see, before eventually the face turned back to her. "Members of the Witch's Council are nearby. They were aware of some of the events you have described." Elsie took this to mean that the Witch's Council hadn't figured out some of what she and Amanda had discovered. "Thank you for informing us." Then the cauldron went black again.

Elsie stared, open-mouthed. That was it? No 'we're on our way to interrogate everyone in town now?' No 'here's how to defend yourself if anything happens?' Well, a fat lot of use that was, then. Elsie texted Phoebe an update, and received an eyeball emoji back. A few minutes later, Phoebe called.

"Hello?"

"You've done everything you can," her cousin's voice came through the phone without a greeting. "You need to leave it now. The Witch's Council has been informed. It's not your place to try to mess with something this big. Just keep your head down and stay out of trouble, OK?"

Elsie made to argue, but her cousin cut her off, "I mean it, whatever is causing those trees to die, not to mention the animal—," Elsie could hear the swallowed down tears in her cousin's voice. Phoebe had a special connection to animals, and Elsie knew the idea of anyone hurting innocent beings would be horrifying to Phoebe. "—is seriously bad news. By yourself, you have no chance against something like that. You said last time this happened there was a big storm and then everything went back to normal. Just let things take their course and hopefully it'll all be over soon."

"But—,"

"No buts. I'm serious Else. This is above either of our pay grades."

Elsie sighed. She knew her cousin was right, but the idea of standing by and doing nothing was hard to swallow. At least Beltane was just around the corner, she reasoned, so this should all be over soon.

Amanda was furious when Elsie told her what the Witch's Council had said, and Phoebe's response. Elsie had thought she would put up a fight, but all three women were out of ideas. Eventually they resolved to keep an eye on things, and if anything else big happened, Elsie would call the Council again and demand they come and help. Elsie went to bed anxious and drained. She dreamed all night of blue flashes of light and incredible pain.

73

Elsie

Elsie was distracted for the next week. Pie in the Sky was still quiet. On the upside, there had been no more dark magic. She was grateful for the respite, but a nagging worry at the back of her mind told her the dark magic was building to something bigger.

She wondered again if she should tell Soren of her suspicions. He was a teacher, and his family was one of the founders of Glen Haven. He might know more than they did. Amanda was still nervous about letting him in though, so for now, Elsie decided that she could sit tight.

The shop was quiet, so she sent Lily home early. She decided to experiment with some new flavours to keep her mind off things. She was in a daydream, mixing batter out the back, when a vial of lurid orange powder was waved in front of her face. "What's this?" She asked, turning to see Soren standing behind her, a cheeky grin on his face.

"Just a little something I whipped up for you." Soren said, his white teeth flashing brilliantly.

Elsie's stomach fluttered involuntarily. It was so kind of Soren to bring her a gift. "What does it do?" She asked, taking the vial and holding it up to inspect.

"It will encourage customers to come back to your shop," he said. "Just blow it in the wind outside your shop, and anyone who walks past will be enticed inside to buy some of your delicious baking."

"But that's terrible!" Elsie said, handing the vial back to Soren and stepping away. "I told you, I don't want to use magic on other people. It's not in my code."

Soren leaned on the workbench nonchalantly. "What is this code you speak of?" He asked, looking curiously at her. "You say that you are driven by this code, but what purpose does it serve?"

"It keeps me on the right path," Elsie replied. Everyone in her family had a code that they developed over time. Many of the lessons or guidelines in Elsie's code had been passed down from one generation to the next. Some she knew had come from her father, some from her grandmother, but others had come from her great great aunties and ancestors from long ago. Whenever a witch in her family turned twenty-one, they received a scroll from each of their parents, complete with notations of who each element of the code had come from. They would then make their own code, which would guide them in their decisions, and especially in their witchcraft, for the rest of their life.

Even though Elsie's mum wasn't a witch, she had contributed her own scroll, and several of her suggested items made their way into Elsie's chosen code. Elsie's code included consent to all receivers and users of her magic (with the caveat that if it was a purely innocuous, small spell, such as a spell for good luck, then this was not always needed), that she would always strive to do what was right, considering others and herself as deserving of love and compassion, and last year Elsie had added to her code that she should make the most of opportunities, as life was short. That had been added after her dad had died so suddenly.

Elsie knew that her father had been a kind and generous man, and that he had lived a good life. She also knew, though, that there had been plenty of things he had put off doing because they were hard or scary, or because he thought he would have time later. He and her mother had once planned a train trip across the length of Australia, but when his sister got sick, they canceled the train ticket so he could look after her. Fortunately, auntie Tracy recovered, but her dad never got around to re-booking that train trip. Elsie didn't want to have regrets like that.

The final item of the code was to treat all beings with respect and love; that had been on her mum's list, and as soon as Elsie read it, she knew that was something she would aspire to for the rest of her life.

Of course, you could always change or update your code. Many witches even chose to review their code at the beginning of every spring, as they thought of their intentions and their aspirations for the coming year. However, most witches stuck pretty closely to their original codes, making only small adjustments as they grew wiser and more experienced. How would influencing people to come into her shop align with her code?

Soren was still looking at her expectantly, so she explained as best she could.

"That sounds pretty... restrictive," Soren said, raising his eyebrows at her seductively. "What about things like having fun, making the most of your skills and abilities? Using what you have to get along?'"

Elsie's face must have shown her displeasure at what Soren had just said, because he said, "OK, I understand. You want to be a good person, I can see that. You are kind and intelligent, and," Elsie felt her cheeks flush, "you obviously want to leave a good mark on the world." Elsie nodded. "Tell me though, is it fair that that angry man, Mr Arnold, scared your customers away?"

Elsie's anger flared inside her, "no!" she said hotly. Her shop had been practically empty since Reginald had come in and all but threatened her customers away again. Elsie might have stood up to the man, with a little magical help, but the customers in her shop had gone before they saw Reginald change his tune. Since Amanda had been so upset about Elsie using the potion, she hadn't used it since, and Reginald had already been into the store twice more this week, scaring away several more of the customers.

"It strikes me that if that Arnold man is using his power and influence to unfairly scare people away from the shop, it would be reasonable for you to use the resources at your disposal to bring them back. After all, you would only be reinstating the status quo."

Elsie had to admit he made a good point, and the letter advising of the increased rent on the shop was burned into her brain like a brand. "They can still make their own decisions? It's not brainwashing them or anything like that?" She asked anxiously.

"They can still make their own decisions. All it will do is compel them to come inside the store," Soren confirmed, leaning over to peck Elsie on the cheek before striding away. She watched his retreating back with interest. This man certainly challenged her and made her think in new and different ways. There was a lot to be said for that. Popping the vial down next to her batter, she resumed her baking, pondering Soren's words.

Amanda walked into the kitchen, pulling her hair into a ponytail and coming over to where Elsie had set out an array of aluminium bowls with various ingredients in each. She gave Elsie a peck on the cheek, and then, noticing the vial, picked it up and sniffed it curiously.

"Careful," Elsie said, grabbing the bottle from Amanda's hands and replacing the cork carefully.

"Why? Is it really expensive or something? It looks like ground rust."

Elsie felt a red flush creeping up her neck and into her cheeks. "It's not expensive exactly," she said evasively. "But it is hard to come by."

"In what way?" Amanda asked," studying Elsie.

"It's a potion," Elsie said, not wanting to admit to Amanda something that she knew would upset her, but also not wanting to lie.

Amanda looked at her in confusion. "What kind of potion?" she asked.

Elsie let out a long breath. "It's a potion to encourage people to come back to the shop." She said, forcing herself to look into Amanda's eyes, even though she really didn't want to.

"What?" Amanda said the word so quietly Elsie almost didn't hear her. "Elsie, what are you doing? What happened to not using magic on people without their consent?"

"It's just a little spell," Elsie said, the flush in her cheeks growing. "I have to look after myself, Amanda, and this is just another way that I can use my talents to encourage people to come back."

"But you're not encouraging them to do anything," Amanda said, her face white. "You're making them. You are literally bewitching them into doing your will. How can you be ok with that?"

Elsie's heart fell at Amanda's words. It really wasn't that big a deal. "I just want them to come back." She said to the floor.

"And they will, because your food is good, not because you cast some spell on them." Amanda hadn't raised her voice, but Elsie could feel the heat in her words.

"You wouldn't understand," she said. "You don't care if people like you. You're so determined to put up walls that you wouldn't let people in even if they tried. Excuse me for not having a heart of granite." Even as she said it, Elsie regretted the words. She wanted to take them back, wanted to tell

Amanda that she was sorry, she didn't mean it, and she knew Amanda had a heart of gold. But she didn't.

Amanda stood there, mouth open like a goldfish, for several long moments. "You're right," she said eventually. "I don't understand."

74

Amanda

Every instinct in Amanda's body was telling her to run, but she tried to engage her brain. She took three deep breaths and then looked at Elsie calmly. "I have seen people be corrupted by people who claim to be their friends. It's gradual, but if you don't stop it, you'll end up in all kinds of trouble."

"I'm so, so sorry that happened to you,." Elsie said, her voice soft and full of concern. "But just because it happened to you doesn't mean that it's going to happen to me. Soren isn't some criminal mastermind trying to manipulate me into committing crimes with him or burying bodies in my backyard. He's just a lonely witch, making friends with another lonely witch."

"I don't trust him. He's using you." Amanda said as gently as she could. "I don't know what for yet, but he's using you."

"Not everyone has an ulterior motive. Why is it so hard for you to believe that he would just want to be my friend?"

"But he's changing you, Elsie," Amanda said. "Can't you see that? What happened to your code? What happened to consent to magic? How would you have felt if I had had some of that potion? Or Wanda?"

Elsie's face paled. "I would never let that happen." She said.

"Why not?" Amanda said, holding Elsie's gaze. "If it's ok for you to give it to the rest of the townsfolk, why not me? I thought you said it was safe?"

"It *is* safe," Elsie protested, "I just wouldn't want to risk you being manipulated by the potion. Especially as it wasn't even made by me."

"Then why is it ok for the other people to have it?" Amanda asked.

"You're not my conscience," Elsie said, stepping into Amanda's space, her violet eyes flaring. "You don't get to decide how I use my magic. Can't you just leave alone things that you don't understand?" Elsie was breathing hard, glaring at Amanda, and the dishes in the kitchen started to wobble. Amanda saw several plates hover up behind Elsie. Was Elsie doing that on purpose, or was it just that she was losing control of her emotions, and her magic?

Amanda stilled. "You're right," she said eventually. "I don't understand. I don't understand how you can go from being such a kind, thoughtful person with more integrity in her little finger than anyone else in this town, to a profit-driven, manipulative witch who think that humans are beneath her."

"Oh so it's because I'm a witch? Now the truth comes out!"

"It's not because you're a witch," Amanda huffed, wrapping her coat around her like a security blanket. "It's because you don't trust that you're good enough for people to like you without you manipulating them with magic. It's because whatever that sleaze-ball says, you do without a second thought. It's because the woman I thought I knew turns out to be just as selfish and unprincipled as everyone else."

Elsie glared at her. "My shop, this town, they mean *so* much to me. I am prepared to fight for them. You say I've changed, well maybe I have. But I don't think change is a bad thing. I'm doing what I need to to protect my business. People aren't getting hurt. It's just one tiny potion."

"And what about the next thing that Soren asks you to do?" Amanda said coolly. A look flitted across Elsie's face and she knew she was right. "You see, he's using you Elsie. You don't need to fall for his charms. You don't have to do what he tells you to do."

For a moment, it almost looked like Elsie was going to collapse into Amanda's arms and agree that this whole thing was a mess that she didn't need to be a part of.

Then Elsie looked around her, her spine straightening, a coldness transforming her face, and Amanda knew she had lost her.

"Please," Amanda begged. "Just walk away. Don't get dragged any further into this."

"I'm not you, Amanda," Elsie said, her voice quiet and stony. "I'm not going to run away just because something gets uncomfortable."

Amanda felt her heart break into a thousand tiny pieces, the shards stabbing into her. Her chest felt like it was being shredded from the inside. But Amanda was a Masters. She didn't show pain. She lifted her chin, rolled back her shoulders, and walked out the door.

75

Elsie

Elsie felt a tiredness that seemed to transcend physicality. Checking the time, she messaged Wanda, not wanting to go home.

Fancy going out for dinner tonight? Elsie typed. *We could drive over to Plimmer Valley and make an evening of it?*

Wanda messaged back moments later. *Sounds great! Amanda too?*

Elsie grimaced. Of course Wanda would assume they'd invite Amanda. Well tough, Amanda could figure out her own plans for the evening. Elsie wasn't her babysitter. Besides, it would be nice to spend some time just her and Wanda. Elsie needed all the friends she could get. She messaged back, *No Amanda tonight. I'm closing up now. Shall I meet you at the shop in twenty minutes?* Wanda replied with a thumbs up, and Elsie got to work sweeping and cashing up the till.

Elsie was waiting on the curb when a tall, well-dressed man clad all in black with white blonde hair walked down the road. He waved when he saw Elsie, and Soren walked over to her, a huge smile on his perfectly featured face.

"Hi," Elsie said, a little tired to deal with any more magic talk this evening.

"Hello," Soren said cheerily. "Are you ok?" He asked, looking at her more closely. "Did something happen?"

"Oh, it's nothing," Elsie said sighing. "I just had a bit of a fight with Amanda."

Soren tipped his head to the side, "Your flatmate?"

"She's not just my flatmate, she's my—" Elsie had nearly said 'girlfriend,' but after that fight she didn't really know what they were. Besides, although they hadn't exactly hidden their relationship, they also hadn't talked about how public they would be about it. There were extra challenges to being openly affectionate as a queer couple, and things with Amanda were still new.

Her feelings for Amanda had been, were, significant, but she didn't want to say anything about their relationship status without checking with Amanda first. "-friend," She ended lamely.

Soren nodded. "I see. Can I ask you what the fight was about?"

Elsie looked around, but there was nobody else on the street at this time of evening. "She was upset about the potion you gave me," Elsie she said quietly.

Soren's pale eyebrows shot up, almost disappearing under the flop of white hair hanging artfully across his brow. "She knows you're a witch?" He asked. "She knows, *I'm*, a witch?"

Elsie felt a little guilty for outing Soren's magic to Amanda without his permission. She had thought, because Amanda had taken her being a witch so well, that it would be the same with Soren. But she could see now that she should have asked him first if he was comfortable with her sharing that information.

"She does," Elsie said. "I'm sorry, I should have asked before I told her about you."

Soren waved this away. "Thank you," he said. "But I'm not concerned about the damage that one non-magical human could do. I am surprised, however. My experience of having non-magical friends is limited, but those I did have ended up being rather...." he motioned in a circle with his hand as if looking for the right word, "jealous?"

Elsie nodded.

"Either that or scared. People tend to fear what they don't understand, and non-magical humans do not understand magic."

Just then Wanda pulled up in her beat up old Nissan Leaf, winding her window down to greet the two.

"Hi Wanda," Elsie said, glad for the interruption. "Soren, this is my friend Wanda, Wanda, this is Soren."

"Well hello there!" Wanda said, glancing from Soren to Elsie and back. "And is Soren coming to dinner too?"

Elsie froze. She knew that Amanda wouldn't like her going out with Soren instead of her, not after the fight they had just had. But on the other hand, she just wanted to let off some steam, and Soren was standing there looking so—, there was no other word for it—, hopeful.

She had obviously paused a second too long, because Soren's face fell, and he began backing away. " I wouldn't want to intrude," he said, glancing at the ground. In that moment, Elsie made up her mind. If Amanda had wanted to come to dinner, she shouldn't have stormed off. And who was she to decide who Elsie could and couldn't spend time with? "You're not intruding, jump in."

Elsie thought she saw a flicker of disdain cross Soren's face as he reached for the car door handle, but it was gone in an instant, and he was all smiles. "Thank you, you're so kind," he said, opening the door for Elsie before going around the other side to climb in himself.

As Wanda pulled in at Lilac House, hours later Elsie was struck with an overwhelming feeling of loneliness at the thought of going inside by herself. It was late, and Amanda would almost certainly be in bed. "Night cap?" She asked Wanda, and the woman smiled. "If by night cap you mean a cup of tea, then yes, thank you." That was a relief, Elsie didn't actually know if she had any spirits to offer Wanda, the alcoholic kind, at least. She certainly had a lot of tea though. Leading the way through to the kitchen, Elsie was surprised to see that Amanda was still up, sitting in the kitchen quietly drinking a cup of tea and reading a book about native trees. Elsie's heart did a little flip when she saw her, and she had to make a conscious effort not to go and kiss the woman.

"Well that was lovely," Wanda said, from behind Elsie, "I'm glad your friend Soren was able to come as well. He's an interesting fellow isn't he? Oh hello Amanda."

Elsie wanted to scream. Of course Wanda wasn't to know that this was the exact worst thing that she could have said, but still.

"You went for dinner with Soren?" Amanda asked, looking up in surprise. Wanda looked between the two of them, seeming to realise she had said just the wrong thing. Her mouth dropped open, and then she hastily made her way towards the kettle. Elsie wanted to explain, to tell Amanda they had just bumped into him, it wasn't like that. But Soren's words echoed in her head '*She doesn't control you.*' So instead she simply said, "Yes, he joined us for dinner."

Amanda's face visibly fell, and Elsie felt terrible. She hadn't meant to hurt this woman, she was just... angry? Confused? She felt like she was being pulled in two directions and didn't know which way to go.

"Right. I did try to text and call you a few times but...." Amanda trailed off, picking up her cup of tea and heading out of the room. "Anyway, I'll head to bed. Big day tomorrow." As she got to the door, she turned, a look of such hurt in her eyes that Elsie wanted to reach out and hug her. Elsie wanted so badly to reach out, to fix it, but at the same time she was overjoyed to have a friend who was a witch, and Amanda was being unfair about Soren. She just stood there numbly, and Amanda nodded her head again, her mind seemingly made up about something. Elsie's heart sank as Amanda left the room, but she didn't follow her.

Amanda and Elsie had slept in the same bed every night since they had gotten together. Tonight, though, Amanda didn't come to Elsie's room. Elsie stood outside Amanda's door for several long minutes, before eventually telling herself that Amanda needed to sleep, and that they could talk things out tomorrow.

Elsie checked her phone as she was lying in bed. With a jolt she saw a string of messages and missed calls from Amanda from earlier in the day. The first one read, *Sorry for storming off. I needed some space after that conversation. Are you ok?* Half an hour later there was another message. *Shall we get some dinner together and just talk? It's been a big few weeks.* Then two hours after that: *I'm guessing you're getting food out, so I'll rustle something up here myself.* Elsie felt bile rising in her throat. Amanda had tried reaching out, several times. Even though that was hard for her. Elsie's phone had been in her bag during dinner, but she should at least have messaged Amanda to say she wouldn't be home. It was petty and selfish of her not to. And for Amanda to find out that instead of taking the olive branch she had offered, Elsie had gone for dinner with Wanda and Soren. This was a disaster.

Elsie put her head in her hands. She felt awful. Regardless of their disagreement, she had treated Amanda very badly by not even responding to her messages. She typed and untyped about a hundred messages on her phone, unable to find the words to say what she wanted to say. Eventually, she simply said "I'm so sorry," and added a hug emoji. She kept her eyes glued to her phone. Amanda saw the message, but after ten minutes, Elsie had to admit to herself that no response was coming.

Elsie lay in bed all night, tossing and turning, unable to sleep, her mind whirring. Had Amanda been right? Had she gone too far with Soren's potion? Or was this just some non-magical human trying to control her magic? Either way she felt terrible for how she had treated Amanda. She resolved to speak to her in the morning, even setting her alarm at the ungodly hour of 6am to make sure she didn't miss Amanda before she headed to work.

The next morning, though, Amanda was nowhere to be found. On impulse, she went to Amanda's room, the door to which was slightly ajar. She pushed the door open, a feeling of dread rising inside her. The bed was neatly made, but the few items which had previously been hanging in wardrobe were gone. Elsie looked around the space. There was nothing on the floor, no empty tea cup beside the bed, no pair of red converse sneakers kicked off under the bed. There was no sign that anyone had been in this room at all. Just like that, Amanda was gone.

76

Amanda

Amanda squashed her feelings down. She would keep herself busy and not allow herself to think until she no longer felt as if her heart had been yanked from her chest and shoved straight into the InSinkErator.

Elsie's face flitted, unbidden across her mind, and she gritted her teeth as she unpacked her bags once again. She had just begun to feel settled in Lilac House. That should have been a sign; she should have known better than to allow herself to get comfortable.

Hot tears ran down her cheeks, and she swiped them away angrily. Why had she let her guard down, let herself open up and become vulnerable again? She had thought Elsie was different, that she got her. But if she could turn her back on Amanda so quickly just because someone else showed her some attention, then she really wasn't the person Amanda had thought she was.

Amanda angrily threw her clothes into various drawers in her latest room, slamming them closed in a huff. "Hey! Watch what you're doing up there," came Murray's sharp voice from downstairs. "Those drawers belonged to my great grandfather."

Sheepishly, Amanda poked her head out of the room and peered down the staircase at her host. "Sorry, Murray," she said, hanging her head in shame. "I got a bit carried away."

Murray walked up the stairs, a slow, careful shuffle. Amanda couldn't tell if it was his old bones or the stairs that were creaking as he ascended. When he got to the landing, he looked at Amanda. "I'm sorry," she said again, her face flushing with embarrassment. Murray was being so kind letting her stay, the least she could do was show him and his things some respect.

"That's alright, youngin," Murray's voice was softer now. "I know you've had a hard time of it recently. Why don't you come downstairs and have a cup of tea? You can finish your unpacking later." Gratefully, Amanda followed his slow progress back down the stairs and into the home's tiny kitchen.

It was nothing like Elsie's expanse of silver and purple. Here the walls were a soft, buttery yellow, the cupboards were faded, and the ceiling looked like it had been overseeing cooking without being cleaned for far too long. The floor was that strange brown and orange geometric tile pattern that had been hugely popular in the 70s. There was a vase with fresh irises on the countertop, and the room was tired but welcoming.

Amanda perched awkwardly on one of the high kitchen stools while Murray busied himself in the kitchen. He boiled the kettle and got two big white mugs out of a cabinet above the kettle. They were sturdy, functional things, nothing like the delicate, personalised cups and mugs of Elsie's kitchen. *Stop thinking about her.* Amanda told herself firmly, just as Murray pulled out a box of what Amanda knew at a glance was Elsie's famous lavender and lemon shortbread. Murray looked at the box and went to put them away, muttering an apology under his breath. "No, it's ok," Amanda heard herself saying. It had only been a few days, but she already missed Elsie's baking. She knew, disappointingly, that the delicious cookies would help her feel better. Murray put a few shortbread biscuits onto a plate, then carried them over to a small two person table pushed against the wall.

Amanda picked up the mugs of tea and brought them over, while Murray grabbed some almond milk from the fridge. Amanda raised an eyebrow, but Murray just glared at her as if willing her to comment on his recent shift from his precious cow's milk. The plate, Amanda noticed, was much more delicate than the mugs were. It had scalloped edges and a floral pattern, and was made of good quality china. Murray must have noticed Amanda's look, because he said simply, "Hatty used to like good china, especially plates. I don't have the heart to use her matching tea cups these days. They were always too small for a proper mug of tea anyway, but she would never stand for me serving guests biscuits on anything other than one of her nice china plates."

Amanda smiled. "Did she like flowers?" She asked, nodding toward the irises on the kitchen counter, and back to the single pink peony on the table she and Murray were now sitting at.

"Aye, she did," Murray said, his voice softening just a tad as he looked at the peony on the table. "She would always have fresh flowers in the house, no matter how strapped we were. If we had money, she would see Fiona at the florist, if not, she would go wandering in the hills until she found enough wild flowers to keep the place nice. The house always smelt of flowers, no matter what time of year."

"She sounds lovely," Amanda said, noticing an extra sheen in Murray's eyes, and studiously taking a sip of tea to allow him a moment.

Murray swallowed hard. "She was. Best woman I ever knew."

"It must have been hard, losing her," Amanda said softly.

"Three years ago next month and not a day goes by that I don't miss her," Murray said, picking up a biscuit and taking a bite. "However," he said as he swallowed, "it is not my love life that is causing you to slam drawers and huff and gruff about the place like an angry teenager."

Amanda flushed. "I'm so sorry Murray," she said, taking a sip of the English Breakfast tea, and trying not to imagine the orange and ginger brew she might have been having at Elsie's.

Murray waved her apology away. "Now I'm not one for messing in people's business." Murray took another bite of his shortbread, a few golden crumbs clinging to his moustache for dear life. "But if you want someone to talk to, I have learned to be a good listener."

Amanda realised that Harriet must have been quite a woman. She guessed Murray came across as grumpy because of his grief. She could see that underneath his rough exterior, he was a good man, with a kind heart. Heck, taking her in like this showed incredible generosity, especially when he clearly had little to spare. She sighed. It seemed a little strange to her that this elderly gentleman was offering what would generally be referred to as 'girl talk', but she was exhausted, and she could do with a friend right about now.

Slowly, haltingly, the whole sorry story, minus, of course, Elsie being a witch, was drawn out of her like an infection from a wound. It was a little tricky to explain Elsie's commonality with Soren without going into the magic thing, but Murray seemed to get the general gist about a 'connection', and didn't push for the details. Amanda was pleasantly surprised that Murray took her lesbianism entirely in his stride. "Love is love, no matter what it looks like," was all he said, when she explained that she and Elsie had been in the beginning stages of a relationship. "And then this bloke sweeps in and steals your girl?" he said gruffly, when Amanda stiltingly explained that Elsie's relationship with Soren had led her to feel entirely replaced.

"I don't think they're in a relationship," she said, fidgeting with the frayed hem of her jumper. "But she seemed to have less and less time for me, and honestly, I barely even recognise her anymore." Amanda ran her hand through her hair, sighing. "Elsie used to be the kindest, most thoughtful person I'd ever met. Yes, there was a part of that that was maybe a little too people-pleasing, but she used to really care. Now Soren's got her doing all kinds of things that the old Elsie never would have done."

Murray nodded his understanding. "I told you I didn't like that boy right from the beginning," he said, when Amanda finished. "The Dahl family has a bit of a mixed reputation in town. They all packed up and moved on years ago, back to Sweden, I think. But the homestead is still there. Why young Soren chose now to come home, I don't know."

Amanda hadn't thought of that. She understood moving away from your family, and Glen Haven certainly had its own charming appeal. But why would Soren, a young, thirty-something witch, decide to go come back to that this tiny little village? She didn't know how long he was in town for, if he had a job, anything. But it didn't sit well with Amanda that he was back for no apparent reason. And he had gravitated instantly to Elise. What was that about? Elsie was nothing like him, except that she was a witch. Soren was rich and flashy, whereas Elsie was, — well, had been — so much more down to earth.

"Do you know much about his family?" She asked, a knot of discomfort bedding itself into her stomach.

"They were one of the founding families of the village as it is now. Said to be amongst the first Europeans to settle in this area. You must have noticed the range of languages of place names around here." Amanda had noticed that, actually. There were indigenous place names, English place names, and several Swedish place names, especially up in the forests. She nodded for Murray to go on. "Rumour has it that years ago, the Dahls had some kind of feud. Tried to take power in the village that wasn't theirs, drove some people off their land. Legend goes that in doing so, they were cursed. The land that had always been plentiful was barren within a year of that fight. You heard of the great blight of 1913?" Amanda nodded her head, sitting forward. "Legend always blamed that family for it. Not true, I'm sure, but the legend only existed because they were pretty nasty people. It's said that some members of the family repented, seeking forgiveness from mother earth for their sins against her and her people. That they poured a lot of money into the town probably helped too," Murray snickered. "Others in the family, however, allegedly became convinced it was their job to seek revenge on the town that cursed them. They created an evil coven, and were even said to kill those who refused to join them, bleeding them dry in some sort of crazed ritual sacrifice under the full moon. Of course," Murray said, slurping down the last of his tea and rising with a creak, "that was a long time ago. The Dahl people have lived in that homestead on and off over the years. Town lore is that when the wrong people are in town, there are droughts or diseases which break out. It's part of the reason that townsfolk are so wary of new people."

Amanda swallowed hard. "Ritual sacrifices?" She repeated, her throat dry.

"That's what the stories say, sure," said Murray. "I mean, I know they say there's a grain of truth to all myths, but honestly I think this particular myth is just taking the Dahl family's legacy a little too far." He placed a hand on Amanda's shoulder in a fatherly way. "For what it's worth, though, I agree with you. That boy is no good. I hope Elsie comes to see that herself." Amanda felt a sense of foreboding in her bones and, looking down at her teacup, saw what looked like a cross in its leaves.

77

Elsie

Elsie hated her shop. She hated the sun. She hated baking, and most of all, she hated any reason she could possibly have to leave her warm, comfortable bed. She had spent the two days following Amanda's departure in bed, only leaving to go to the toilet or to the kitchen, and even then she left it as long as she could before moving from the protective shelter of her duvet.

She had put a note up at Pie in the Sky saying she was sick and would be back soon, or rather, she had asked Lily to. Dark Witch or not, Elsie was still paying her. She hoped she would be back soon, although the way she was currently feeling, it was likely that she would never leave Lilac House again. She knew shutting the shop would be terrible for business, but she simply couldn't face human interaction. Right now, all Elsie was capable of doing was crying, eating tubs of ice cream, and watching reruns of the Gilmore Girls.

Her stomach hurt constantly, though Elsie couldn't be sure if that was because of the heart-ache or because she was subsisting entirely on Duck Island's peanut butter cookie dough ice cream. Wanda had popped by a few times and tried to feed her more nutritious things, bringing in offerings of soup and various vegetable casseroles, but Elsie didn't have the energy for it. Peanut butter cookie dough ice cream could be spooned into her mouth directly from the tub. It was cold, delicious, and comforting. And sometimes it froze Elsie's brain, which frankly was a welcome relief from the constant thoughts of Amanda running through her head and heart, making her feel like she had been squished in a box and ineffectually hacked in half by a very poor magician, guts hanging out for all to see.

Elsie had eventually gotten up the nerve to text Amanda again, to apologise properly. Once she started messaging, she had been unable to stop. Amanda hadn't answered her seven phone calls or any of her nineteen text messages. Elsie finally decided that twenty text messages was the limit at which pining turned into stalking, and, instead of messaging Amanda, she simply glared at her phone for hours out of every day. Sometimes she punished it, and herself, by locking it in a drawer, before rushing back to check it an hour later, only to see that Amanda had still not replied.

Sometimes she was still mad at Amanda. OK, so Elsie had messed up, but avoiding Elsie was exactly what Amanda had said she wouldn't do any more. She was being so childish, refusing to even acknowledge Elsie's existence.

She had heard from Soren a few times, but he just wanted to go casting, and Elsie wasn't in the mood. Philo came in and snuggled next to her for hours of every day. In a moment of weakness, Elsie had let him up onto the bed one night, and now every time he trotted into the room he wiggled his bottom excitedly and leapt onto the bed, almost always knocking over Elsie's laptop, spilling a half-eaten tub of ice cream, or landing painfully on Elsie's foot.

It was nice, though, having Philo for company. He would lie next to her on the bed and rest his gigantic head on her tummy or chest, almost cutting off her airflow. Philo didn't say much for the first few days after their breakup, obviously sensing Elsie's need for quiet and comfort.

Eventually, almost a week into her self-imposed exile, Wanda bustled into her room, coffee and a few pieces of toast on a tray. Elsie burst into tears again at the memory of her stealing Amanda's weird peanut butter banana agave toast. Wanda shushed gently and then raised Elsie's head to look at her. "Honey, you have got to take a shower." Wanda said, pulling Elsie to her feet and ushering her towards the bathroom. "And if Philo is going to sleep on your bed every night, then we should probably change the sheets, too."

Rude Philo's voice said inside her head. *You smell worse than I do.* Hesitantly, Elsie lifted her arm and sniffed. Philo was right. She did smell worse than him. She had gotten as far as changing underwear most days, and she was pretty sure that this t-shirt was only a couple of days old. Then again, looking down at the various brown stains on it, she couldn't quite be sure of that.

She came out from the shower to find fresh sheets on her bed, and clothing laid out for her. Whether it was by Wanda or her clothes themselves, Elsie couldn't be sure. She donned the familiar black leggings and purple

251

crop top anyway, pulling an enormous brown sweater over the top for comfort as much as warmth.

As she walked downstairs, she heard Wanda in the kitchen, chatting amiably to Philo. The smell of coffee filled her nostrils, and Elsie was propelled forwards. Wanda looked up and smiled when Elsie entered the room. "There she is, our little gremlin back from the dead."

"Gremlins are undead," Elsie murmured under her breath, but Wanda didn't seem to hear her. "Now I know that you don't want to face the world yet," Wanda began, "but lying in bed pining for Amanda won't bring her back." Elsie made a non-committal noise as she took the coffee Wanda passed her. It was in her favourite mug, the purple and green one with stars on it that was about as big as a bowl, and Elsie buried her face in its warm embrace.

Looking at the pile of bills on her counter, Elsie groaned. Maybe she should just put Lilac House on the market and move back home to Christchurch. She had tried her hardest, but she didn't have the energy to keep running the shop anymore. She just wanted to run away and lick her wounds. Thinking of her home town made Elsie's heart sink even farther. Her dad was gone, Phoebe was still in America, and her mum was just as distant as ever. She hadn't even called Elsie on the winter solstice. Not, Elsie admitted, that she had called her mother, either. If Elsie couldn't fix her relationship with Amanda, maybe she could at least do something about the other broken relationship in her life.

Wanda, with the perception of a mind-reader, had made herself scarce while Elsie was still being revived by coffee. Reaching into her pocket, she grabbed her phone, and taking a deep breath, dialled.

78

Elsie

Elsie's mother answered almost immediately, before Elsie had the chance to second-guess herself.

"Hi, mum" Elsie said, her voice cracking.

"Elsie, honey, what's wrong?" Elsie could hear noise in the background, and then a door closing, and the noise quieted down. She sniffled, tears forming in her eyes.

"I'm sorry we dragged you into our magical world," Elsie said, the words falling out of her mouth.

"What?"

"I mean, I know I didn't have a choice about being born a witch," Elsie sniffled loudly, "but I'm sorry that magic was such a big part of our lives. I know it always made you feel left out and inferior."

There was a pause, and then, "Where is this coming from, honey?"

"There was this girl, woman. I really liked her, but I messed it up. I got carried away with magic and I thought it wouldn't work because she's a normy," Elsie was rambling now but she couldn't stop, "then I accused her of thinking that magic was evil and she told me I cared too much about what other people think and it all fell apart." Elsie dissolved into sobs, and her mother made gentle shushing noises down the phone.

When her tears eventually subsided, her mother said quietly. "I was never jealous of your magic, Elsie."

"You weren't?"

"No. I loved that you had magic. I was perfectly content with my herbs and my music and everything else."

"But you always seemed so sad when dad and I would go off flying, or when Phoebe and I would go off and make potions."

"It wasn't the magic I was jealous about."

"It wasn't?"

"No." Her mother said softly, "I was sad that you didn't include me. I was sad that you didn't think I was worth spending time with just because I didn't have magic."

Elsie felt shame creep up her throat like bile. "But you didn't want to join in, you didn't even come for winter solstice."

"You didn't invite me."

Elsie thought back. She had invited her mother, hadn't she? They had celebrated the winter solstice as a family every year for as long as Elsie could remember. She had no recollection of the first solstice without her dad. But since Elsie had moved to Glen Haven, she had just assumed Nancy would come and spend the festive seasons with her. She had been devastated that her mother hadn't been to visit even once in the year that she had been there. But had she actually invited her?

"I thought you hated our magical traditions." She whispered.

"I loved celebrating with you all." Her mother's voice was equally subdued. "I knew you only included me because your father insisted, but it was so special to me to share that time with you all." Elsie recalled her mother happily hanging ribbons on the trees at summer solstice, carefully weaving beautiful wreaths during the winter solstice, and filling the house with flowers at Beltane. Elsie had thought that her mother was grudgingly involved in their magical traditions. Had she misread the situation this whole time?

"I'm sorry." She whispered. Fresh tears falling down her face. How had she been so stupid?

"I'm sorry too," Nancy said, and Elsie could hear tears in her mother's voice.

They talked a little more, and Elsie asked if her mother would come over for Christmas and stay for a while. She hadn't heard so much excitement in her mother's voice in well over a year, and Elsie felt ashamed at not realising her mother needed her, just as much as she needed her mother.

They ended the call with a promise to speak soon, and Elsie felt a little lighter. She was glad to have mended fences with her mother, but Elsie was overwhelmed by the knot in her stomach at the idea that she had misread the situation so badly. Had she allowed her misconceptions about how her mother felt about magic to taint her view of Amanda? Elsie had tried getting in contact with Amanda, but short of turning up on her doorstep with a boombox, a move which she didn't think Amanda would appreciate, she didn't think there was anything else she could do. Tears rolling down her cheeks, Elsie realised that she had lost Amanda for good. A hole gaped in her heart at the thought.

On the counter was a letter from the property owner advising her she was late on her rent for Pie in the Sky. The shop had made a loss last week, and Elsie was at the point of giving up. She resolved to give it one more month. If she had to return home with her tail between her legs, at least her mother would be happy to see her now.

79

Amanda

Amanda threw herself into her work at the community garden. She spent every day in the garden, rain or shine. Spring was around the corner, and Amanda was bordering on obsessive in her attentiveness to the plants. She was already thinking of further improvements she could make to the place. She was also in the garden centre almost every other day, picking up an order or putting in a new one.

A week ago, Amanda had seen a tree fallen over in the greenhouse at Higgs Twiggs. Seeing that neither Mrs Higgs nor her son were around, Amanda had picked the plant back up, and then had accidentally lost several hours watering and pruning the various plants. Once she realised Mrs Higgs didn't mind, she had started popping in virtually every day. She ordered plants, rearranged shelves, and spent hours upon hours nursing the various shrubs, trees, and flowers back to health.

She was grateful for the distraction, but it wasn't really helping Amanda's mood. Normally, Amanda would have loved the work she was doing, but at the moment, she felt like she was frantically swimming against a tide to keep from drowning, rather than floating along in her happy place. She was spending long days in the garden centre and the community garden, often working from 8 in the morning until 4 or 5 in the evening. At lunchtime, she would go for a punishing run in the hills, before heading back to the community garden to ensure that no weeds had sprung up during her absence.

Her plan was to exhaust herself so much that all she could do was work, eat, or sleep. And it worked, sometimes. Thoughts of Elsie still filled her mind every day, but Amanda had been burned badly enough to know that there was no going back. She had read some of Elsie's messages, and felt a pang of longing for her with each one. After a little while, Amanda had muted their conversation. She couldn't risk hoping again. She definitely couldn't risk trusting Elsie again, and Amanda knew that the more she read, the more connected to Elsie she would feel, and the harder it would be to stay away. Elsie would change her mind again soon enough. She had cast Amanda aside once, she would doubtless do it again the instant someone else more interesting came along.

Murray had told Amanda she could stay for as long as she wanted, but she still felt bad taking up room in his cramped house. She stayed away as much as she could, giving him space. She also took to cooking a few meals a week. Her cooking had improved since she'd moved in with Elsie, but Amanda tried hard not to think about that as she sautéed vegetables or chopped tofu.

She wasn't sleeping well, despite her gruelling routine. Twice, Murray had come downstairs thinking there was an intruder in the house, only to find Amanda, her nose stuck in the fridge, trying to fill the ache in her heart with snacks. He had been wielding an umbrella the first time he caught her in the kitchen. Amanda couldn't help wondering how effectual that would've been had there been an actual intruder.

Murray, bless him, had been very good to Amanda. The coffee at Beth's Bakehouse was nowhere near as good as Elsie's, but Amanda simply couldn't bring herself to go into Pie in the Sky. Instead, she walked to work each morning with a sub-par coffee in a bright orange takeaway cup shaped like a pumpkin, trying to ignore the fact that Elsie had bought her the vessel. Once a week, though, on their day off, Murray would go to Pie in the Sky and get two takeaway coffees. Amanda guessed it would be fairly obvious to Elsie who the large vanilla latte in the pumpkin cup was for, but at least she didn't have to face her in person. She and Murray would stroll down to the river, sipping their coffees in companionable silence, remarking occasionally on the bird-life.

Murray was very knowledgeable about native birds. There were a few species, such as the southern black robin, that Amanda wasn't familiar with, as they were endemic only to the South Island. Amanda recruited Murray to help with her display at Higgs' Twiggs, and he got rather into it.

None of her myriad distractions softened the pain in her heart, though. Amanda had been in a few relationships before, several for longer than the fleeting thing she and Elsie had had. Somehow, this felt different. Amanda had never shared so much with someone before. Elsie had made her feel safe, seen. Never had Amanda felt at home like she had at Lilac House. Murray was very welcoming, but nothing compared to walking in the door after a long day and seeing the person you love. She missed their Netflix binge sessions, their long walks with Philo, missed those few precious days she had with Elsie when they had laid together, sharing the highs and lows of the day, before falling asleep in each other's arms.

On top of her heartbreak, the date of her brother's hearing was coming up, and Pierce was on her case every other day, trying to convince her to testify. A million thoughts swirled in Amanda's head as she tried to decide what to do. She did not want to testify against those men. She didn't want to risk her life, blow the cover she had so carefully crafted here, give the thugs a chance to track her down, or worse, follow her back to Glen Haven. But a nagging thought at the back of Amanda's mind kept telling her she was still running.

80

Elsie

The sun was just beginning to set, painting the sky a dusky pink, as Elsie locked up the Pie in the Sky. A few wisps of clouds looked down on them gently, the air crisp and still. She pulled her red-riding-hood jacket tighter around herself. She swore the winter wasn't this cold last year. "It's a perfect night for enchanting."

"Oh, hi Soren," Elsie said, turning around in surprise as he came up behind her. She was worn out, but she didn't want to upset one of the few friends she had in this town. "I don't know if I really feel like enchanting tonight. It'd be nice to hang out, though. Could we do something else instead?"

A flash of what Elsie thought might have been annoyance flashed across Soren's face, but it was gone too quickly for her to be sure. "Sorry," she said hurriedly. "Maybe we could have a coffee or something and then I can see how I'm feeling?" It was a beautiful night, and Elsie really should practice her magic. Maybe some coffee and company would perk her up a bit.

Soren looked at her for a moment, his face unreadable. Then, at last, he smiled.

"OK, that sounds like a good idea. I think the night might cast its spell on you yet." They walked to Soren's house, chatting a little as they went. Soren had been researching some new spells. Elsie wondered again if she should tell Soren about the Dark Witch. She had told Amanda she wouldn't, but- Elsie's heart was heavy thinking of what she had lost - given that ship had sailed, maybe it would be wise to tell her witch friend about it? Elsie resolved that if anything else dark magicky happened, she would talk to Soren about it. He was so wise and knew more spells than Elsie could imagine. Maybe he would have some ideas.

Soren led them through to the sitting room. "Why don't you sit down while I make us some drinks?" He asked, waving his hand casually at the fireplace to bring dancing flames bursting into life.

"Thanks," Elsie said. "I'm exhausted."

"Long day?"

Elsie slumped into one of the huge leather couches facing the fireplace. "You can say that again," she said. "The shop is still struggling, so I've had to let Lily go, which I feel awful about. I've been trying out as many pies and cupcake recipes and different flavour combinations as I can to entice customers back in. It feels like I'm fighting an uphill battle at the moment."

"Did you use the potion I gave you?"

Elsie's stomach clenched. She should have seen that coming. She didn't want to be rude and tell Soren that she had decided not to use the potion, that she was trying to look at herself and reassess her morals. She didn't want to offend him, but Elsie thought that probably she and Soren weren't completely aligned when it came to their attitude towards using magic. "I didn't," she said, hoping not to upset him too much. "Sorry Soren, it was such a lovely thought, but I've decided I need to be a bit more careful about what I do with my magic. I don't want to do anything that hurts people, or manipulates them."

She turned and saw Soren purse his lips. He was at a drinks trolley, pouring various liquids into two crystal glasses that probably cost more than a week's wages. "I see," Soren said slowly, looking up at her over the amber liquid. "Well, I was planning on doing something different this evening. Nothing to do with manipulating people at all. It's a spell I have been working up to for a while now. It takes energy out of the earth and allows the spell caster to utilise that as magical energy. It's really very clever."

A jolt of fear shot through Elsie. Soren pointed a finger at each of their drinks, and a sphere of ice appeared. An ice witch! Elsie recalled how cold that poor calf was mere moments after it had died. Hurriedly, she turned back to the fireplace so Soren wouldn't see the look of horror and realisation on her face.

He was the Dark Witch! It was Soren! And now he wanted Elsie to help him draw the magic from the earth. Elsie needed to get out of here. She had to call the Witch's Council and let them know what was going on. But she couldn't let Soren know she had figured him out.

"That sounds interesting," she said, trying not to let disgust seep into her words. "Was that spell in your family's Book of Shadows?" Soren stepped around the couch, handing her an amber drink with a slice of orange, a dash of something red in the bottom and a single, round ice cube resting in the liquid.

"It was. My great-great-grandfather used it here once before." Soren said. Elsie took a deep, steadying sip of the liquid. Soren hadn't asked her what she wanted to drink, and now that she knew what he was capable of, she didn't want to upset him by turning down the cocktail and asking for a tea or coffee instead. The alcohol burned her throat on the way down and she let out a tiny gasp.

"W-why did your family leave Glen Haven?" Elsie asked, desperate to find out as much as she could, and to keep Soren distracted from her fear and despair.

"Oh, I think grandfather had a falling out with one of the other families here," Soren said airily. "He upset a few people with his decision-making. This happens when you're strong-willed sometimes. Anyway, I'm sure that's all water under the bridge now." Changing topics abruptly, Soren said, "I'm pleased to see you're not spending time with that Amanda person anymore. I know she had a bit of a thing for you, but she clearly didn't understand your need to practice magic."

Elsie felt a stab of remorse at the mention of Amanda's name. She had messed everything up with her, and it turned out that Amanda had been right about Soren all along! If Elsie ever got out of this, she would go to Murray's house and beg for forgiveness. She'd break down the door if she had to.

Elsie didn't know how she had ever found Soren so compelling. He was arrogant, looking down on other people and seeing himself as superior just because he had magic. She took another big swig of her drink, hoping to get out of Soren's creepy family home as quickly as possible. The chandelier, massive fireplace and imposing black leather furniture, which had seemed so impressive on her first visit, now felt oppressive and dark. Heaviness spread throughout her body. She wasn't used to drinking hard liquor, but she didn't want to sip her drink slowly, either. She had another big sip, and Soren continued. "Non-magical folk have no concept of the kind of life we lead. They don't understand what it is to wait up and forage under the full moon, to read the bones of an animal to predict which way to go, they don't know about spells or potions, let alone flying and all the other parts of being and having magic."

Elsie tried not to grimace as Soren all but confirmed that he had been the one to practice Dark Divination. "But we still have more in common with non-magical people than we do differences,." Elsie said, yawning. "We still enjoy food, exercise, nature, we still dance, create art, fall in love." Once again Amanda's face drifted across Elsie's mind, and Soren scoffed, almost as if he could see what she was thinking.

"Of course, we have some things in common with non-magical folk. But let's be real, life would be better if it was all witches, vampires, and werewolves, if we didn't have to hide who we were for fear of retribution, if we could just all embrace magic fully and live, unhidden and untethered."

"I do wish we didn't have to hide our magic," Elsie said slowly, trying to figure out how much to say. She didn't want to suddenly agree with everything Soren said or he would get suspicious, but she didn't want to piss him off, either. "But things are getting better. There haven't been witch hunts for hundreds of years. And plenty of non-magical people now see the benefits of tarot, tea leaves, and the medicinal properties of herbs. I believe there will be a day when witches and non-magical people can live happily side by side." As an after-thought, she added, "I'm not so sure about the werewolves and vampires, though."

Soren laughed, but it wasn't a friendly laugh. It was a cruel, harsh laugh. "You silly girl," he said, and Elsie stiffened. "Don't you know we are superior to humans? How can you be content to simply not be hunted and burned at the stake? Do you not wish for our kind to flourish, unconstrained by the chains of fitting in with the non-magical world? To have the chance to grow and expand into something beautiful, something altogether much *greater* than any of the non-magical folk could imagine?"

Elsie had had enough. She took a final sip of her drink and set the empty glass on the side table, moving to get up. "I'm afraid you and I have very different views on what the ideal world would look like," she said, unable to keep the abruptness from her tone. Her body felt sluggish, and she tried once more to get up from the couch. "I think I'll be g-going now." Why were her legs not moving? Why was she struggling to speak?

"Ah, I see the effects of the little something I put into your drink are beginning to take effect," Soren said with a sardonic smile. "Excellent. You will help me, Elsie Hazelwood, whether you would like to or not. Tonight is not only a full moon, but a blood moon as well. Those don't come around very often, and I will not be wasting the opportunity to cast the Transcendential spell just because you have the ideals of a twelve-year-old girl." Elsie glared at Soren, trying once more to move. Nothing happened, except her head felt foggy. Her body was paralysed, and she was gripped with terror as she listened. "If you won't help me of your own free will, there are other ways that I can get you to help me. All I need is a little blood." He stood, picked up her empty glass, and started towards the kitchen. Then he turned. "Well, quite a lot of blood, actually." Elsie's last thought before she passed out was a resounding, silent *help!*

81

Amanda

The door to Murray's cottage slammed open, and Amanda saw Lily standing there, her purple hair a crazed mess atop her head, her eyes wild. "Woah!" Amanda said, taking a step back, almost splashing her evening cup of peppermint tea down herself. What was Lily doing here? She looked like a maniac.

"He's got Elsie," Lily said, without preamble.

Amanda froze. "Who's got Elsie?" she asked, though she already knew. A million thoughts raced through her head at once. Was Elsie OK? What did Lily know? Could she trust her?

Lily grabbed her hand saying only, "I'll explain on the way, we have to go." Amanda yanked a jacket off a hook on the wall as she was hauled out the door. She was following Lily back up the street before she even knew what she was doing.

"Lily, what's going on?" she asked, fear and confusion mixing with anger in her chest.

"Soren has Elsie, and I think he's going to sacrifice her under the Blood Moon," Lily said, turning for a moment to face Amanda, fear all over her pale face. Amanda felt the bottom drop out of her stomach. "What?" she said, her brain scrambling to catch up. "Why would he sacrifice..."

"I left my jumper at the shop, so I went back this evening to grab it. I saw Elsie leaving with Soren and, well, I followed them."

"You followed them?" Amanda asked, incredulity in her voice.

Lily waved an impatient hand. "I've been keeping an eye on them both for a while, trying to work out who was casting the dark magic. I was pretty sure it was just Soren, but he and Elsie seemed so close I thought perhaps they were both in it together. So I followed them to see if I could figure out what they were doing."

Amanda was stung by the observation that Elsie and Soren were so close. Her mind was reeling at Lily's words, trying to piece things together. "You were keeping an eye... so why were you wearing the amulet? What about the icy soil in the Community Garden?"

Lily looked confused, then she clicked her finger. "I knew Elsie had recognised my necklace!" Amanda just stared. "To stop the evil witch from knowing I was a witch, of course. And the ground wasn't icy from me. I saw it and figured it had been drained. I've been trying to figure out what's causing all this creepy stuff for ages." Lily pulled on Amanda's hand, urging her to hurry, but she glanced back over her shoulder at Amanda. "Why did you think I was wearing it?"

"We thought you might have been the evil witch and you were wearing the amulet to stop anyone finding you out." A surprised laugh escaped from Lily's lips. "You thought it was me?"

Amanda shrugged. She was going to say, 'Well, you thought it could have been Elsie, so it wasn't exactly unreasonable,' but Lily cocked her head to one side thoughtfully.

"Maybe Soren used one, though," she said. "To hide the kind of magic he used."

OK, Amanda needed to know what was going on. She stopped in the middle of the footpath, pulling Lily back and turning her to face her. "OK, so, you were following Elsie and Soren. What happened?"

"They went inside Soren's house. I thought about casting a spell to see what they were doing, but I was worried they might sense it, so I waited outside for a while. They were in there for about an hour," Amanda could feel jealously and anger bubbling up inside of her, but she clamped it down. Now was not the time. Elsie was in danger, or, at least, that's what she thought was happening. Lily hadn't exactly been clear so far.

Lily was still talking, "I was about to give up and go home when I saw the back door open. Soren brought Elsie out to his car, but he had to carry her. She looked like she was passed out. Then he opened the boot, looked around, and threw her in."

Fear gripped Amanda. "Do you know where he took her?" She asked in a tiny whisper, "or why?"

Lily shook her head. "I saw him drive up the street, but I don't know where they went. As for what he was planning on doing, I don't know for sure, but I don't think it's good. The dark magic around here recently, the bone ritual, the animal sacrifices—,"

Amanda balked, "Animal sacrifices?"

"The sheep and cows that went missing," Lily said, her usually pale face even paler now as she looked at Amanda with a mixture of fear and sorrow. "They were sacrificed down by the river. I felt the magic, and I felt their blood being mixed into the river."

Amanda looked at her in confusion and horror. Had Elsie known about this? "Water witch," Lily said by way of explanation. Her fingers anxiously twirled the many silver rings on her long fingers as she talked. "I think all of those sacrifices are leading to something else, and I'm worried that something is Elsie."

Amanda thought she might actually throw up. She fought the feeling down, forcing herself to focus. "OK, so what's the plan?" she asked.

Lily looked uncertain. "I think if we go to Pie in the Sky, I can try to scry and see if I can figure out where they are."

"You can figure out where Elsie is?" Amanda asked.

Lily bit her bottom lip nervously. "I can try to. I'm still learning. Hopefully it will at least give us an idea of where she—..." A memory came crashing into Amanda's mind; Her joking with Elsie about GPS.

"Change of plan," she said, taking off at a run. "We're going to get Philo."

"Philo?" Lily yelled from behind her.

"Her Familiar," Amanda said over her shoulder.

"Her Familiar is a dog!?"

But Amanda just kept running, all the way to Lilac House. She pounded on the door like a woman possessed. Maybe she was. There was a scrambling of paws and the sound of barking. "Philo, it's me." Amanda said, and the barking got louder. Amanda fished a key from a chain around her neck, refusing to mentally engage with the fact that she had been wearing the key around her heart for the past two weeks. The door opened and Philo bounded out, leaping in nervous circles, barking loudly.

Lily took a step back, but Amanda crouched in front of the dog, gently holding him still. "Philo, we know Elsie's in trouble. Soren has her. Can you help us find her?" Philo lifted his head and barked once at the ceiling, and then he was off like a shot, Amanda and Lily trailing behind him.

82

Elsie

Elsie awoke in the dark. She was moving. It was bumpy. Her head was sore. How much had she had to drink last night? She tried to sit up and her head hit something hard. *Ow!* In a rush of panic, the events in Soren's sitting room came back to her. She moved again, but her hands and feet were bound. Listening, Elsie could hear a car's engine, and over it, was that, Elvis? Fear and anger tore through Elsie. She was in Soren's car. Soren, her friend, who it turned out was actually the Dark Witch who had been causing all this pain all over Glen Haven. Amanda had seen through him straight away. How could Elsie have been so stupid?

Elsie's heart ached at the thought of Amanda. Why hadn't she listened to her? Why had she let herself become so consumed by the idea of making friends, witch friends, that she had treated Amanda so badly? She could berate herself later. Right now, Elsie needed to get out of here. She needed to escape and alert the Witch Council of Soren's plan. Testing the ropes around her wrists and ankles, she was dismayed by how little give there was in them. Concentrating with all her might, she loosened the bindings ever so slightly. She brought her hands to her mouth, wondering if she could bite her way free. She ground her teeth against the rope again and again, but it would take her a long time to break through. The car stopped, and Elsie's chest tightened in fear.

The boot opened and Elsie saw the pale face of Soren looking down at her, his icy eyes dancing. "Oh good, you're awake. That means you'll be able to walk."

Soren lifted Elsie out of the trunk, apparently unfazed by the glare she gave him as he did so. Soren unbound her feet so she could walk, and Elsie considered running. Unfortunately, she had no idea where she was, and with no car and the grogginess of Soren's enchantment still effecting her, she didn't think she would get far.

Soren pushed her forward, and looking around, she realised with a start that they were in Viskande. It looked like the track up to the pond of reflection. Everything was bathed in the moon's light, and if she hadn't been so terrified, Elsie would have thought how beautiful it was. She needed to wait for the effects of the enchantment to wear off before she made a run for it.

It must have taken an hour to get to the pool of reflection. Elsie was sluggish from the effects of the enchantment, but Soren grew impatient, pushing her along whenever she slowed. When they reached the pond, Soren set up a cauldron the size of a bathtub and began an incantation. Elsie could feel the darkness growing around her, the temperature dropping even lower as Soren continued his spell. When his back was turned, Elsie tried to sneak away, but a twig snapped loudly under foot, and Soren spun around, his blue eyes flashing in the moonlight. He was using a wand to help focus his attention on this spell, and he pointed it at Elsie now, a snarl escaping his lips. Elsie flew through the sky towards him, his spell drawing her in against her will. As she landed, she dove towards Soren, grabbing his wand from his hand. Wands were reinforced with magic, but Elsie's fear and anger emphasised her own magic. With great effort, she snapped the thing. Soren let out a shriek and pulled something from his cloak. It glinted in the moonlight and Elsie realised in terror that it was a dagger. She tried to run away, but Soren grabbed her, and she screamed as the blade tore through her skin. The world around her went black again.

83

Amanda

Philo bounded ahead of Amanda, nose to the ground, tail down. The blood moon was high in the sky now, its light the only thing illuminating their path. They ran through Viskande, up the hill that Amanda had walked all those weeks ago. It was hard going, but they kept going without pause.

When they got to the top, Amanda's blood froze. There, just in front of the pond of reflection, was a figure in a long, black cloak. He was holding a book of shadows, reading from it as he stirred the contents of an enormous cauldron that was levitating above bright blue flames. Something about it made Amanda feel sick, and she heard Lily gagging beside her.

She looked frantically for Elsie, but couldn't see her anywhere. Philo shot forward once more, and Amanda raced to catch up with him. As they rounded the bend of the pond, she saw a pile of material in a heap at Soren's feet, and in horror Amanda realised that there was someone in them. As they got closer, Amanda recognised Elsie's long, braided hair, and the blood red coat that she called her 'red riding hood' jacket. Elsie wasn't moving. For an awful moment, Amanda feared they were too late.

Soren was so engrossed in what he was doing that he didn't look up at all until Philo had leapt at him. Soren fell back with a thump, and the flames underneath the cauldron instantly went out. Philo stood, his front paws on Soren's chest, pinning him down, growling like Cereus.

"Get off me!" Soren yelled, trying to push Philo away, but the dog held his ground, barking fiercely in Soren's face. Amanda ran to Elsie, checking her pulse urgently. It was faint, but it was still there. In terror, she looked down and saw that there was a long slice along Elsie's arm, which was bleeding profusely. Amanda's heart nearly stopped, and she tore her shirt off, tying it around Elsie's arm as tightly as she could to try to stop the bleeding. Elsie was very pale, her breathing barely there.

"What did you do to her?" She roared, running over to Soren and punching him square in the jaw as Philo moved to guard Elsie.

Soren held his jaw in his hands, cursing. Then suddenly Amanda was flying through the sky, propelled by magic of brutal force. She landed with a heavy thump, and looked up to see Soren walking over to where Philo stood, gently licking Elsie's face to rouse her.

Philo rounded on Soren, his teeth bared, but Soren sent the dog flying with another wave of his hand. He picked Elsie up, throwing her over his shoulder as he walked towards the cauldron. "Ideally, I would wait until her blood has fully drained from her before I boil her," he said, his blue eyes shining in the moonlight. "But I can see you won't allow me the luxury of waiting for that to happen, so I guess I will have to make do." He hoisted Elsie as if to throw her in the cauldron, which was once again bubbling.

Amanda and Philo were both running for him at full speed. As they ran, the water from the pond suddenly rose and coiled itself around Soren, creating bonds of water which held him in place. Another ribbon of water carefully plucked Elsie out of Soren's grasp and lay her gently on the ground. Amanda and Philo halted, and Amanda turned to see Lily, arms out in front of her, waving them like she was conducting an orchestra. Her face looked strained, and Amanda thought she probably couldn't hold it for long.

Soren was visibly straining against his restraints, and before long, he pulled an arm free. Amanda moved towards Elsie, who let out a small groan. Before Amanda could reach her, she dropped to the ground, her body convulsing in pain. Next to her she heard a desperate yelping, as whatever was happening to her must have been happening to Philo as well. In the distance, she heard Lily let out a gasp, and there was a great splash as the pond water rushed down hill back into its hole, no longer moving to Lily's will. There was a snarling next to her and a snapping, and the pain stopped. She looked over to see that Philo had bitten Soren brutally on the leg. This must have broken the spell, and she wobbled to her feet again. Philo was snarling and snapping violently at Soren, who kicked out as he struggled on his back to get away.

Amanda chanced a glance at Lily. She was lying, panting, on the ground a few feet away. Exhaustion was written across her features. It had clearly taken it out of her to conjure the water like that, and against a powerful witch such as Soren, no less.

Soren made it to his feet, and with another wave of his hand, he threw Philo across the clearing. Amanda heard a crash and a squeal in the distance, and then silence. Soren was injured, but he clearly wasn't going down without a fight. Amanda didn't care what his magic might do to her. She couldn't let him hurt Elsie, couldn't let him destroy this place with his dark magic. Amanda was sick to death of people like him getting away with whatever they wanted. Not anymore.

She ran towards Soren once more, fists raised. As she approached, Soren twitched his fingers, and Amanda felt heat and pain coursing through her body. Her clothes were on fire, a hot, bright red flame that appeared out of nowhere. Amanda screamed and, without thinking, leapt into the pond.

She sank to the bottom, flailing wildly to put out the flame. The pond was deeper than she expected, and she kicked hard, lungs straining, as she dragged herself back to the surface. Her limbs ached, but she fought to bring her head above the surface of the water.

As her face breached the surface, she looked around frantically and saw Soren pulling himself over to Elsie, the flames beneath the cauldron re-lit. *Oh, no you don't.* Amanda hauled herself out of the water, striding over to Soren, ready to fight him with every last breath in her body. He had reached Elsie now, and was about to lift her up when he turned and saw Amanda striding toward him. "Don't you ever give up?" Soren asked in a tight, angry whisper.

"Too easily sometimes, it seems." Amanda said, "but not today. You—"

But she didn't get any further. Soren pointed a finger at her and once again Amanda was convulsing in pain. She felt herself being lifted off the ground and saw with horror that she was floating over towards the cauldron. "If you care about her so much, you can join her," Soren said, a wicked smile on his face, his teeth gleaming in the darkness.

There was a flash of purple light, and Amanda dropped to the ground with a jolt. A band of violet light tightened itself like a lasso around Soren, binding his arms tightly to his sides.

Amanda looked around and saw to her surprise that Elsie was on her feet. She was leaning badly to one side, and seemed to be in an incredible amount of pain, but the look of determination on her face left Amanda in no doubt that it was she would who had cast the binding spell. "Leave them alone." Elsie said in a slow, rasping voice.

"You pathetic, weak-willed woman," Soren spat. "You could have joined me in my quest for power. We could have been in this together. But no, your ridiculous 'code' was more important to you than all the wonderful things we could do together. We could have been brilliant!"

Elsie let out a sardonic laugh, "Nothing you do will ever be brilliant, Soren. You're selfish and evil. Amanda warned me about you. I only wish I had listened to her sooner and saved us all this mess."

"You can be high and mighty all you want," Soren said, still struggling against the bonds that held him, "but you know you enjoyed that sense of power. You liked being able to influence people and bend them to your will. You can't hide that part of yourself forever."

Elsie looked sick. "You're right," she said. "I enjoyed having people like me, and I was too willing to do anything to have that. I've got a lot of soul-searching to do before I can look myself in the mirror again, but I can tell you I have learned my lesson. Making people like you through magic isn't real. I was lucky enough to have someone who cared about me for who I am, not what I could do for them or because of some potion. I got so caught up in being popular that I forgot to value being seen, being known." She glanced at Amanda, her eyes soft. "Maybe even being loved."

Soren rolled his eyes. "Spare me," he spat. "You can't hold me like this forever. You'll have to either kill me or let me go. And if you let me go, you know you'll be looking over your shoulder every day for the rest of your life. Because I will be there, biding my time, waiting for the opportunity to strike."

"She might not be able to hold you, but we can."

Amanda turned to see Wanda and Catherine striding towards them. "Sorry we're late dear," Wanda said to Elsie. "It's terribly difficult to get a babysitter at this time of night." Amanda stared as Wanda and her sister simultaneously brought wands from their pockets and pointed them at Soren. A thread of turquoise and another of bright yellow wound themselves around Soren's body, and he gasped.

"You're witches too!" Amanda cried out in disbelief.

"Of course," Wanda said, looking over at Amanda with a smile. "Thanks for holding the fort until we got here." Catherine walked towards Elsie and gently lifted her wounded arm. Amanda saw soft waves of yellow light, and then the makeshift bandage on her arm fell away. The wound was completely healed!

Catherine moved to check on Lily, who was still lying on the forest floor.

"You nearly had us fooled, Soren." Wanda said, her voice full of disdain. "Trying to hint, rather unsubtly I might add, that Elsie might have caused all this damage was a clever touch." Amanda's eyes widened, and her fist itched to punch Soren again. "The Witch's Council will not look favourably on your behaviour, Mr Dahl." Soren's face paled, and he strained harder against the bindings.

"The Witch's Council?" Elsie asked in surprise, "you're the ones they said they had in the area?"

Catherine nodded, almost regally. "We have been aware of the dark magic here for some time, but Soren covered his tracks well. You might have gotten away with it if this power trio hadn't interrupted you." She turned to Elsie, "Are you lot alright getting home if we take him in now?"

Elsie looked at Amanda, who shrugged and nodded. "Sure," Elsie said.

"Your arm is healed, but whatever magic Soren used to drug you is still in your system. You will need rest." Catherine warned Elsie. Wanda waved her hand over the cauldron and it shrank down before Amanda's eyes. Once it was the size of a small teacup, she picked it up and put it in her pocket. Then she and her sister waved their wands, and Soren flew overhead until he was floating in front of them.

"I had no idea you two were witches." Elsie said, staring at them.

"Yes, we were hiding our magic. Sorry we didn't tell you earlier, dear," Wanda said.

"We wanted to be sure you hadn't been corrupted by that vile creature." The other woman said.

Elsie looked at the ground, embarrassed. Amanda glanced over at Soren and saw him muttering something, his fingers twitching. A ball of ice began forming between his fingertips and Amanda saw him look towards Elsie. Rearing back, she punched him square in the face, and the ice-ball dropped to the ground, harmless.

"She's handy to have around," Catherine said, looking at Soren's unconscious face with a raised eyebrow.

"She is," Elsie said, melting Amanda's heart with her smile. The two Council women walked off, Soren floating above them. Elsie threw her arms around Amanda's neck, and Amanda held her back reflexively. What was it about Elsie's embrace that made Amanda feel so at home? After a moment, Elsie pulled back. "Where's Philo?" she cried. There was a blur of white as Philo flew at Elsie, licking her face and wagging his tail uncontrollably. Elsie laughed and knelt next to him, patting his head and whispering, "thank you" into the soft fur of his neck. "I don't know what I would have done without you." Philo, a little calmer now, gave a low snuffle.

There was a grumble from the ground somewhere to Amanda's left, and she heard Lily say, "No no, don't worry, I can get up by myself." Amanda laughed, shuffling over to help Lily to her feet.

"Thank you," Elsie said, giving Lily an awkward hug. "And uh- sorry for thinking you were the dark witch."

"Back at you," Lily shrugged, and Elsie laughed again. There was a moment of awkward silence and then Lily looked at Philo and said, "Maybe we should give these two a minute." Philo sat in front of Elsie like a protective guard dog.

Elsie bent and kissed his head, before saying "Thank you, that would be great." Philo growled, but he followed Lily away. Then Elsie and Amanda were alone.

84

Elsie

Elsie's breathing was short and fast. "I think you're in shock." Amanda said, leading her to a tree and helping her sit down against it. There was a moment of silence, and then, "I'm sorry," they both said at the same time. Elsie laughed nervously, her body shaking.

"We can talk about it later," Amanda said, feeling Elsie's forehead with the back of her hand. The rough warmth of Amanda's touch was almost more than Elsie's heart could stand. "Right now, we should probably get you to a hospital." Amanda continued, her face a picture of concern.

"We should," Elsie said, "but I need to say something first." Amanda looked at her, her expression unreadable. Elsie's stomach clenched at the thought that this might be her only shot at winning Amanda back. After two weeks, the sight of this woman still stopped her in her tracks. Elsie didn't know if her heart was beating so fast from shock, or if it was the very clear realisation of everything she had had, and what she had lost.

"I never should have gotten so carried away with Soren-" Amanda made to interject, but Elsie held up a hand. "Please, let me finish," she said. Amanda nodded. "I should have listened to you when you said that he was bad news. I thought you were just jealous because I was spending so much time with him. I thought you were jealous because he was a witch."

"Well, I was," Amanda mumbled. One corner of Elsie's mouth hitched up.

"You and I have spent months getting to know one another. I trust you. I care about you, stupid amounts. I should have listened when you said you had a bad feeling about him. I should have listened when my gut told me *I* had a bad feeling about him." Elsie ran her hands over her face in frustration. "I ignored all the warning signs with Soren because I was so desperate to have someone understand me. What I forgot is that magic isn't *me*. And Soren didn't understand me at all, not really. Sure, he understood potions and flying

276

and cauldron etiquette, but he doesn't understand that I need at least two coffees in the morning before I'm capable of human interaction. He doesn't know that flowers lift my heart and fill my house with them. Heck, he tried to get me to use magic to get more customers at Pie in the Sky rather than believing in me the way you did."

"He was also a raging murderer," Amanda said in a quiet voice. Elsie burst out laughing, causing a dull ache in her ribs. She reached out and gently took Amanda's hand. "I got so caught up in the idea of having a fellow witch in my life, of being accepted by the town, of not having to worry about the shop. I lost track of the things that really matter, like companionship, my values, love." Elsie whispered the last word. Amanda was looking at the ground as Elsie spoke, but she looked up at that last word.

"I am so, so sorry for hurting you the way I did." She continued, "I treated you terribly. I know I don't deserve it, but do you think you could ever forgive me?"

Amanda looked anguished.

"Of course I forgive you," she said, her eyes brimming with tears. Relief flooded Elsie's body, and she leaned in to kiss Amanda. Amanda pulled back. "I forgive you, but I also think you're right. You deserve to be with a witch, someone who can understand you. And if I am ever to fall in love again," she said softly, Elsie's heart fluttered at the 'l' word, but this was all wrong, "then I will deserve someone who thinks I'm enough just as I am."

"Amanda, I—"

"You chose Soren over me. You chose money, popularity, over your own code. I loved you Elsie, still love you, but just because the first witch who came along was evil and trying to take over the world doesn't mean the next one won't be much nicer." Elsie's brain was fluttery and confused by pain, by sorcery, but now it was clinging to that one little word. Had Amanda really just said that she *loved* Elsie? Elsie knew she had to try. She couldn't let this be the end.

Amanda's face was pale and sad, her usually bright complexion ashen. "You don't need me, Elsie. You have Lily, heck, you have Wanda and Catherine as it turns out. The garden is tidy, you have the shop, you have—," Elsie turned Amanda's face towards her, her eyes hot with tears.

"I want you, Amanda. I don't care so much about making friends in this town anymore. You've taught me it's ok to embrace who you are, to be unapologetically that person, and to trust that the right people will come along. Yes, hopefully Wanda and Catherine will want to be friends, maybe even Lily too, once this all dies down. But I don't just need witches in my life, Amanda, I need love. I love you. I have since that day by the beach. Sooner, probably. I was so scared of loving a normy because I thought my mum was miserable being the only normy in our family. I thought she hated magic."

"And doesn't she?"

"It turns out she just didn't like being left out." Elsie was embarrassed by how poorly she had misread things for so long. "We kept going off and doing magic stuff without her, not including her. The solstice was the only thing that we always did as a family. Turns out she was pretty heartbroken I hadn't invited her to celebrate the solstice here this year. She didn't want to overstep, so she said she had plans. I feel like such an idiot."

Elsie reached for Amanda's hand, holding it in both of hers. "I have learned my lesson. You have been so amazing with all this witch stuff. I'm sorry I stopped including you. If you'll give me another chance, I promise I won't make that mistake again."

Tears streamed down Amanda's face, and Elsie pulled her in close. Her body was cold, and Elsie conjured a blanket of warm air to wrap around them both. Then a thought occurred to Elsie. "You don't hate magic now, do you? I should've asked before." Elsie went to remove the magical blanket, but Amanda grabbed her hands.

"I don't hate magic," Amanda said. "But I am scared."

"Me too," Elsie said. "You nearly ripped my heart out when you left like that, and ghosted me."

Amanda hung her head. "I'm sorry. I've never felt like this before Elsie. I don't usually let people in, heck, you know about my past. I haven't exactly had great models for relationships."

Elsie sniffled. "I want to be better," Amanda said, "but I'm going to need your help. I've spent my whole life putting up walls, barely ever letting anyone in, and running as soon as they let me down."

"I will let you down sometimes, Amanda. I'm only human." Amanda raised an eyebrow, and Elsie laughed. "Well, I'm only a witch. We're not perfect. You'll need to learn to forgive, to talk through things. You can take time out to think, but I'm going to need you to come back and talk to me afterwards. Can you do that?"

Amanda took Elsie's face in her hands and kissed her. A deliciously slow kiss that took Elsie's breath away. "I take it that's a yes?" Elsie asked, and Amanda kissed her again. After several heavenly minutes, Amanda pulled back. "I have to go." She said.

"What?" Elsie's heart froze,

"I have to testify." Amanda said, "I want to stop running and face up to things. That means not running from my past, either."

Elsie clutched her chest. "You nearly killed me," she said. Amanda looked abashed. "Actually," Elsie said thoughtfully, "I had an idea about how I can help you with that particular problem, if you'll let me."

Amanda opened her arms wide. "I'm a new woman." She said, "accepting help is one of my new leaves." She looked around the forest, at the golden leaves scattered at their feet, the first buds of spring beginning to open. "pun not intended." Elsie rolled her eyes.

85

Amanda

Three weeks later

The court room was stiflingly hot. Amanda tugged at the collar of her shirt. The scratchy fabric was making her uncomfortable, and the blazer was restricting her ribcage, slowly suffocating her. She had been trying to go for a 'power suit' vibe. Elsie had always made it seem like dressing up gave her an extra burst of energy, and Amanda was prepared to try anything to get her through the day. So far, the suit just felt like it was out to get her.

She opened the folder on her lap again, re-reading the notes she had made for the hundredth time. She would read her evidence into the court record. Her hands were already sweating. "Alright?" Pierce's voice shattered her thoughts, and she looked up, startled.

"Yes, yep, yeah," Amanda said, trying to subtly wipe her sweaty hands on the figure-hugging black trousers she was wearing.

Pierce's blue eyes softened. "It's going to be ok," he said. The Court Registrar strode in, calling the room to attention and directing them to stand for the entrance of the judge, and Pierce made his way to his seat at the prosecution table. Next to her, Elsie squeezed her hand, and they both stood. The judge, a chestnut- haired woman with bright red lipstick and sharp eyes, surveyed the room. The Registrar told them they could be seated, and Amanda all but collapsed back into her chair with a thump.

When the Registrar announced the case name, Police v Theo Masters, her stomach retched. She tasted the acrid flavour of regurgitated banana in her mouth, and forced it back down, trying to breathe. Two guards in grey uniforms led her brother into the courtroom. Theo glanced around, and when he saw her, his face registered confusion. Then she saw realisation dawn, and his face turned thunderous. "You!" He yelled, pushing his face against the glass barrier which kept prisoners from the rest of the courtroom.

Amanda shrank back in her seat, her breath coming hard and fast, heart pounding. Blood rushed in her ears, and she could only vaguely hear the judge calling for order. She squeezed her eyes tight, clenching her hands in her lap and trying to count, to focus on anything other than her brother's shouts, his eyes. Darkness hemmed her in, and she tore her jacket off, no longer able to handle the feeling of suffocation. She couldn't have a panic attack. Not here, not now. Her mind was racing.

She felt soft hands on hers. Opening her eyes, she saw a violet pair looking back at her. Even in her current state, she would recognise those eyes anywhere.

Elsie, who at Amanda's insistence had cast a glamour on herself so nobody would recognise her, knelt in front of her, her eyes never leaving Amanda's. "Breathe with me," Elsie said, through an ocean of white noise. Amanda nodded, breathing in as Elsie slowly counted to four, and then out again for four. Her mind started to race, thinking about her brother, the danger she would be in, the danger Elsie could be in. Amanda went to speak, but Elsie simply placed Amanda's hand on her heart, reminding her to be present, to listen to Elsie's heartbeat, to focus only on the breath and the counting.

Eventually, Amanda calmed down enough that her eyes cleared. Elsie held out a small golden chain with a teardrop- shaped purple gem and placed it in Amanda's hand. "Amethyst is a natural channeller of peace and calmness. I thought it might help."

Amanda swallowed another lump in her throat. Incapable of speaking, she nodded her thanks to Elsie, clutching the pendant for dear life.

Finally glancing up, Amanda saw the judge had regained control of the courtroom. Pierce was standing behind Elsie, looking anxiously at Amanda. "I'm OK," Amanda said. "Just a little wobble." Pierce didn't quite look convinced, but the judge was calling for everyone to resume their seats, so he nodded and moved back to the prosecution table.

The hearing lasted the entire day, and Elsie sat at Amanda's side for the whole thing. She didn't speak, but she would squeeze Amanda's hand now and then, or offer an encouraging smile. When Amanda was sworn in to give her evidence, her brother began hurling insults at her again. The judge had to warn him he would be removed from the courtroom if he didn't "cease speaking immediately." Amanda shivered as Theo ran a finger across his throat, his cold eyes on hers, when the judge turned her back. She kept focussing on her breathing, looking directly at Elsie sitting in the front row. The glamour meant she looked different. Her hair was blonde, and she was several inches taller, but her eyes were unchanged. Amanda held her gaze, drawing strength from having the woman she loved here with her.

86

Elsie

"How do you feel?" Elsie asked, as she and Amanda walked into the court's bathroom. After checking the room was empty, Elsie flicked a finger to magically lock the door. They couldn't risk anyone seeing what they were up to.

Amanda's face was pale, but she still had that determined glint in her eye. "I'm glad it's over, that's for sure." She said, drawing Elsie in for a hug. "Thank you so much for being here with me." Elsie squeezed back, still unable to believe that this incredible, brave woman was hers. "Nowhere I would rather be," Elsie said, her fingers brushing Amanda's cheek gently.

Amanda laughed, "Well, that makes one of us. I don't want to spend another minute in Kerikeri. Let's get out of here."

Reaching into her bag and pulling out a mini cupcake, Elsie raised her eyebrows at Amanda. "You sure you still want to do this?" She asked. It had been Elsie's suggestion to use an invisibility spell to get out of Kerikeri without being followed by Theo's thugs, and they had discussed the plan in detail several times. After her recent mistakes with magical boundaries, she wanted to be extra sure Amanda was still OK with the plan. Amanda kissed her gently on the lips, and took the enchanted cupcake from her hand, biting into it with a smile. Elsie watched as Amanda disappeared before her eyes.

The plan was carefully curated. Nobody but Elsie knew that Amanda George was actually Amanda Masters, so once they got back to Glen Haven, Amanda would be safe. The plan to get there was elaborate, to ensure that nobody stayed on their tail.

Elsie, in a different glamour, would leave the court in Elsie's car. Amanda, invisible, would sit in the front with her. They shouldn't be followed, with Elsie looking like a completely different person from the one who supported Amanda during her testimony, and Amanda, for all anyone watching them knew, still in the bathroom. Regardless, they would take no risks on the way home. They had several stops mapped out on the route home for additional chicanery. At each point, Elsie would change her glamour, stock Amanda up on invisibility cupcakes, and even glamour their vehicle to ensure that there was no chance of being seen. When they reached the bottom of the North Island, they would drive the car onto the ferry, and then continue their trip down the South Island. It would take two days, with at least six stops scheduled for re-glamourising. But when they got home there would be no sign of Amanda Masters, and they could continue life in Glen Haven in peace.

The three weeks between their ordeal with Soren and now had been full of a lot of talking, and Elsie's mind was still reeling. Amanda had agreed to move back into Lilac House again, but this time as partners, not flatmates. Amanda had bought Higgs' Twiggs with the money from her nursery, allowing Mrs Higgs to retire in peace. She had promised Mrs Higgs that her son would have a job there any time he wanted one. She had also, much to Elsie's surprise, made another suggestion. She asked Elsie to consider moving Pie in the Sky to the garden centre. Now the blight was over, the plants were thriving once more. A cafe in the garden centre would be surrounded by real flowers, their fragrance filling the space. The garden centre would draw more customers for the cafe, and vice-versa. Amanda had said instead of paying rent for the cafe, Elsie could do the accounts for Higgs' Twiggs. Elsie was thrilled! Her little shop wouldn't close, and she could continue to win over the people of Glen Haven with her pies and cupcakes. Plus, hopefully Beth wouldn't see a garden centre cafe as direct competition. Elsie beamed as she thought of decking out her new space, and all the flower-themed baking she could do. Perhaps she could get Wanda and Catherine to help her with the renovations.

It turned out Wanda and Catherine were powerful witches from the Council. They had known Elsie's grandmother, and had been keeping an eye on Elsie in honour of their old friend. Along with Lily, it seemed that Elsie now had a small coven in Glen Haven. They were planning on doing some extra spells at the upcoming Beltane festival, to ensure the ill-effects of Soren's magic were wiped away, and to welcome in the spring.

That was wonderful, but as Elsie's fingers grasped around the invisible hand next to her in the car, she couldn't help but feel that she had won the jackpot. "What are you thinking about?" Amanda's voice came from the apparently empty passenger seat.

"Just reflecting on the past few months," Elsie said. "To think that three weeks ago I almost died, and now I'm here with you, heading home to Lilac House, spring in the air. I just feel so happy. So full of hope. It's surreal."

Elsie felt a rough hand trail gently down her cheek. They stopped at a red light and Elsie turned towards Amanda. She leaned forward, conscious for half a second how strange this would look if any cars came up behind them. "I love you, Amanda Masters," she whispered. Amanda's lips brushed hers, Elsie leaned in farther, and they kissed, warm and slow. "I love you too, Elsie Hazelwood," Amanda said, and Elsie's heart almost exploded. She laced Amanda's fingers through hers, putting the car in drive. They were going home.

The End.

Epilogue
Elsie

Elsie sat in the kitchen, turning her teacup in her hands. She tipped it over, asking what her day would hold. As she brought the teacup up to her face to examine it, she tilted her head to the side. A dove. Well, that was a little on the nose, she thought, smiling to herself.

Two hours later, she met Amanda at the door to the kitchen. Amanda was in a tailored white three-piece suit, her mahogany hair tied in an elegant knot above her head, and a dash of red across her lips that highlighted her rosy complexion. "Wow," Elsie breathed.

"Wow is right," Amanda said, looking Elsie up and down appreciatively.

Elsie was in a sleek, floor length dress with a low back and lace accents. Her hair was braided as usual over one shoulder, but today she had tiny sprays of baby's breath woven through it, bewitched to glimmer in the sunlight. Amanda held out her arm and Elsie took it. Philo was waiting at the door, looking very dapper with a black bow tie in place of his usual turquoise collar.

The garden walls were covered in the lilac vines the house was known for, sprays of pale purple bright against the dark brick behind. The celebrant was set up under the elm tree, which was draped with a huge sheet of white gauze. Along either side of their makeshift aisle sat rows of chairs. As they walked together up the aisle, Elsie looked around and saw the faces of so many people she cared about. Her mum and Phoebe sat up the front, with Murray and Ms Watters in corresponding seats on the other side of the aisle. Samantha, Sally, and the rest of the yoga gang were all beaming at them. Her coven; Wanda, Catherine, and Lily were there too, Wanda's two boys dressed in little tuxedo onesies. Elsie's heart felt incredibly full. This might not be the whole town, but these were people she knew loved her, who would be there for her and Amanda when the going got tough. She understood now that being popular wasn't the same as being known and being loved, just as you are. She had Amanda to thank for that.

Elsie squeezed Amanda's arm, and whispered "how are your feet?" Amanda looked down at her white keds.

"I thought you said these shoes would be ok?" her face was a picture of concern, and Elsie chuckled quietly.

"Not too cold?" She asked, and Amanda actually reached behind them and pinched her bum! Elsie let out a little squeak and had to take a moment to stop herself from bursting out laughing.

"My feet are just fine, thank you," Amanda said. "Because I got shoes that are fit for walking in. Not like those stunning but honestly terrifying things on your feet." Amanda nodded down at Elsie's chic silver stilettos, with a heel so sharp she could use it to cut their cake. "But I promise you, any running I do from now on will be with you, not away from you."

Elsie had a witty comeback. She did. But as she looked into the eyes of this woman who had taught her so much, who had opened Elsie up to believing she was loveable, and who loved her so well. The woman who was working so hard to overcome her own demons to continue to love her well, all she could do was lean over and plant a kiss on her lips. Ready to take on this new adventure together.

Can't bear to leave Glen Haven? Phoebe returns home in Lavender Loathing, check it out here: https://books2read.com/u/bOjEPg

Don't miss out!

Visit the website below and you can sign up to receive emails whenever Rosie Evylin publishes a new book. There's no charge and no obligation.

https://books2read.com/r/B-A-TACBB-DWQPC

BOOKS 2 READ

Connecting independent readers to independent writers.

About the Author

Rosie lives in New Zealand and writes whimsical stories about magic and emotions. Her children's stories are inspired by two very special little people in her life.

Read more at https://www.rosieevylin.com.

www.ingramcontent.com/pod-product-compliance
Lightning Source LLC
Chambersburg PA
CBHW021216250626
47155CB00008B/2825